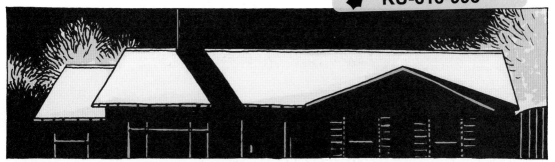

GET IT TOGETHER, ABRAHAM.

YOU'VE BEEN OUT THERE BEFORE...

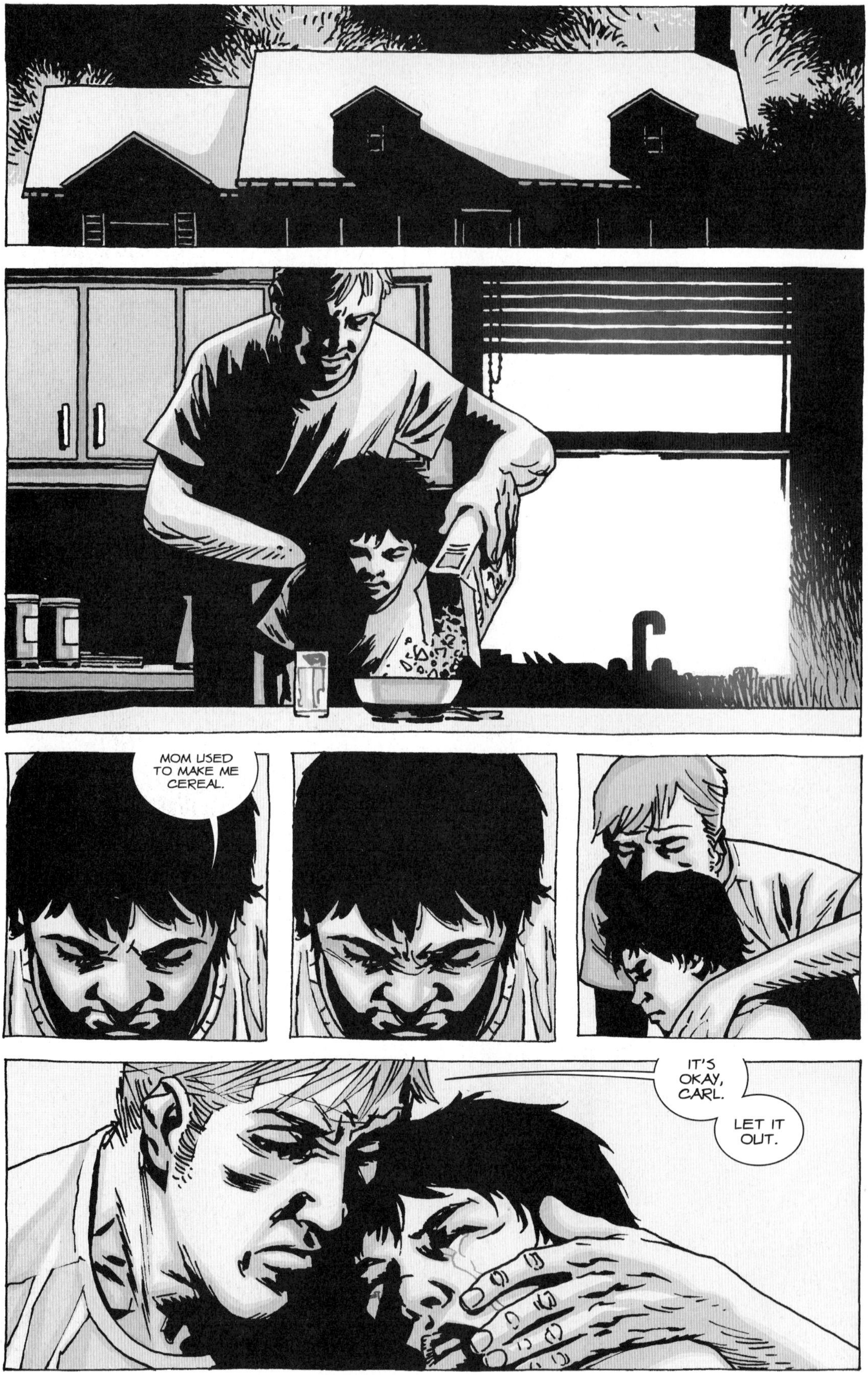
MOM USED TO MAKE ME CEREAL.
IT'S OKAY, CARL.
LET IT OUT.

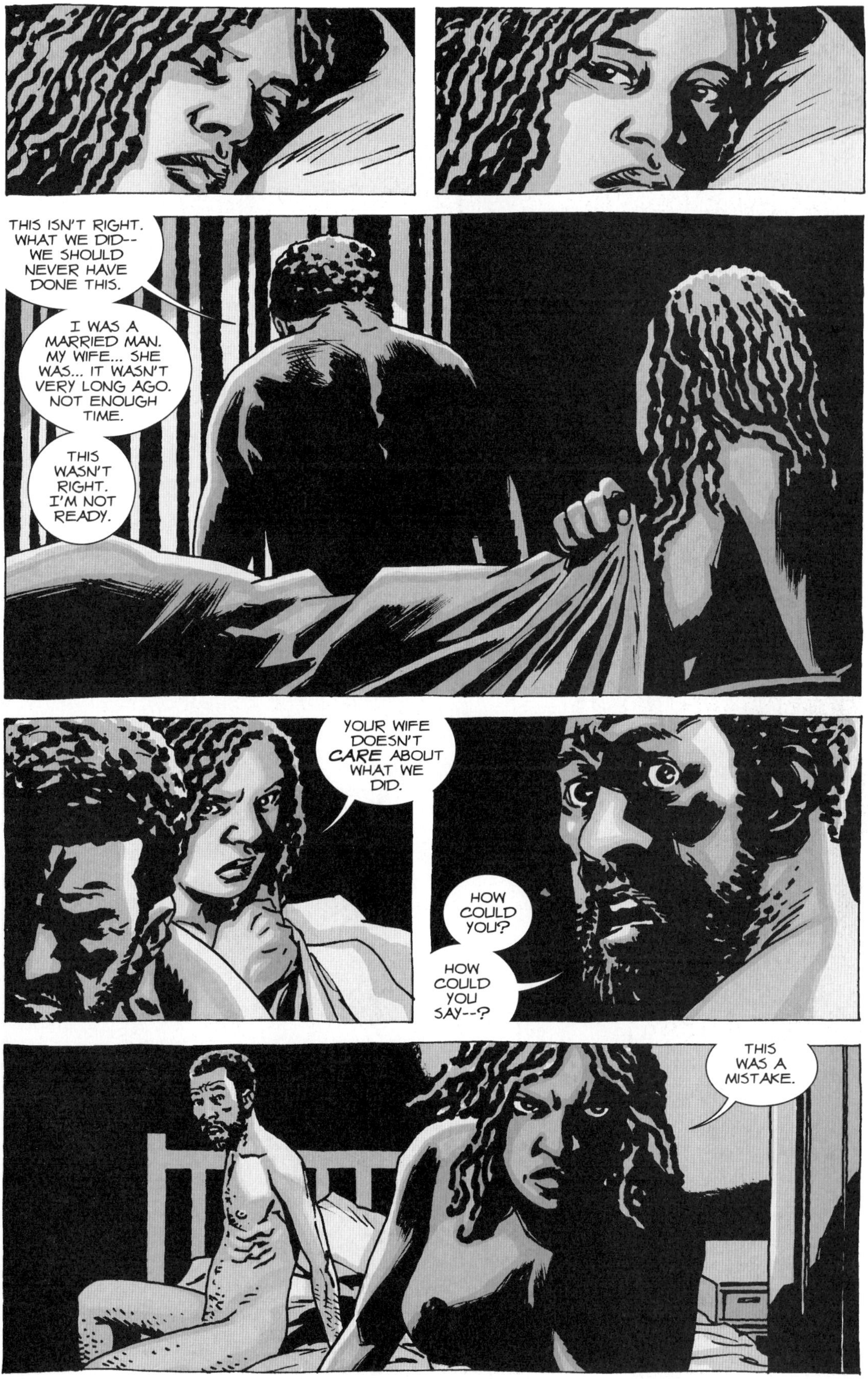
THIS ISN'T RIGHT. WHAT WE DID-- WE SHOULD NEVER HAVE DONE THIS.
I WAS A MARRIED MAN. MY WIFE... SHE WAS... IT WASN'T VERY LONG AGO. NOT ENOUGH TIME.
THIS WASN'T RIGHT. I'M NOT READY.
YOUR WIFE DOESN'T CARE ABOUT WHAT WE DID.
HOW COULD YOU?
HOW COULD YOU SAY--?
THIS WAS A MISTAKE.

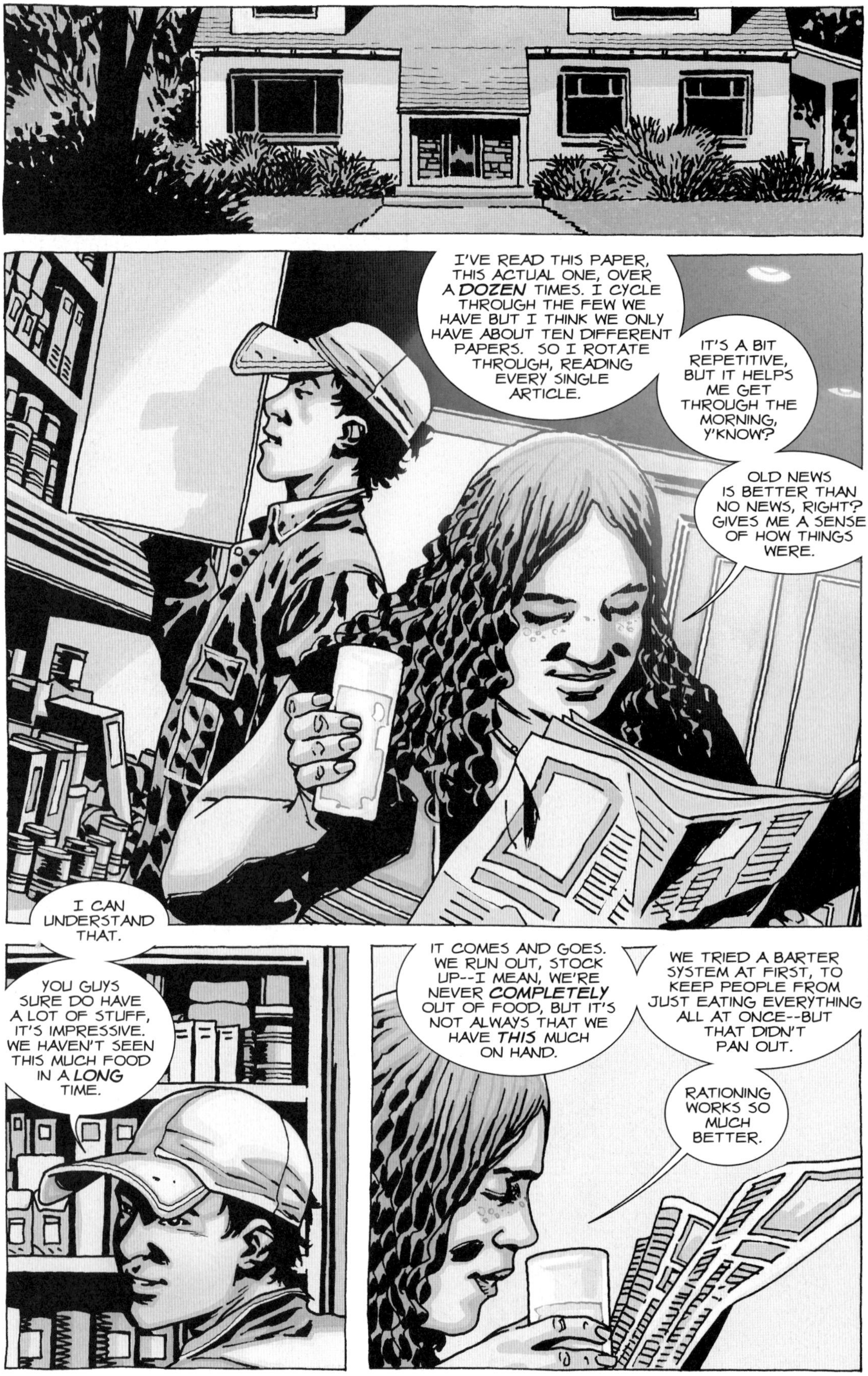
I'VE READ THIS PAPER, THIS ACTUAL ONE, OVER A DOZEN TIMES. I CYCLE THROUGH THE FEW WE HAVE BUT I THINK WE ONLY HAVE ABOUT TEN DIFFERENT PAPERS. SO I ROTATE THROUGH, READING EVERY SINGLE ARTICLE.
IT'S A BIT REPETITIVE, BUT IT HELPS ME GET THROUGH THE MORNING, Y'KNOW?
OLD NEWS IS BETTER THAN NO NEWS, RIGHT? GIVES ME A SENSE OF HOW THINGS WERE.
I CAN UNDERSTAND THAT.
YOU GUYS SURE DO HAVE A LOT OF STUFF, IT'S IMPRESSIVE. WE HAVEN'T SEEN THIS MUCH FOOD IN A LONG TIME.
IT COMES AND GOES. WE RUN OUT, STOCK UP--I MEAN, WE'RE NEVER COMPLETELY OUT OF FOOD, BUT IT'S NOT ALWAYS THAT WE HAVE THIS MUCH ON HAND.
WE TRIED A BARTER SYSTEM AT FIRST, TO KEEP PEOPLE FROM JUST EATING EVERYTHING ALL AT ONCE--BUT THAT DIDN'T PAN OUT.
RATIONING WORKS SO MUCH BETTER.

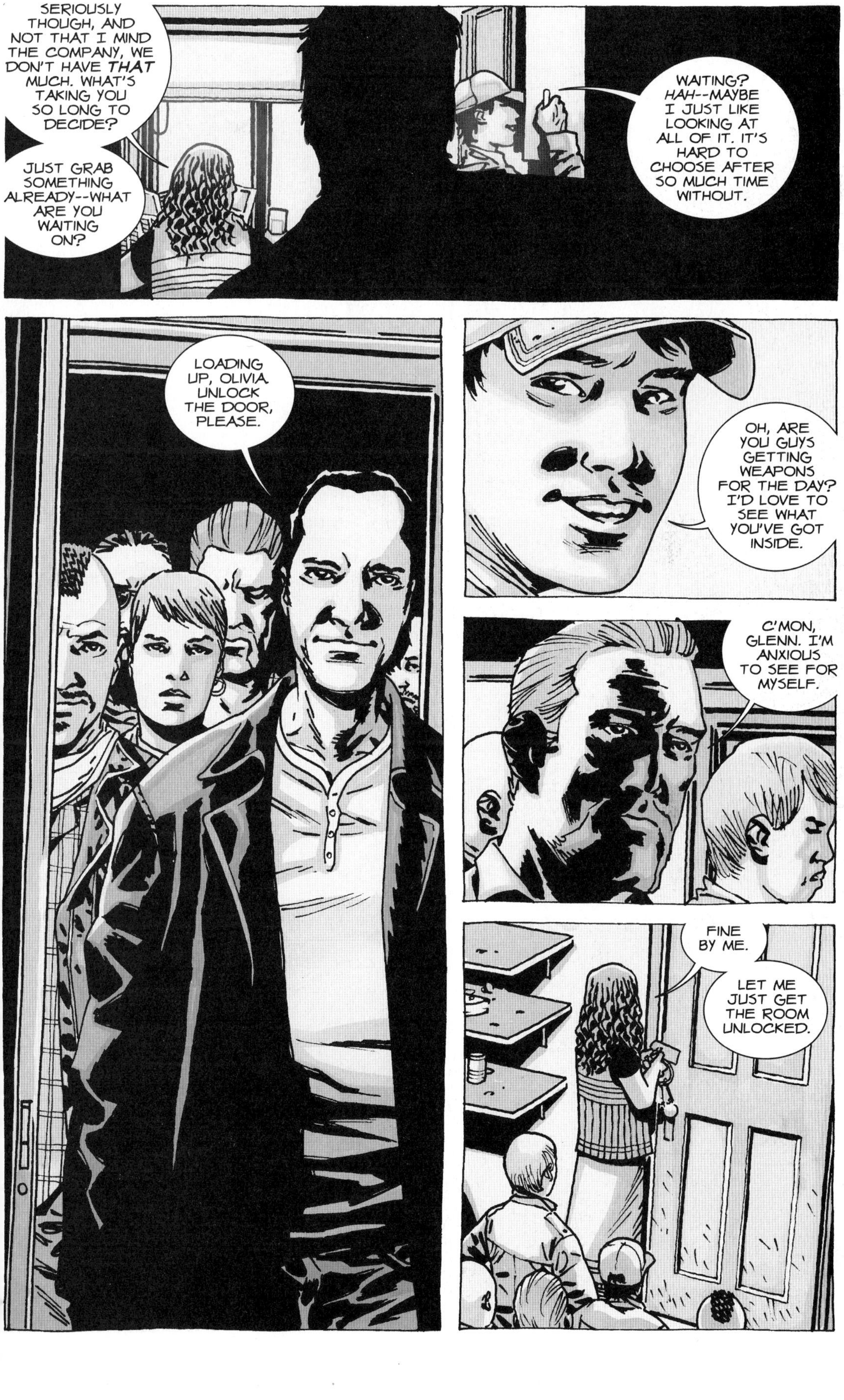
SERIOUSLY THOUGH, AND NOT THAT I MIND THE COMPANY, WE DON'T HAVE *THAT* MUCH. WHAT'S TAKING YOU SO LONG TO DECIDE?
JUST GRAB SOMETHING ALREADY--WHAT ARE YOU WAITING ON?
WAITING? *HAH*--MAYBE I JUST LIKE LOOKING AT ALL OF IT. IT'S HARD TO CHOOSE AFTER SO MUCH TIME WITHOUT.
LOADING UP, OLIVIA. UNLOCK THE DOOR, PLEASE.
OH, ARE YOU GUYS GETTING WEAPONS FOR THE DAY? I'D LOVE TO SEE WHAT YOU'VE GOT INSIDE.
C'MON, GLENN. I'M ANXIOUS TO SEE FOR MYSELF.
FINE BY ME.
LET ME JUST GET THE ROOM UNLOCKED.

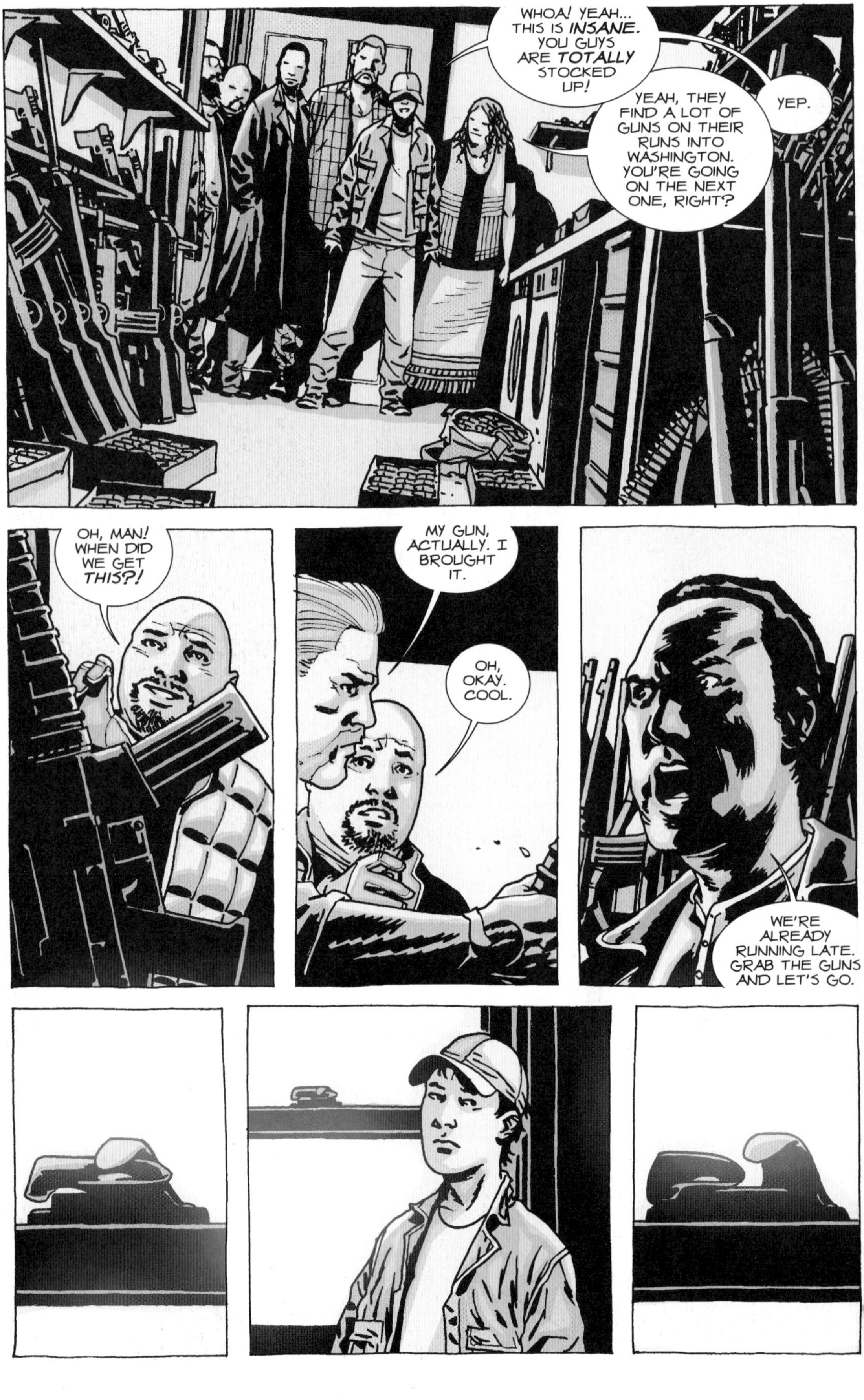
WHOA! YEAH... THIS IS INSANE. YOU GUYS ARE TOTALLY STOCKED UP!
YEP.
YEAH, THEY FIND A LOT OF GUNS ON THEIR RUNS INTO WASHINGTON. YOU'RE GOING ON THE NEXT ONE, RIGHT?
OH, MAN! WHEN DID WE GET THIS?!
MY GUN, ACTUALLY. I BROUGHT IT.
OH, OKAY. COOL.
WE'RE ALREADY RUNNING LATE. GRAB THE GUNS AND LET'S GO.

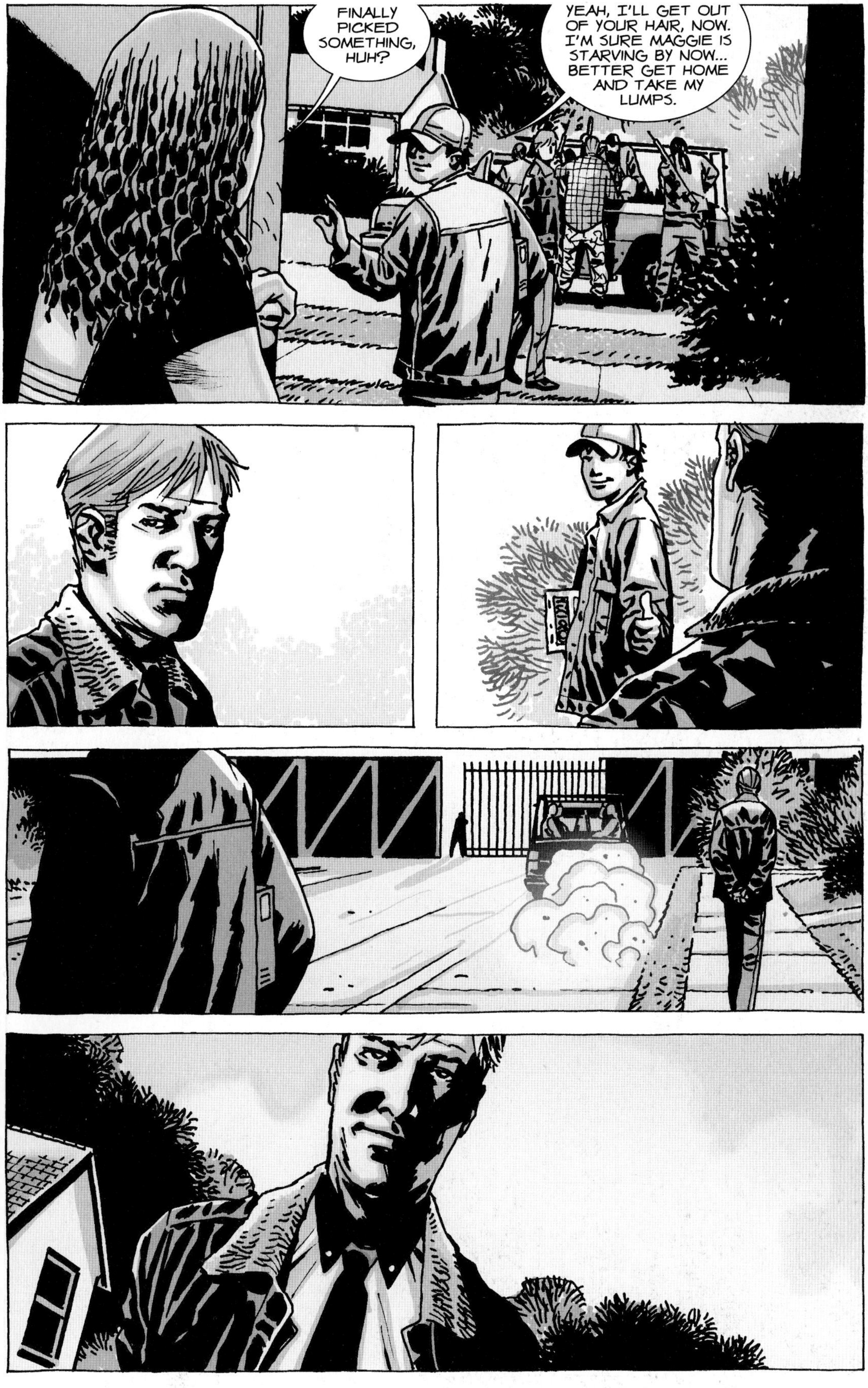
FINALLY PICKED SOMETHING, HUH?
YEAH, I'LL GET OUT OF YOUR HAIR, NOW. I'M SURE MAGGIE IS STARVING BY NOW... BETTER GET HOME AND TAKE MY LUMPS.

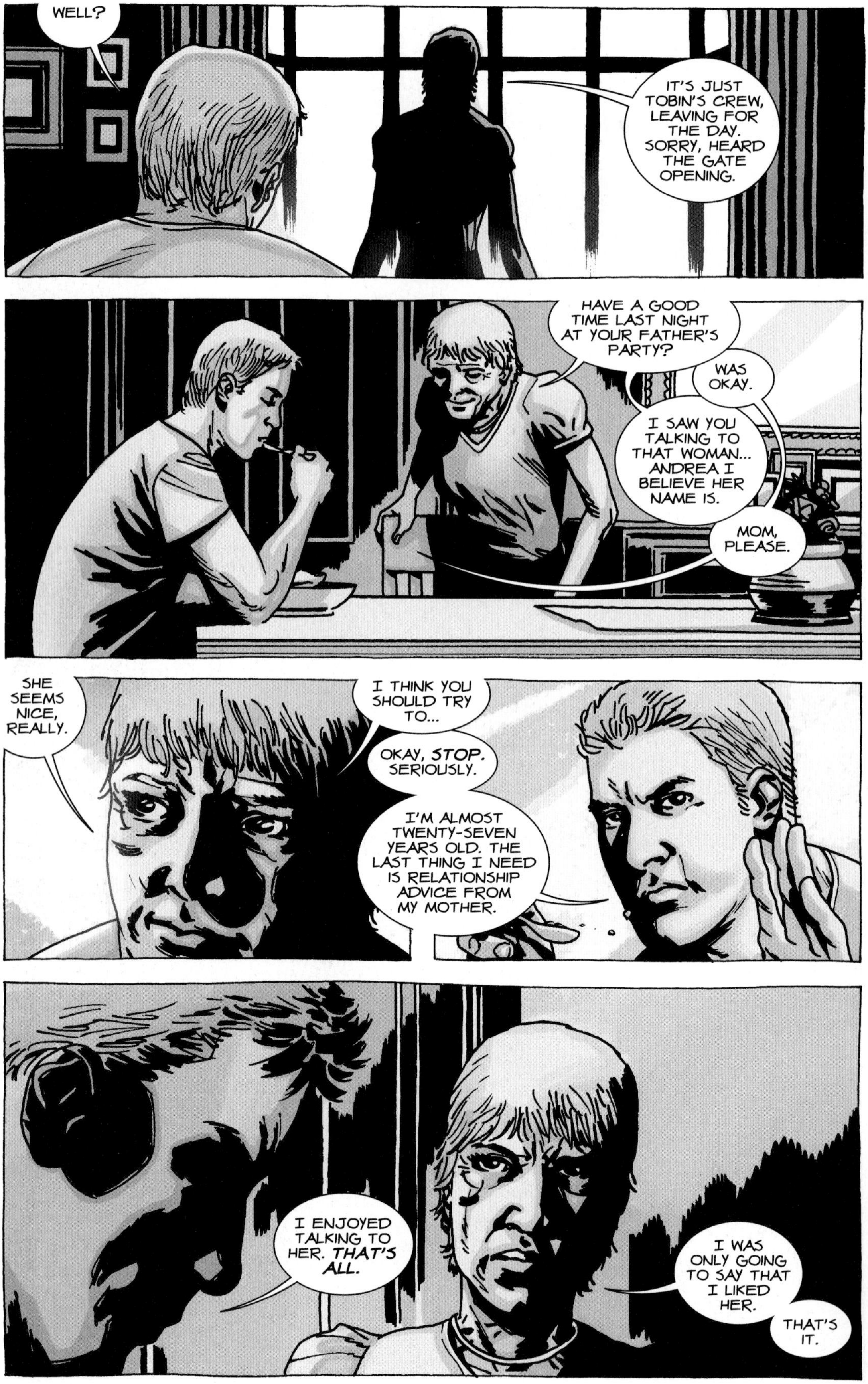
WELL?
IT'S JUST TOBIN'S CREW, LEAVING FOR THE DAY. SORRY, HEARD THE GATE OPENING.
HAVE A GOOD TIME LAST NIGHT AT YOUR FATHER'S PARTY?
WAS OKAY.
I SAW YOU TALKING TO THAT WOMAN... ANDREA I BELIEVE HER NAME IS.
MOM, PLEASE.
SHE SEEMS NICE, REALLY.
I THINK YOU SHOULD TRY TO...
OKAY, STOP. SERIOUSLY.
I'M ALMOST TWENTY-SEVEN YEARS OLD. THE LAST THING I NEED IS RELATIONSHIP ADVICE FROM MY MOTHER.
I ENJOYED TALKING TO HER. THAT'S ALL.
I WAS ONLY GOING TO SAY THAT I LIKED HER.
THAT'S IT.

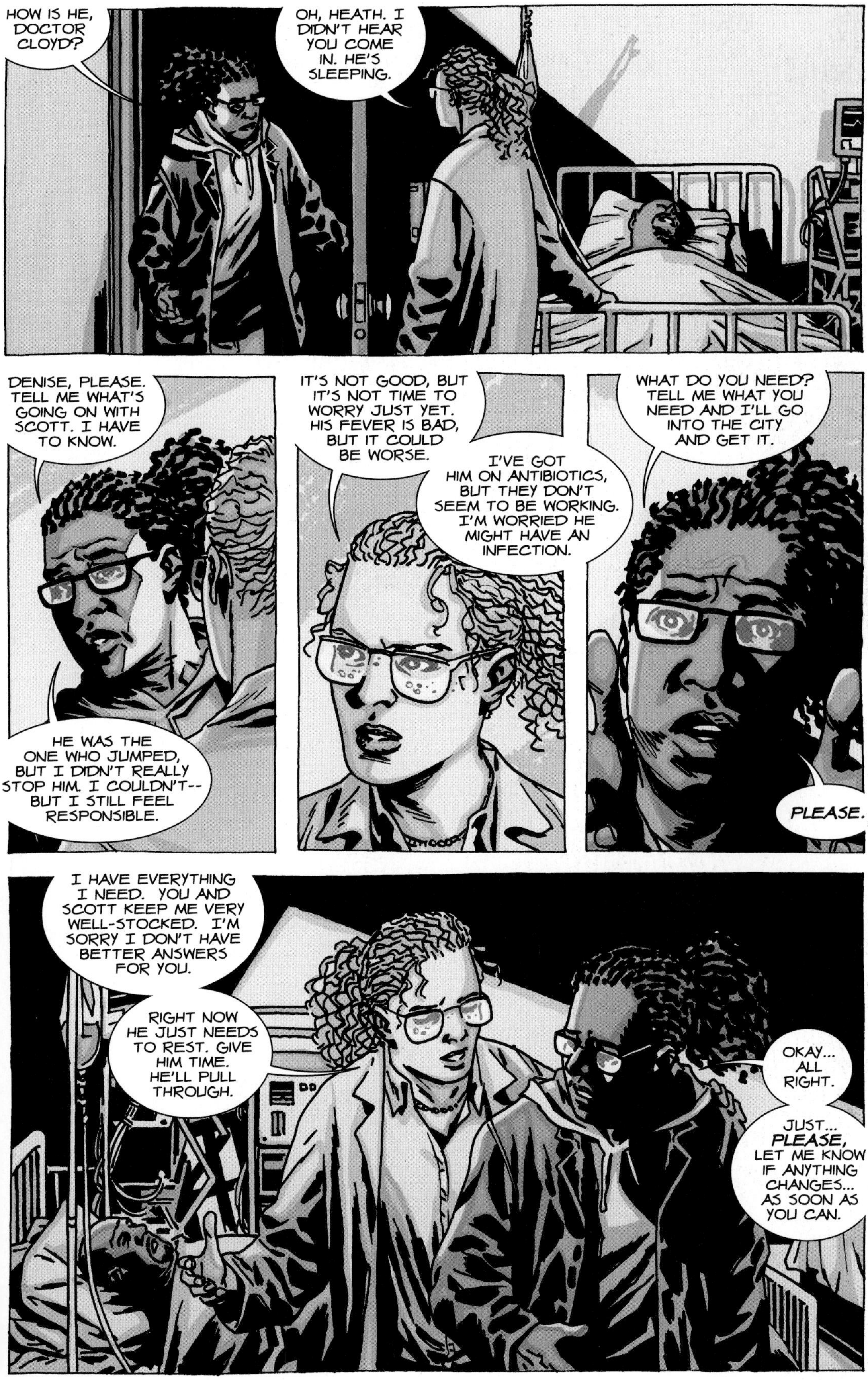
HOW IS HE, DOCTOR CLOYD?
OH, HEATH. I DIDN'T HEAR YOU COME IN. HE'S SLEEPING.
DENISE, PLEASE. TELL ME WHAT'S GOING ON WITH SCOTT. I HAVE TO KNOW.
HE WAS THE ONE WHO JUMPED, BUT I DIDN'T REALLY STOP HIM. I COULDN'T-- BUT I STILL FEEL RESPONSIBLE.
IT'S NOT GOOD, BUT IT'S NOT TIME TO WORRY JUST YET. HIS FEVER IS BAD, BUT IT COULD BE WORSE.
I'VE GOT HIM ON ANTIBIOTICS, BUT THEY DON'T SEEM TO BE WORKING. I'M WORRIED HE MIGHT HAVE AN INFECTION.
WHAT DO YOU NEED? TELL ME WHAT YOU NEED AND I'LL GO INTO THE CITY AND GET IT.
PLEASE.
I HAVE EVERYTHING I NEED. YOU AND SCOTT KEEP ME VERY WELL-STOCKED. I'M SORRY I DON'T HAVE BETTER ANSWERS FOR YOU.
RIGHT NOW HE JUST NEEDS TO REST. GIVE HIM TIME. HE'LL PULL THROUGH.
OKAY... ALL RIGHT.
JUST... PLEASE, LET ME KNOW IF ANYTHING CHANGES... AS SOON AS YOU CAN.

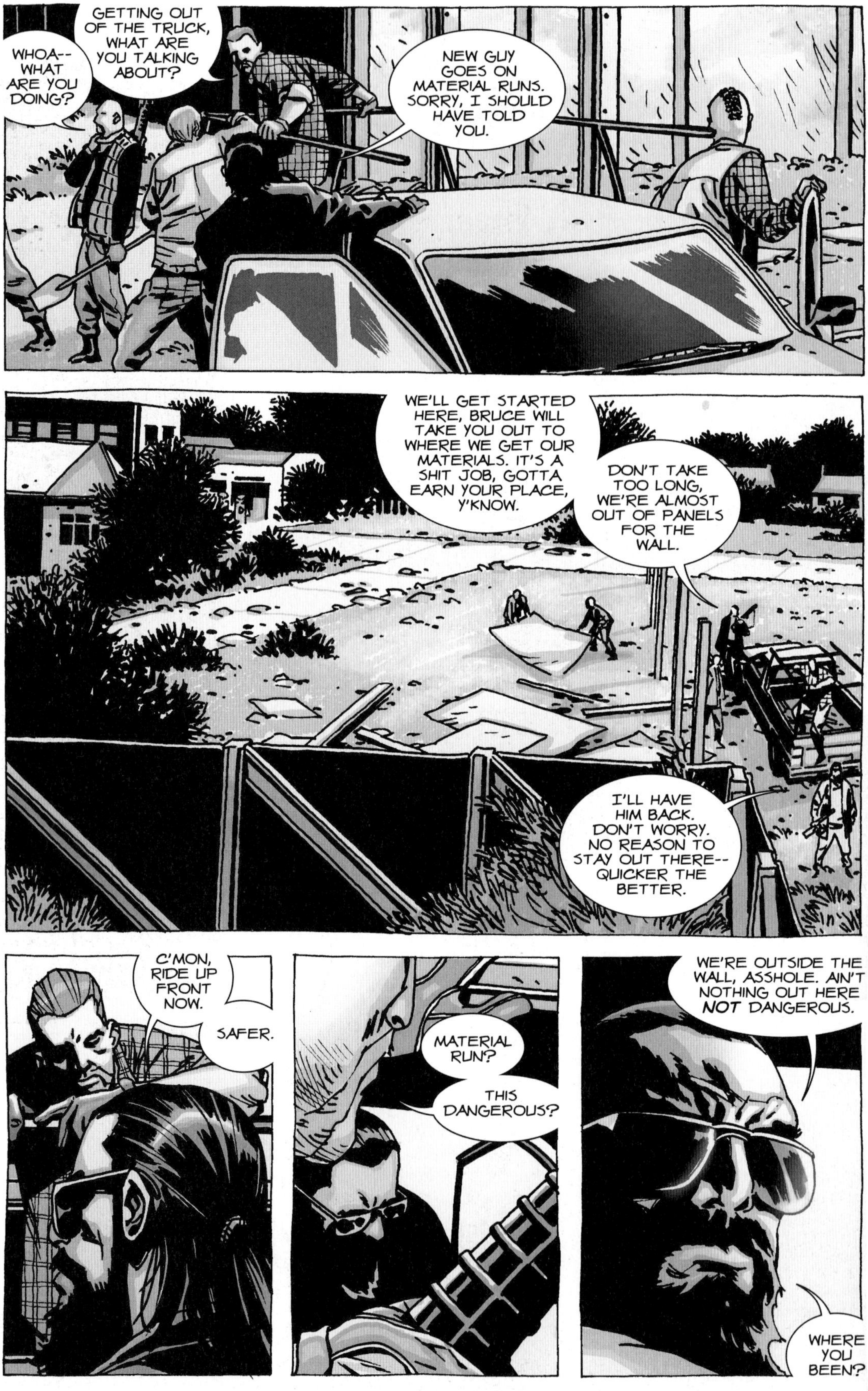
WHOA-- WHAT ARE YOU DOING?
GETTING OUT OF THE TRUCK, WHAT ARE YOU TALKING ABOUT?
NEW GUY GOES ON MATERIAL RUNS. SORRY, I SHOULD HAVE TOLD YOU.
WE'LL GET STARTED HERE, BRUCE WILL TAKE YOU OUT TO WHERE WE GET OUR MATERIALS. IT'S A SHIT JOB, GOTTA EARN YOUR PLACE, Y'KNOW.
DON'T TAKE TOO LONG, WE'RE ALMOST OUT OF PANELS FOR THE WALL.
I'LL HAVE HIM BACK. DON'T WORRY. NO REASON TO STAY OUT THERE-- QUICKER THE BETTER.
C'MON, RIDE UP FRONT NOW.
SAFER.
MATERIAL RUN?
THIS DANGEROUS?
WE'RE OUTSIDE THE WALL, ASSHOLE. AIN'T NOTHING OUT HERE NOT DANGEROUS.
WHERE YOU BEEN?

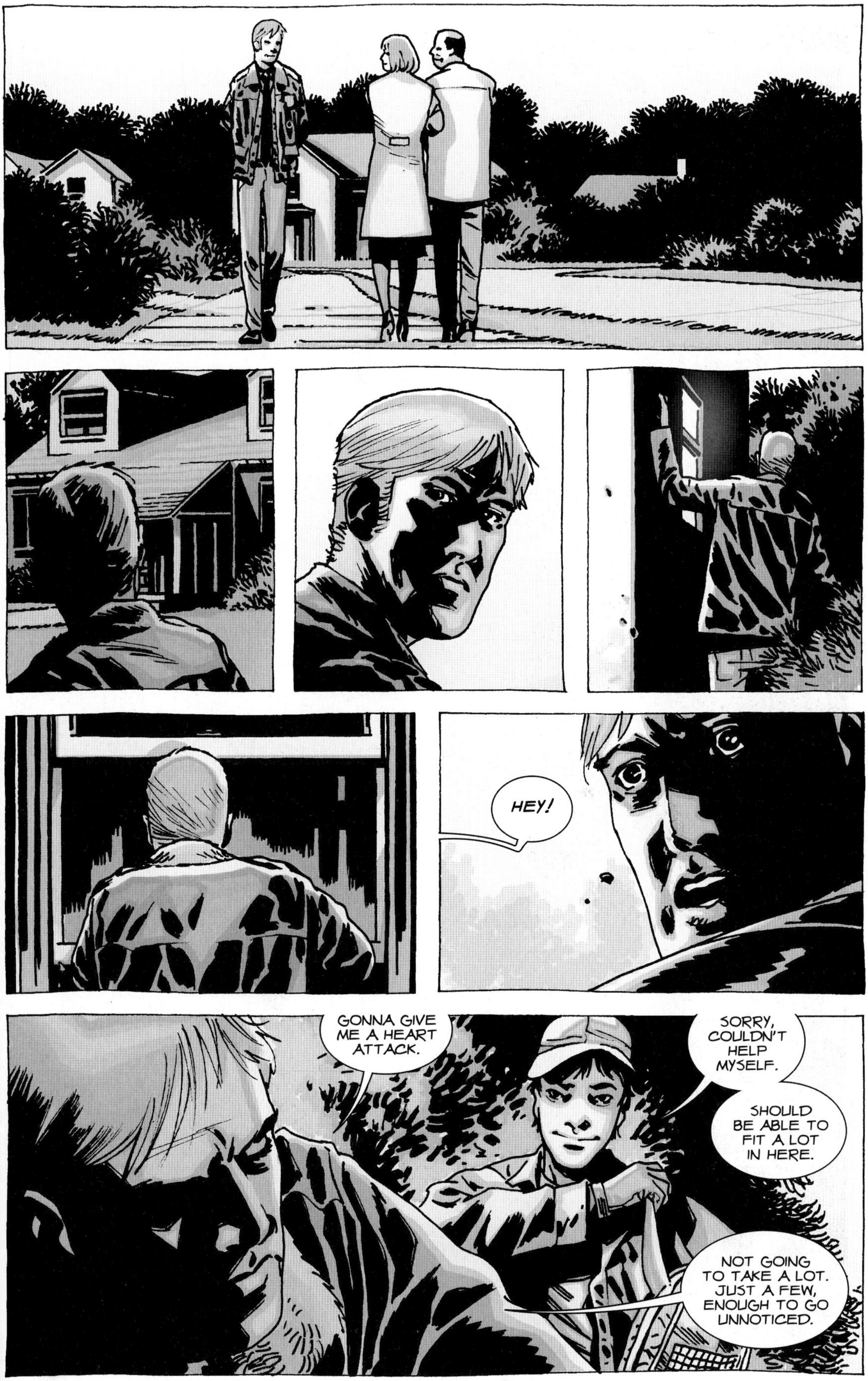
HEY!
GONNA GIVE ME A HEART ATTACK.
SORRY, COULDN'T HELP MYSELF.
SHOULD BE ABLE TO FIT A LOT IN HERE.
NOT GOING TO TAKE A LOT. JUST A FEW, ENOUGH TO GO UNNOTICED.

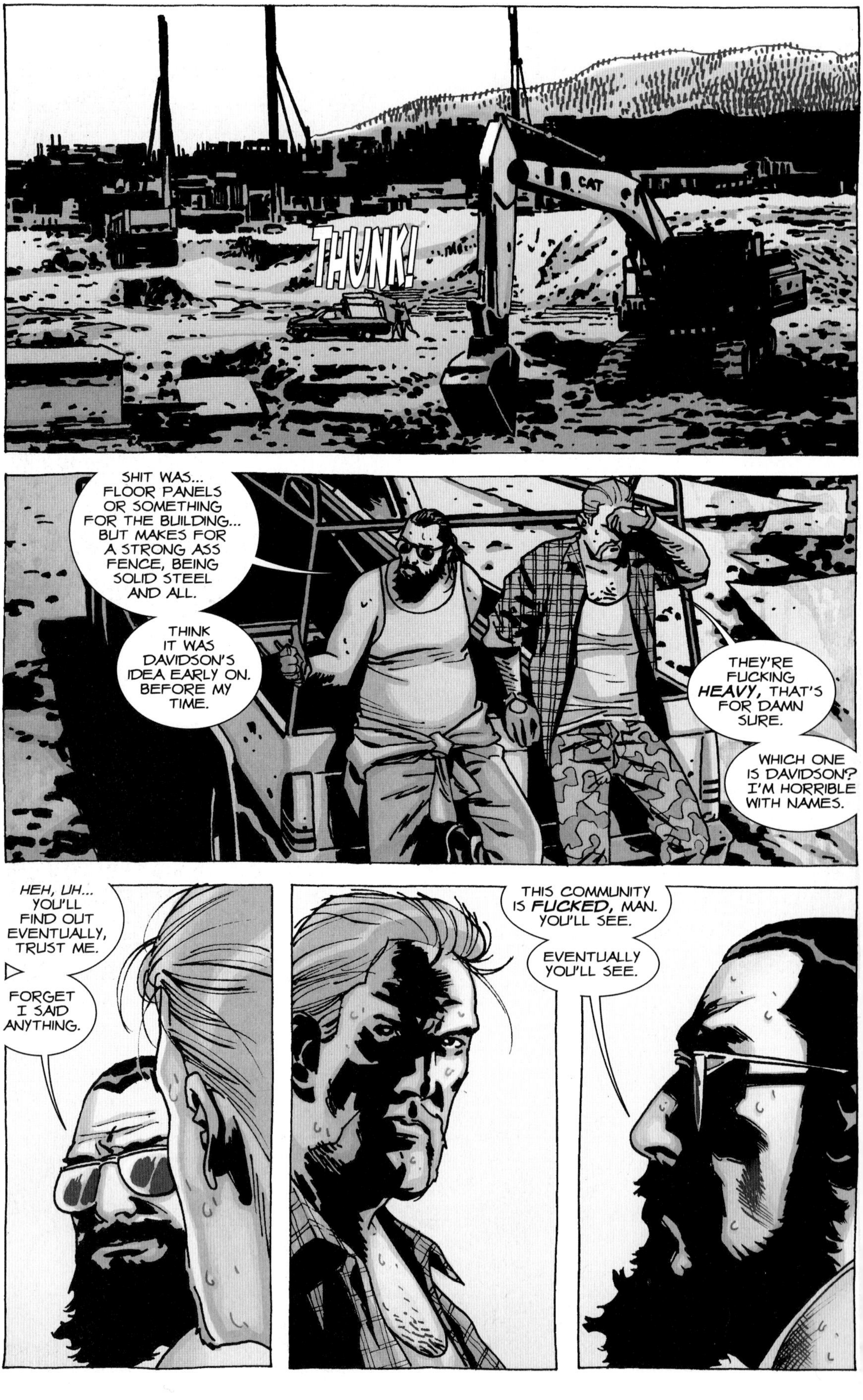
THUNK!
SHIT WAS... FLOOR PANELS OR SOMETHING FOR THE BUILDING... BUT MAKES FOR A STRONG ASS FENCE, BEING SOLID STEEL AND ALL.
THINK IT WAS DAVIDSON'S IDEA EARLY ON. BEFORE MY TIME.
THEY'RE FUCKING HEAVY, THAT'S FOR DAMN SURE.
WHICH ONE IS DAVIDSON? I'M HORRIBLE WITH NAMES.
HEH, UH... YOU'LL FIND OUT EVENTUALLY, TRUST ME.
FORGET I SAID ANYTHING.
THIS COMMUNITY IS FUCKED, MAN. YOU'LL SEE.
EVENTUALLY YOU'LL SEE.

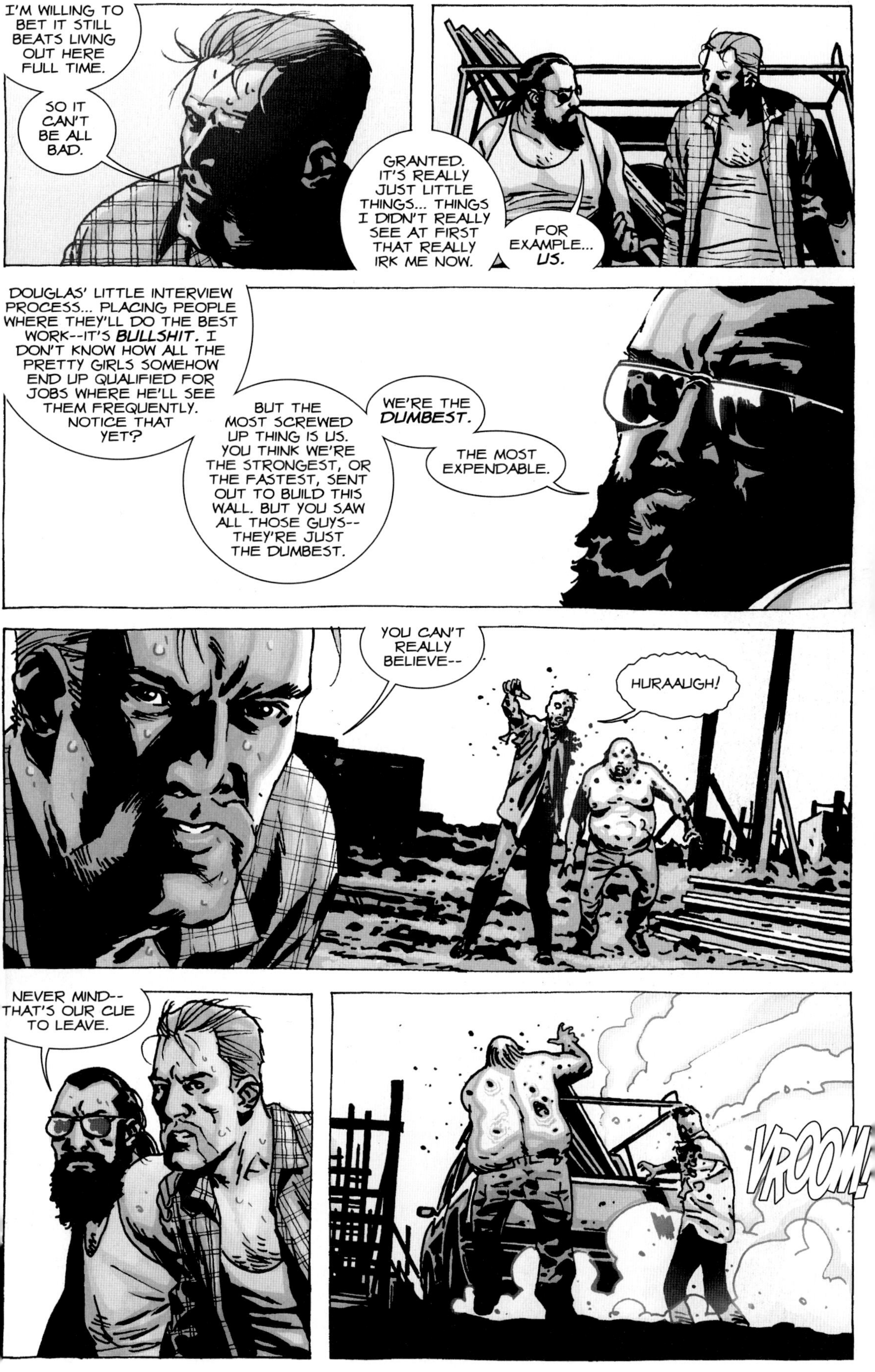
I'M WILLING TO BET IT STILL BEATS LIVING OUT HERE FULL TIME.
SO IT CAN'T BE ALL BAD.
GRANTED. IT'S REALLY JUST LITTLE THINGS... THINGS I DIDN'T REALLY SEE AT FIRST THAT REALLY IRK ME NOW.
FOR EXAMPLE... US.
DOUGLAS' LITTLE INTERVIEW PROCESS... PLACING PEOPLE WHERE THEY'LL DO THE BEST WORK--IT'S BULLSHIT. I DON'T KNOW HOW ALL THE PRETTY GIRLS SOMEHOW END UP QUALIFIED FOR JOBS WHERE HE'LL SEE THEM FREQUENTLY. NOTICE THAT YET?
BUT THE MOST SCREWED UP THING IS US. YOU THINK WE'RE THE STRONGEST, OR THE FASTEST, SENT OUT TO BUILD THIS WALL. BUT YOU SAW ALL THOSE GUYS-- THEY'RE JUST THE DUMBEST.
WE'RE THE DUMBEST.
THE MOST EXPENDABLE.
YOU CAN'T REALLY BELIEVE--
HURAAUGH!
NEVER MIND-- THAT'S OUR CUE TO LEAVE.
VROOM!

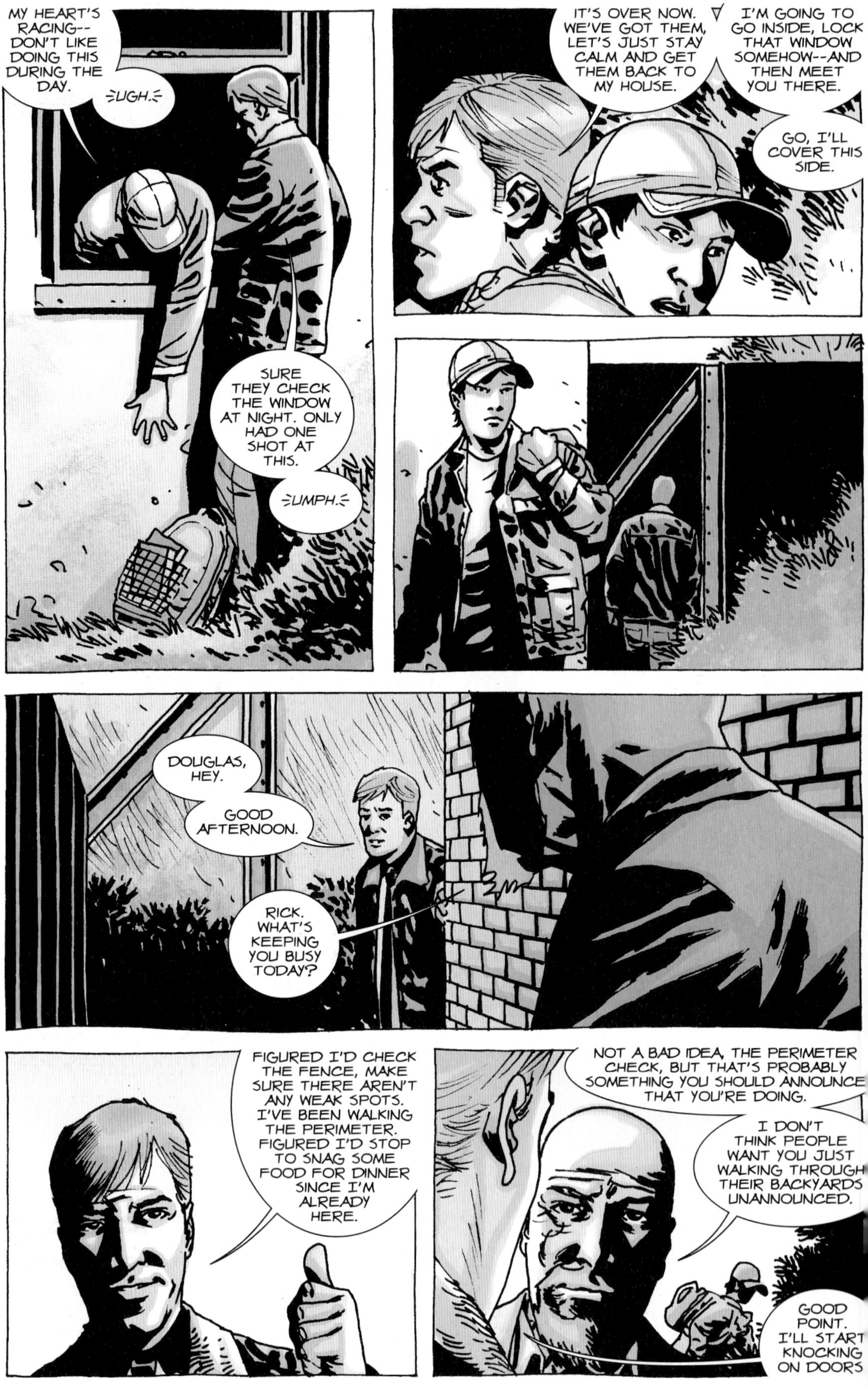
MY HEART'S RACING-- DON'T LIKE DOING THIS DURING THE DAY.
UGH.
SURE THEY CHECK THE WINDOW AT NIGHT. ONLY HAD ONE SHOT AT THIS.
UMPH.
IT'S OVER NOW. WE'VE GOT THEM, LET'S JUST STAY CALM AND GET THEM BACK TO MY HOUSE.
I'M GOING TO GO INSIDE, LOCK THAT WINDOW SOMEHOW--AND THEN MEET YOU THERE.
GO, I'LL COVER THIS SIDE.
DOUGLAS, HEY.
GOOD AFTERNOON.
RICK. WHAT'S KEEPING YOU BUSY TODAY?
FIGURED I'D CHECK THE FENCE, MAKE SURE THERE AREN'T ANY WEAK SPOTS. I'VE BEEN WALKING THE PERIMETER. FIGURED I'D STOP TO SNAG SOME FOOD FOR DINNER SINCE I'M ALREADY HERE.
NOT A BAD IDEA, THE PERIMETER CHECK, BUT THAT'S PROBABLY SOMETHING YOU SHOULD ANNOUNCE THAT YOU'RE DOING.
I DON'T THINK PEOPLE WANT YOU JUST WALKING THROUGH THEIR BACKYARDS UNANNOUNCED.
GOOD POINT. I'LL START KNOCKING ON DOORS

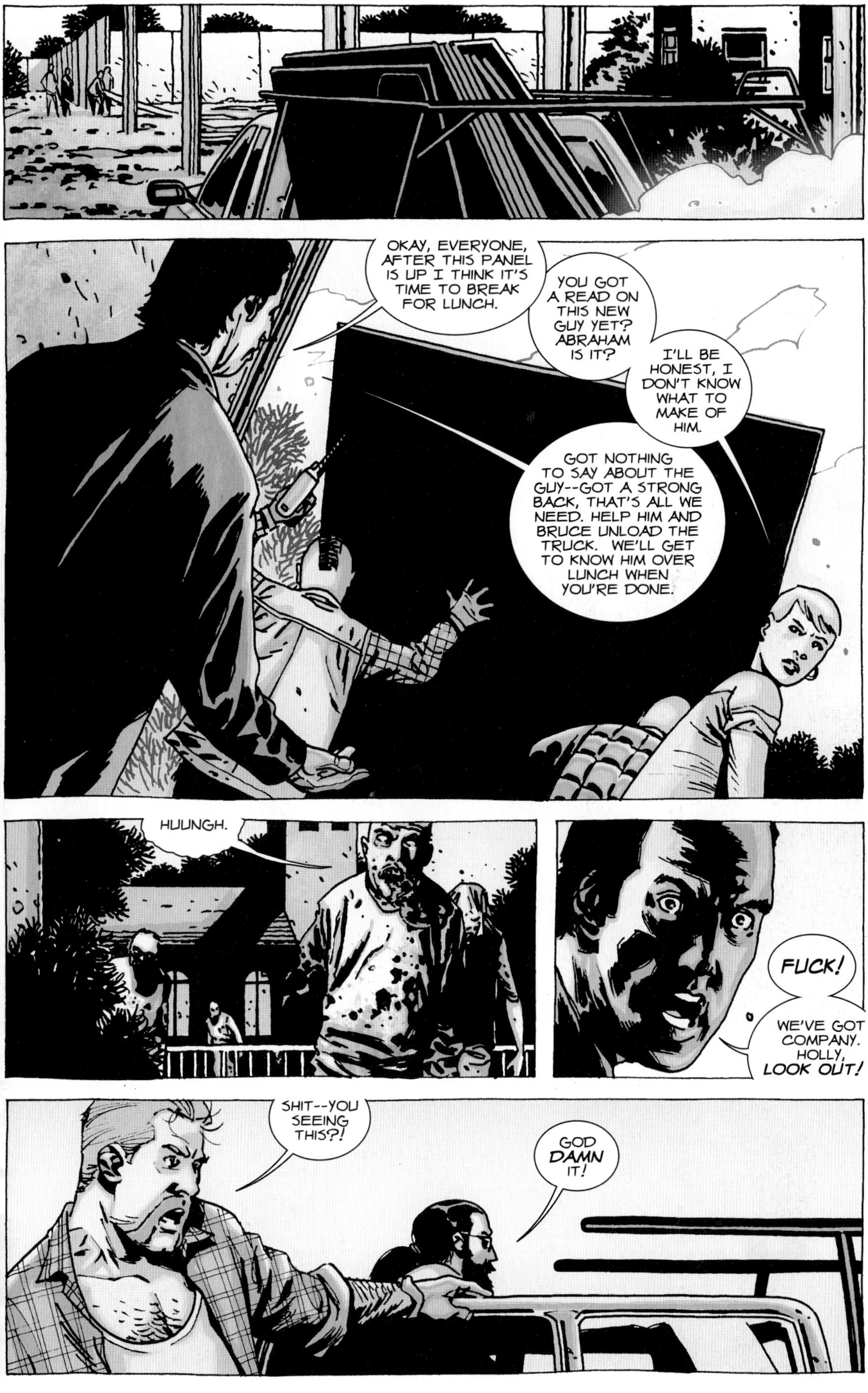
OKAY, EVERYONE, AFTER THIS PANEL IS UP I THINK IT'S TIME TO BREAK FOR LUNCH.
YOU GOT A READ ON THIS NEW GUY YET? ABRAHAM IS IT?
I'LL BE HONEST, I DON'T KNOW WHAT TO MAKE OF HIM.
GOT NOTHING TO SAY ABOUT THE GUY--GOT A STRONG BACK, THAT'S ALL WE NEED. HELP HIM AND BRUCE UNLOAD THE TRUCK. WE'LL GET TO KNOW HIM OVER LUNCH WHEN YOU'RE DONE.
HUUNGH.
FUCK!
WE'VE GOT COMPANY. HOLLY, LOOK OUT!
SHIT--YOU SEEING THIS?!
GOD DAMN IT!

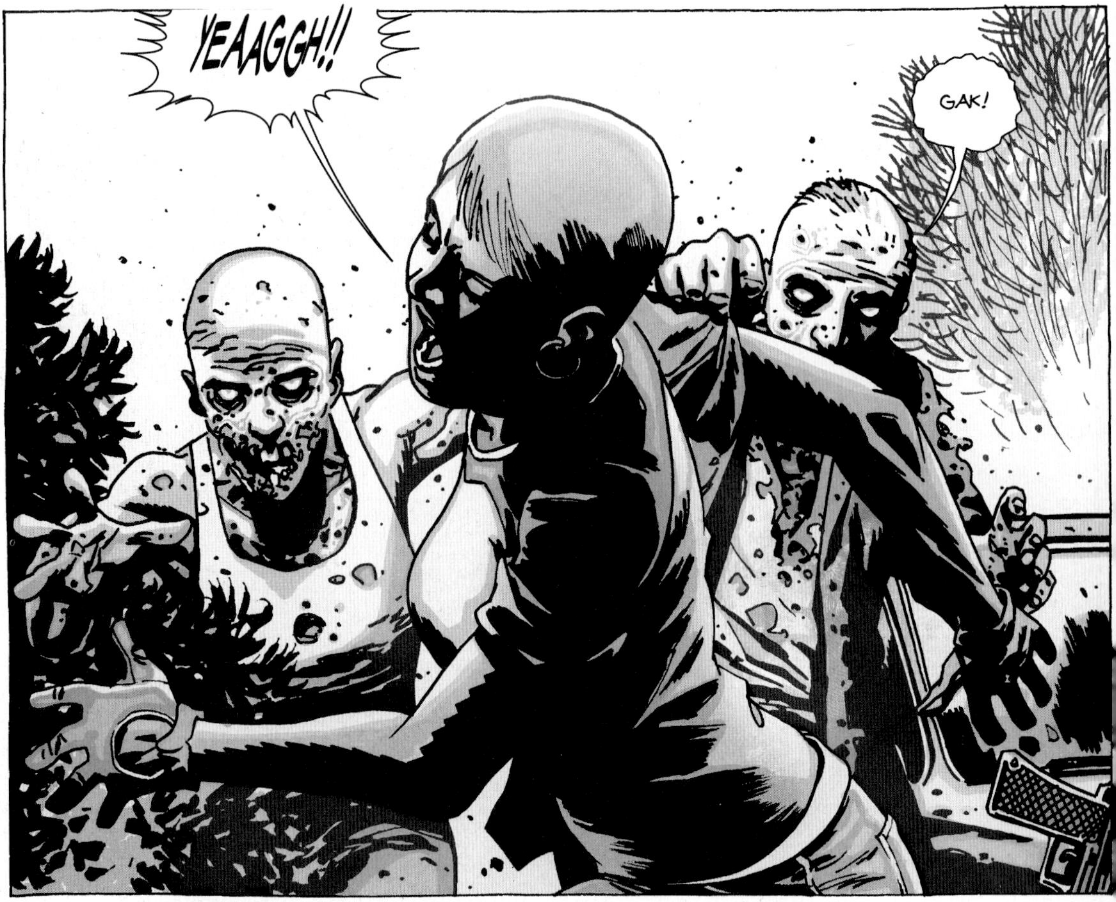
YEAAGGH!!
GAK!

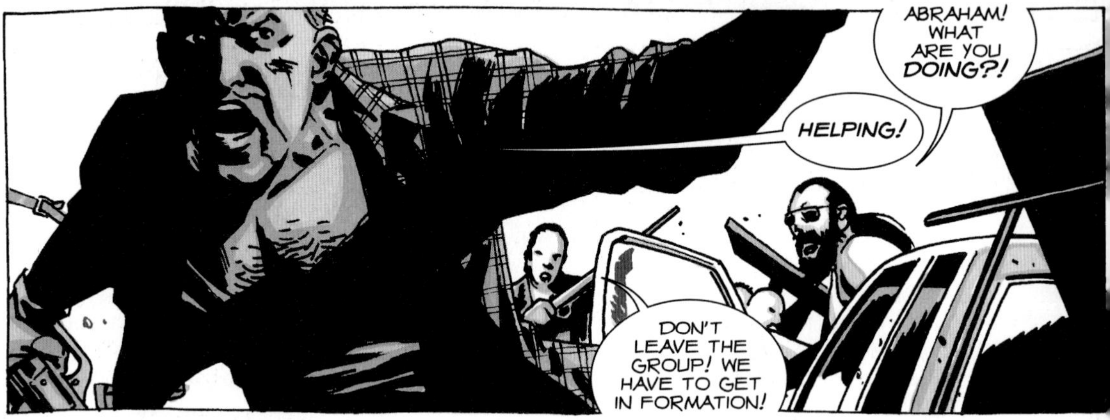
ABRAHAM! WHAT ARE YOU DOING?!
HELPING!
DON'T LEAVE THE GROUP! WE HAVE TO GET IN FORMATION!

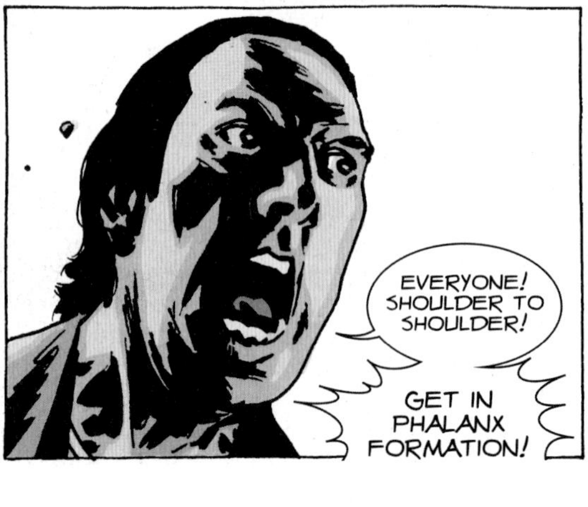
EVERYONE! SHOULDER TO SHOULDER!
GET IN PHALANX FORMATION!

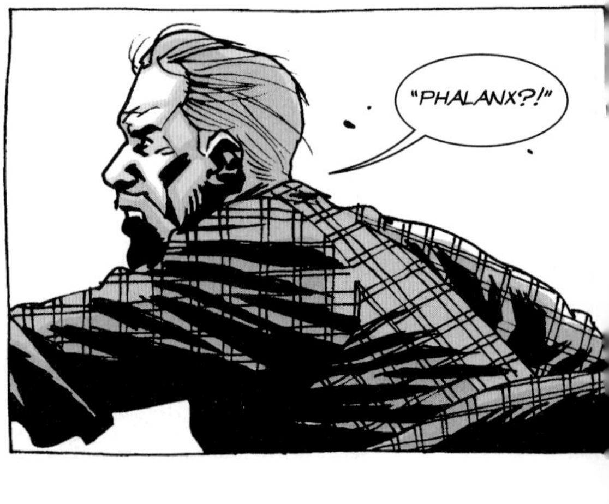
"PHALANX?!"

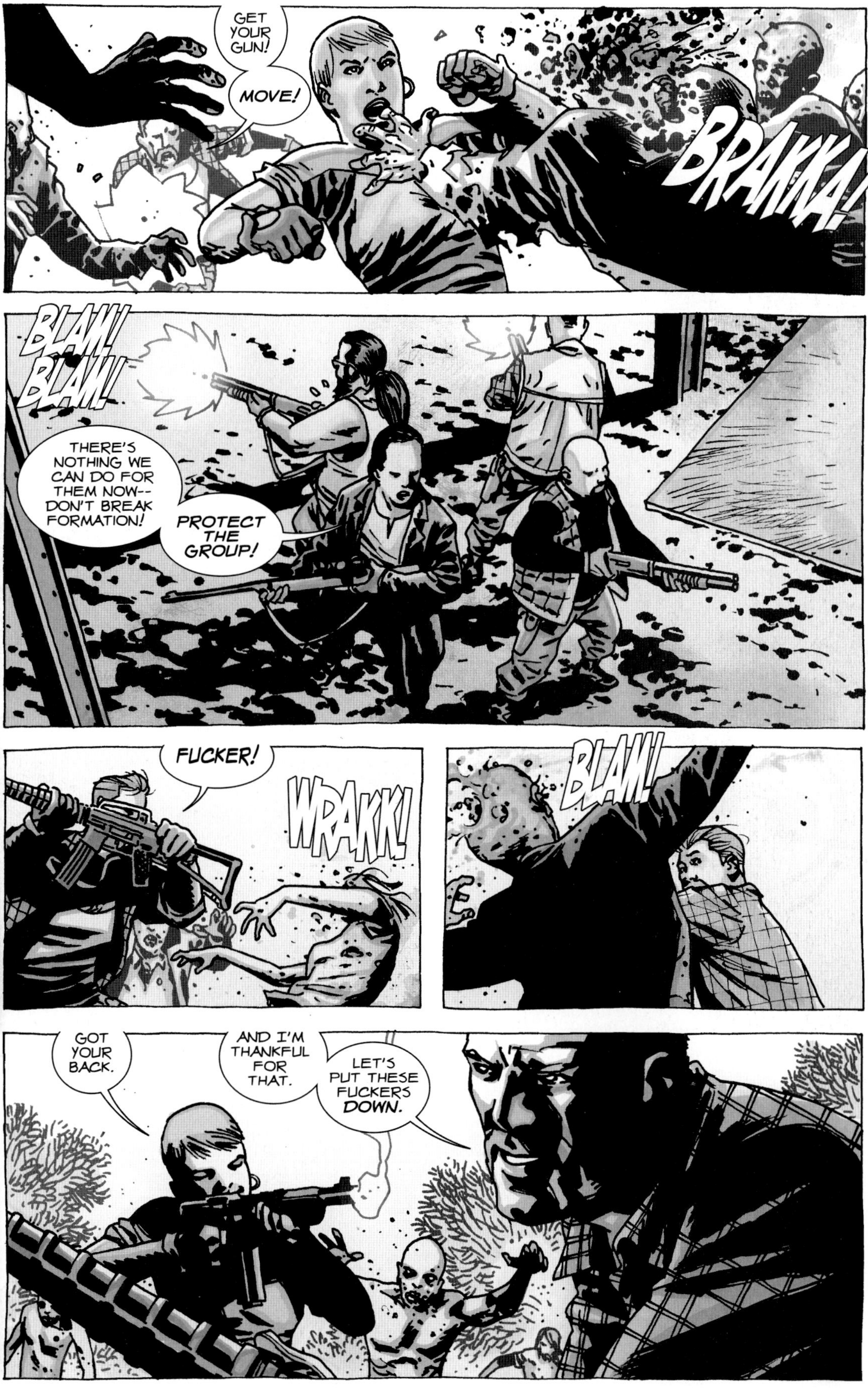
GET YOUR GUN!
MOVE!
BRAKKA!
BLAM! BLAM!
THERE'S NOTHING WE CAN DO FOR THEM NOW-- DON'T BREAK FORMATION!
PROTECT THE GROUP!
FUCKER!
WRAKK!
BLAM!
GOT YOUR BACK.
AND I'M THANKFUL FOR THAT.
LET'S PUT THESE FUCKERS DOWN.

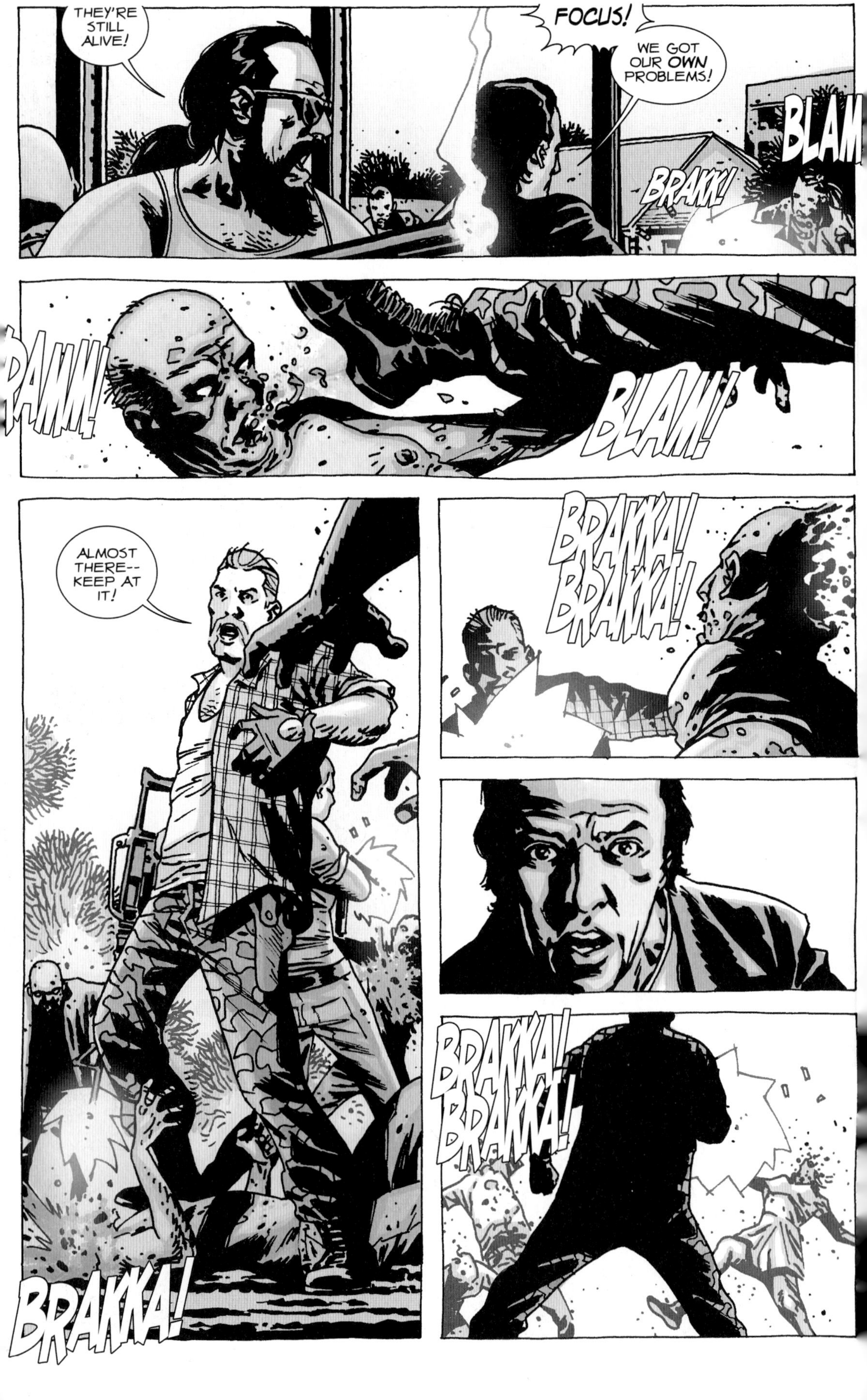
THEY'RE STILL ALIVE!
FOCUS!
WE GOT OUR OWN PROBLEMS!
BRAKK!
BLAM
BLAM!
ALMOST THERE-- KEEP AT IT!
BRAKKA!
BRAKKA! BRAKKA!
BRAKKA! BRAKKA!

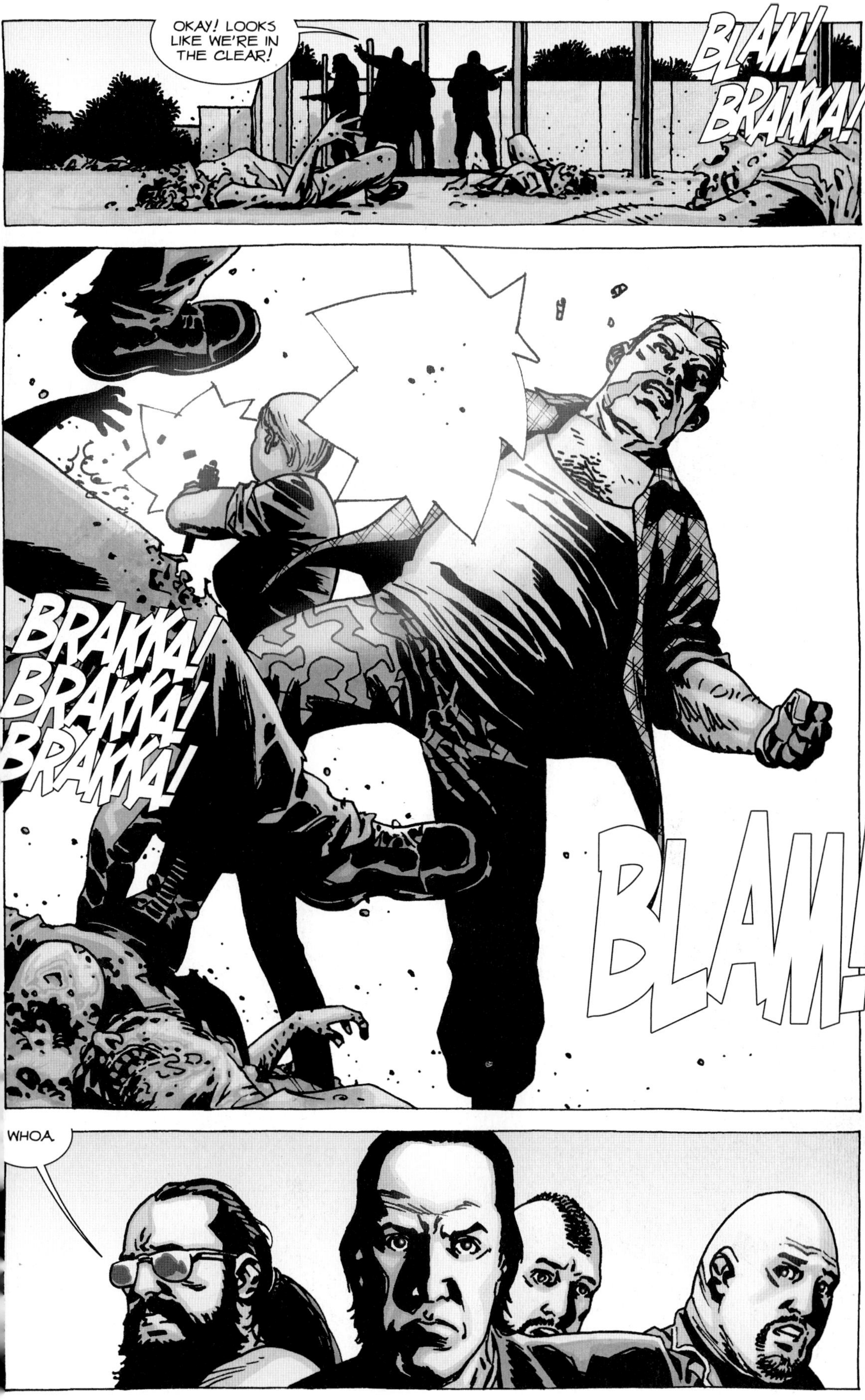
OKAY! LOOKS LIKE WE'RE IN THE CLEAR!
BLAM! BRAKKA!
BRAKKA! BRAKKA! BRAKKA!
BLAM!
WHOA.

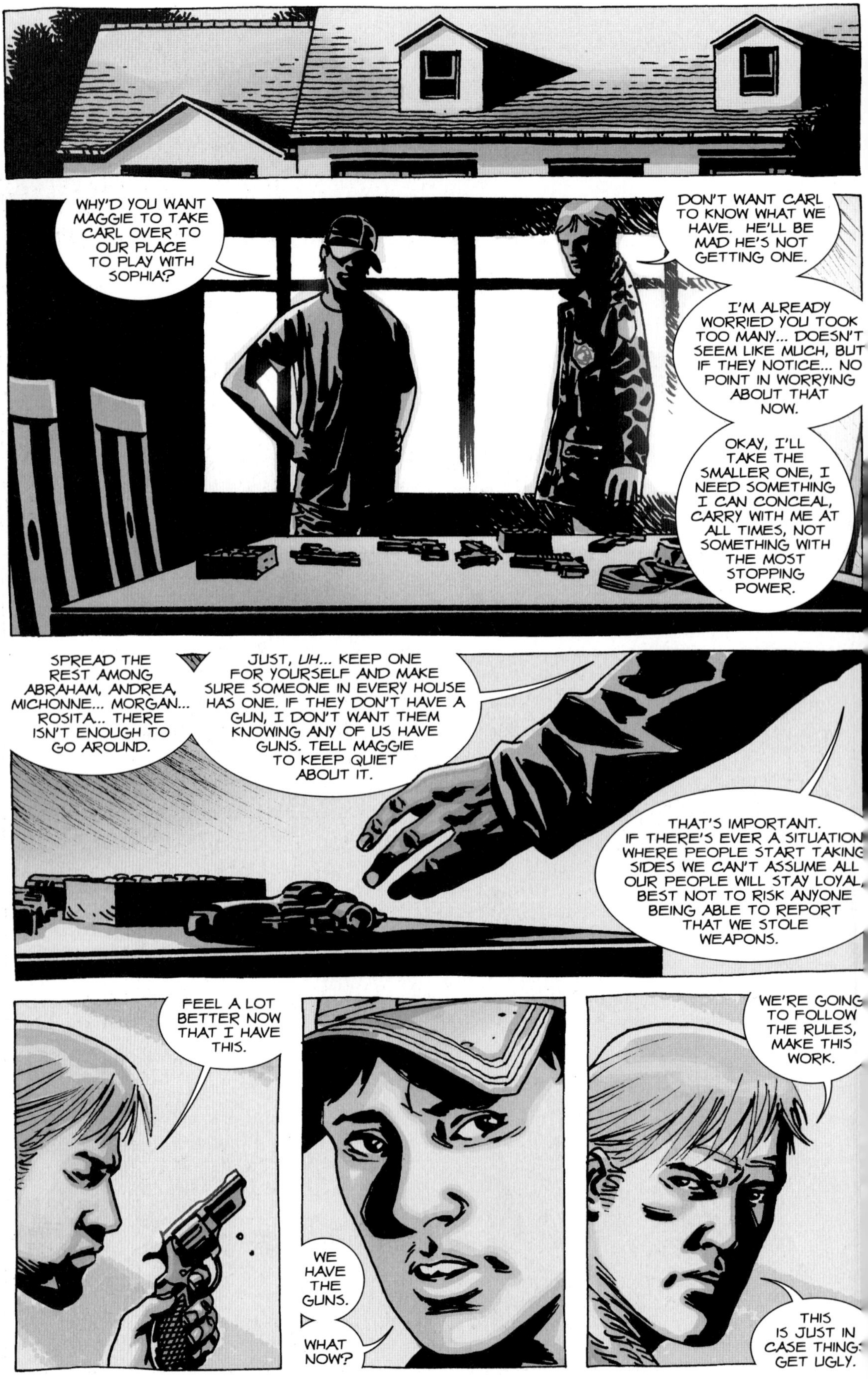
WHY'D YOU WANT MAGGIE TO TAKE CARL OVER TO OUR PLACE TO PLAY WITH SOPHIA?
DON'T WANT CARL TO KNOW WHAT WE HAVE. HE'LL BE MAD HE'S NOT GETTING ONE.
I'M ALREADY WORRIED YOU TOOK TOO MANY... DOESN'T SEEM LIKE MUCH, BUT IF THEY NOTICE... NO POINT IN WORRYING ABOUT THAT NOW.
OKAY, I'LL TAKE THE SMALLER ONE, I NEED SOMETHING I CAN CONCEAL, CARRY WITH ME AT ALL TIMES, NOT SOMETHING WITH THE MOST STOPPING POWER.
SPREAD THE REST AMONG ABRAHAM, ANDREA, MICHONNE... MORGAN... ROSITA... THERE ISN'T ENOUGH TO GO AROUND.
JUST, UH... KEEP ONE FOR YOURSELF AND MAKE SURE SOMEONE IN EVERY HOUSE HAS ONE. IF THEY DON'T HAVE A GUN, I DON'T WANT THEM KNOWING ANY OF US HAVE GUNS. TELL MAGGIE TO KEEP QUIET ABOUT IT.
THAT'S IMPORTANT. IF THERE'S EVER A SITUATION WHERE PEOPLE START TAKING SIDES WE CAN'T ASSUME ALL OUR PEOPLE WILL STAY LOYAL, BEST NOT TO RISK ANYONE BEING ABLE TO REPORT THAT WE STOLE WEAPONS.
FEEL A LOT BETTER NOW THAT I HAVE THIS.
WE HAVE THE GUNS.
WHAT NOW?
WE'RE GOING TO FOLLOW THE RULES, MAKE THIS WORK.
THIS IS JUST IN CASE THINGS GET UGLY.

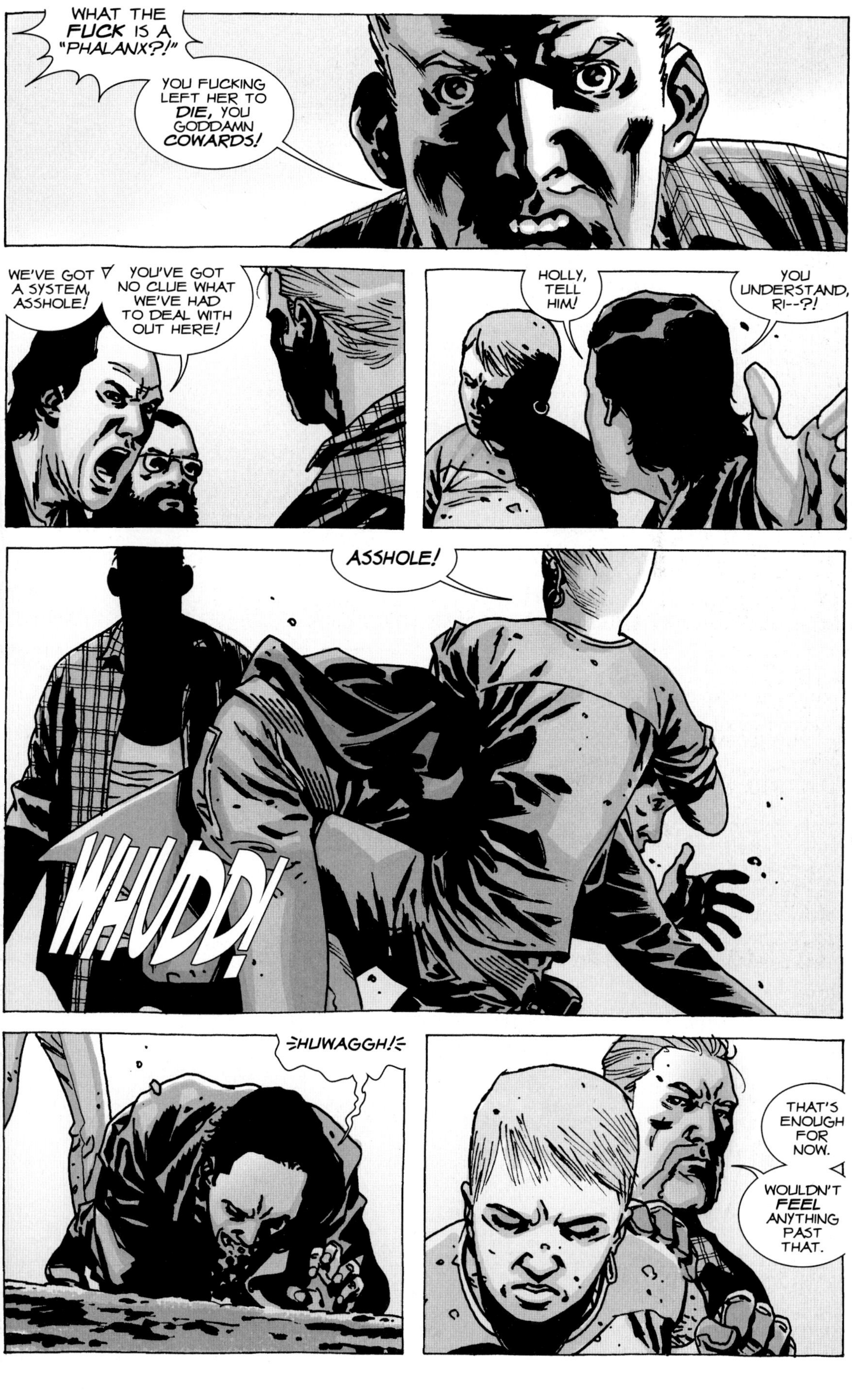
WHAT THE FUCK IS A "PHALANX?!"
YOU FUCKING LEFT HER TO DIE, YOU GODDAMN COWARDS!
WE'VE GOT A SYSTEM, ASSHOLE!
YOU'VE GOT NO CLUE WHAT WE'VE HAD TO DEAL WITH OUT HERE!
HOLLY, TELL HIM!
YOU UNDERSTAND, RI--?!
ASSHOLE!
WHUDD!
HUWAGGH!
THAT'S ENOUGH FOR NOW.
WOULDN'T FEEL ANYTHING PAST THAT.

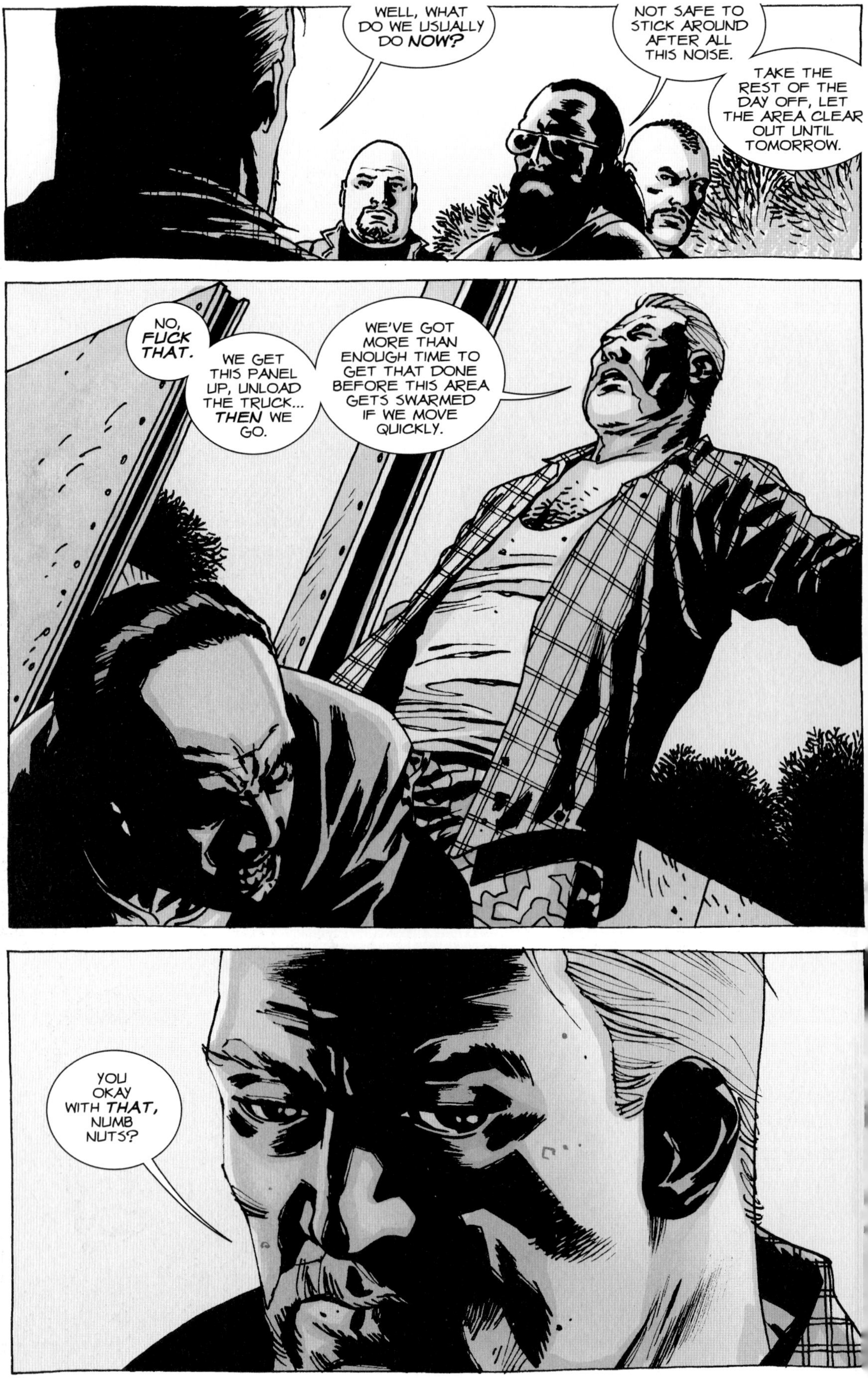
WELL, WHAT DO WE USUALLY DO NOW?
NOT SAFE TO STICK AROUND AFTER ALL THIS NOISE.
TAKE THE REST OF THE DAY OFF, LET THE AREA CLEAR OUT UNTIL TOMORROW.
NO, FUCK THAT.
WE GET THIS PANEL UP, UNLOAD THE TRUCK... THEN WE GO.
WE'VE GOT MORE THAN ENOUGH TIME TO GET THAT DONE BEFORE THIS AREA GETS SWARMED IF WE MOVE QUICKLY.
YOU OKAY WITH THAT, NUMB NUTS?

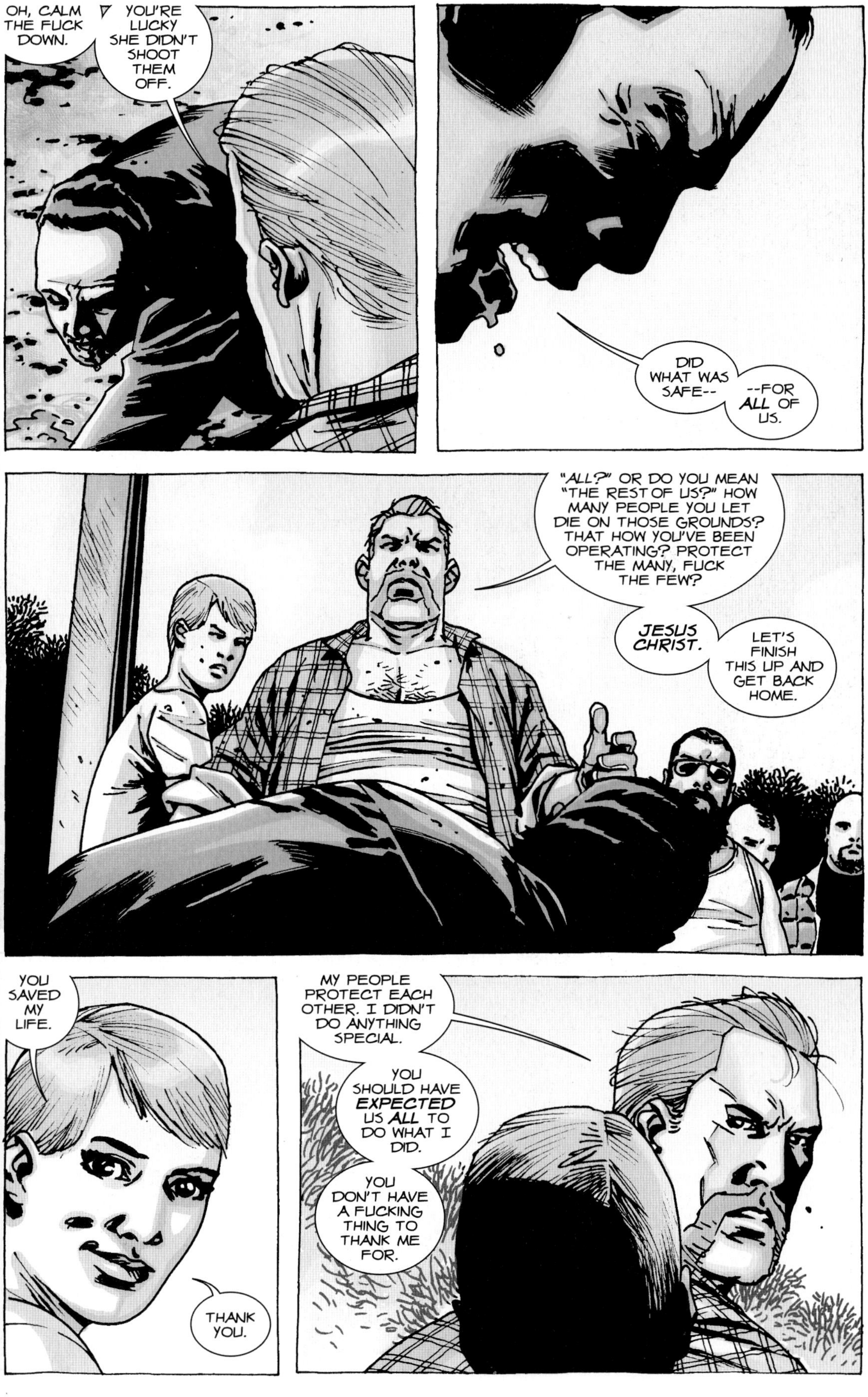
OH, CALM THE FUCK DOWN.
YOU'RE LUCKY SHE DIDN'T SHOOT THEM OFF.
DID WHAT WAS SAFE--
--FOR ALL OF US.
"ALL?" OR DO YOU MEAN "THE REST OF US?" HOW MANY PEOPLE YOU LET DIE ON THOSE GROUNDS? THAT HOW YOU'VE BEEN OPERATING? PROTECT THE MANY, FUCK THE FEW?
JESUS CHRIST.
LET'S FINISH THIS UP AND GET BACK HOME.
YOU SAVED MY LIFE.
THANK YOU.
MY PEOPLE PROTECT EACH OTHER. I DIDN'T DO ANYTHING SPECIAL.
YOU SHOULD HAVE EXPECTED US ALL TO DO WHAT I DID.
YOU DON'T HAVE A FUCKING THING TO THANK ME FOR.

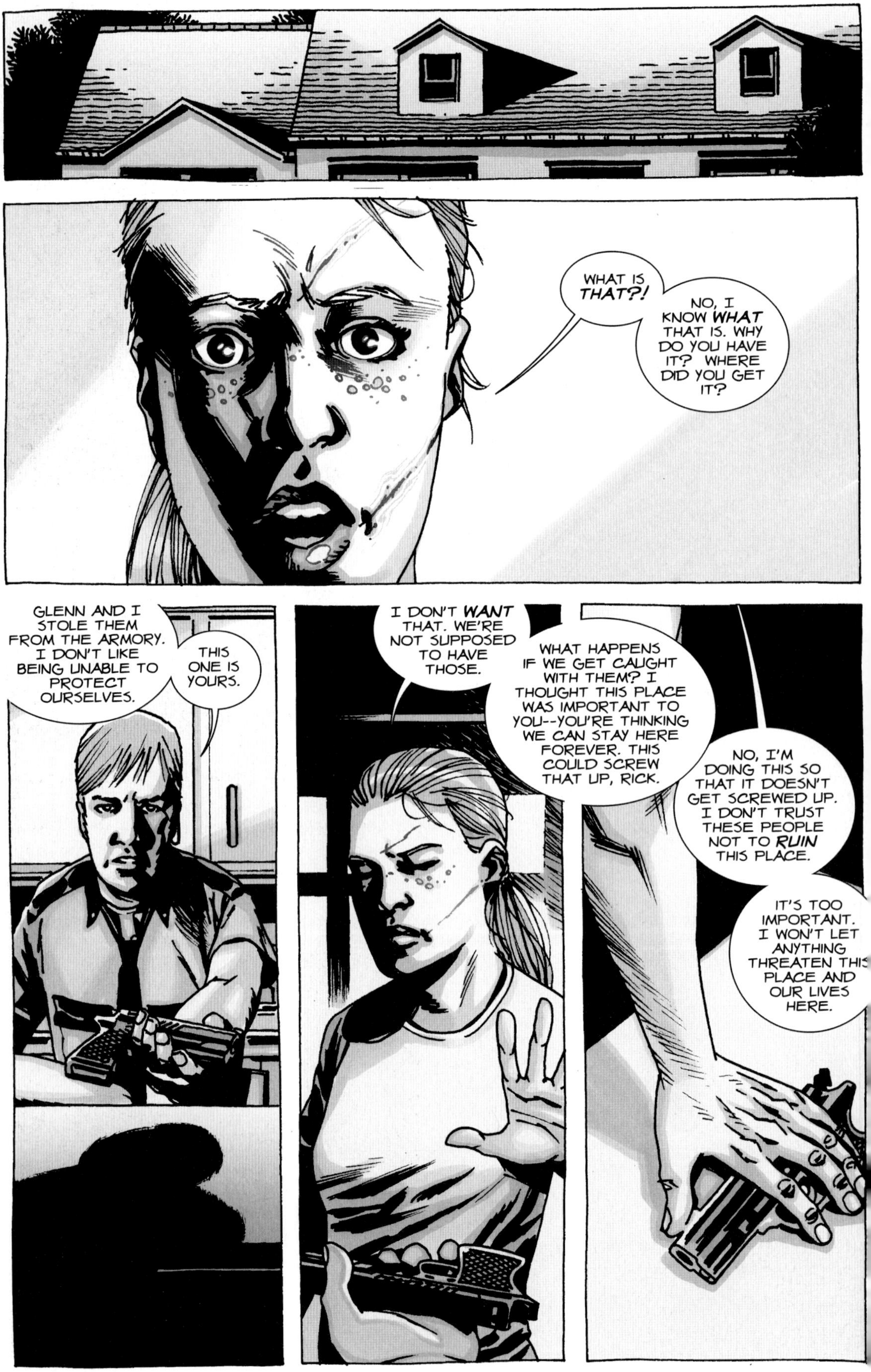
WHAT IS THAT?!
NO, I KNOW WHAT THAT IS. WHY DO YOU HAVE IT? WHERE DID YOU GET IT?
GLENN AND I STOLE THEM FROM THE ARMORY. I DON'T LIKE BEING UNABLE TO PROTECT OURSELVES.
THIS ONE IS YOURS.
I DON'T WANT THAT. WE'RE NOT SUPPOSED TO HAVE THOSE.
WHAT HAPPENS IF WE GET CAUGHT WITH THEM? I THOUGHT THIS PLACE WAS IMPORTANT TO YOU--YOU'RE THINKING WE CAN STAY HERE FOREVER. THIS COULD SCREW THAT UP, RICK.
NO, I'M DOING THIS SO THAT IT DOESN'T GET SCREWED UP. I DON'T TRUST THESE PEOPLE NOT TO RUIN THIS PLACE.
IT'S TOO IMPORTANT. I WON'T LET ANYTHING THREATEN THIS PLACE AND OUR LIVES HERE.

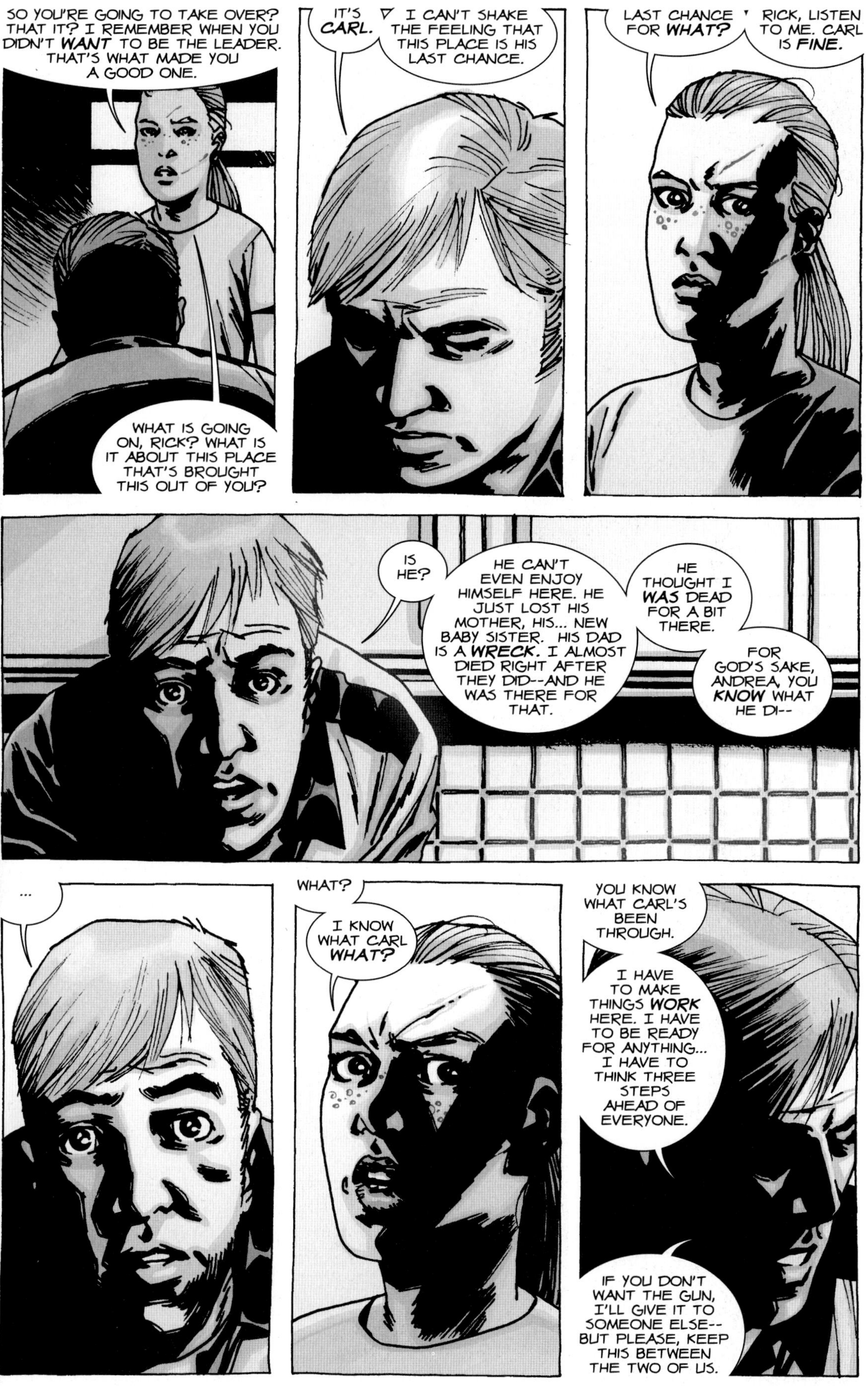
SO YOU'RE GOING TO TAKE OVER? THAT IT? I REMEMBER WHEN YOU DIDN'T WANT TO BE THE LEADER. THAT'S WHAT MADE YOU A GOOD ONE.
WHAT IS GOING ON, RICK? WHAT IS IT ABOUT THIS PLACE THAT'S BROUGHT THIS OUT OF YOU?
IT'S CARL.
I CAN'T SHAKE THE FEELING THAT THIS PLACE IS HIS LAST CHANCE.
LAST CHANCE FOR WHAT?
RICK, LISTEN TO ME. CARL IS FINE.
IS HE?
HE CAN'T EVEN ENJOY HIMSELF HERE. HE JUST LOST HIS MOTHER, HIS... NEW BABY SISTER. HIS DAD IS A WRECK. I ALMOST DIED RIGHT AFTER THEY DID--AND HE WAS THERE FOR THAT.
HE THOUGHT I WAS DEAD FOR A BIT THERE.
FOR GOD'S SAKE, ANDREA, YOU KNOW WHAT HE DI--
...
WHAT?
I KNOW WHAT CARL WHAT?
YOU KNOW WHAT CARL'S BEEN THROUGH.
I HAVE TO MAKE THINGS WORK HERE. I HAVE TO BE READY FOR ANYTHING... I HAVE TO THINK THREE STEPS AHEAD OF EVERYONE.
IF YOU DON'T WANT THE GUN, I'LL GIVE IT TO SOMEONE ELSE-- BUT PLEASE, KEEP THIS BETWEEN THE TWO OF US.

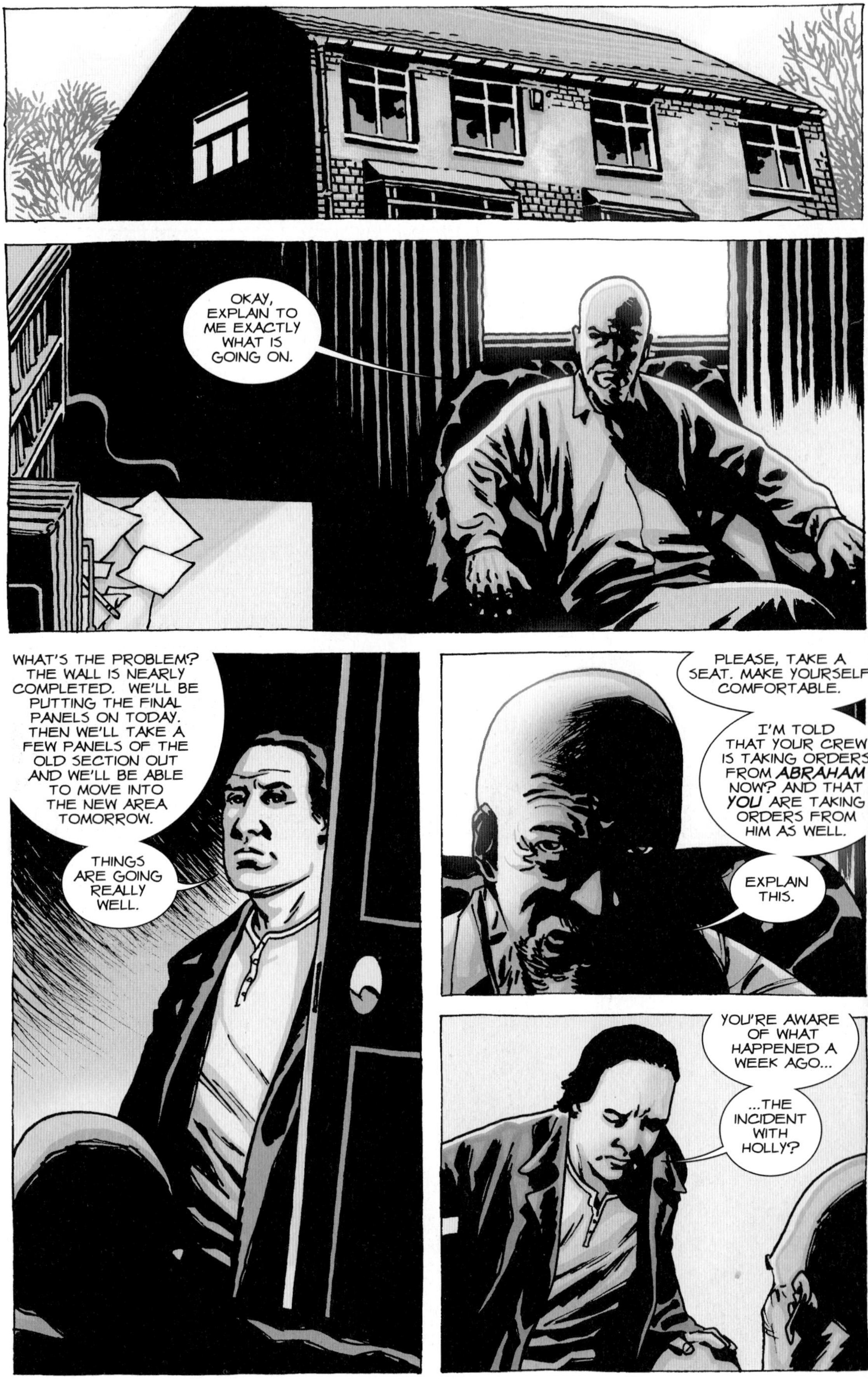
OKAY, EXPLAIN TO ME EXACTLY WHAT IS GOING ON.
WHAT'S THE PROBLEM? THE WALL IS NEARLY COMPLETED. WE'LL BE PUTTING THE FINAL PANELS ON TODAY. THEN WE'LL TAKE A FEW PANELS OF THE OLD SECTION OUT AND WE'LL BE ABLE TO MOVE INTO THE NEW AREA TOMORROW.
THINGS ARE GOING REALLY WELL.
PLEASE, TAKE A SEAT. MAKE YOURSELF COMFORTABLE.
I'M TOLD THAT YOUR CREW IS TAKING ORDERS FROM ABRAHAM NOW? AND THAT YOU ARE TAKING ORDERS FROM HIM AS WELL.
EXPLAIN THIS.
YOU'RE AWARE OF WHAT HAPPENED A WEEK AGO...
...THE INCIDENT WITH HOLLY?

SHE WAS IN DANGER, ABRAHAM SAVED HER.

YOU DIDN'T. I UNDERSTAND YOU FEEL GUILTY ABOUT THIS, BUT IT WASN'T YOUR FAULT. YOU DON'T CONTROL THE WALKERS, YOU CAN'T MAKE THEM ATTACK--HOW CAN YOU BLAME YOURSELF?

DOUGLAS, SHE WOULD BE *DEAD* IF ABRAHAM HADN'T BEEN THERE. I WAS IN CHARGE AND MY PLAN WOULD HAVE GOTTEN HER *KILLED*.

SHE WOULD BE DEAD.

HOW MANY OTHERS DIED BECAUSE I'M A COWARD? DO YOU REMEMBER BARNES? WHAT ABOUT RICHARDS?

YES... AND I REMEMBER CARTER AND JESSICA AND BETH AND DAVIDSON AND A WHOLE LOT MORE.

I REMEMBER EVERYONE WE'VE LOST... BUT I DON'T GO STEPPING DOWN BECAUSE OF IT AND I SURE AS HELL DON'T BLAME MYSELF.

THE PEOPLE HERE DEPEND ON ME... WE DEPEND ON EACH OTHER. YOU BETTER BELIEVE YOUR CREW DEPENDS ON *YOU*.

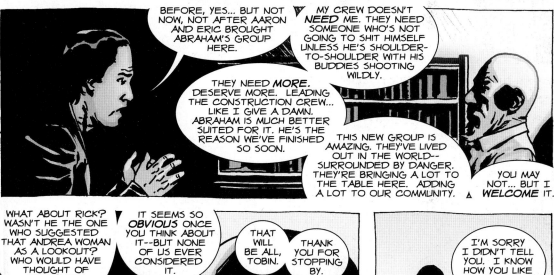

BEFORE, YES... BUT NOT NOW, NOT AFTER AARON AND ERIC BROUGHT ABRAHAM'S GROUP HERE.

THEY NEED *MORE*. DESERVE MORE. LEADING THE CONSTRUCTION CREW... LIKE I GIVE A DAMN. ABRAHAM IS MUCH BETTER SUITED FOR IT. HE'S THE REASON WE'VE FINISHED SO SOON.

MY CREW DOESN'T *NEED* ME. THEY NEED SOMEONE WHO'S NOT GOING TO SHIT HIMSELF UNLESS HE'S SHOULDER-TO-SHOULDER WITH HIS BUDDIES SHOOTING WILDLY.

THIS NEW GROUP IS AMAZING. THEY'VE LIVED OUT IN THE WORLD-- SURROUNDED BY DANGER. THEY'RE BRINGING A LOT TO THE TABLE HERE. ADDING A LOT TO OUR COMMUNITY.

YOU MAY NOT... BUT I *WELCOME* IT.

WHAT ABOUT RICK? WASN'T HE THE ONE WHO SUGGESTED THAT ANDREA WOMAN AS A LOOKOUT? WHO WOULD HAVE THOUGHT OF THAT? YOU CERTAINLY DIDN'T.

IT SEEMS SO *OBVIOUS* ONCE YOU THINK ABOUT IT--BUT NONE OF US EVER CONSIDERED IT.

THAT WILL BE ALL, TOBIN.

THANK YOU FOR STOPPING BY.

I'M SORRY I DIDN'T TELL YOU. I KNOW HOW YOU LIKE TO BE IN THE LOOP.

AS FAR AS I'M CONCERNED-- ABRAHAM HAS *EARNED* MY POSITION ON THE CONSTRUCTION CREW.

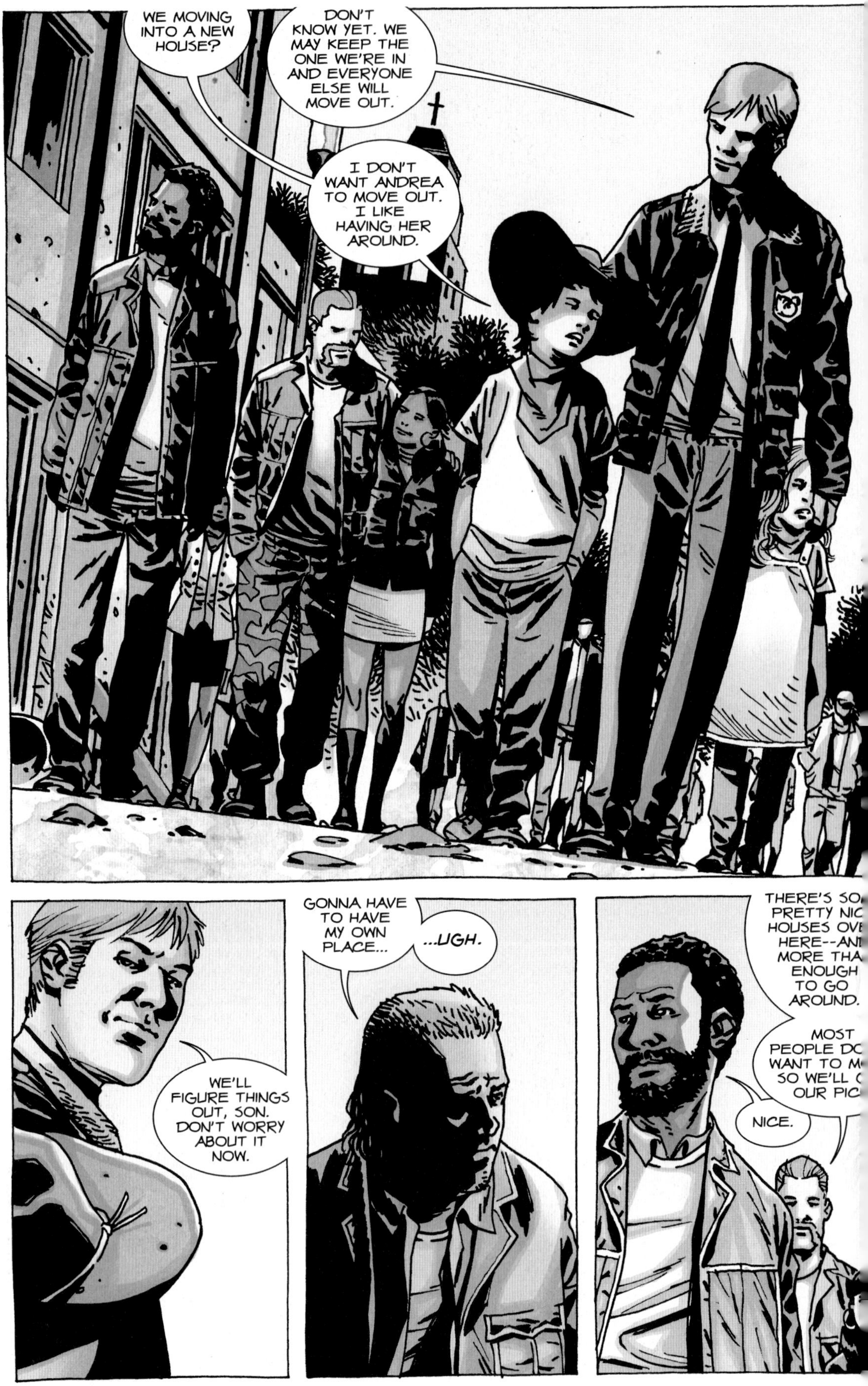

WE MOVING INTO A NEW HOUSE?
DON'T KNOW YET. WE MAY KEEP THE ONE WE'RE IN AND EVERYONE ELSE WILL MOVE OUT.
I DON'T WANT ANDREA TO MOVE OUT. I LIKE HAVING HER AROUND.
WE'LL FIGURE THINGS OUT, SON. DON'T WORRY ABOUT IT NOW.
GONNA HAVE TO HAVE MY OWN PLACE...
...UGH.
THERE'S SO PRETTY NIC HOUSES OVE HERE--AN MORE THA ENOUGH TO GO AROUND.
NICE.
MOST PEOPLE DO WANT TO M SO WE'LL OUR PIC

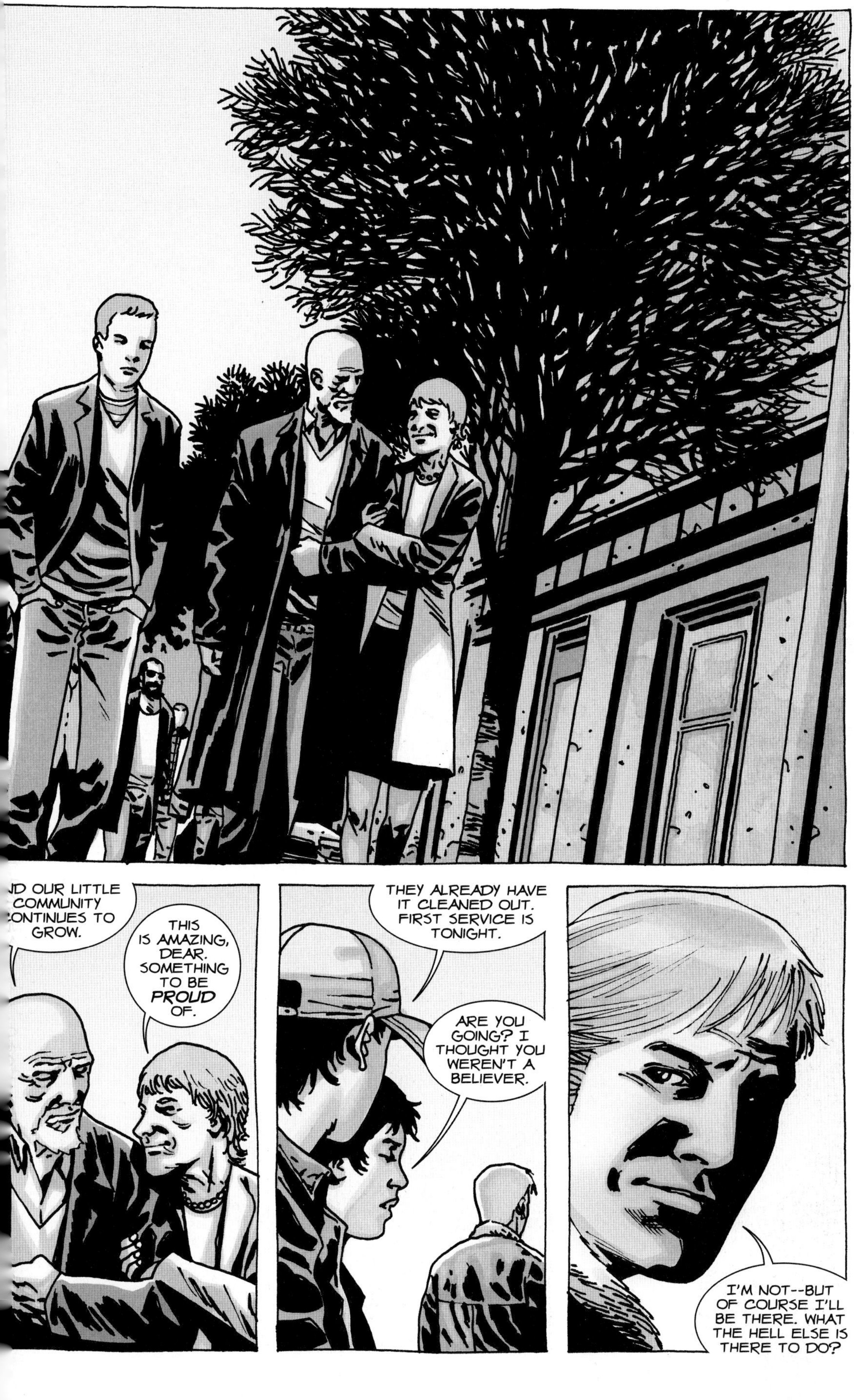

ND OUR LITTLE COMMUNITY CONTINUES TO GROW.
THIS IS AMAZING, DEAR. SOMETHING TO BE *PROUD* OF.
THEY ALREADY HAVE IT CLEANED OUT. FIRST SERVICE IS TONIGHT.
ARE YOU GOING? I THOUGHT YOU WEREN'T A BELIEVER.
I'M NOT--BUT OF COURSE I'LL BE THERE. WHAT THE HELL ELSE IS THERE TO DO?

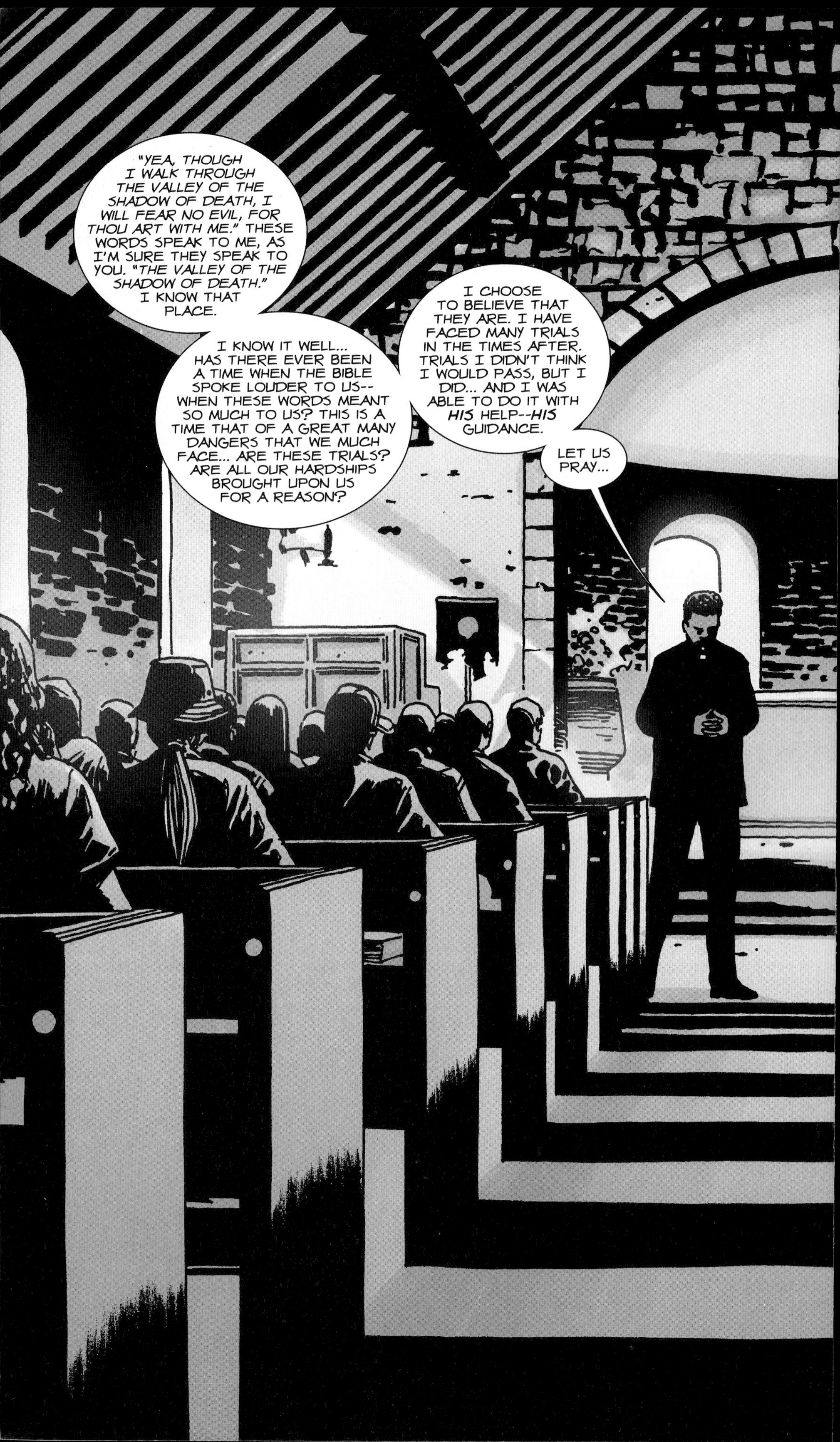
"YEA, THOUGH I WALK THROUGH THE VALLEY OF THE SHADOW OF DEATH, I WILL FEAR NO EVIL, FOR THOU ART WITH ME." THESE WORDS SPEAK TO ME, AS I'M SURE THEY SPEAK TO YOU. "THE VALLEY OF THE SHADOW OF DEATH." I KNOW THAT PLACE.
I KNOW IT WELL... HAS THERE EVER BEEN A TIME WHEN THE BIBLE SPOKE LOUDER TO US-- WHEN THESE WORDS MEANT SO MUCH TO US? THIS IS A TIME THAT OF A GREAT MANY DANGERS THAT WE MUCH FACE... ARE THESE TRIALS? ARE ALL OUR HARDSHIPS BROUGHT UPON US FOR A REASON?
I CHOOSE TO BELIEVE THAT THEY ARE. I HAVE FACED MANY TRIALS IN THE TIMES AFTER. TRIALS I DIDN'T THINK I WOULD PASS, BUT I DID... AND I WAS ABLE TO DO IT WITH HIS HELP--HIS GUIDANCE.
LET US PRAY...

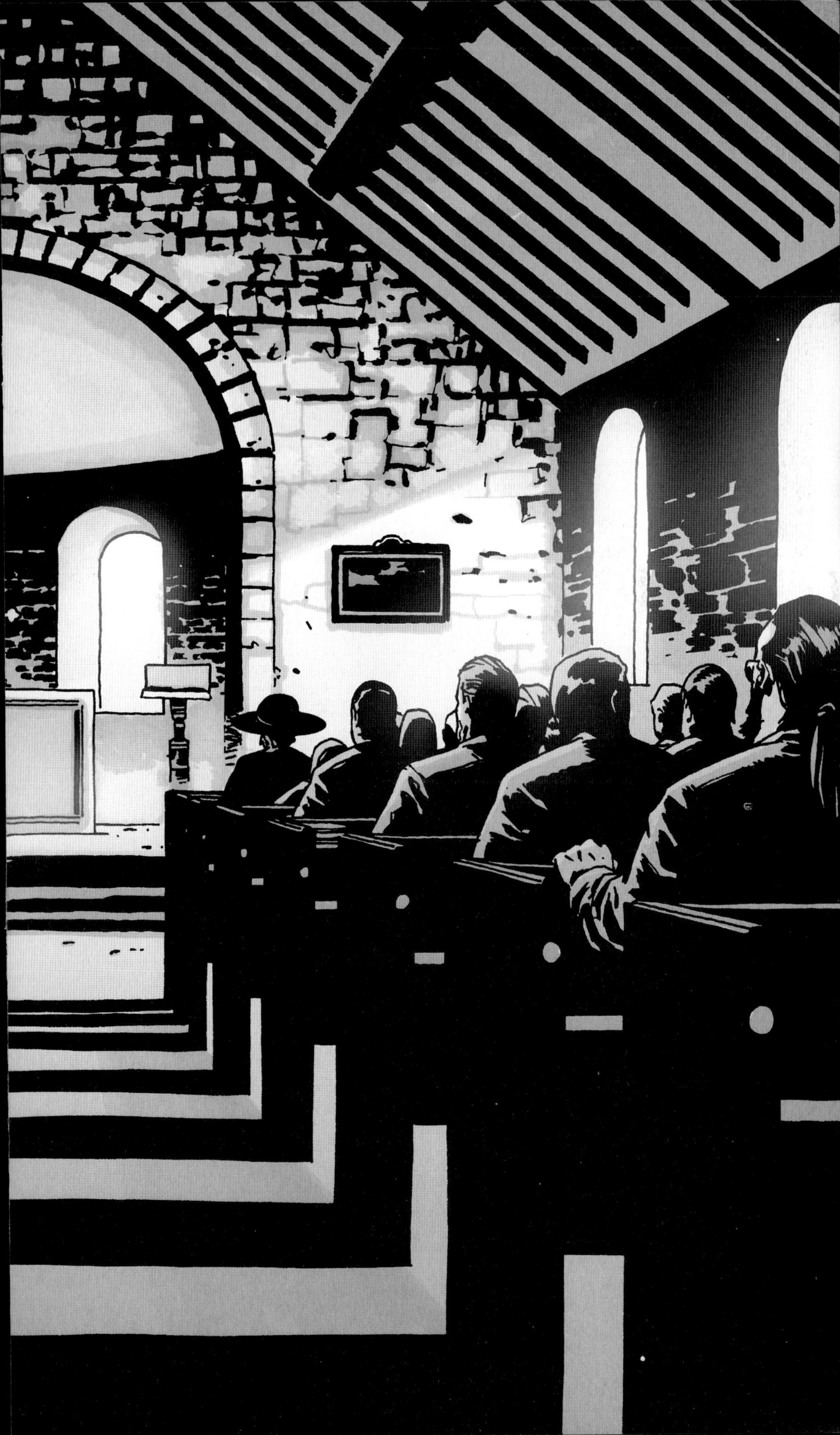

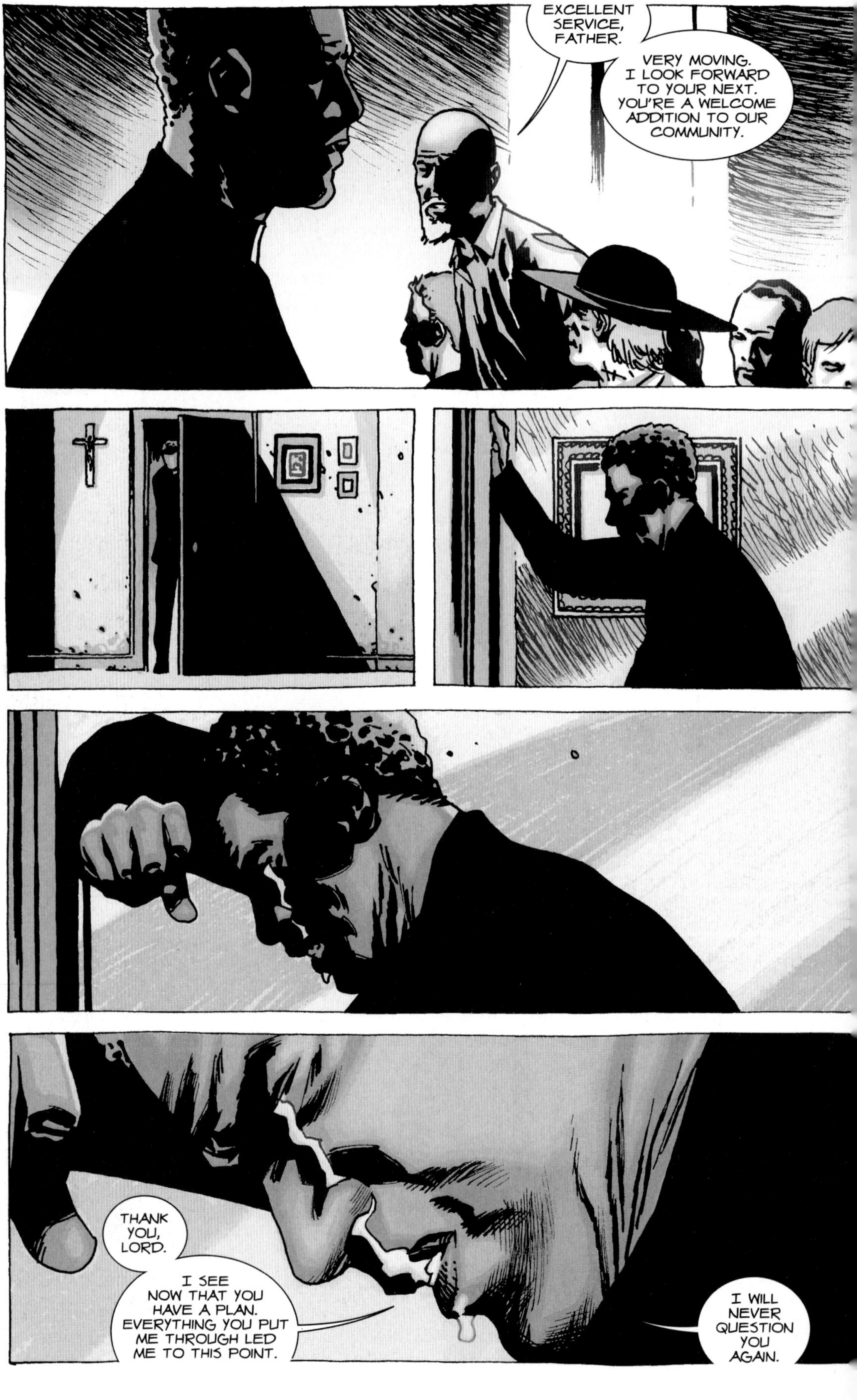
EXCELLENT SERVICE, FATHER.
VERY MOVING. I LOOK FORWARD TO YOUR NEXT. YOU'RE A WELCOME ADDITION TO OUR COMMUNITY.
THANK YOU, LORD.
I SEE NOW THAT YOU HAVE A PLAN. EVERYTHING YOU PUT ME THROUGH LED ME TO THIS POINT.
I WILL NEVER QUESTION YOU AGAIN.

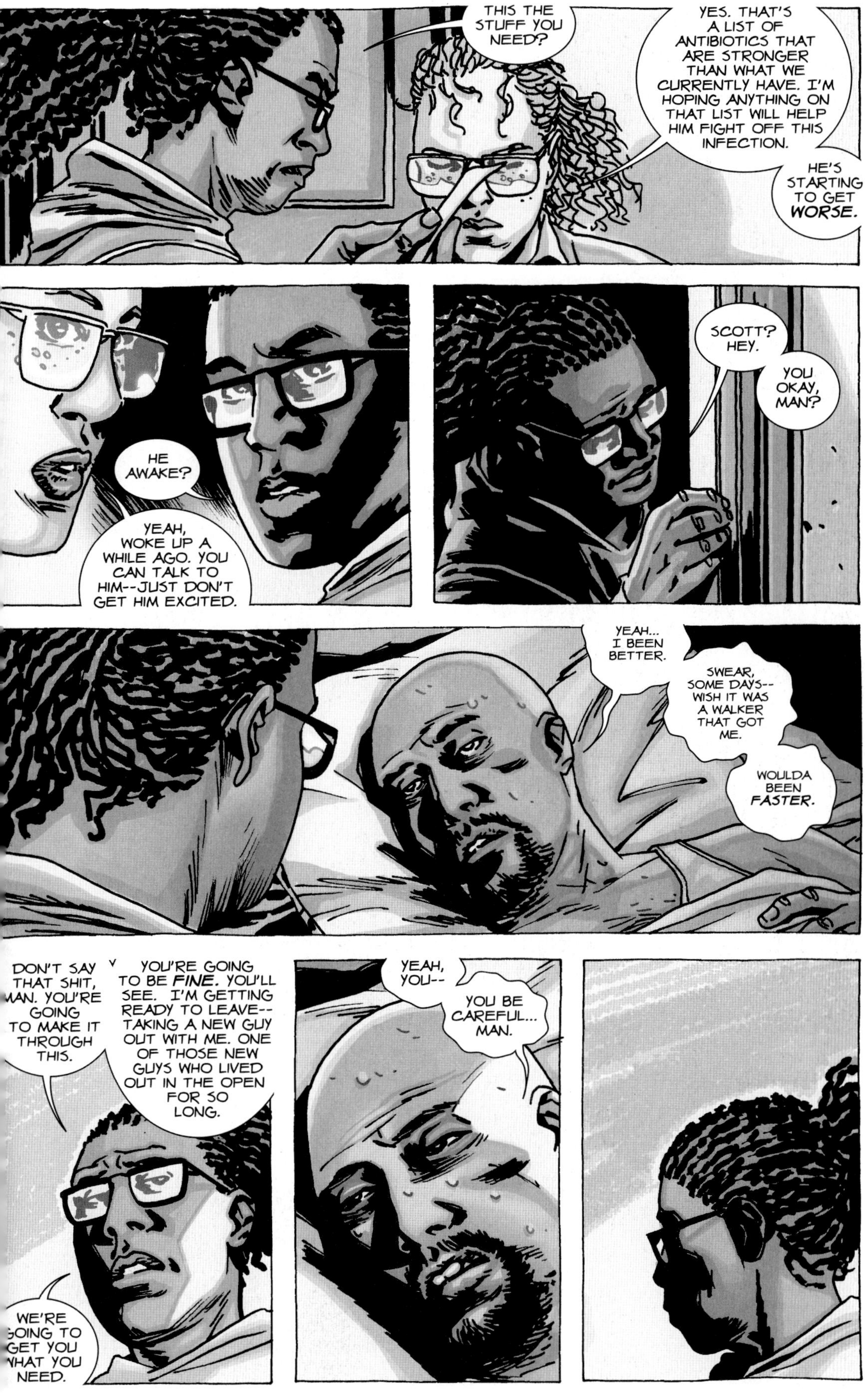
THIS THE STUFF YOU NEED?
YES. THAT'S A LIST OF ANTIBIOTICS THAT ARE STRONGER THAN WHAT WE CURRENTLY HAVE. I'M HOPING ANYTHING ON THAT LIST WILL HELP HIM FIGHT OFF THIS INFECTION.
HE'S STARTING TO GET WORSE.
HE AWAKE?
YEAH, WOKE UP A WHILE AGO. YOU CAN TALK TO HIM--JUST DON'T GET HIM EXCITED.
SCOTT? HEY.
YOU OKAY, MAN?
YEAH... I BEEN BETTER.
SWEAR, SOME DAYS-- WISH IT WAS A WALKER THAT GOT ME.
WOULDA BEEN FASTER.
DON'T SAY THAT SHIT, MAN. YOU'RE GOING TO MAKE IT THROUGH THIS.
YOU'RE GOING TO BE FINE. YOU'LL SEE. I'M GETTING READY TO LEAVE-- TAKING A NEW GUY OUT WITH ME. ONE OF THOSE NEW GUYS WHO LIVED OUT IN THE OPEN FOR SO LONG.
WE'RE GOING TO GET YOU WHAT YOU NEED.
YEAH, YOU--
YOU BE CAREFUL... MAN.

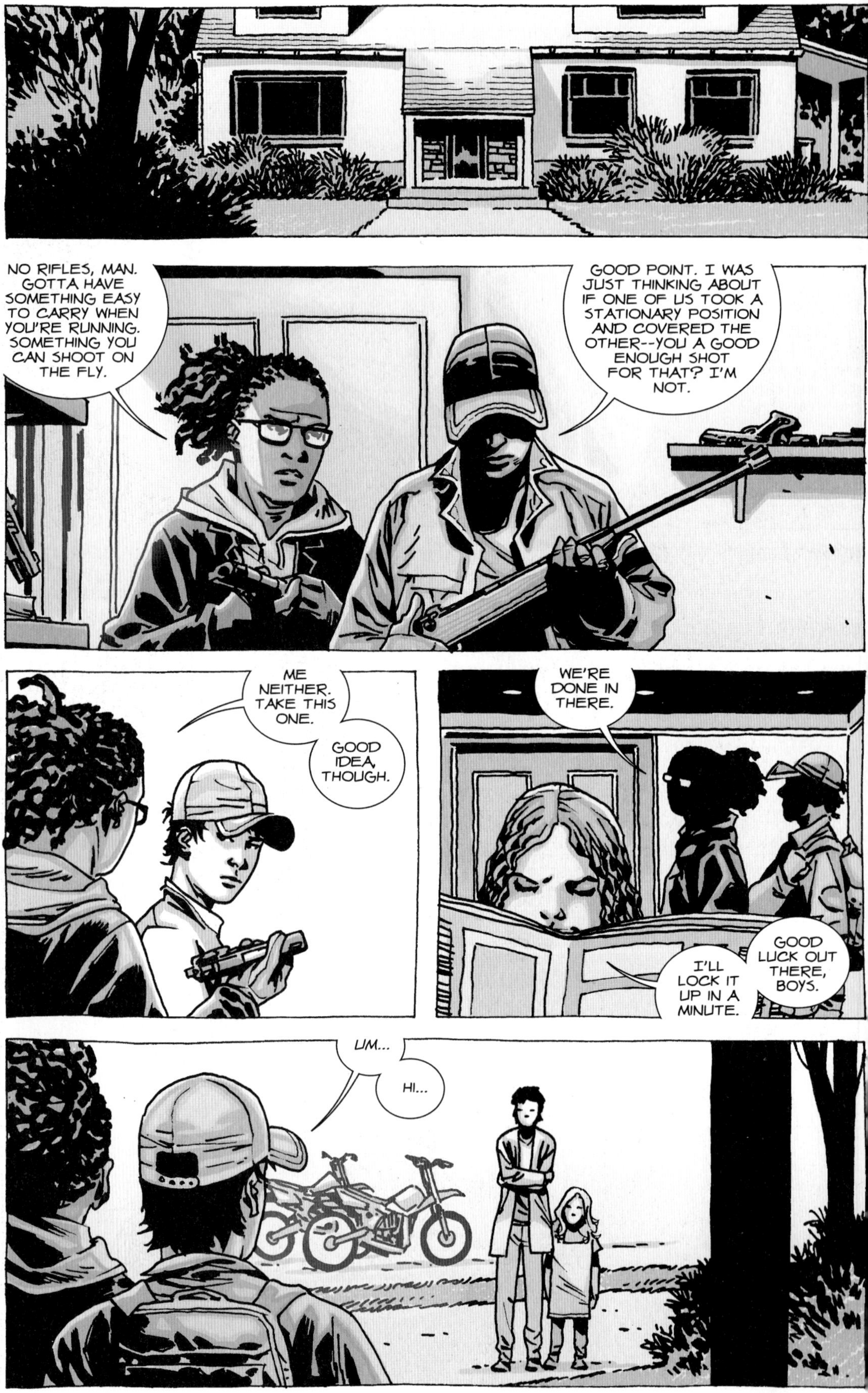
NO RIFLES, MAN. GOTTA HAVE SOMETHING EASY TO CARRY WHEN YOU'RE RUNNING. SOMETHING YOU CAN SHOOT ON THE FLY.
GOOD POINT. I WAS JUST THINKING ABOUT IF ONE OF US TOOK A STATIONARY POSITION AND COVERED THE OTHER--YOU A GOOD ENOUGH SHOT FOR THAT? I'M NOT.
ME NEITHER. TAKE THIS ONE.
GOOD IDEA, THOUGH.
WE'RE DONE IN THERE.
I'LL LOCK IT UP IN A MINUTE.
GOOD LUCK OUT THERE, BOYS.
UM...
HI...

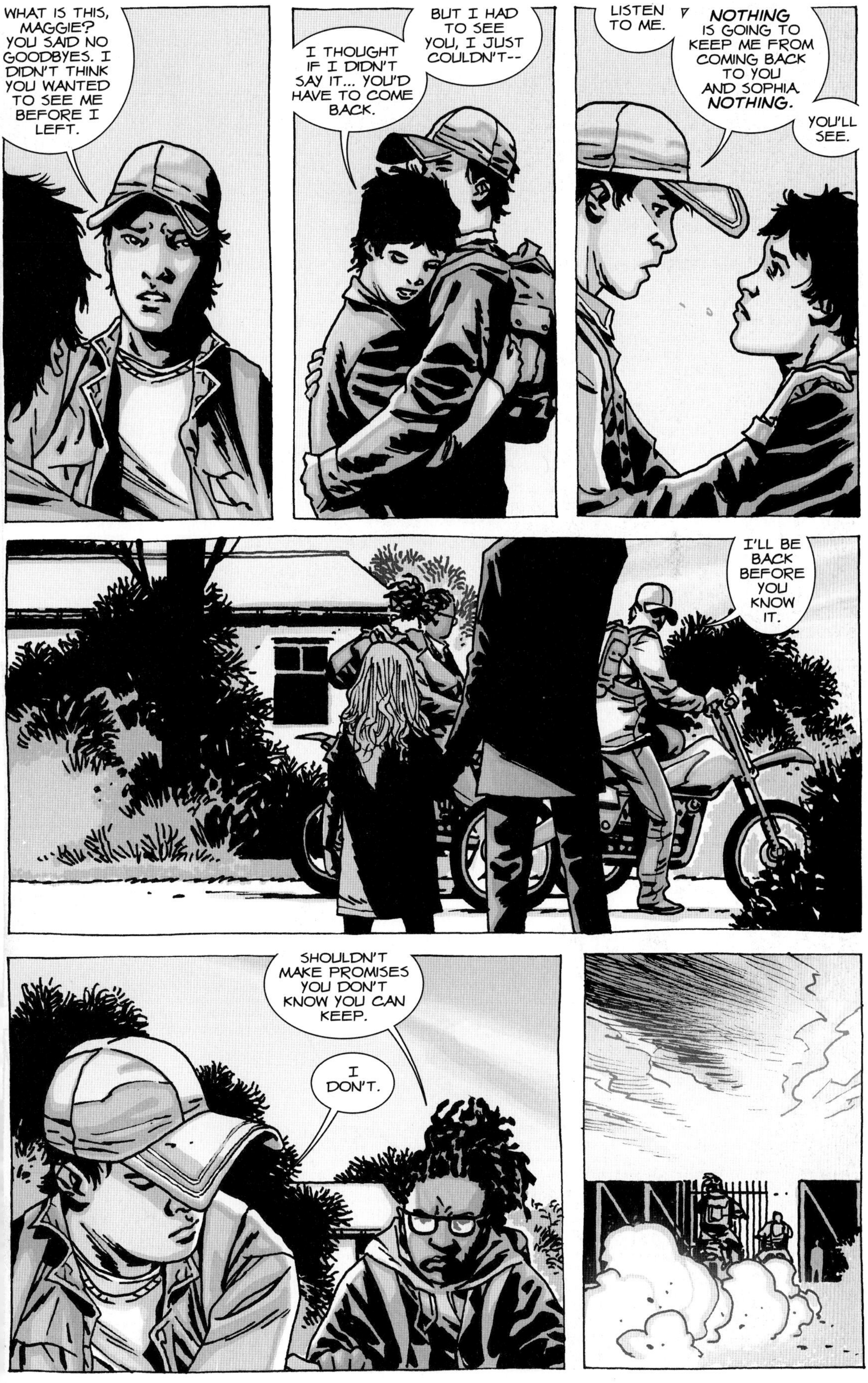
WHAT IS THIS, MAGGIE? YOU SAID NO GOODBYES. I DIDN'T THINK YOU WANTED TO SEE ME BEFORE I LEFT.
I THOUGHT IF I DIDN'T SAY IT... YOU'D HAVE TO COME BACK.
BUT I HAD TO SEE YOU, I JUST COULDN'T--
LISTEN TO ME.
NOTHING IS GOING TO KEEP ME FROM COMING BACK TO YOU AND SOPHIA. NOTHING.
YOU'LL SEE.
I'LL BE BACK BEFORE YOU KNOW IT.
SHOULDN'T MAKE PROMISES YOU DON'T KNOW YOU CAN KEEP.
I DON'T.

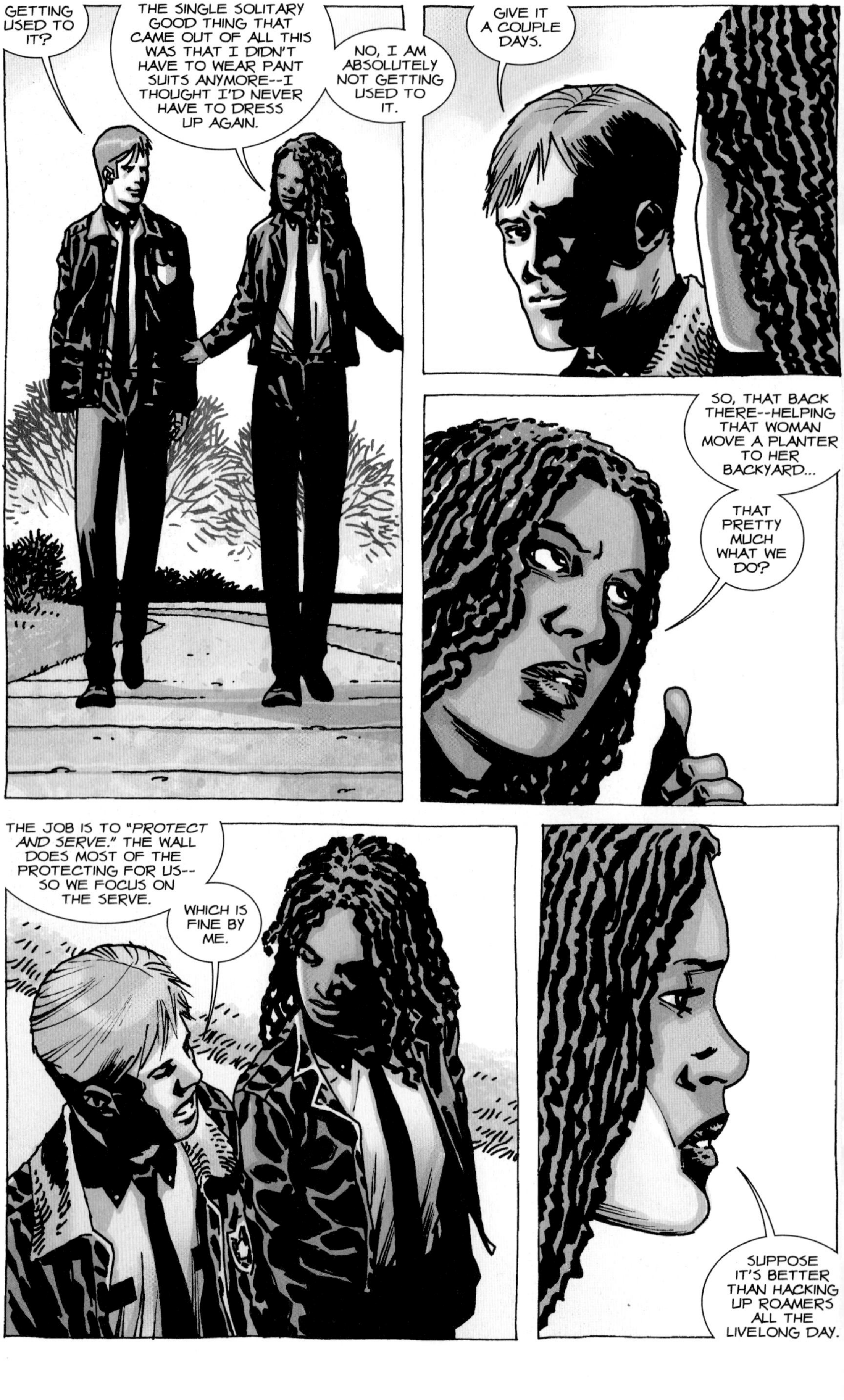
GETTING USED TO IT?
THE SINGLE SOLITARY GOOD THING THAT CAME OUT OF ALL THIS WAS THAT I DIDN'T HAVE TO WEAR PANT SUITS ANYMORE--I THOUGHT I'D NEVER HAVE TO DRESS UP AGAIN.
NO, I AM ABSOLUTELY NOT GETTING USED TO IT.
GIVE IT A COUPLE DAYS.
SO, THAT BACK THERE--HELPING THAT WOMAN MOVE A PLANTER TO HER BACKYARD...
THAT PRETTY MUCH WHAT WE DO?
THE JOB IS TO "PROTECT AND SERVE." THE WALL DOES MOST OF THE PROTECTING FOR US--SO WE FOCUS ON THE SERVE.
WHICH IS FINE BY ME.
SUPPOSE IT'S BETTER THAN HACKING UP ROAMERS ALL THE LIVELONG DAY.

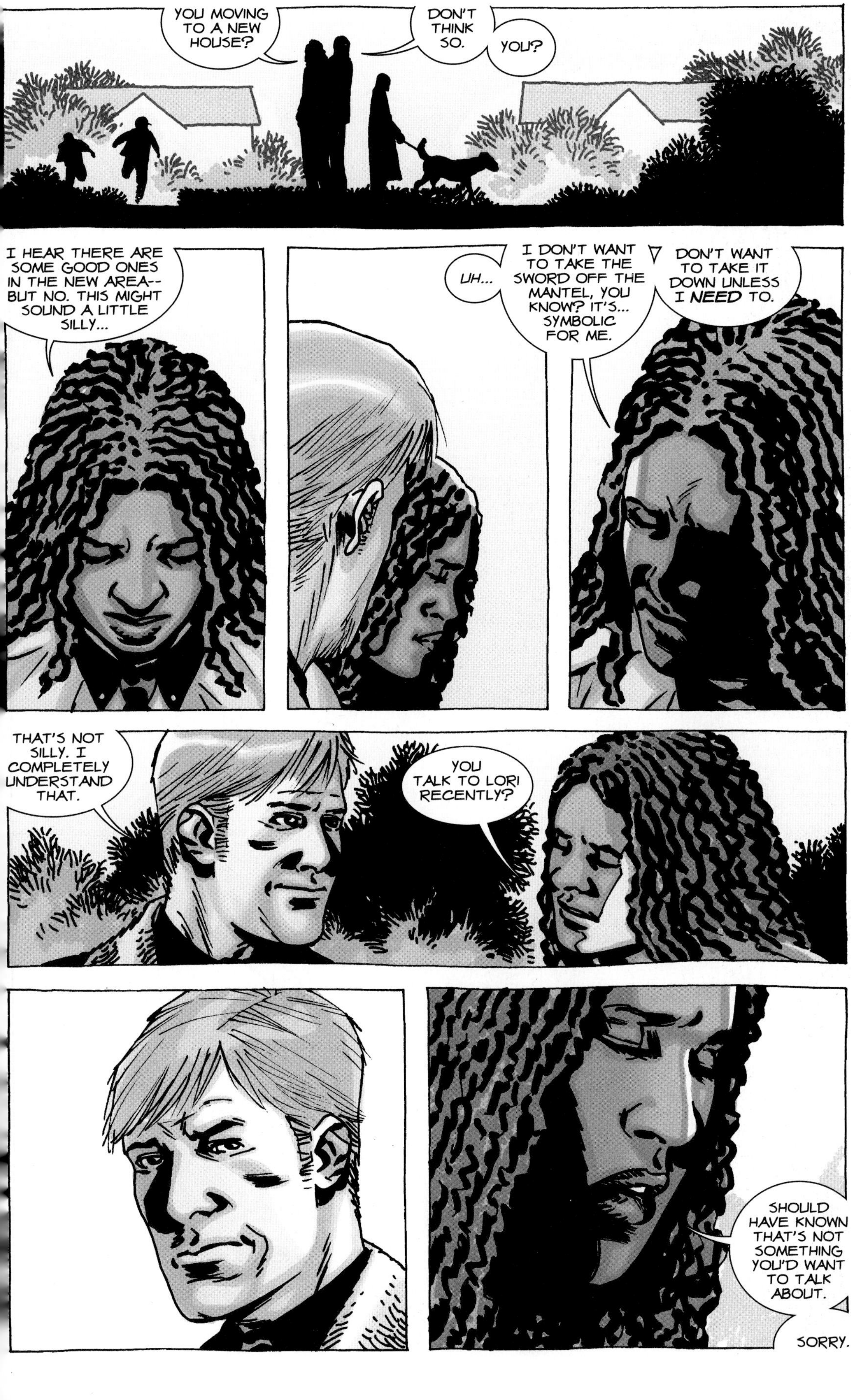
YOU MOVING TO A NEW HOUSE?
DON'T THINK SO.
YOU?
I HEAR THERE ARE SOME GOOD ONES IN THE NEW AREA-- BUT NO. THIS MIGHT SOUND A LITTLE SILLY...
UH...
I DON'T WANT TO TAKE THE SWORD OFF THE MANTEL, YOU KNOW? IT'S... SYMBOLIC FOR ME.
DON'T WANT TO TAKE IT DOWN UNLESS I NEED TO.
THAT'S NOT SILLY. I COMPLETELY UNDERSTAND THAT.
YOU TALK TO LORI RECENTLY?
SHOULD HAVE KNOWN THAT'S NOT SOMETHING YOU'D WANT TO TALK ABOUT.
SORRY.

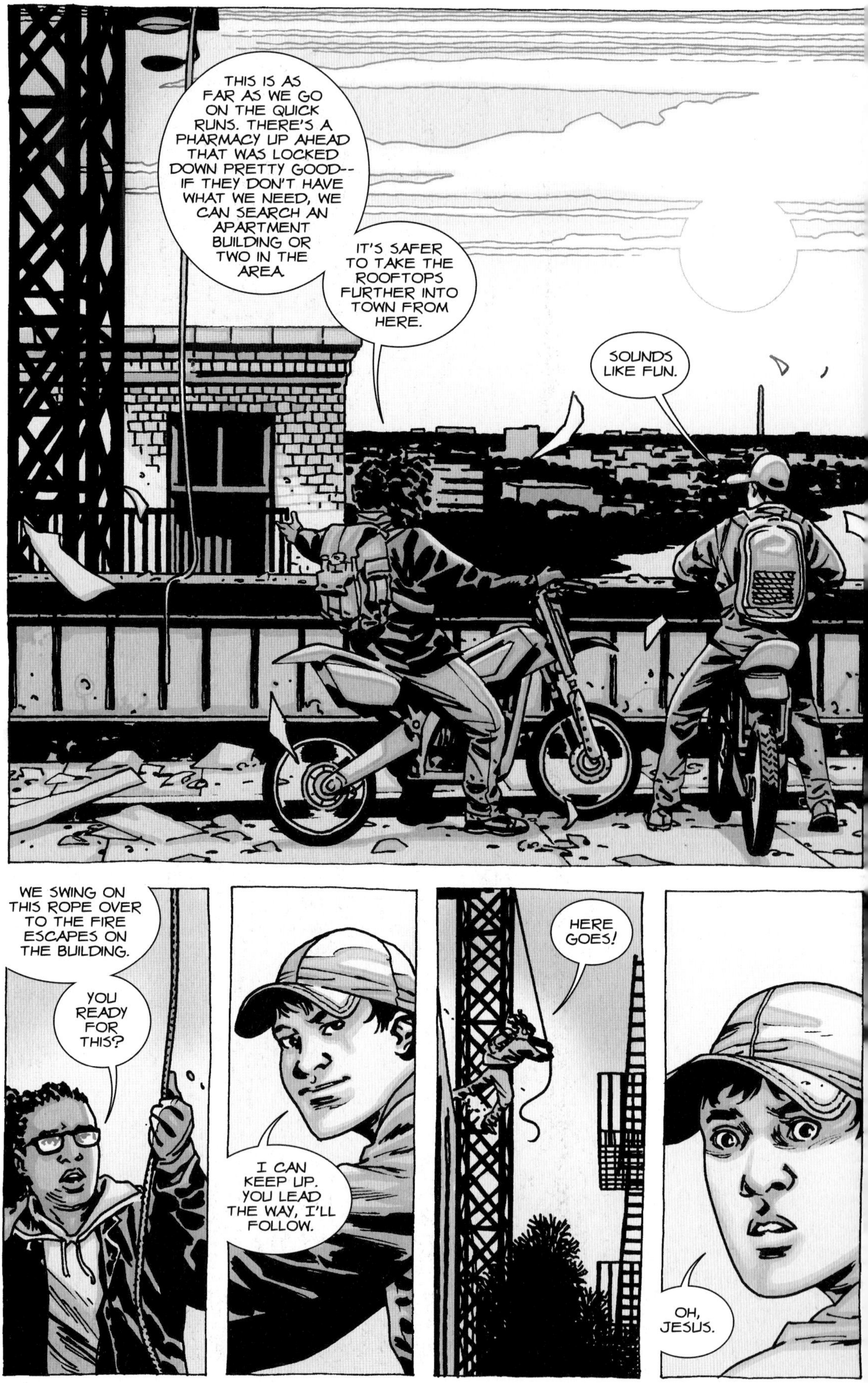
THIS IS AS FAR AS WE GO ON THE QUICK RUNS. THERE'S A PHARMACY UP AHEAD THAT WAS LOCKED DOWN PRETTY GOOD-- IF THEY DON'T HAVE WHAT WE NEED, WE CAN SEARCH AN APARTMENT BUILDING OR TWO IN THE AREA.
IT'S SAFER TO TAKE THE ROOFTOPS FURTHER INTO TOWN FROM HERE.
SOUNDS LIKE FUN.
WE SWING ON THIS ROPE OVER TO THE FIRE ESCAPES ON THE BUILDING.
YOU READY FOR THIS?
I CAN KEEP UP. YOU LEAD THE WAY, I'LL FOLLOW.
HERE GOES!
OH, JESUS.

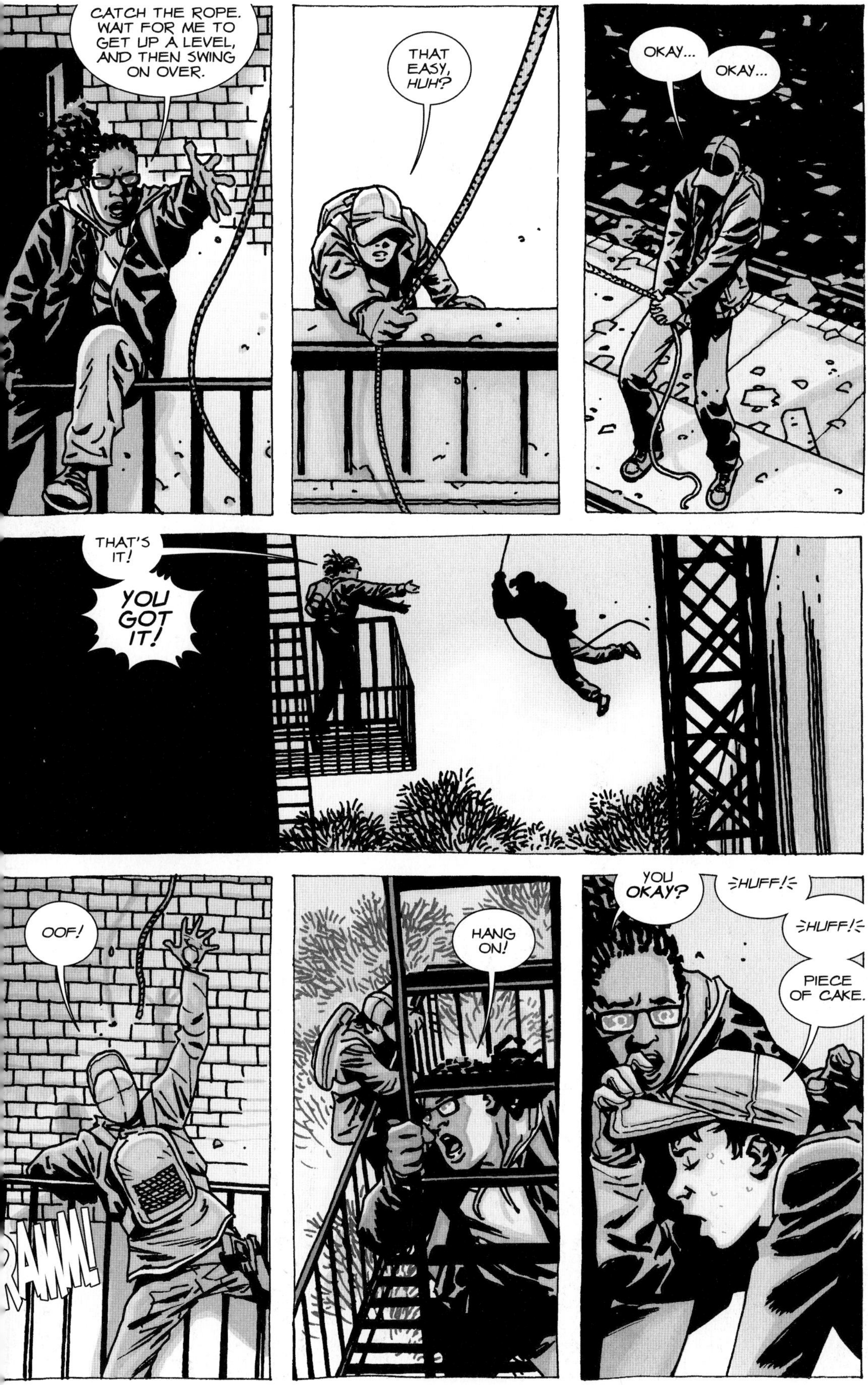
CATCH THE ROPE. WAIT FOR ME TO GET UP A LEVEL, AND THEN SWING ON OVER.
THAT EASY, HUH?
OKAY...
OKAY...
THAT'S IT!
YOU GOT IT!
OOF!
RAMM!
HANG ON!
YOU OKAY?
HUFF!
HUFF!
PIECE OF CAKE.

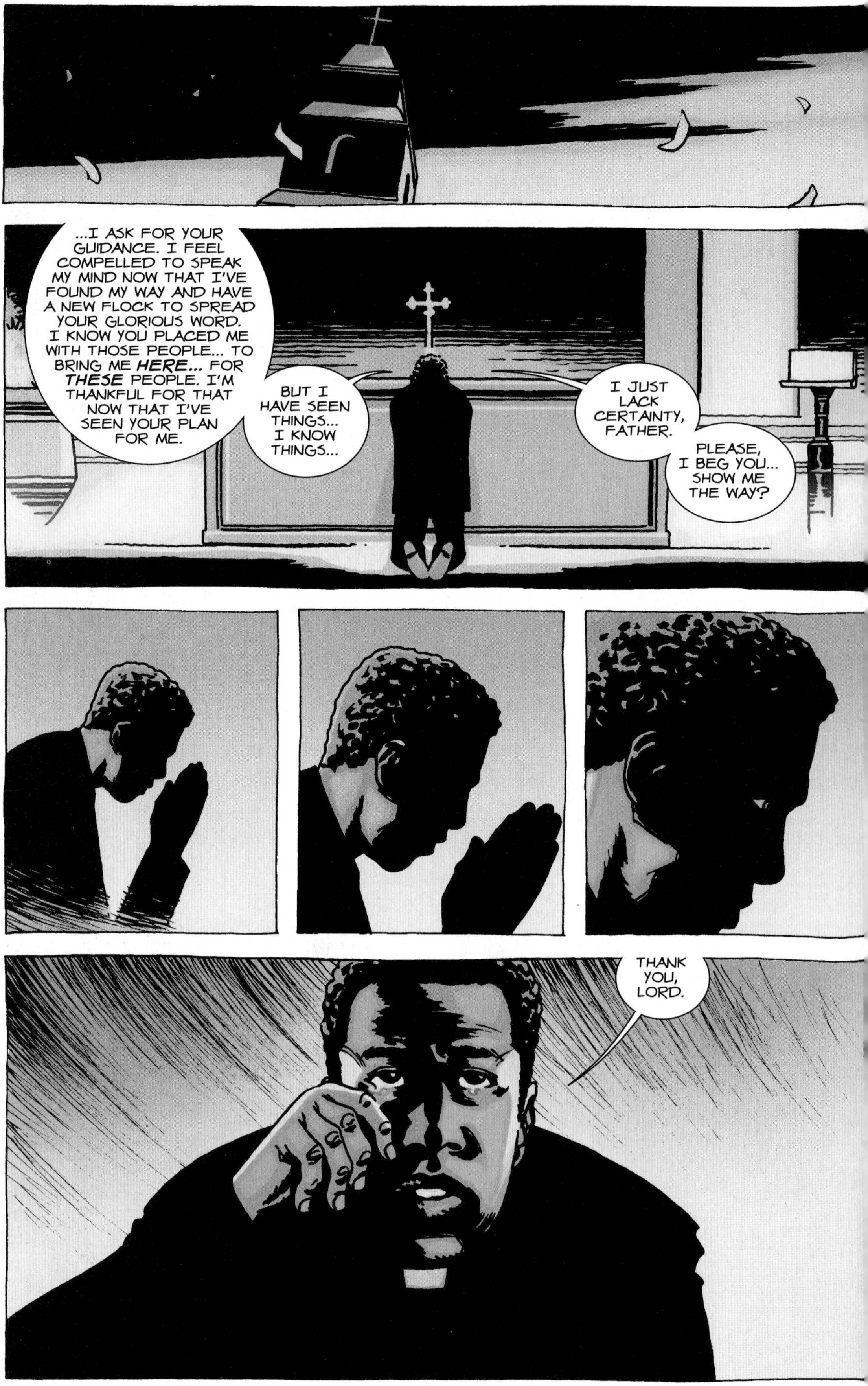
...I ASK FOR YOUR GUIDANCE. I FEEL COMPELLED TO SPEAK MY MIND NOW THAT I'VE FOUND MY WAY AND HAVE A NEW FLOCK TO SPREAD YOUR GLORIOUS WORD. I KNOW YOU PLACED ME WITH THOSE PEOPLE... TO BRING ME HERE... FOR THESE PEOPLE. I'M THANKFUL FOR THAT NOW THAT I'VE SEEN YOUR PLAN FOR ME.
BUT I HAVE SEEN THINGS... I KNOW THINGS...
I JUST LACK CERTAINTY, FATHER.
PLEASE, I BEG YOU... SHOW ME THE WAY?
THANK YOU, LORD.

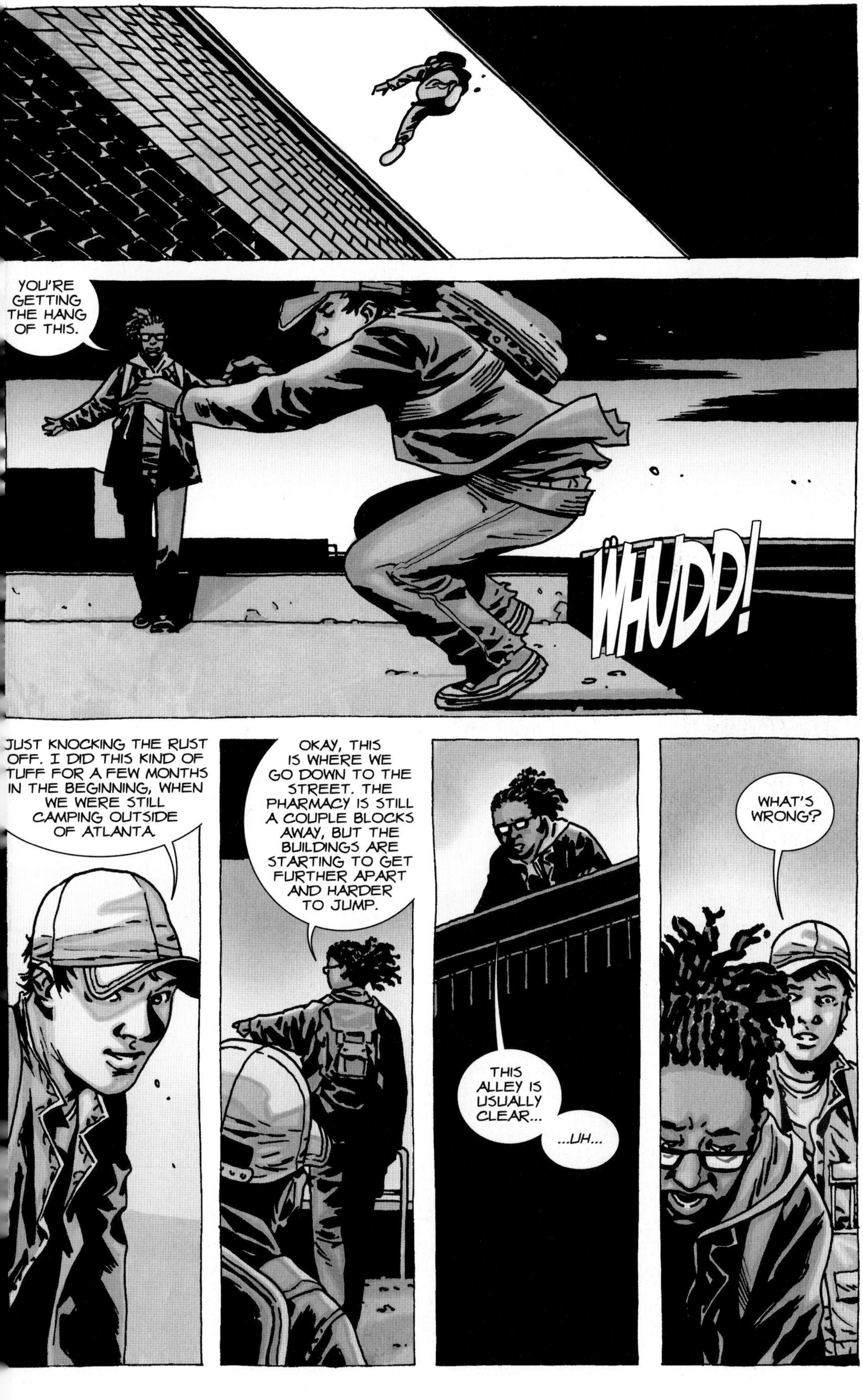

YOU'RE GETTING THE HANG OF THIS.
WHUDD!
JUST KNOCKING THE RUST OFF. I DID THIS KIND OF STUFF FOR A FEW MONTHS IN THE BEGINNING, WHEN WE WERE STILL CAMPING OUTSIDE OF ATLANTA.
OKAY, THIS IS WHERE WE GO DOWN TO THE STREET. THE PHARMACY IS STILL A COUPLE BLOCKS AWAY, BUT THE BUILDINGS ARE STARTING TO GET FURTHER APART AND HARDER TO JUMP.
THIS ALLEY IS USUALLY CLEAR...
...UH...
WHAT'S WRONG?

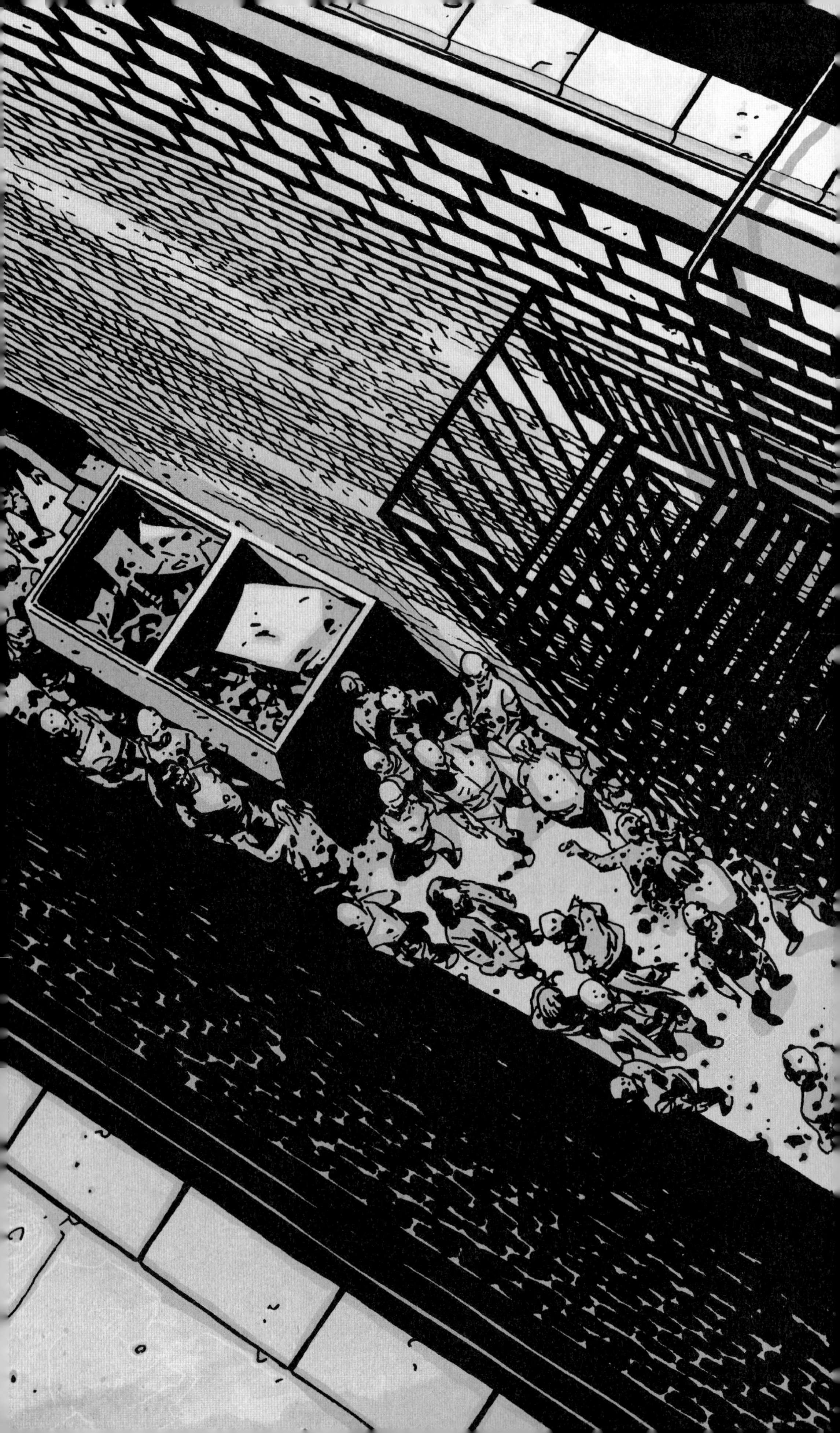

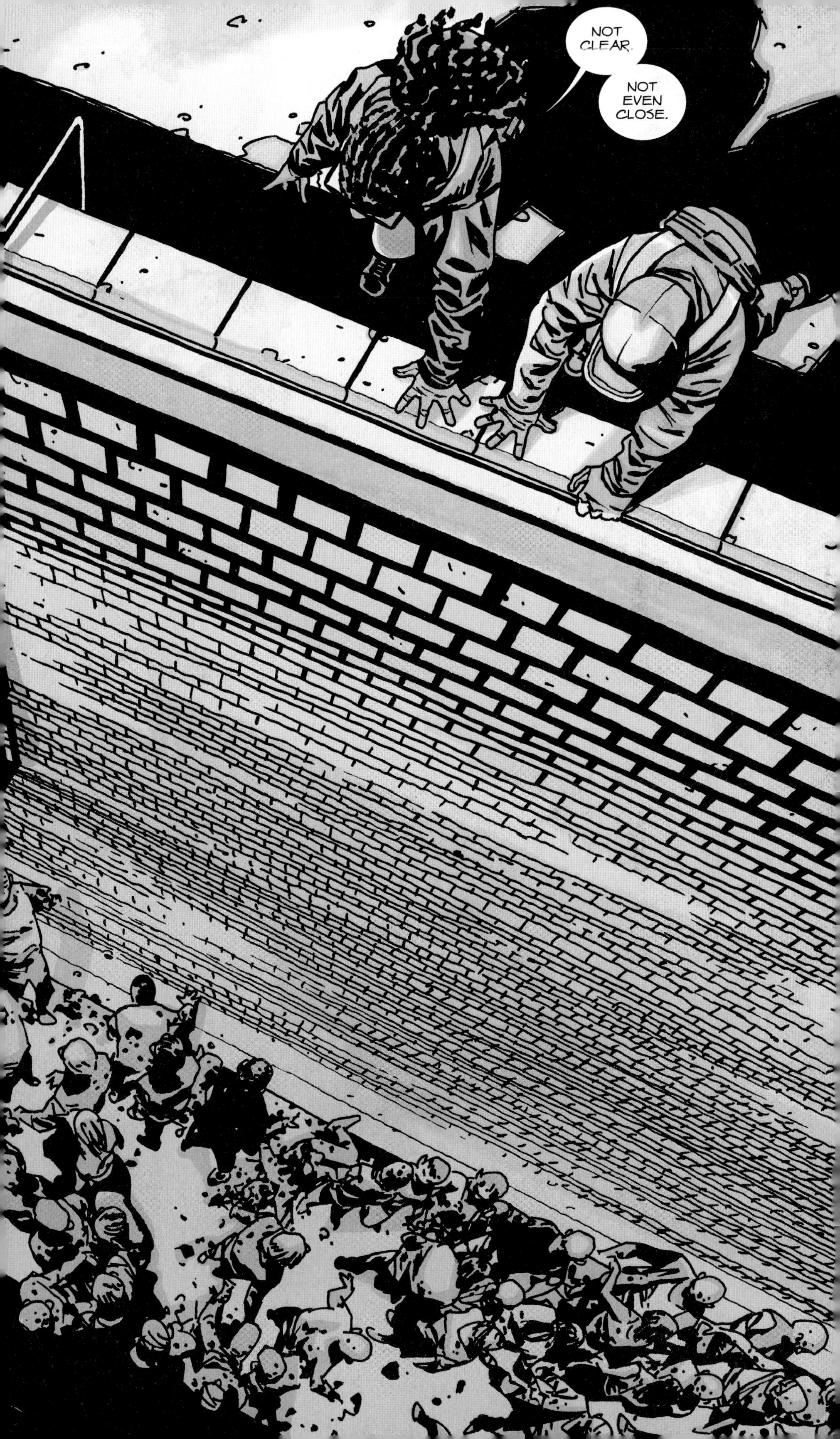
NOT CLEAR.
NOT EVEN CLOSE.

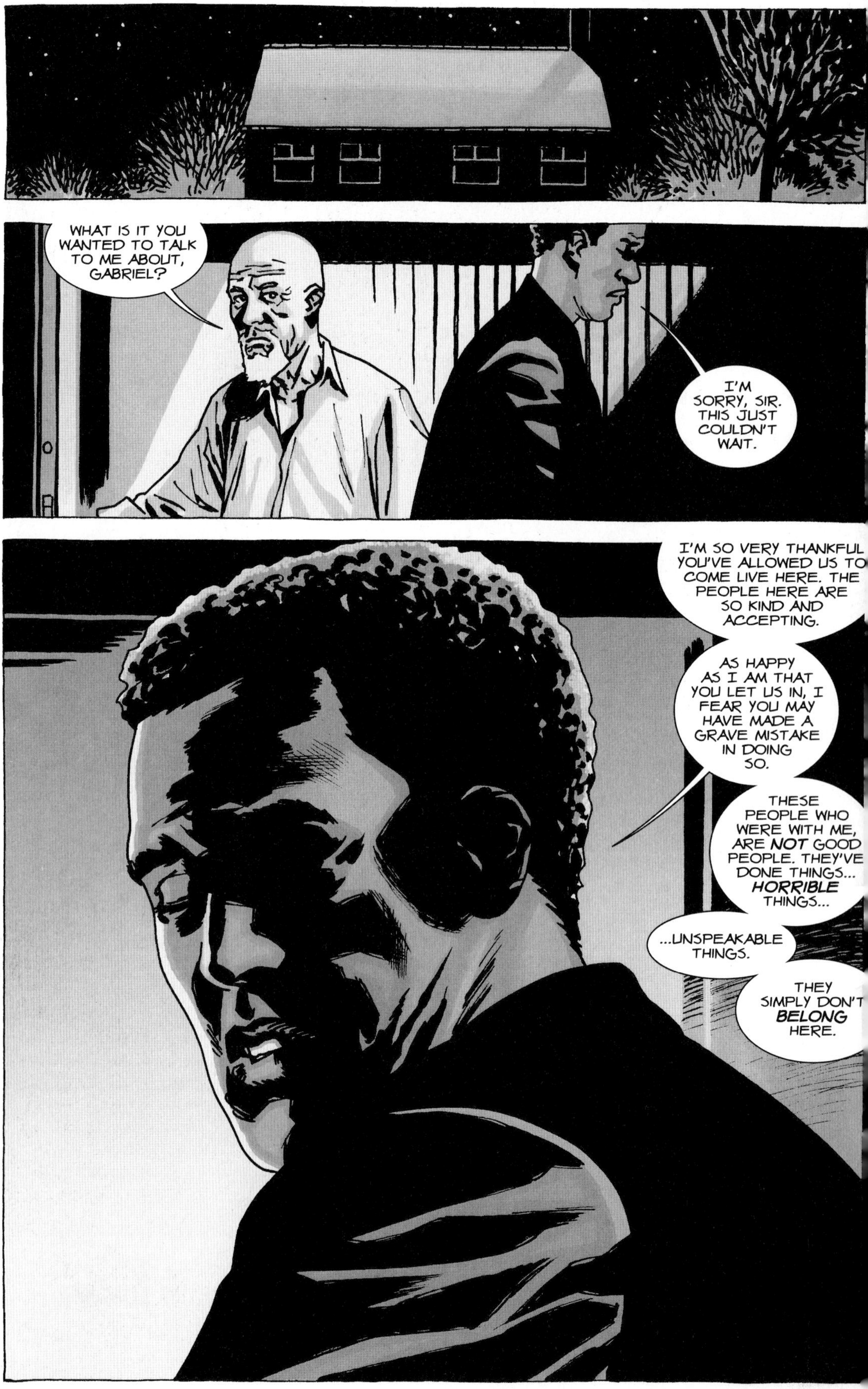
WHAT IS IT YOU WANTED TO TALK TO ME ABOUT, GABRIEL?
I'M SORRY, SIR. THIS JUST COULDN'T WAIT.
I'M SO VERY THANKFUL YOU'VE ALLOWED US TO COME LIVE HERE. THE PEOPLE HERE ARE SO KIND AND ACCEPTING.
AS HAPPY AS I AM THAT YOU LET US IN, I FEAR YOU MAY HAVE MADE A GRAVE MISTAKE IN DOING SO.
THESE PEOPLE WHO WERE WITH ME, ARE NOT GOOD PEOPLE. THEY'VE DONE THINGS... HORRIBLE THINGS...
...UNSPEAKABLE THINGS.
THEY SIMPLY DON'T BELONG HERE.

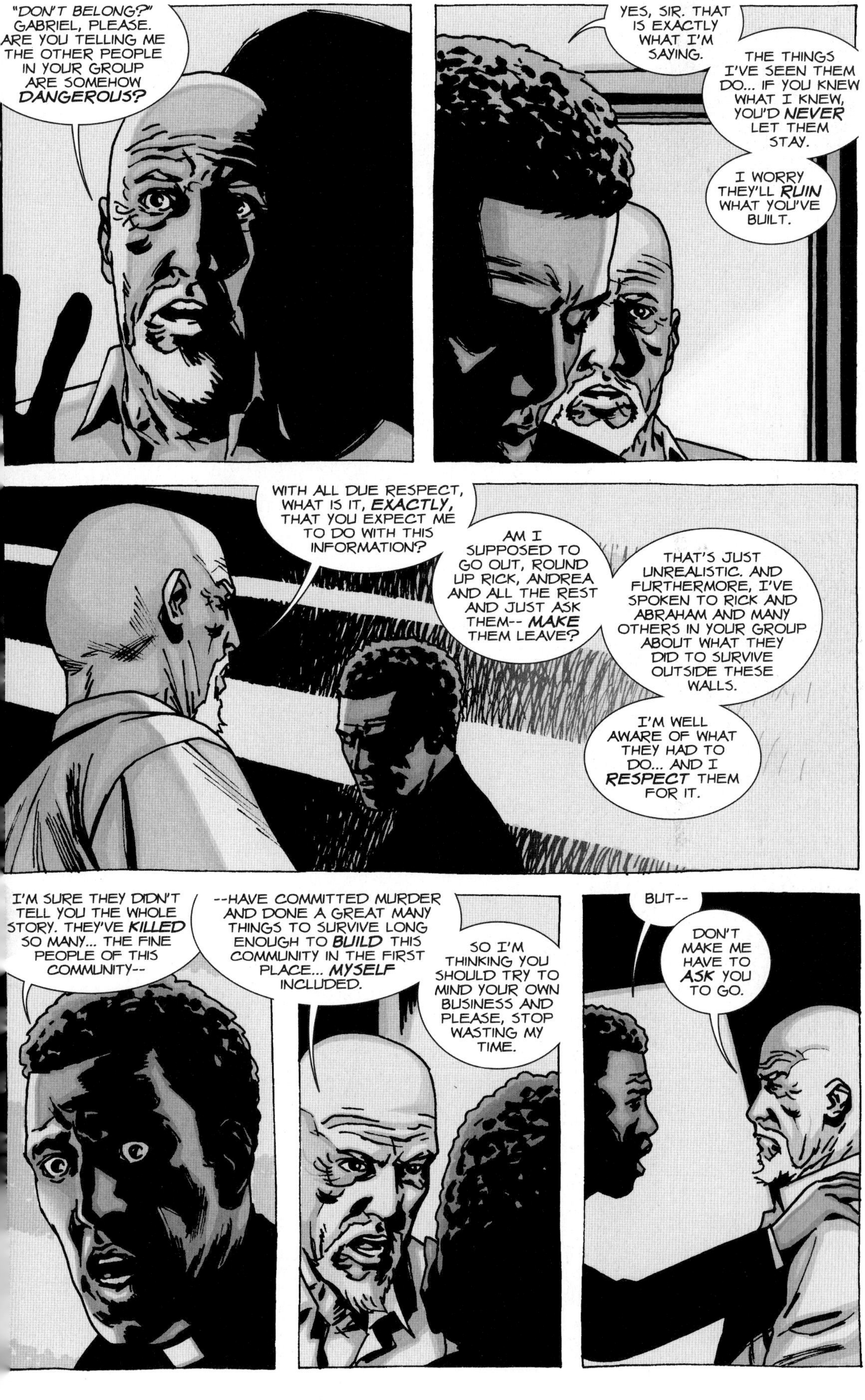
"DON'T BELONG?" GABRIEL, PLEASE. ARE YOU TELLING ME THE OTHER PEOPLE IN YOUR GROUP ARE SOMEHOW DANGEROUS?
YES, SIR. THAT IS EXACTLY WHAT I'M SAYING.
THE THINGS I'VE SEEN THEM DO... IF YOU KNEW WHAT I KNEW, YOU'D NEVER LET THEM STAY.
I WORRY THEY'LL RUIN WHAT YOU'VE BUILT.
WITH ALL DUE RESPECT, WHAT IS IT, EXACTLY, THAT YOU EXPECT ME TO DO WITH THIS INFORMATION?
AM I SUPPOSED TO GO OUT, ROUND UP RICK, ANDREA AND ALL THE REST AND JUST ASK THEM-- MAKE THEM LEAVE?
THAT'S JUST UNREALISTIC. AND FURTHERMORE, I'VE SPOKEN TO RICK AND ABRAHAM AND MANY OTHERS IN YOUR GROUP ABOUT WHAT THEY DID TO SURVIVE OUTSIDE THESE WALLS.
I'M WELL AWARE OF WHAT THEY HAD TO DO... AND I RESPECT THEM FOR IT.
I'M SURE THEY DIDN'T TELL YOU THE WHOLE STORY. THEY'VE KILLED SO MANY... THE FINE PEOPLE OF THIS COMMUNITY--
--HAVE COMMITTED MURDER AND DONE A GREAT MANY THINGS TO SURVIVE LONG ENOUGH TO BUILD THIS COMMUNITY IN THE FIRST PLACE... MYSELF INCLUDED.
SO I'M THINKING YOU SHOULD TRY TO MIND YOUR OWN BUSINESS AND PLEASE, STOP WASTING MY TIME.
BUT--
DON'T MAKE ME HAVE TO ASK YOU TO GO.

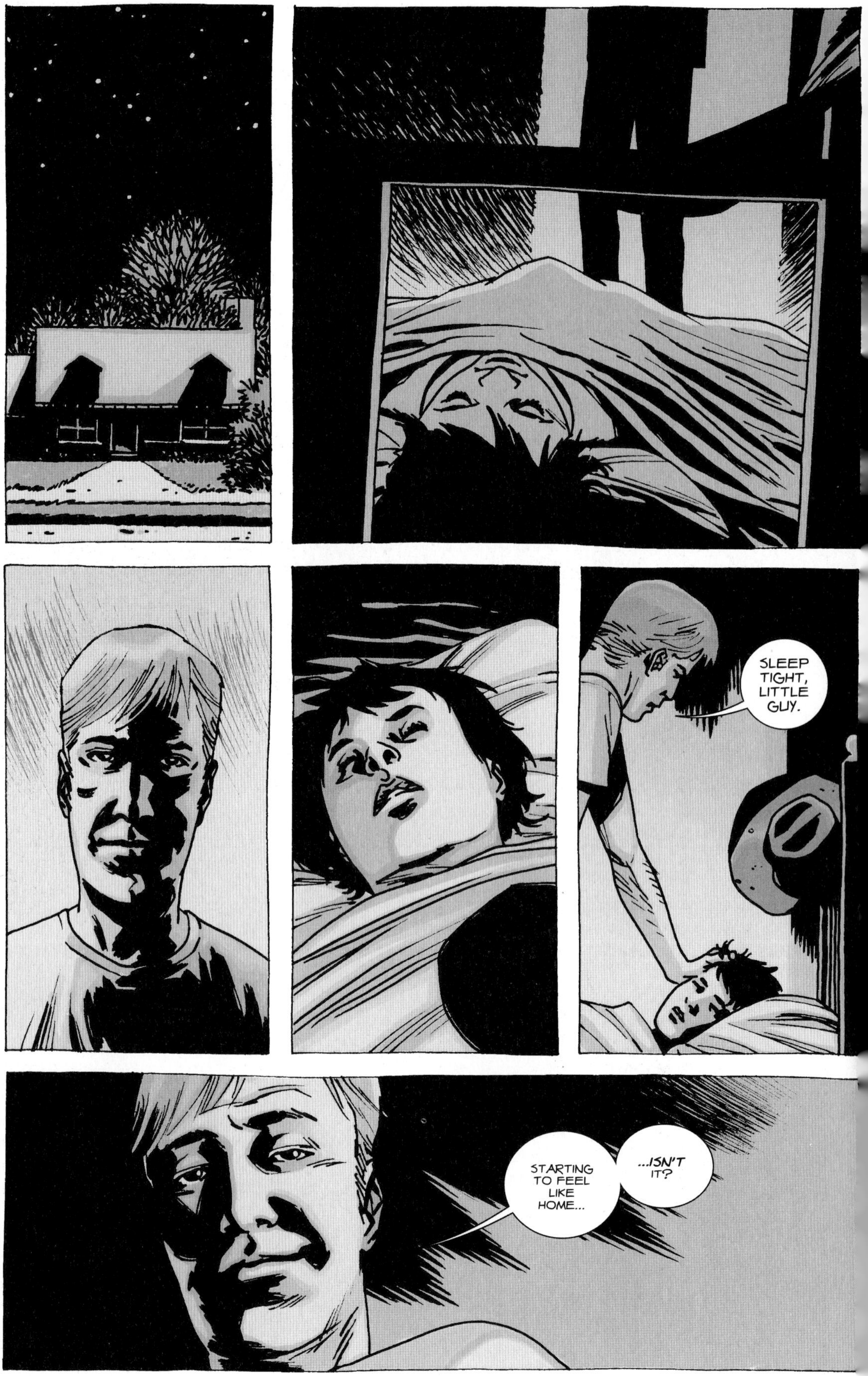
SLEEP TIGHT, LITTLE GUY.
STARTING TO FEEL LIKE HOME...
...ISN'T IT?

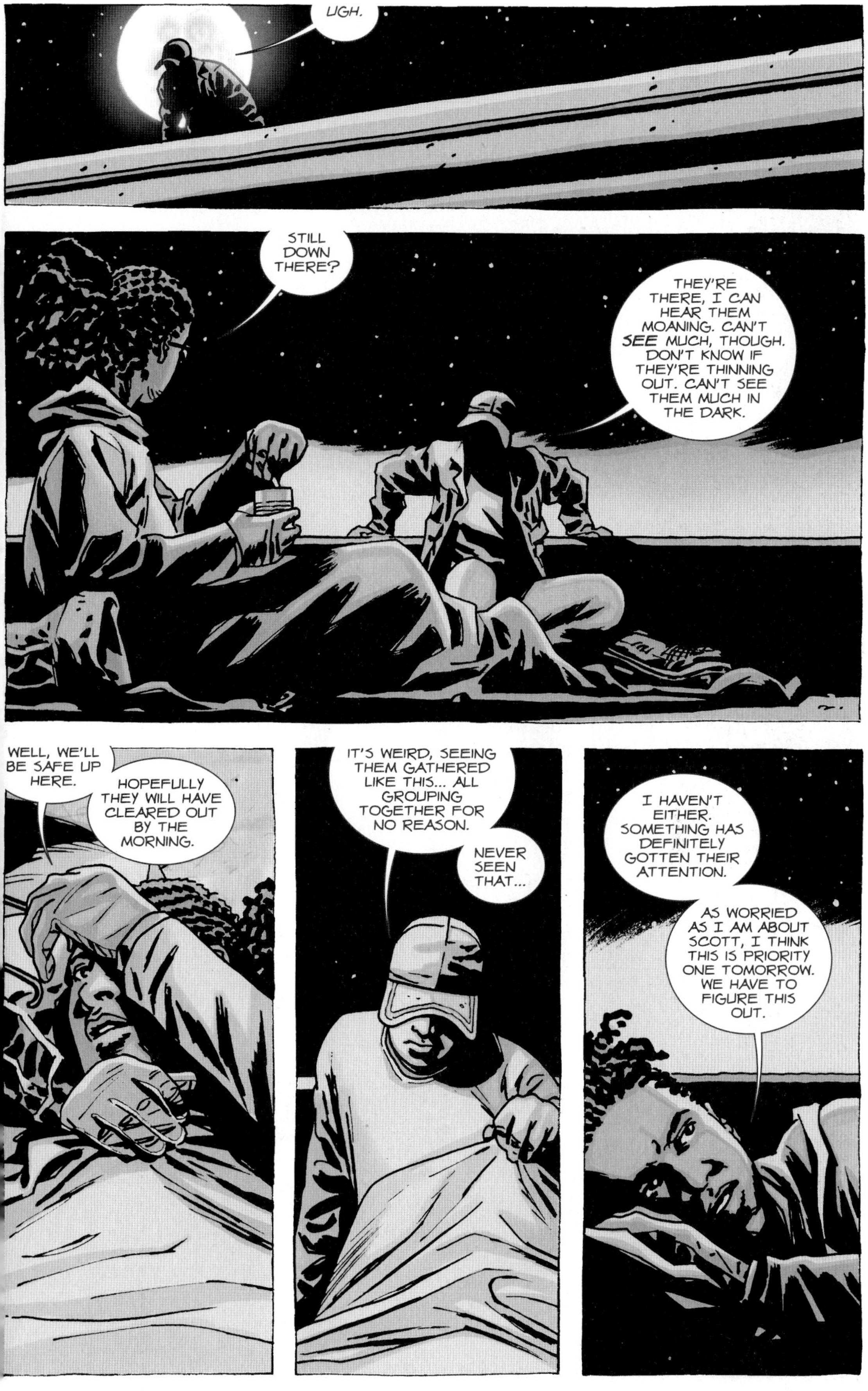
UGH.
STILL DOWN THERE?
THEY'RE THERE, I CAN HEAR THEM MOANING. CAN'T SEE MUCH, THOUGH. DON'T KNOW IF THEY'RE THINNING OUT. CAN'T SEE THEM MUCH IN THE DARK.
WELL, WE'LL BE SAFE UP HERE.
HOPEFULLY THEY WILL HAVE CLEARED OUT BY THE MORNING.
IT'S WEIRD, SEEING THEM GATHERED LIKE THIS... ALL GROUPING TOGETHER FOR NO REASON.
NEVER SEEN THAT...
I HAVEN'T EITHER. SOMETHING HAS DEFINITELY GOTTEN THEIR ATTENTION.
AS WORRIED AS I AM ABOUT SCOTT, I THINK THIS IS PRIORITY ONE TOMORROW. WE HAVE TO FIGURE THIS OUT.

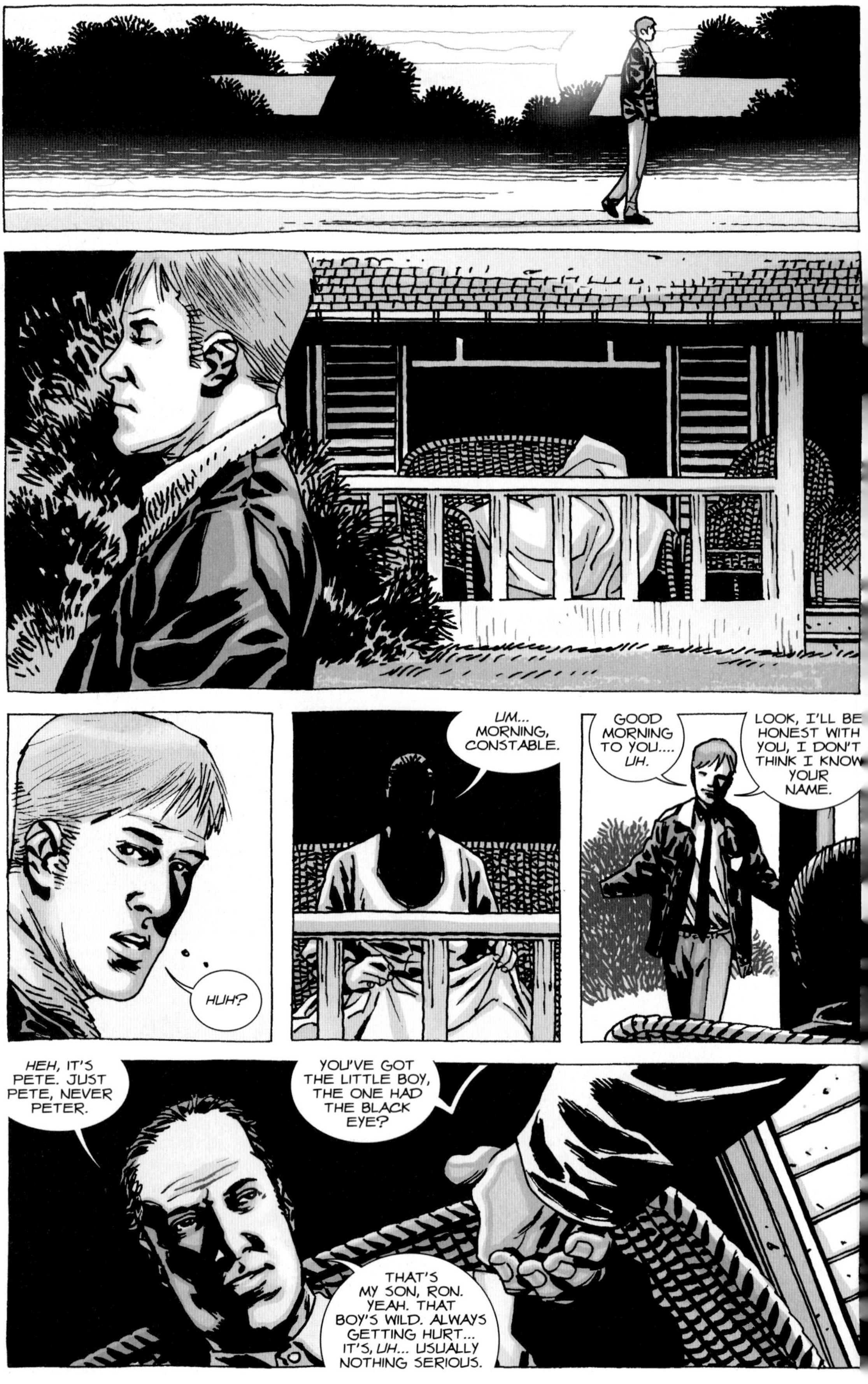
HUH?
UM... MORNING, CONSTABLE.
GOOD MORNING TO YOU.... UH.
LOOK, I'LL BE HONEST WITH YOU, I DON'T THINK I KNOW YOUR NAME.
HEH, IT'S PETE. JUST PETE, NEVER PETER.
YOU'VE GOT THE LITTLE BOY, THE ONE HAD THE BLACK EYE?
THAT'S MY SON, RON. YEAH. THAT BOY'S WILD. ALWAYS GETTING HURT... IT'S, UH... USUALLY NOTHING SERIOUS.

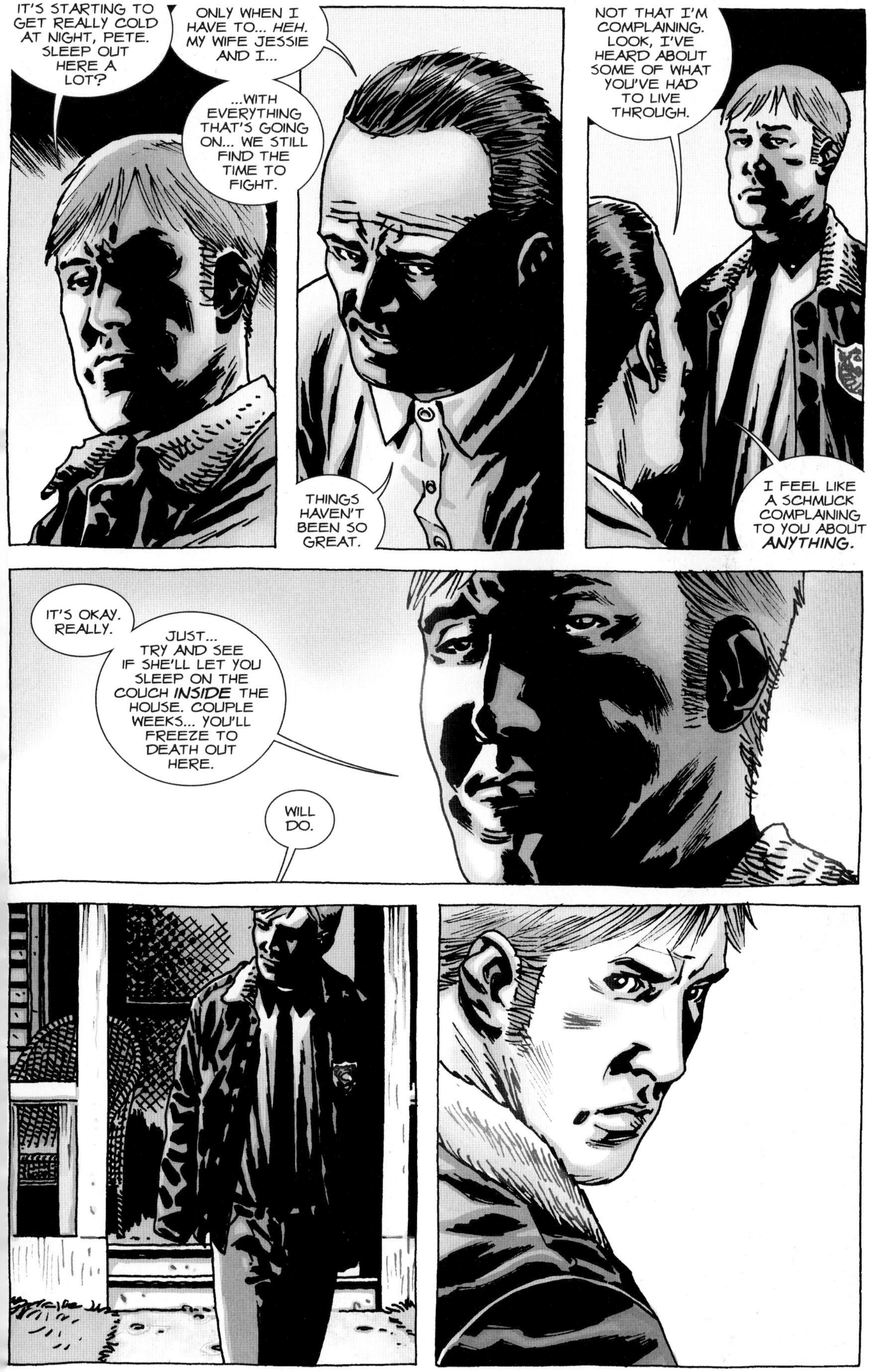
IT'S STARTING TO GET REALLY COLD AT NIGHT, PETE. SLEEP OUT HERE A LOT?
ONLY WHEN I HAVE TO... *HEH.* MY WIFE JESSIE AND I...
...WITH EVERYTHING THAT'S GOING ON... WE STILL FIND THE TIME TO FIGHT.
THINGS HAVEN'T BEEN SO GREAT.
NOT THAT I'M COMPLAINING. LOOK, I'VE HEARD ABOUT SOME OF WHAT YOU'VE HAD TO LIVE THROUGH.
I FEEL LIKE A SCHMUCK COMPLAINING TO YOU ABOUT *ANYTHING.*
IT'S OKAY. REALLY.
JUST... TRY AND SEE IF SHE'LL LET YOU SLEEP ON THE COUCH *INSIDE* THE HOUSE. COUPLE WEEKS... YOU'LL FREEZE TO DEATH OUT HERE.
WILL DO.

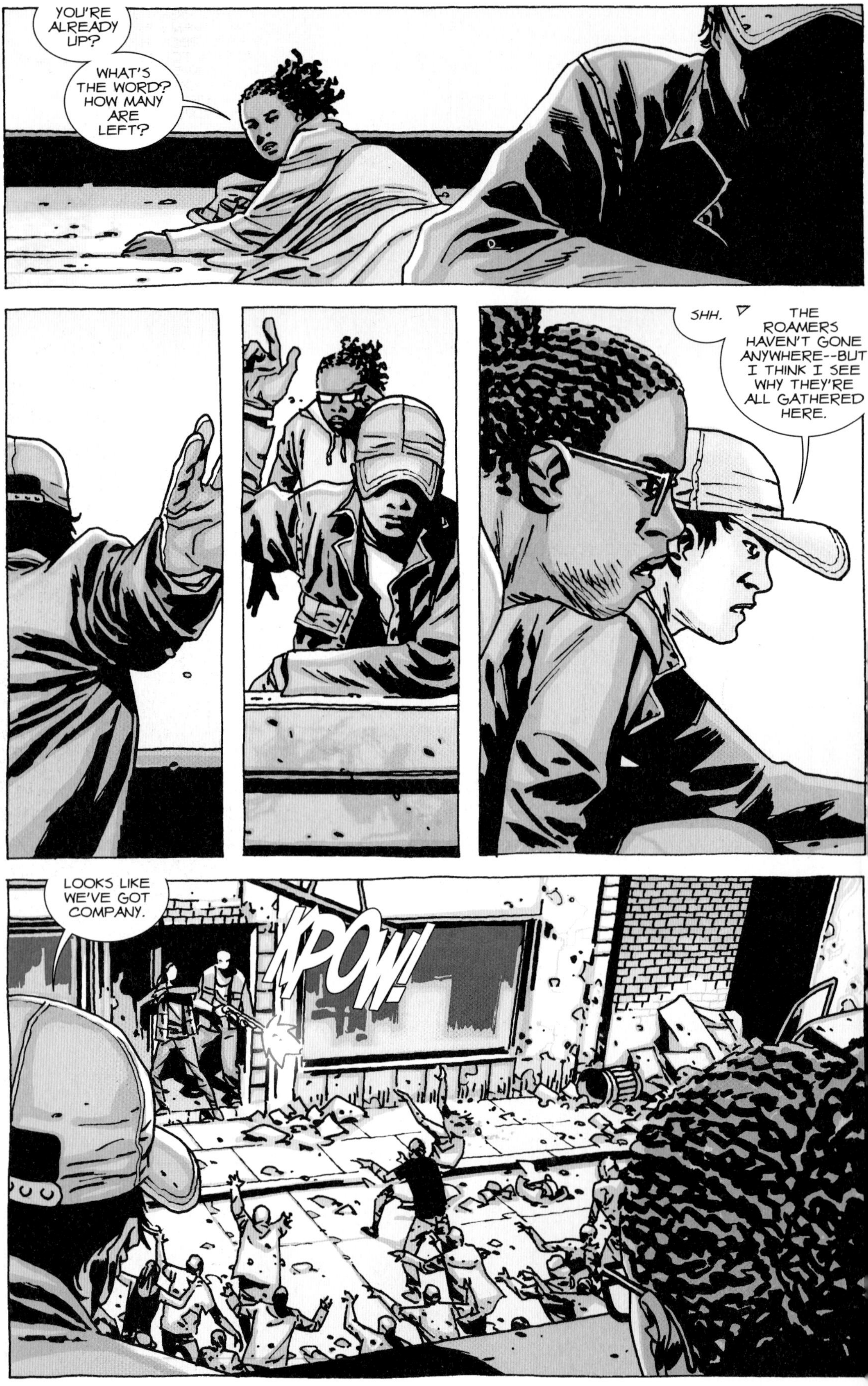
YOU'RE ALREADY UP?
WHAT'S THE WORD? HOW MANY ARE LEFT?
SHH.
THE ROAMERS HAVEN'T GONE ANYWHERE--BUT I THINK I SEE WHY THEY'RE ALL GATHERED HERE.
LOOKS LIKE WE'VE GOT COMPANY.
KPOW!

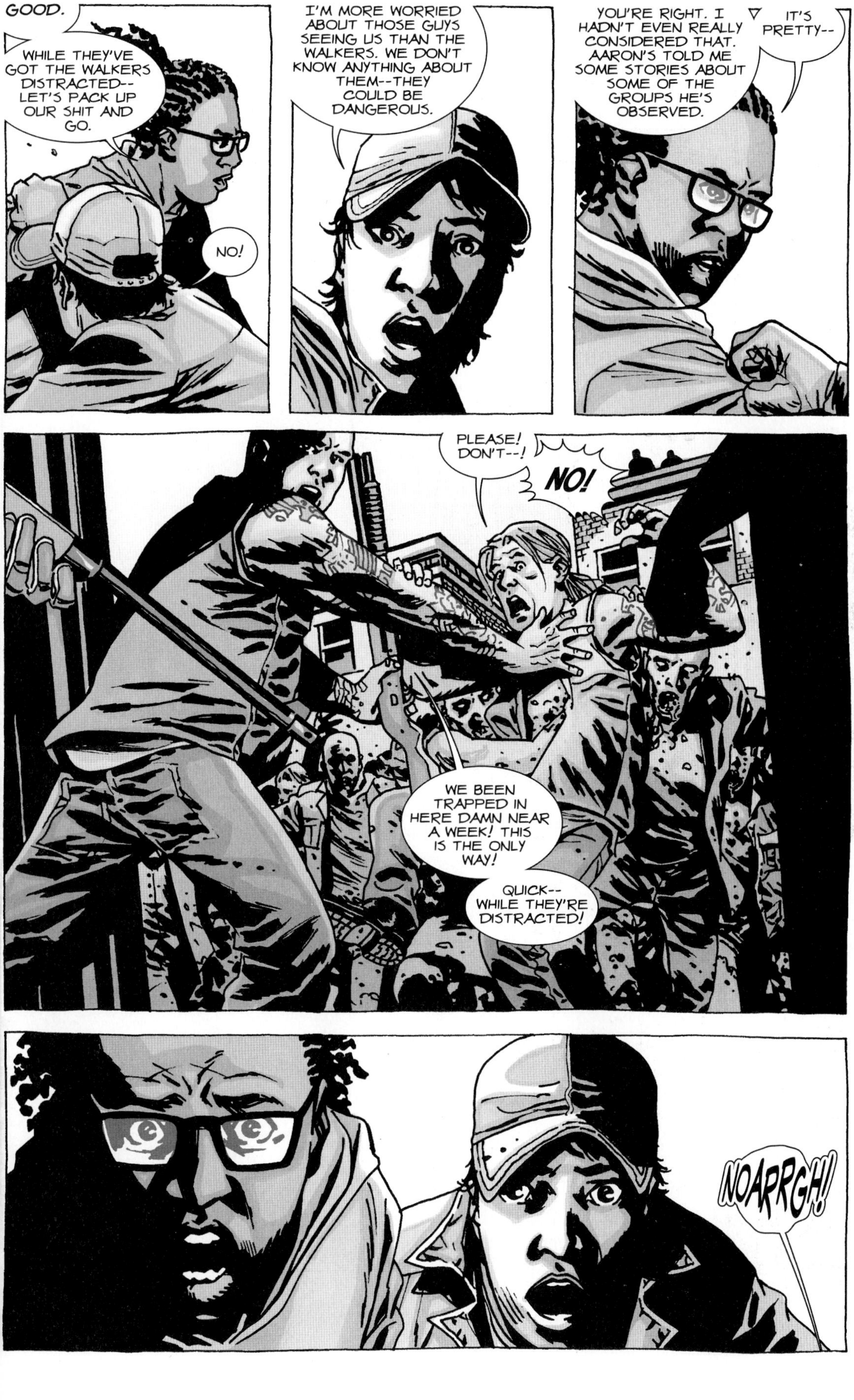
GOOD.
WHILE THEY'VE GOT THE WALKERS DISTRACTED-- LET'S PACK UP OUR SHIT AND GO.
NO!
I'M MORE WORRIED ABOUT THOSE GUYS SEEING US THAN THE WALKERS. WE DON'T KNOW ANYTHING ABOUT THEM--THEY COULD BE DANGEROUS.
YOU'RE RIGHT. I HADN'T EVEN REALLY CONSIDERED THAT. AARON'S TOLD ME SOME STORIES ABOUT SOME OF THE GROUPS HE'S OBSERVED.
IT'S PRETTY--
PLEASE! DON'T--!
NO!
WE BEEN TRAPPED IN HERE DAMN NEAR A WEEK! THIS IS THE ONLY WAY!
QUICK-- WHILE THEY'RE DISTRACTED!
NOARRGH!

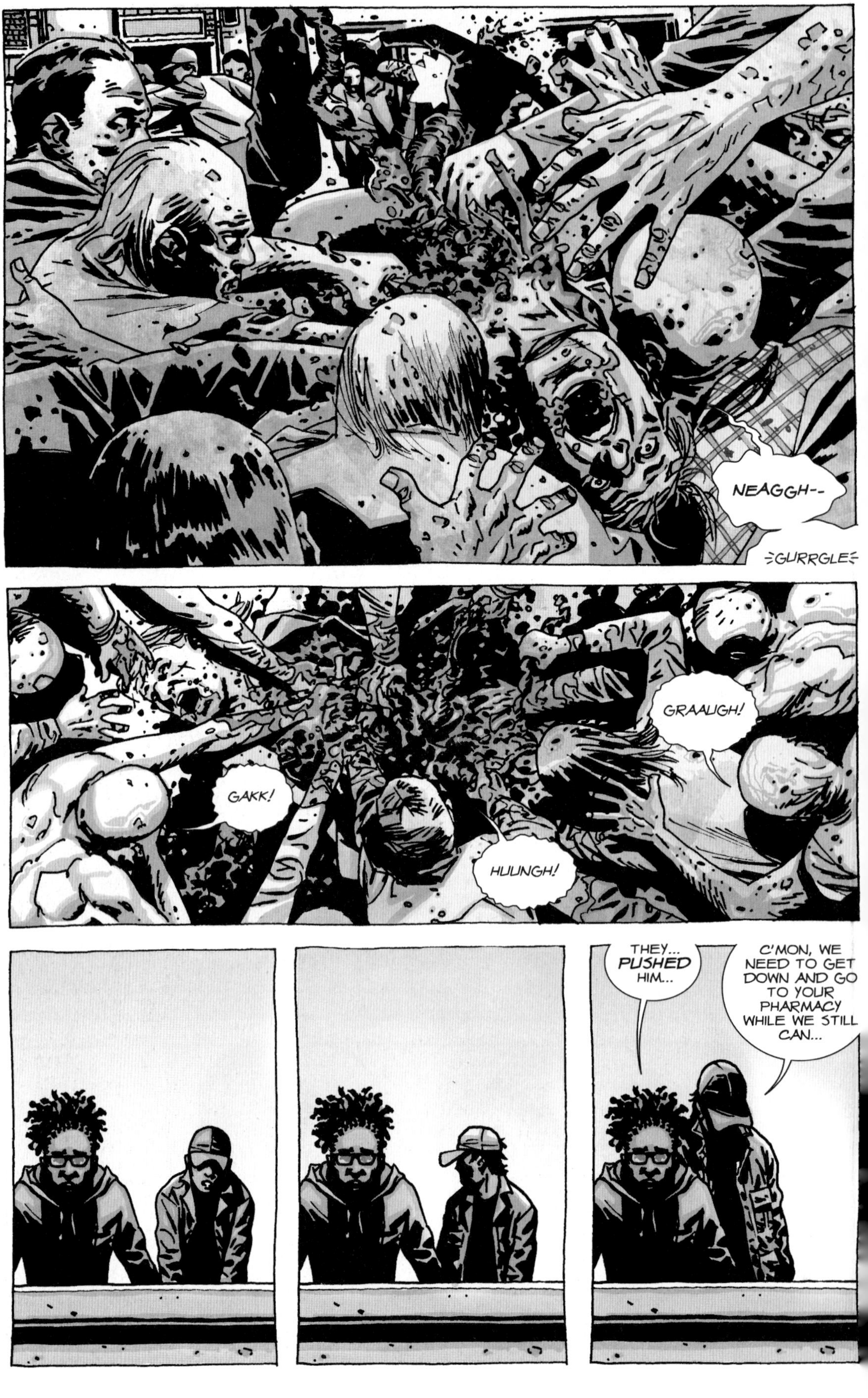
NEAGGH--
GURRGLE
GRAAUGH!
GAKK!
HUUNGH!
THEY... PUSHED HIM...
C'MON, WE NEED TO GET DOWN AND GO TO YOUR PHARMACY WHILE WE STILL CAN...

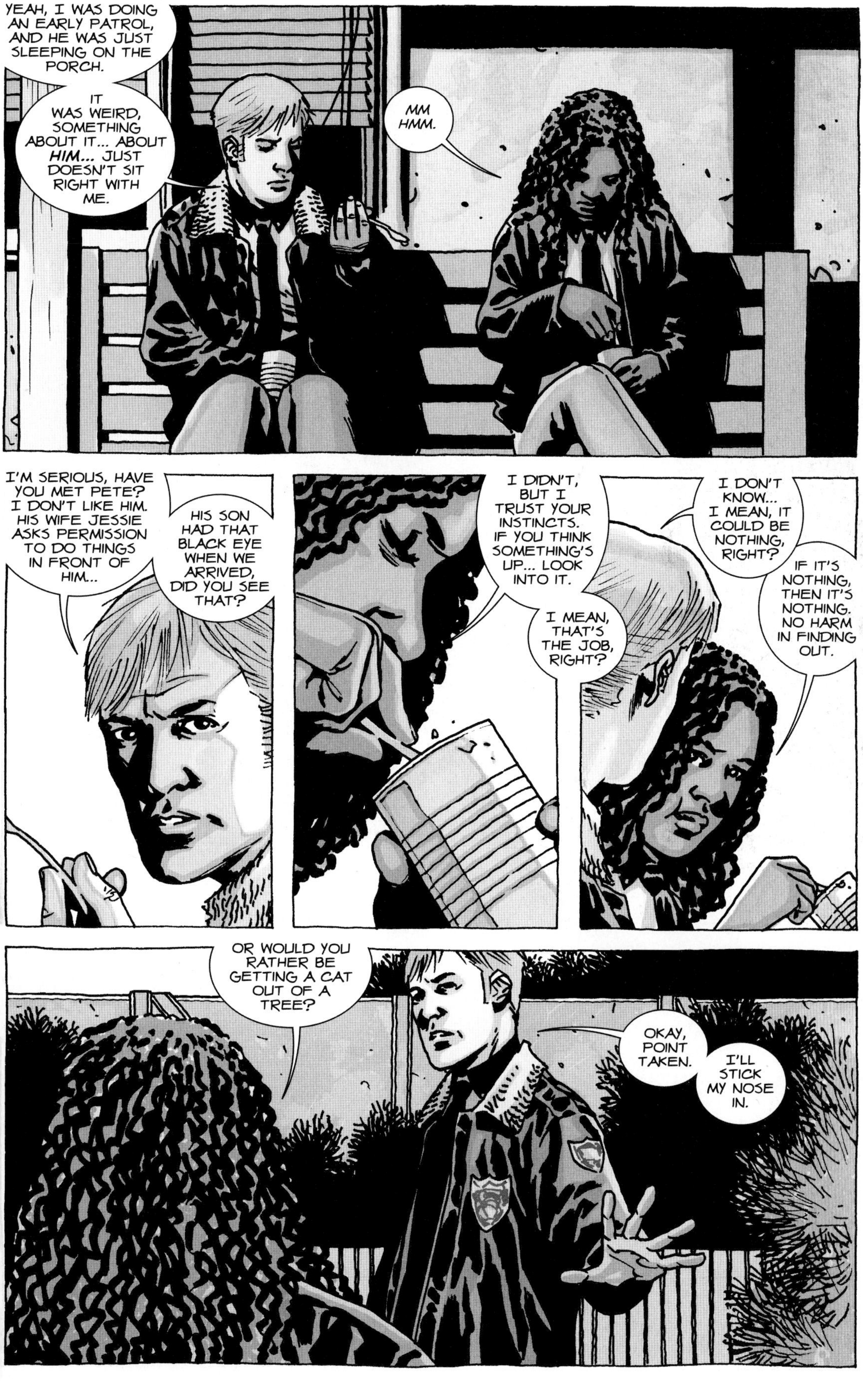
YEAH, I WAS DOING AN EARLY PATROL, AND HE WAS JUST SLEEPING ON THE PORCH.
IT WAS WEIRD, SOMETHING ABOUT IT... ABOUT *HIM...* JUST DOESN'T SIT RIGHT WITH ME.
MM HMM.
I'M SERIOUS, HAVE YOU MET PETE? I DON'T LIKE HIM. HIS WIFE JESSIE ASKS PERMISSION TO DO THINGS IN FRONT OF HIM...
HIS SON HAD THAT BLACK EYE WHEN WE ARRIVED, DID YOU SEE THAT?
I DIDN'T, BUT I TRUST YOUR INSTINCTS. IF YOU THINK SOMETHING'S UP... LOOK INTO IT.
I MEAN, THAT'S THE JOB, RIGHT?
I DON'T KNOW... I MEAN, IT COULD BE NOTHING, RIGHT?
IF IT'S NOTHING, THEN IT'S NOTHING. NO HARM IN FINDING OUT.
OR WOULD YOU RATHER BE GETTING A CAT OUT OF A TREE?
OKAY, POINT TAKEN.
I'LL STICK MY NOSE IN.

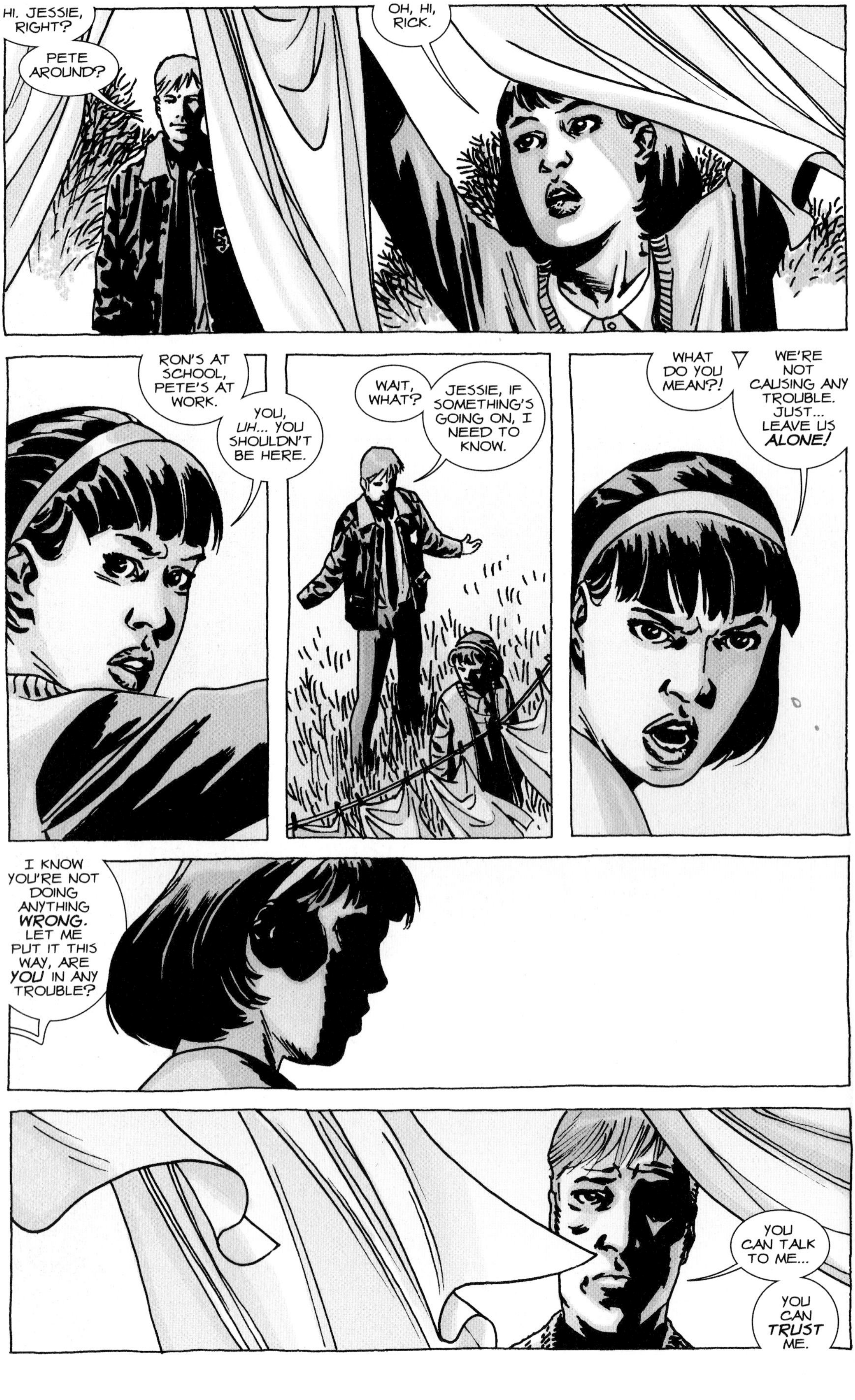
HI. JESSIE, RIGHT?
PETE AROUND?
OH, HI, RICK.
RON'S AT SCHOOL, PETE'S AT WORK.
YOU, UH... YOU SHOULDN'T BE HERE.
WAIT, WHAT?
JESSIE, IF SOMETHING'S GOING ON, I NEED TO KNOW.
WHAT DO YOU MEAN?!
WE'RE NOT CAUSING ANY TROUBLE. JUST... LEAVE US ALONE!
I KNOW YOU'RE NOT DOING ANYTHING WRONG. LET ME PUT IT THIS WAY, ARE YOU IN ANY TROUBLE?
YOU CAN TALK TO ME...
YOU CAN TRUST ME.

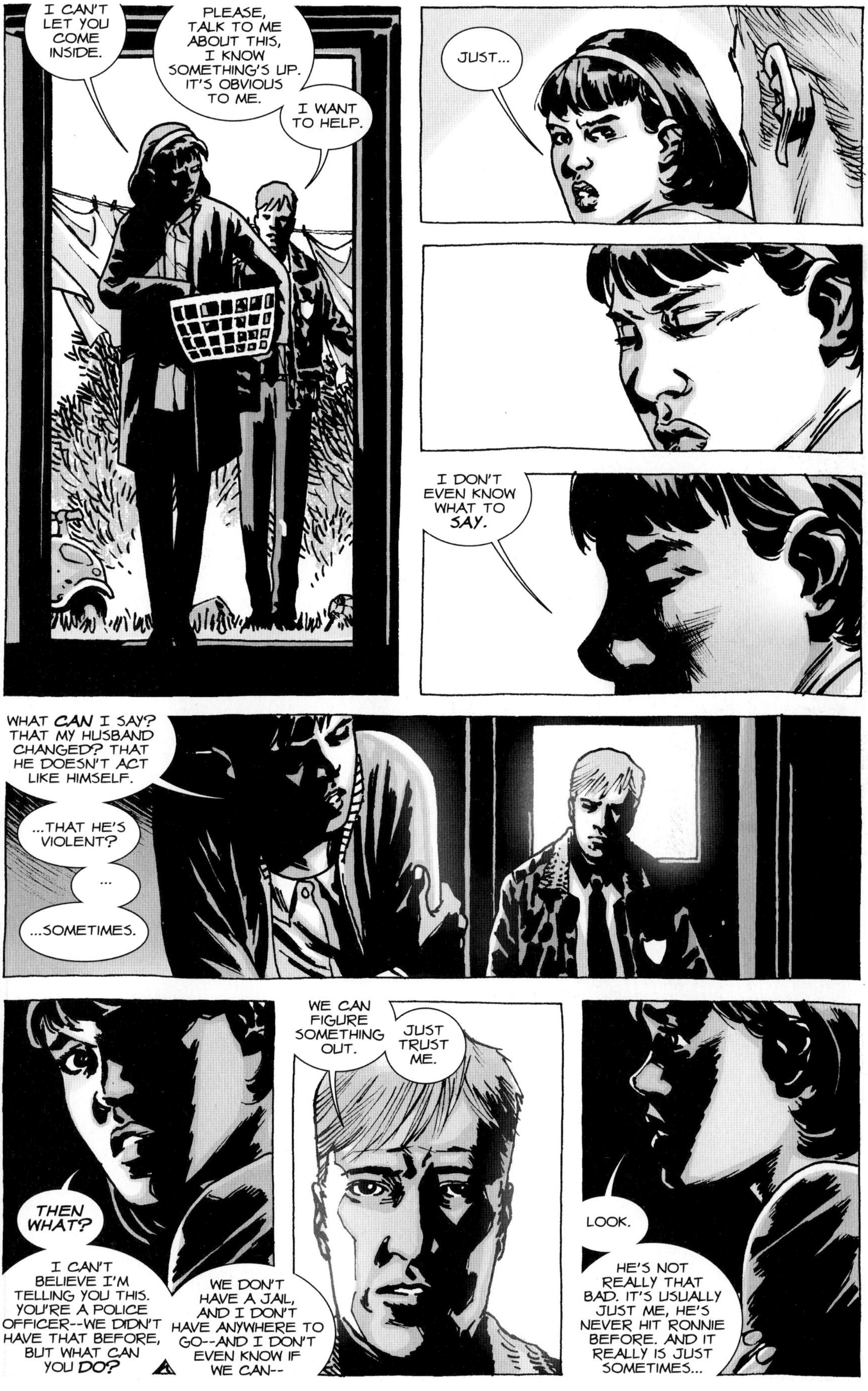
I CAN'T LET YOU COME INSIDE.
PLEASE, TALK TO ME ABOUT THIS, I KNOW SOMETHING'S UP. IT'S OBVIOUS TO ME.
I WANT TO HELP.
JUST...
I DON'T EVEN KNOW WHAT TO SAY.
WHAT CAN I SAY? THAT MY HUSBAND CHANGED? THAT HE DOESN'T ACT LIKE HIMSELF.
...THAT HE'S VIOLENT?
...
...SOMETIMES.
THEN WHAT?
I CAN'T BELIEVE I'M TELLING YOU THIS. YOU'RE A POLICE OFFICER--WE DIDN'T HAVE THAT BEFORE, BUT WHAT CAN YOU DO?
WE DON'T HAVE A JAIL, AND I DON'T HAVE ANYWHERE TO GO--AND I DON'T EVEN KNOW IF WE CAN--
WE CAN FIGURE SOMETHING OUT.
JUST TRUST ME.
LOOK.
HE'S NOT REALLY THAT BAD. IT'S USUALLY JUST ME, HE'S NEVER HIT RONNIE BEFORE. AND IT REALLY IS JUST SOMETIMES...

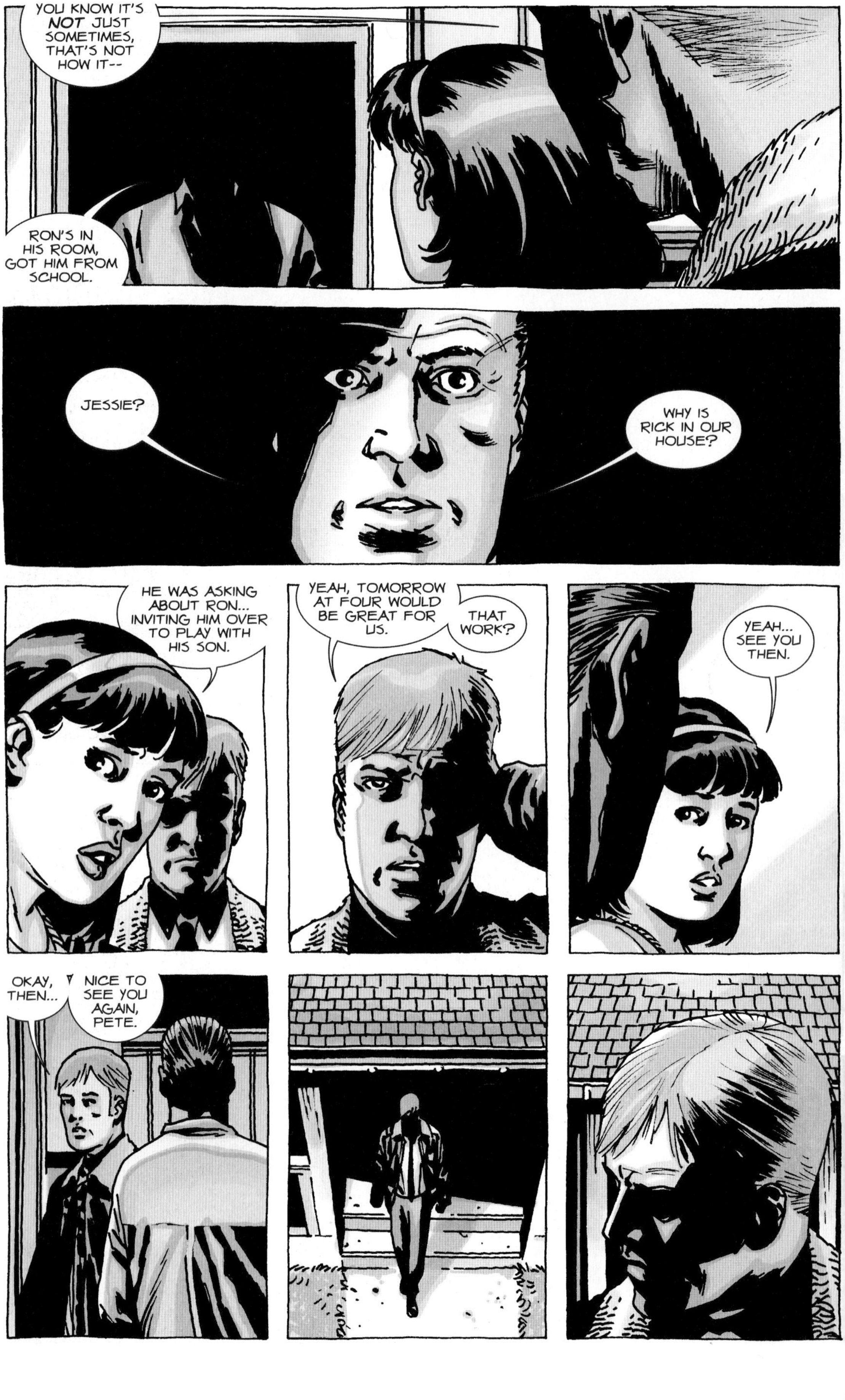
YOU KNOW IT'S NOT JUST SOMETIMES, THAT'S NOT HOW IT--
RON'S IN HIS ROOM, GOT HIM FROM SCHOOL.
JESSIE?
WHY IS RICK IN OUR HOUSE?
HE WAS ASKING ABOUT RON... INVITING HIM OVER TO PLAY WITH HIS SON.
YEAH, TOMORROW AT FOUR WOULD BE GREAT FOR US.
THAT WORK?
YEAH... SEE YOU THEN.
OKAY, THEN...
NICE TO SEE YOU AGAIN, PETE.

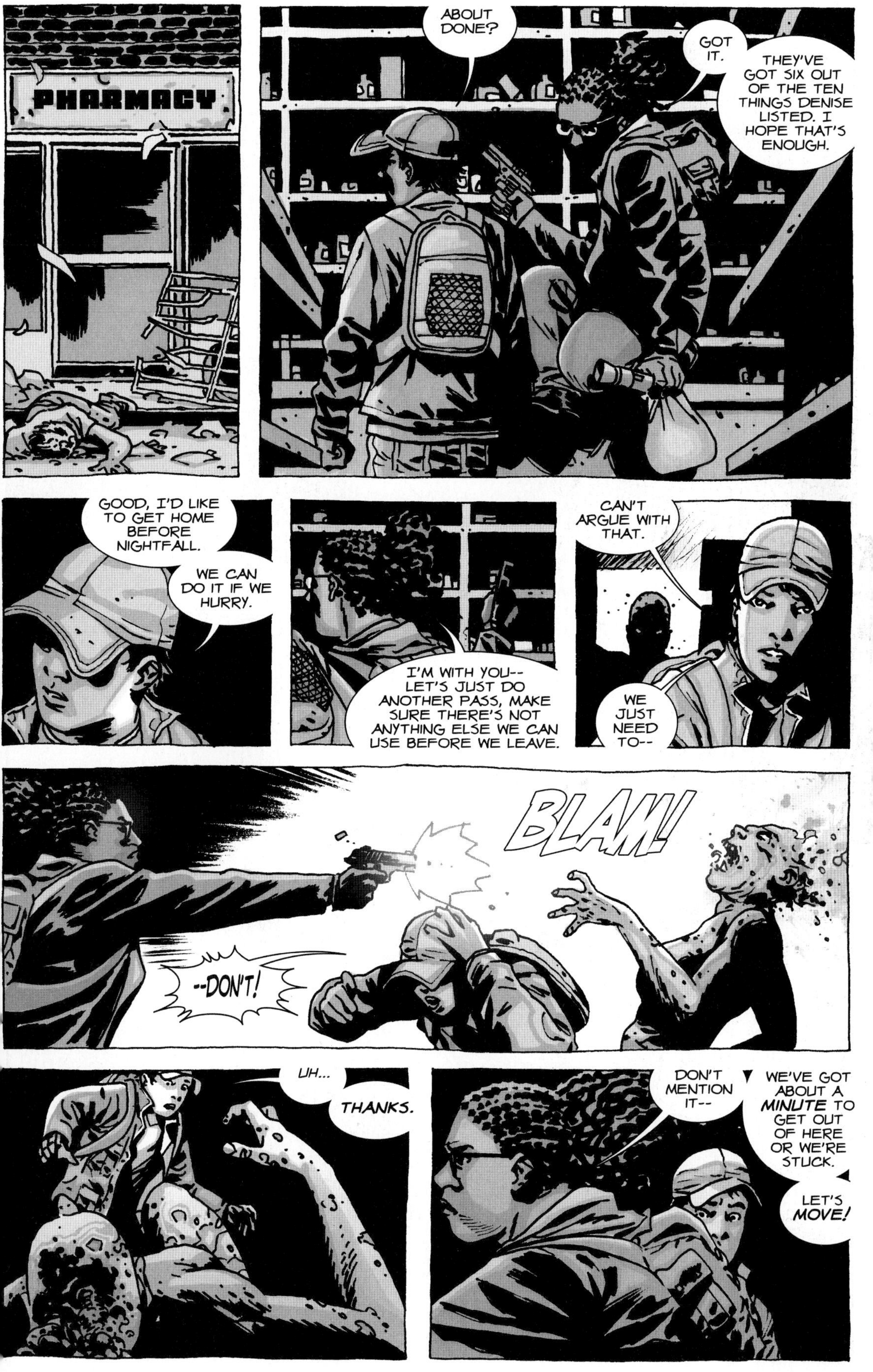
PHARMACY
ABOUT DONE?
GOT IT.
THEY'VE GOT SIX OUT OF THE TEN THINGS DENISE LISTED. I HOPE THAT'S ENOUGH.
GOOD, I'D LIKE TO GET HOME BEFORE NIGHTFALL.
WE CAN DO IT IF WE HURRY.
I'M WITH YOU-- LET'S JUST DO ANOTHER PASS, MAKE SURE THERE'S NOT ANYTHING ELSE WE CAN USE BEFORE WE LEAVE.
CAN'T ARGUE WITH THAT.
WE JUST NEED TO--
BLAM!
--DON'T!
UH...
THANKS.
DON'T MENTION IT--
WE'VE GOT ABOUT A MINUTE TO GET OUT OF HERE OR WE'RE STUCK.
LET'S MOVE!

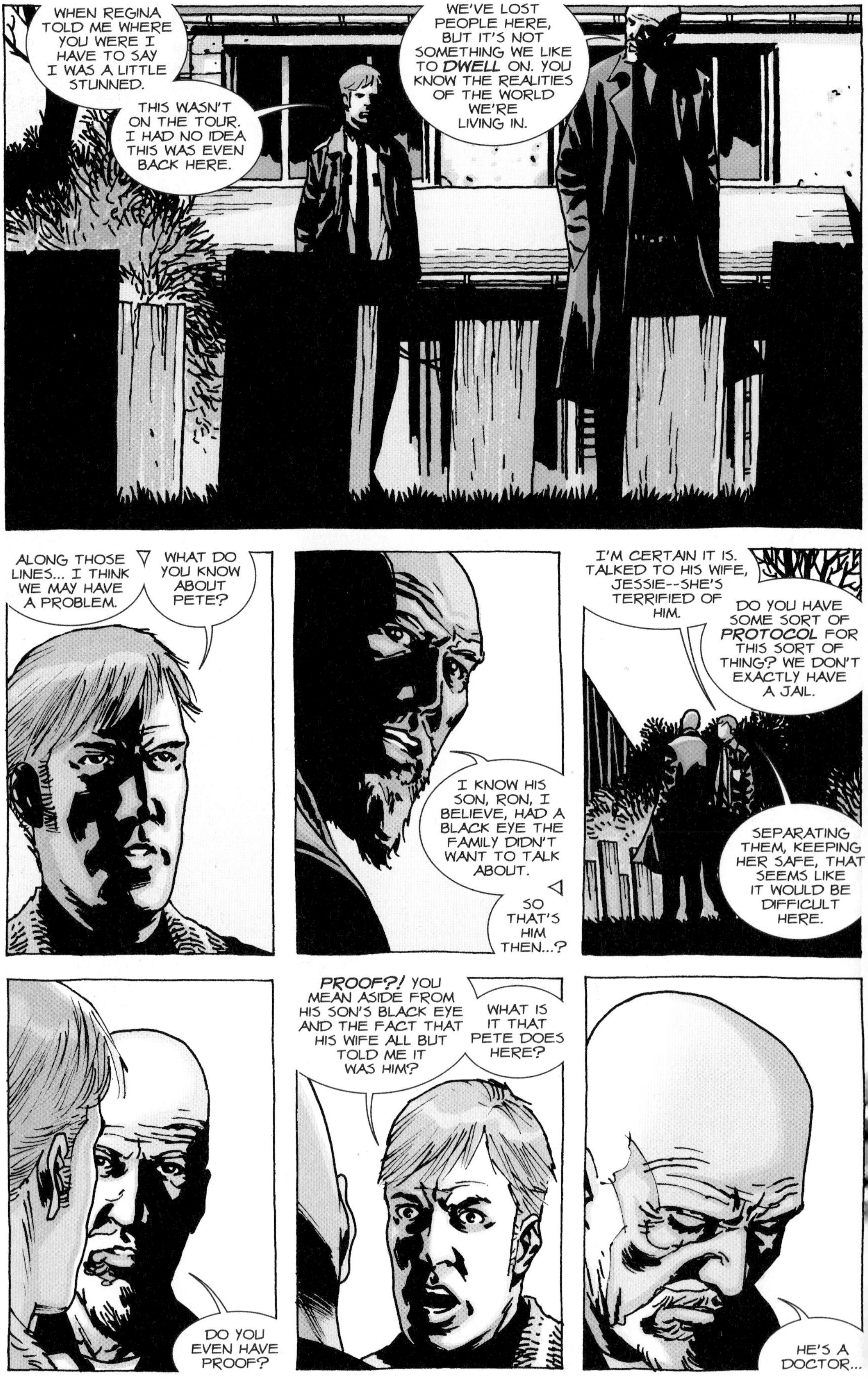
WHEN REGINA TOLD ME WHERE YOU WERE I HAVE TO SAY I WAS A LITTLE STUNNED.
THIS WASN'T ON THE TOUR. I HAD NO IDEA THIS WAS EVEN BACK HERE.
WE'VE LOST PEOPLE HERE, BUT IT'S NOT SOMETHING WE LIKE TO DWELL ON. YOU KNOW THE REALITIES OF THE WORLD WE'RE LIVING IN.
ALONG THOSE LINES... I THINK WE MAY HAVE A PROBLEM.
WHAT DO YOU KNOW ABOUT PETE?
I KNOW HIS SON, RON, I BELIEVE, HAD A BLACK EYE THE FAMILY DIDN'T WANT TO TALK ABOUT.
SO THAT'S HIM THEN...?
I'M CERTAIN IT IS. TALKED TO HIS WIFE, JESSIE--SHE'S TERRIFIED OF HIM.
DO YOU HAVE SOME SORT OF PROTOCOL FOR THIS SORT OF THING? WE DON'T EXACTLY HAVE A JAIL.
SEPARATING THEM, KEEPING HER SAFE, THAT SEEMS LIKE IT WOULD BE DIFFICULT HERE.
DO YOU EVEN HAVE PROOF?
PROOF?! YOU MEAN ASIDE FROM HIS SON'S BLACK EYE AND THE FACT THAT HIS WIFE ALL BUT TOLD ME IT WAS HIM?
WHAT IS IT THAT PETE DOES HERE?
HE'S A DOCTOR...

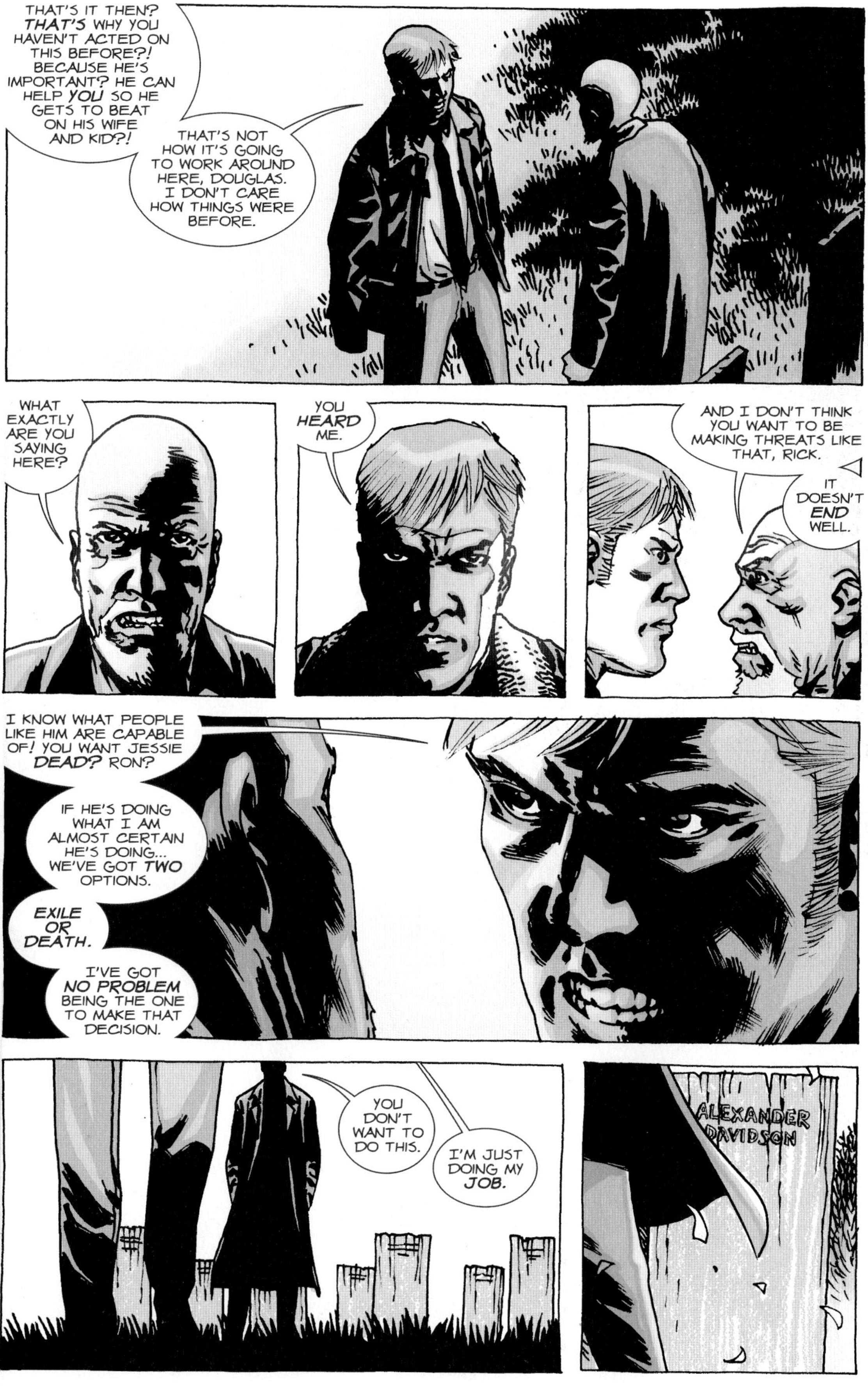
THAT'S IT THEN? THAT'S WHY YOU HAVEN'T ACTED ON THIS BEFORE?! BECAUSE HE'S IMPORTANT? HE CAN HELP YOU SO HE GETS TO BEAT ON HIS WIFE AND KID?!
THAT'S NOT HOW IT'S GOING TO WORK AROUND HERE, DOUGLAS. I DON'T CARE HOW THINGS WERE BEFORE.
WHAT EXACTLY ARE YOU SAYING HERE?
YOU HEARD ME.
AND I DON'T THINK YOU WANT TO BE MAKING THREATS LIKE THAT, RICK.
IT DOESN'T END WELL.
I KNOW WHAT PEOPLE LIKE HIM ARE CAPABLE OF! YOU WANT JESSIE DEAD? RON?
IF HE'S DOING WHAT I AM ALMOST CERTAIN HE'S DOING... WE'VE GOT TWO OPTIONS.
EXILE OR DEATH.
I'VE GOT NO PROBLEM BEING THE ONE TO MAKE THAT DECISION.
YOU DON'T WANT TO DO THIS.
I'M JUST DOING MY JOB.
ALEXANDER DAVIDSON

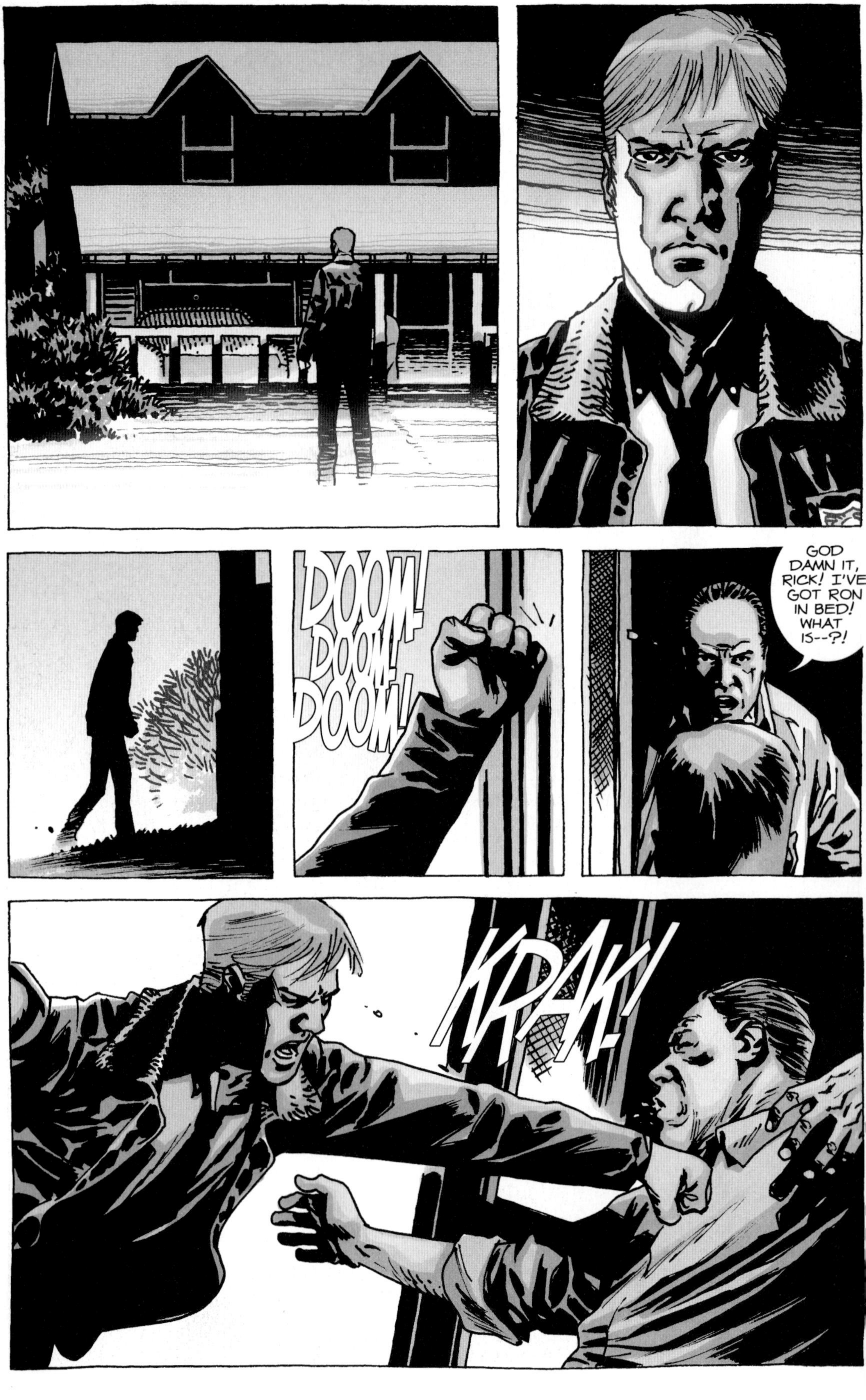
DOOM! DOOM! DOOM!
GOD DAMN IT, RICK! I'VE GOT RON IN BED! WHAT IS--?!
KRAK!

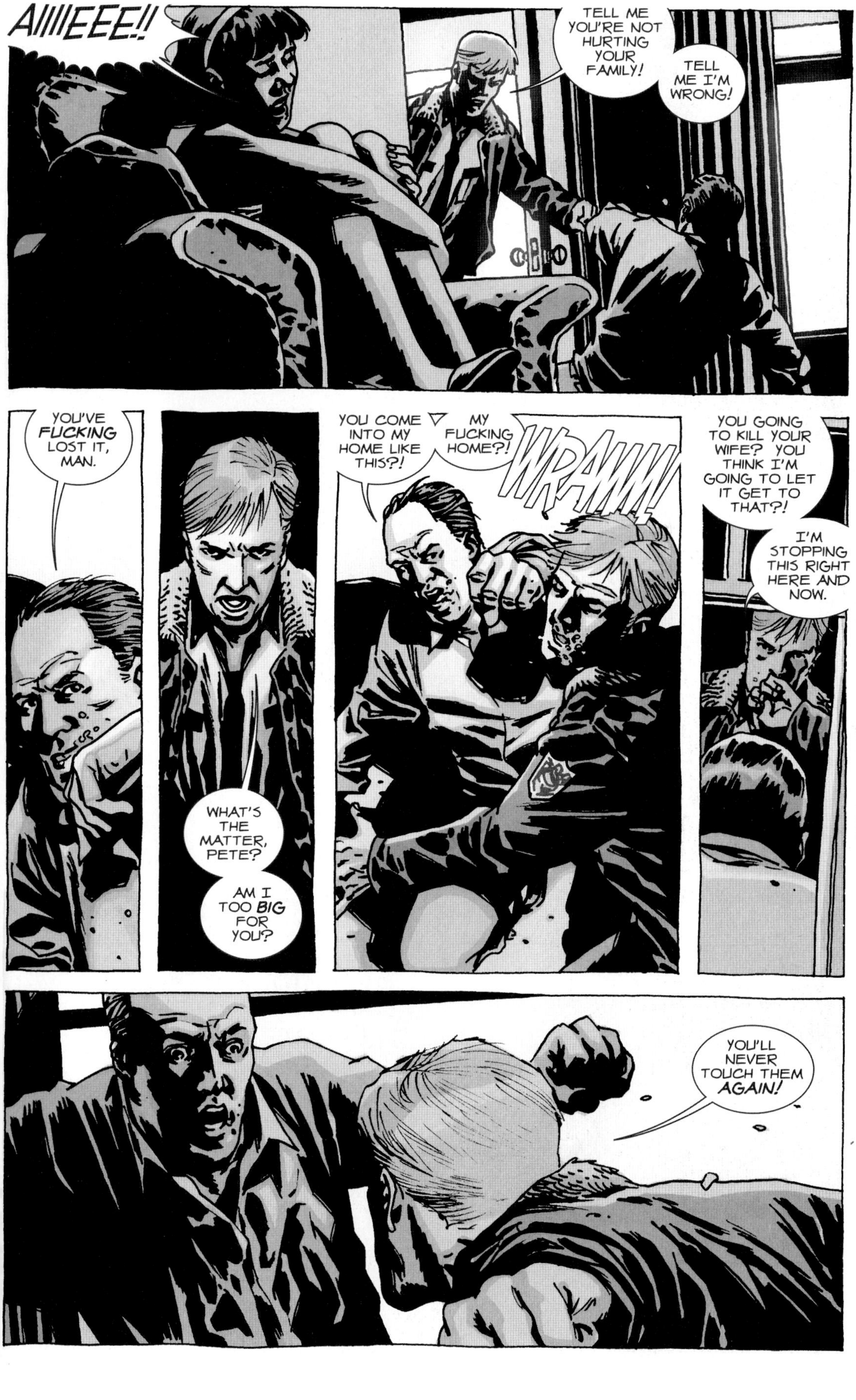
AIIIEEE!!
TELL ME YOU'RE NOT HURTING YOUR FAMILY!
TELL ME I'M WRONG!
YOU'VE FUCKING LOST IT, MAN.
WHAT'S THE MATTER, PETE?
AM I TOO BIG FOR YOU?
YOU COME INTO MY HOME LIKE THIS?!
MY FUCKING HOME?!
WRAMM!
YOU GOING TO KILL YOUR WIFE? YOU THINK I'M GOING TO LET IT GET TO THAT?!
I'M STOPPING THIS RIGHT HERE AND NOW.
YOU'LL NEVER TOUCH THEM AGAIN!

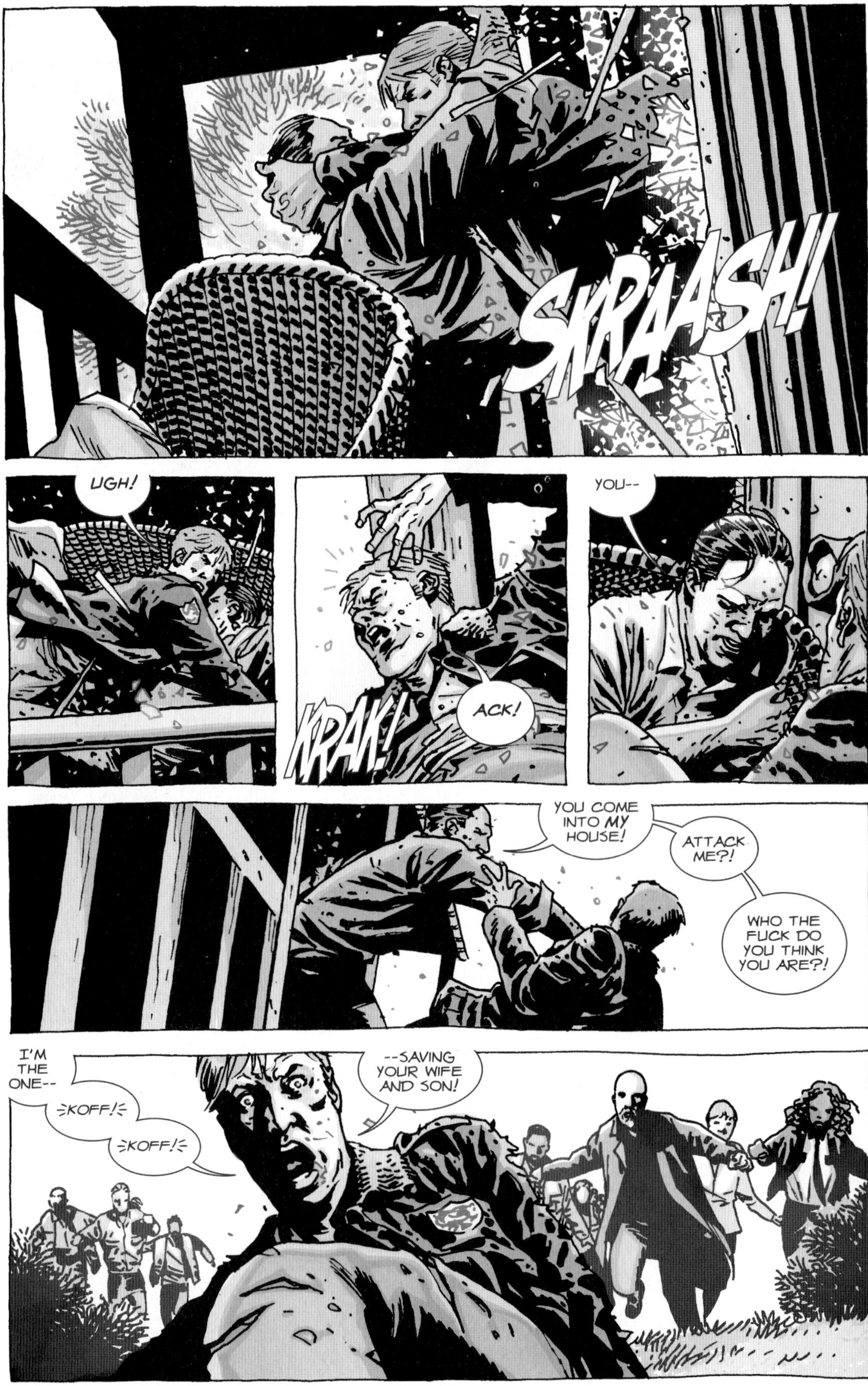
SKRAASH!
UGH!
KRAK!
ACK!
YOU--
YOU COME INTO MY HOUSE!
ATTACK ME?!
WHO THE FUCK DO YOU THINK YOU ARE?!
I'M THE ONE--
--SAVING YOUR WIFE AND SON!
KOFF!
KOFF!

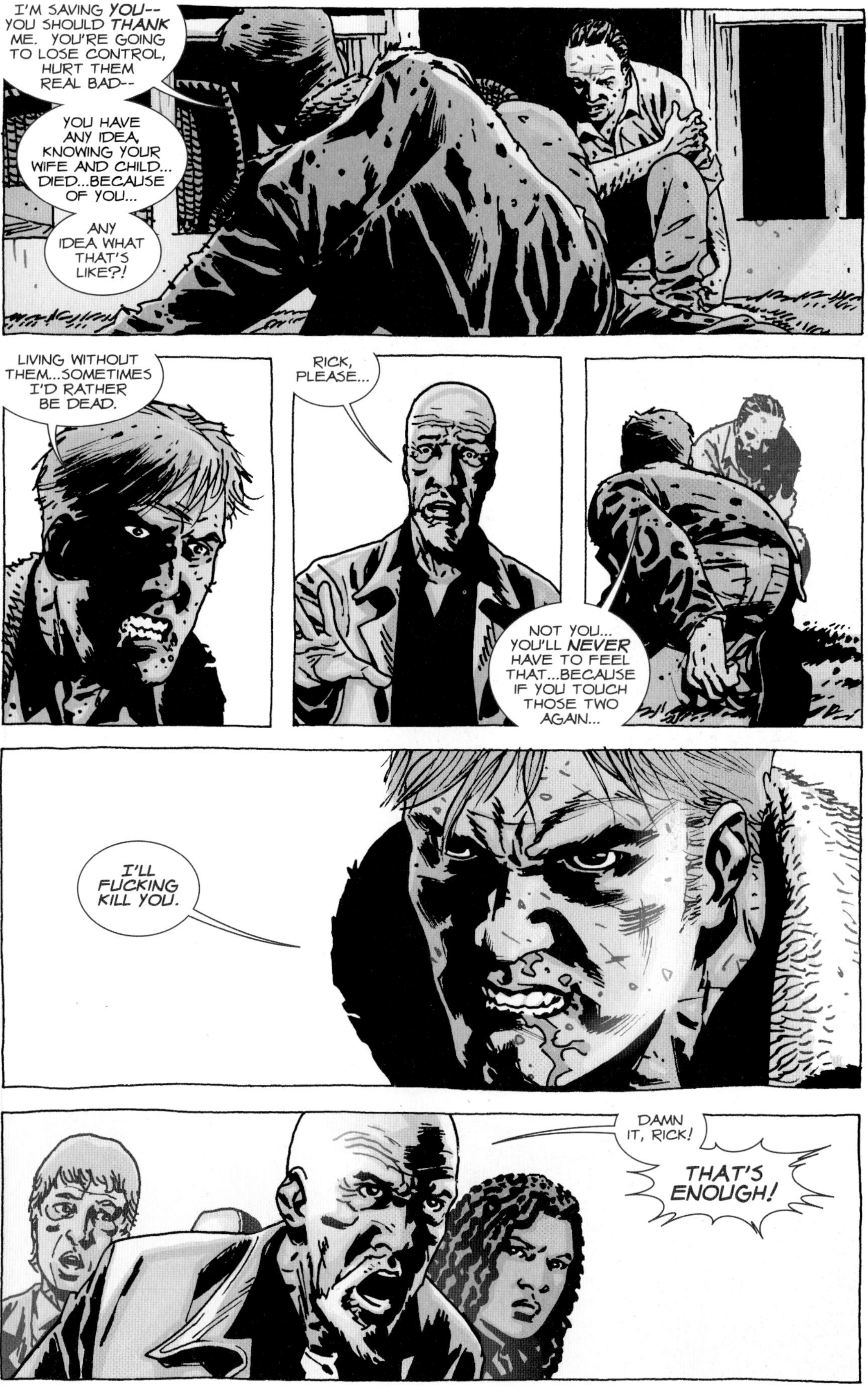
I'M SAVING *YOU*-- YOU SHOULD *THANK* ME. YOU'RE GOING TO LOSE CONTROL, HURT THEM REAL BAD--
YOU HAVE ANY IDEA, KNOWING YOUR WIFE AND CHILD... DIED...BECAUSE OF YOU...
ANY IDEA WHAT THAT'S LIKE?!
LIVING WITHOUT THEM...SOMETIMES I'D RATHER BE DEAD.
RICK, PLEASE...
NOT YOU... YOU'LL *NEVER* HAVE TO FEEL THAT...BECAUSE IF YOU TOUCH THOSE TWO AGAIN...
I'LL FUCKING KILL YOU.
DAMN IT, RICK!
THAT'S ENOUGH!

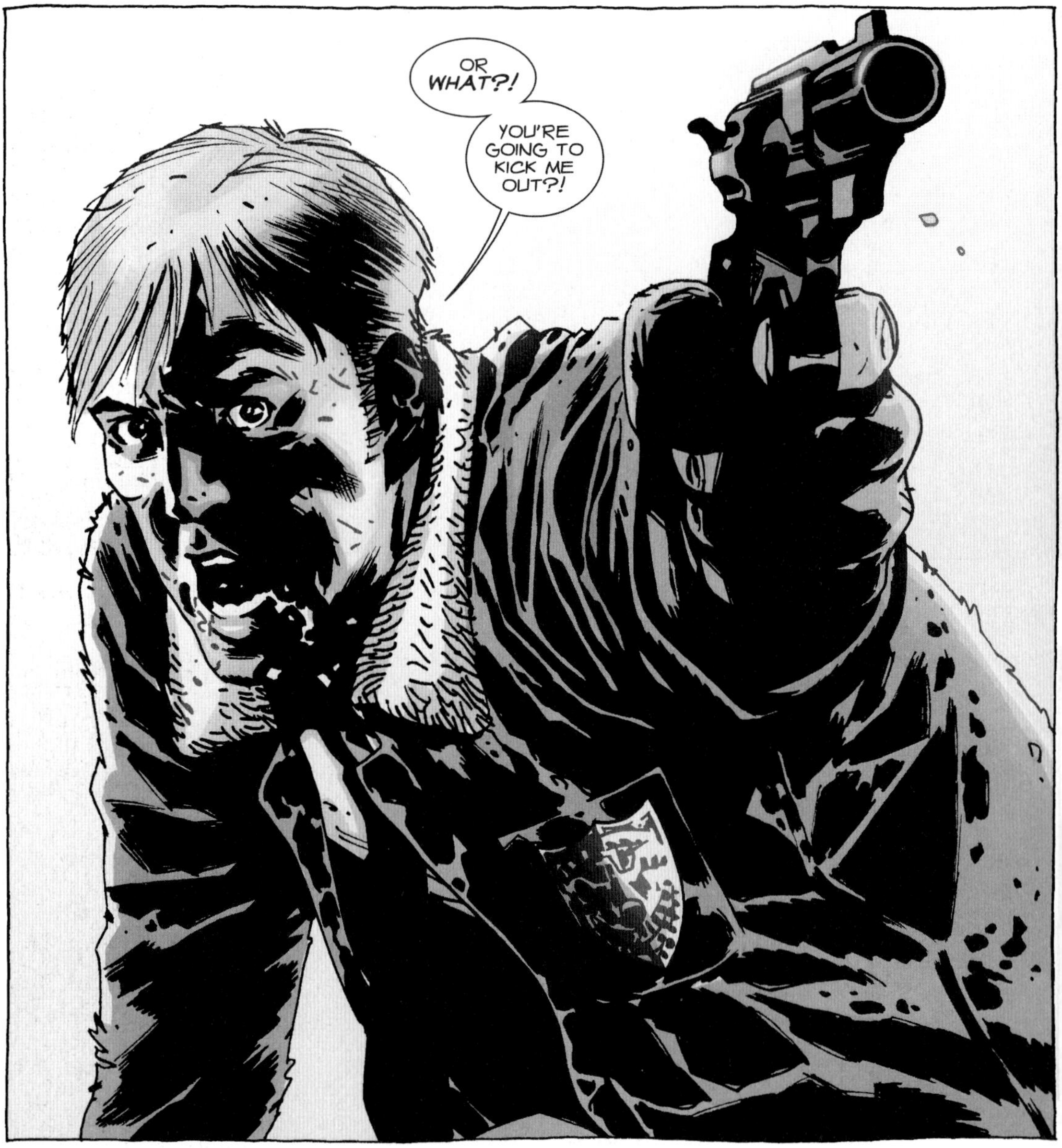
OR WHAT?!
YOU'RE GOING TO KICK ME OUT?!

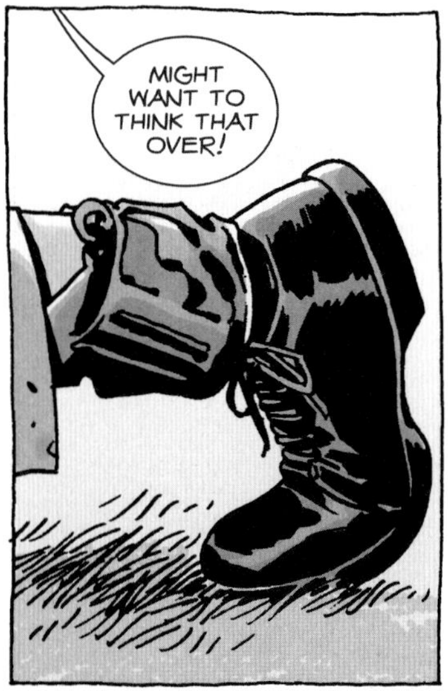
MIGHT WANT TO THINK THAT OVER!

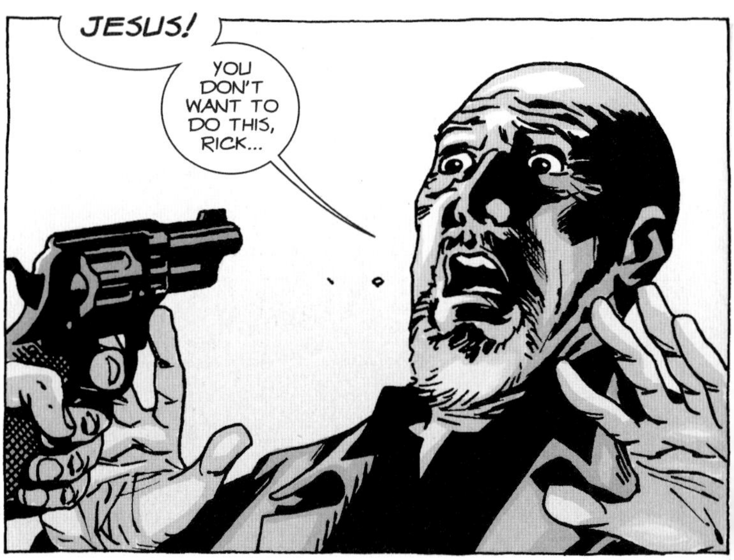
JESUS!
YOU DON'T WANT TO DO THIS, RICK...

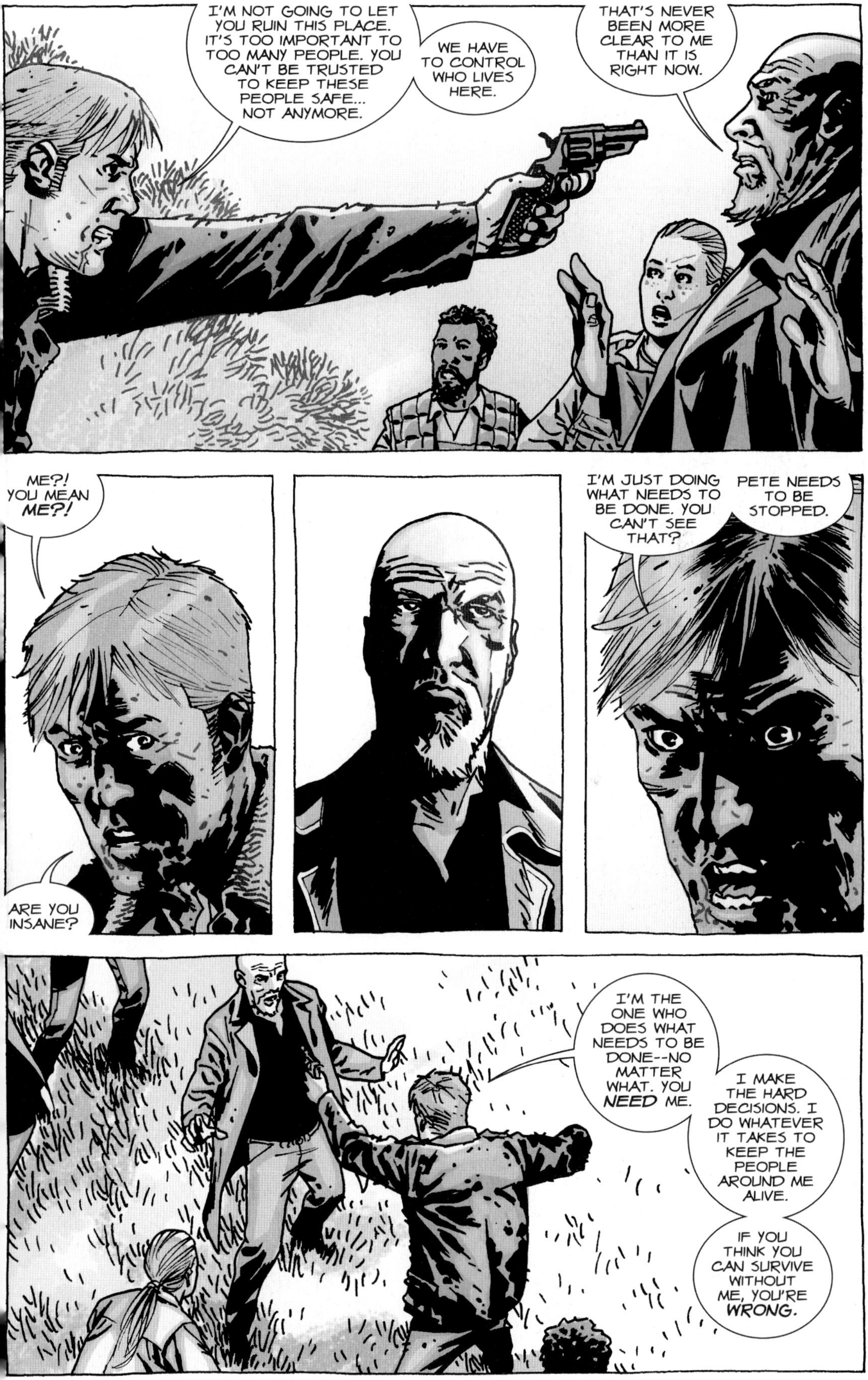
I'M NOT GOING TO LET YOU RUIN THIS PLACE. IT'S TOO IMPORTANT TO TOO MANY PEOPLE. YOU CAN'T BE TRUSTED TO KEEP THESE PEOPLE SAFE... NOT ANYMORE.
WE HAVE TO CONTROL WHO LIVES HERE.
THAT'S NEVER BEEN MORE CLEAR TO ME THAN IT IS RIGHT NOW.
ME?! YOU MEAN *ME?!*
ARE YOU INSANE?
I'M JUST DOING WHAT NEEDS TO BE DONE. YOU CAN'T SEE THAT?
PETE NEEDS TO BE STOPPED.
I'M THE ONE WHO DOES WHAT NEEDS TO BE DONE--NO MATTER WHAT. YOU ***NEED*** ME.
I MAKE THE HARD DECISIONS. I DO WHATEVER IT TAKES TO KEEP THE PEOPLE AROUND ME ALIVE.
IF YOU THINK YOU CAN SURVIVE WITHOUT ME, YOU'RE ***WRONG.***

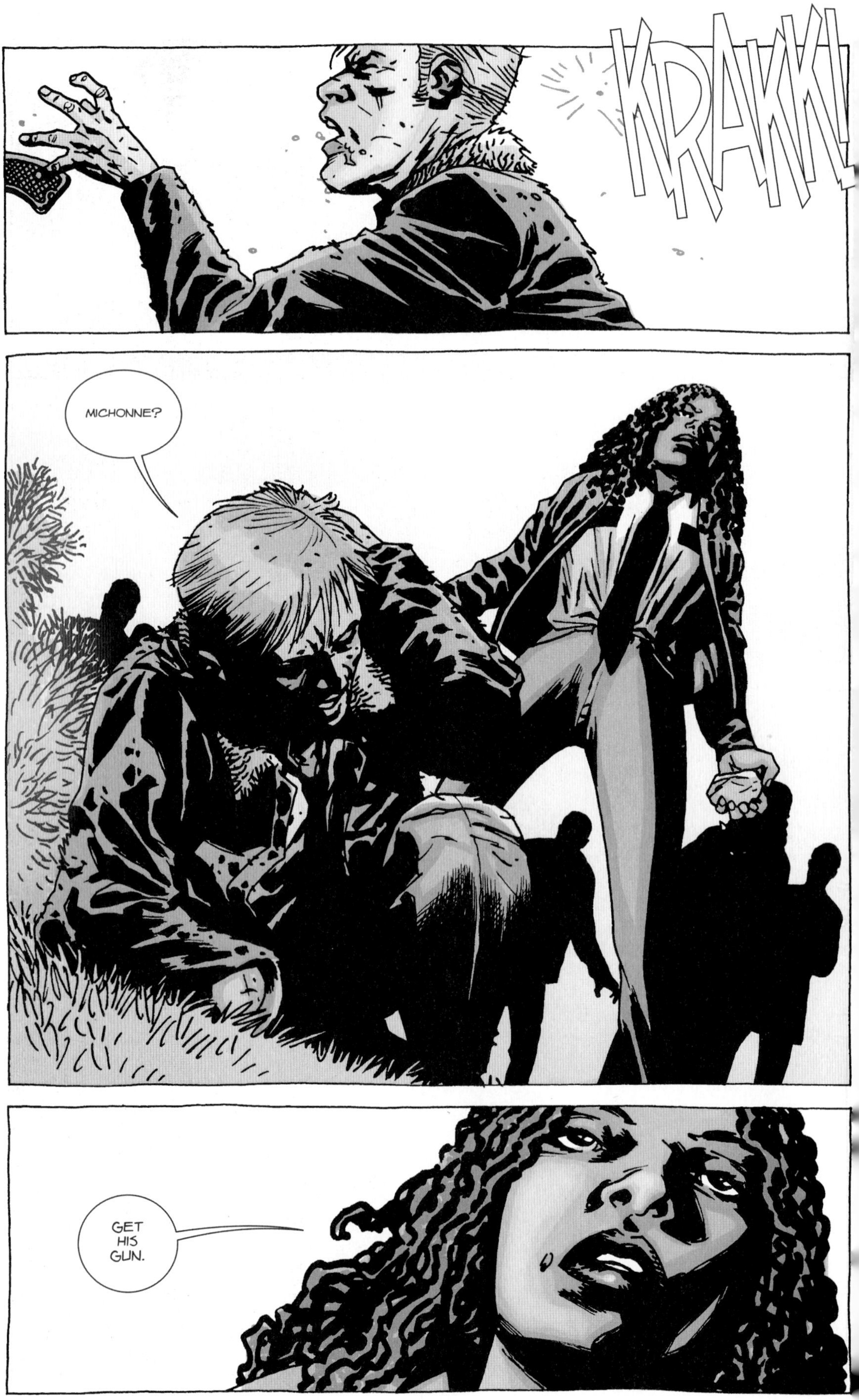
KRAKK!
MICHONNE?
GET HIS GUN.

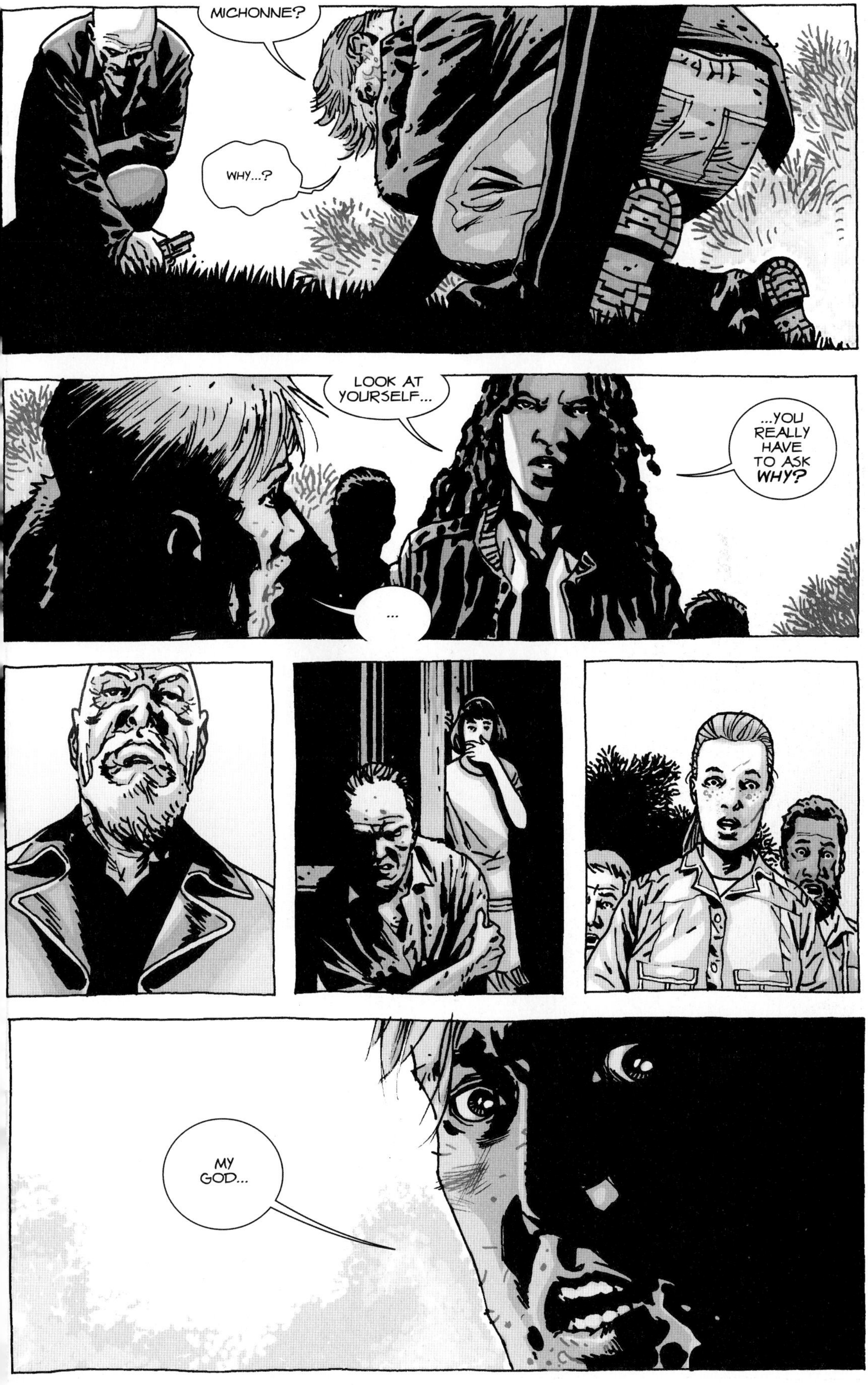
MICHONNE?
WHY...?
LOOK AT YOURSELF...
...YOU REALLY HAVE TO ASK WHY?
...
MY GOD...

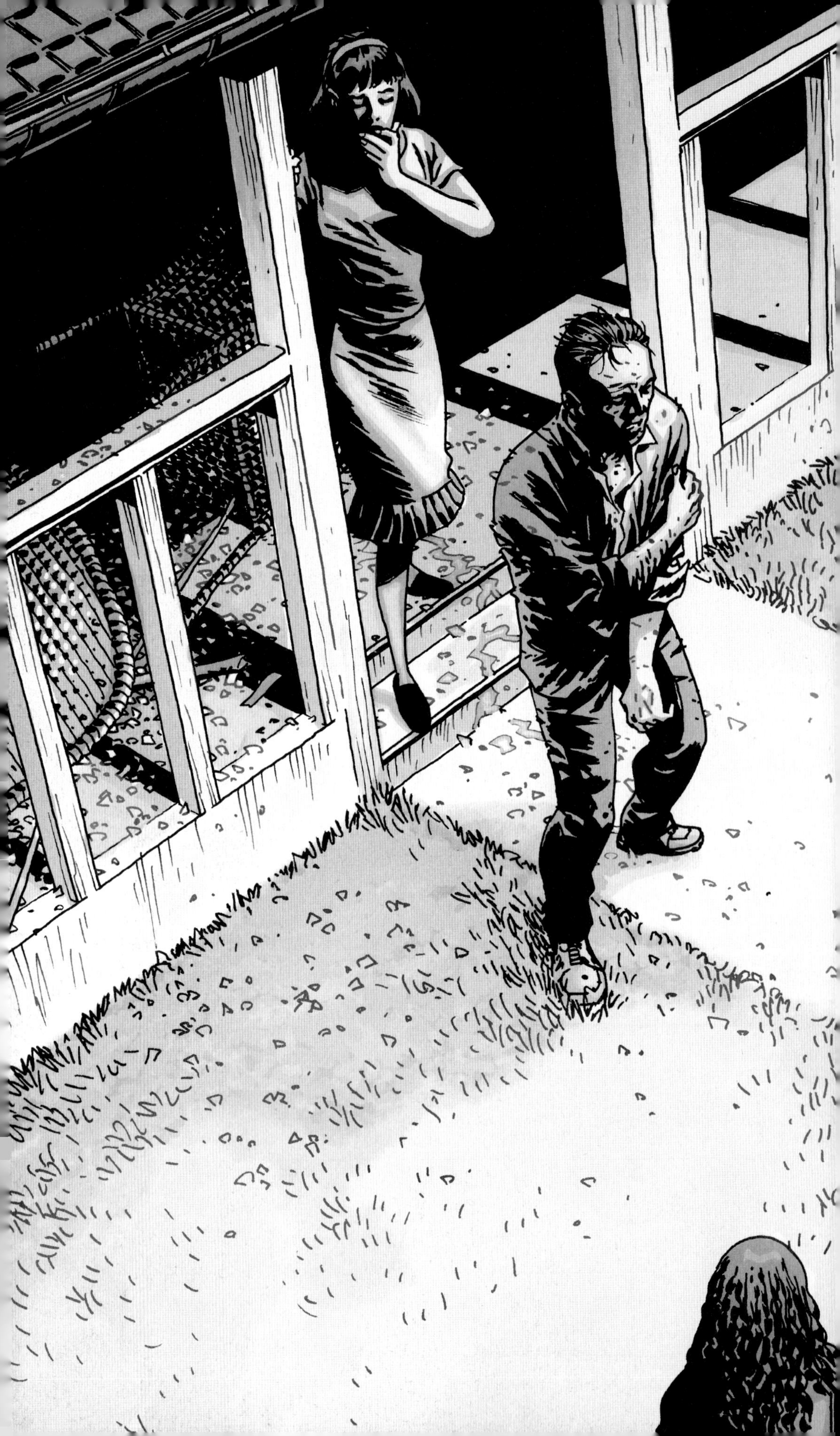

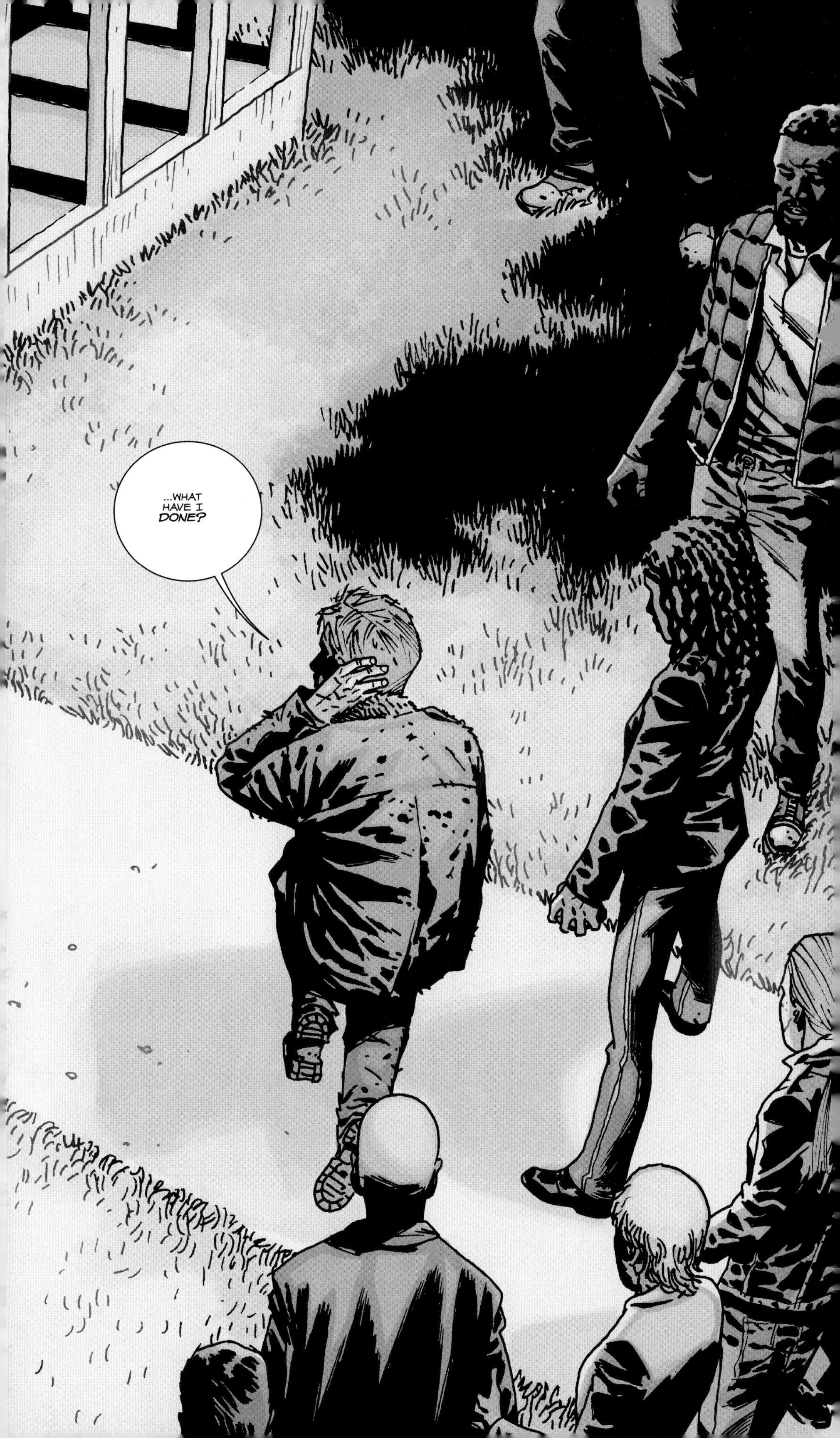
...WHAT HAVE I DONE?

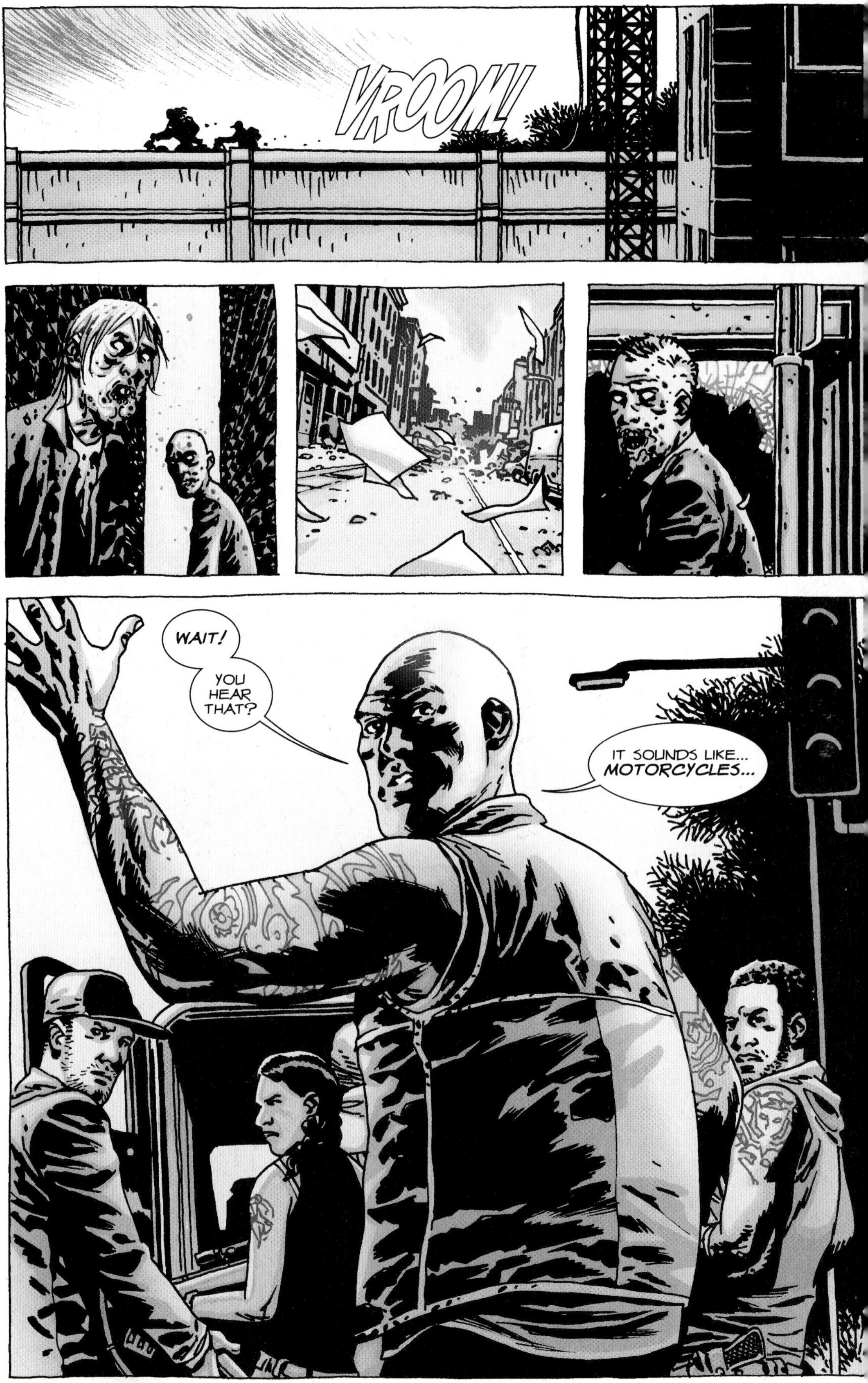
VROOM!
WAIT!
YOU HEAR THAT?
IT SOUNDS LIKE... MOTORCYCLES...

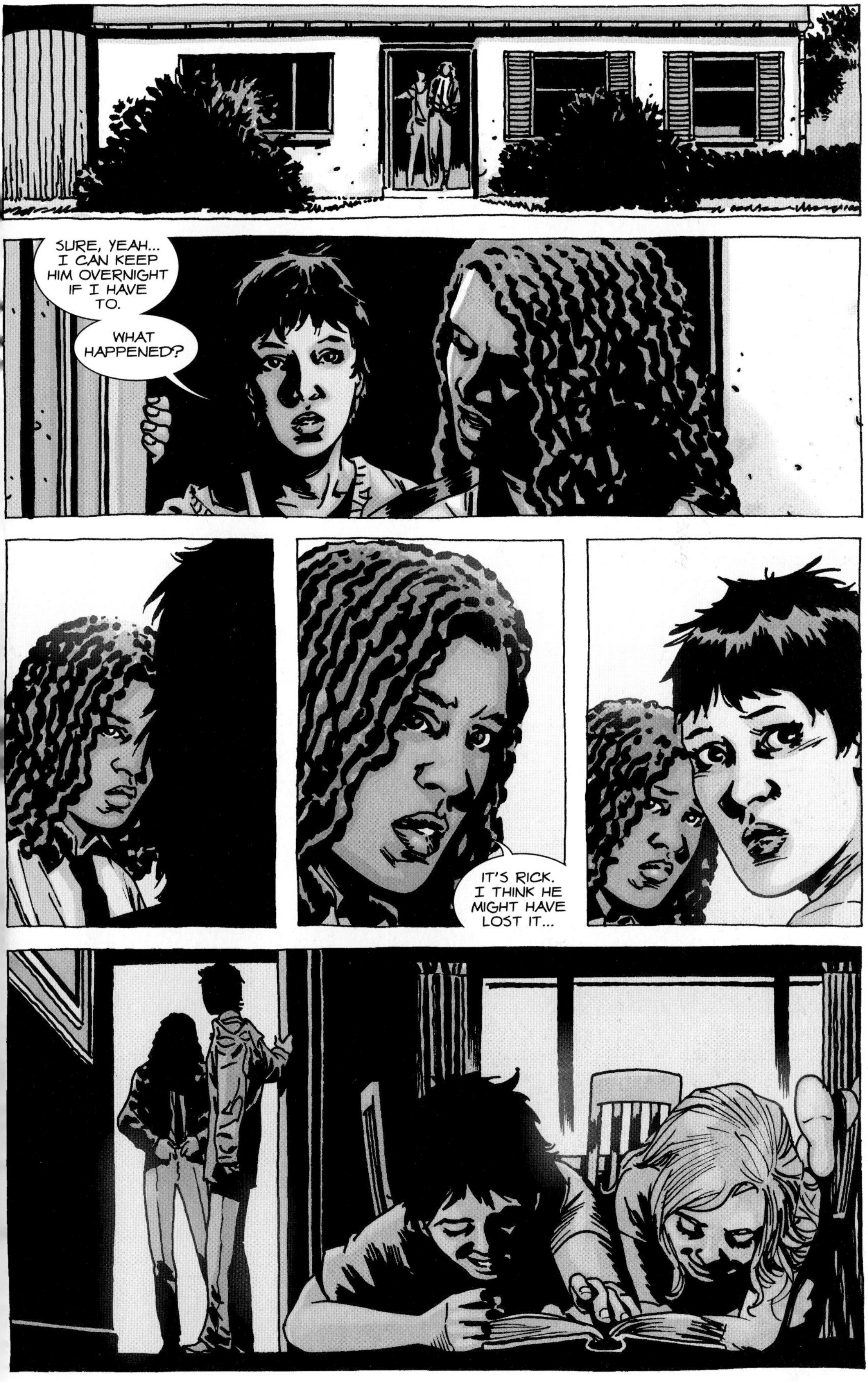
SURE, YEAH... I CAN KEEP HIM OVERNIGHT IF I HAVE TO.
WHAT HAPPENED?
IT'S RICK. I THINK HE MIGHT HAVE LOST IT...

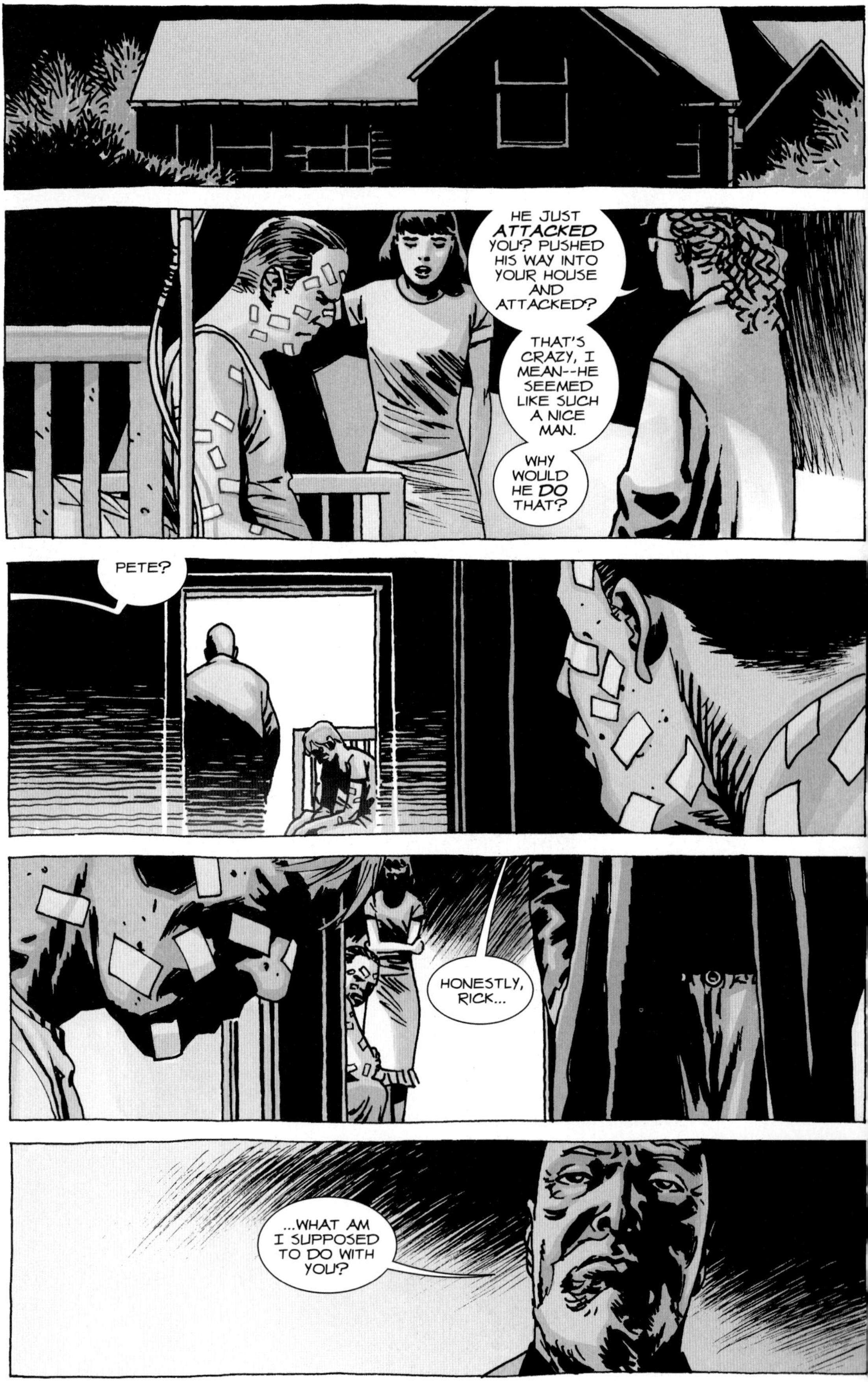
HE JUST ATTACKED YOU? PUSHED HIS WAY INTO YOUR HOUSE AND ATTACKED?
THAT'S CRAZY, I MEAN--HE SEEMED LIKE SUCH A NICE MAN.
WHY WOULD HE DO THAT?
PETE?
HONESTLY, RICK...
...WHAT AM I SUPPOSED TO DO WITH YOU?

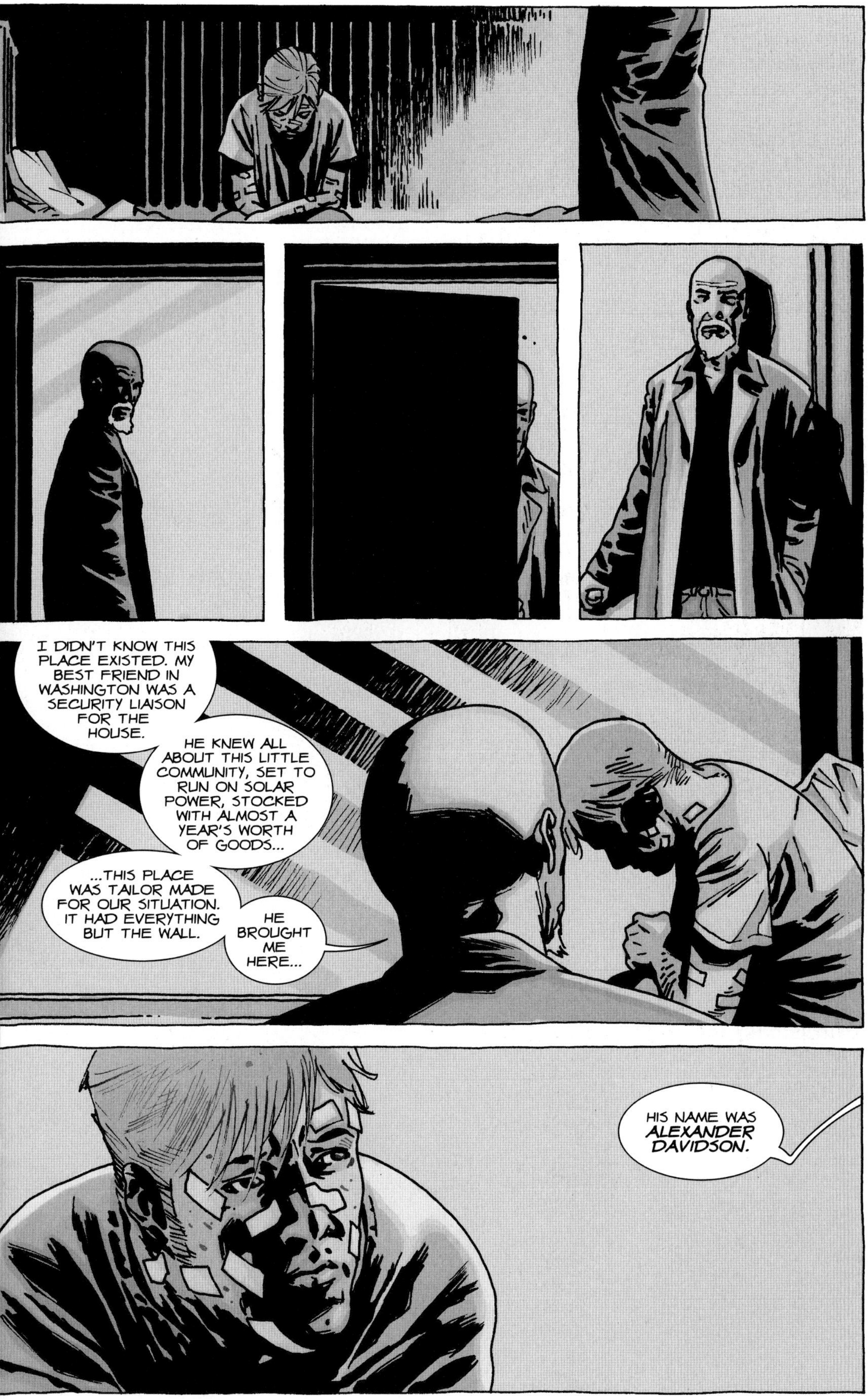
I DIDN'T KNOW THIS PLACE EXISTED. MY BEST FRIEND IN WASHINGTON WAS A SECURITY LIAISON FOR THE HOUSE.
HE KNEW ALL ABOUT THIS LITTLE COMMUNITY, SET TO RUN ON SOLAR POWER, STOCKED WITH ALMOST A YEAR'S WORTH OF GOODS...
...THIS PLACE WAS TAILOR MADE FOR OUR SITUATION. IT HAD EVERYTHING BUT THE WALL.
HE BROUGHT ME HERE...
HIS NAME WAS *ALEXANDER DAVIDSON.*

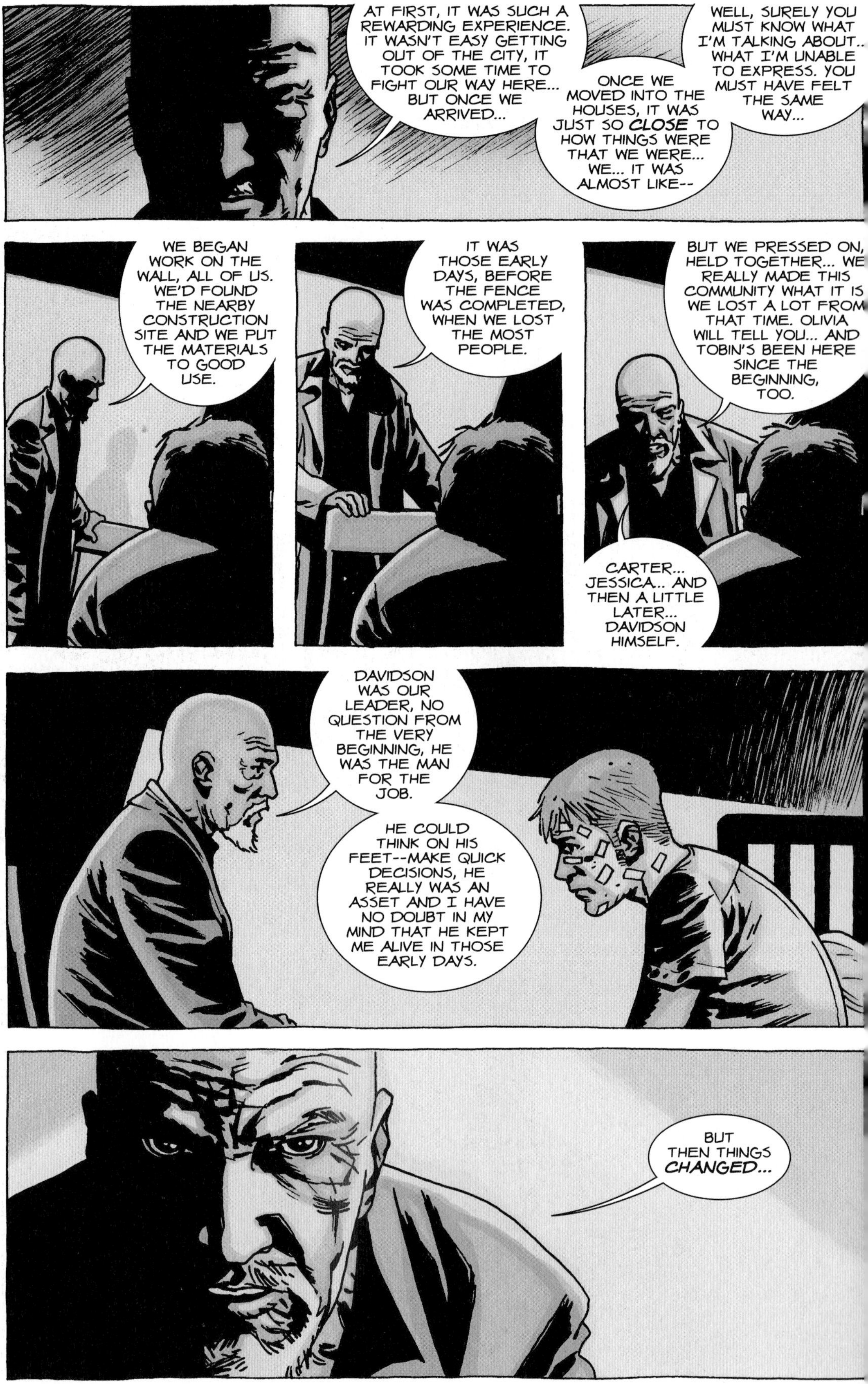
AT FIRST, IT WAS SUCH A REWARDING EXPERIENCE. IT WASN'T EASY GETTING OUT OF THE CITY, IT TOOK SOME TIME TO FIGHT OUR WAY HERE... BUT ONCE WE ARRIVED...
ONCE WE MOVED INTO THE HOUSES, IT WAS JUST SO CLOSE TO HOW THINGS WERE THAT WE WERE... WE... IT WAS ALMOST LIKE--
WELL, SURELY YOU MUST KNOW WHAT I'M TALKING ABOUT... WHAT I'M UNABLE TO EXPRESS. YOU MUST HAVE FELT THE SAME WAY...
WE BEGAN WORK ON THE WALL, ALL OF US. WE'D FOUND THE NEARBY CONSTRUCTION SITE AND WE PUT THE MATERIALS TO GOOD USE.
IT WAS THOSE EARLY DAYS, BEFORE THE FENCE WAS COMPLETED, WHEN WE LOST THE MOST PEOPLE.
BUT WE PRESSED ON, HELD TOGETHER... WE REALLY MADE THIS COMMUNITY WHAT IT IS. WE LOST A LOT FROM THAT TIME. OLIVIA WILL TELL YOU... AND TOBIN'S BEEN HERE SINCE THE BEGINNING, TOO.
CARTER... JESSICA... AND THEN A LITTLE LATER... DAVIDSON HIMSELF.
DAVIDSON WAS OUR LEADER, NO QUESTION FROM THE VERY BEGINNING, HE WAS THE MAN FOR THE JOB.
HE COULD THINK ON HIS FEET--MAKE QUICK DECISIONS, HE REALLY WAS AN ASSET AND I HAVE NO DOUBT IN MY MIND THAT HE KEPT ME ALIVE IN THOSE EARLY DAYS.
BUT THEN THINGS CHANGED...

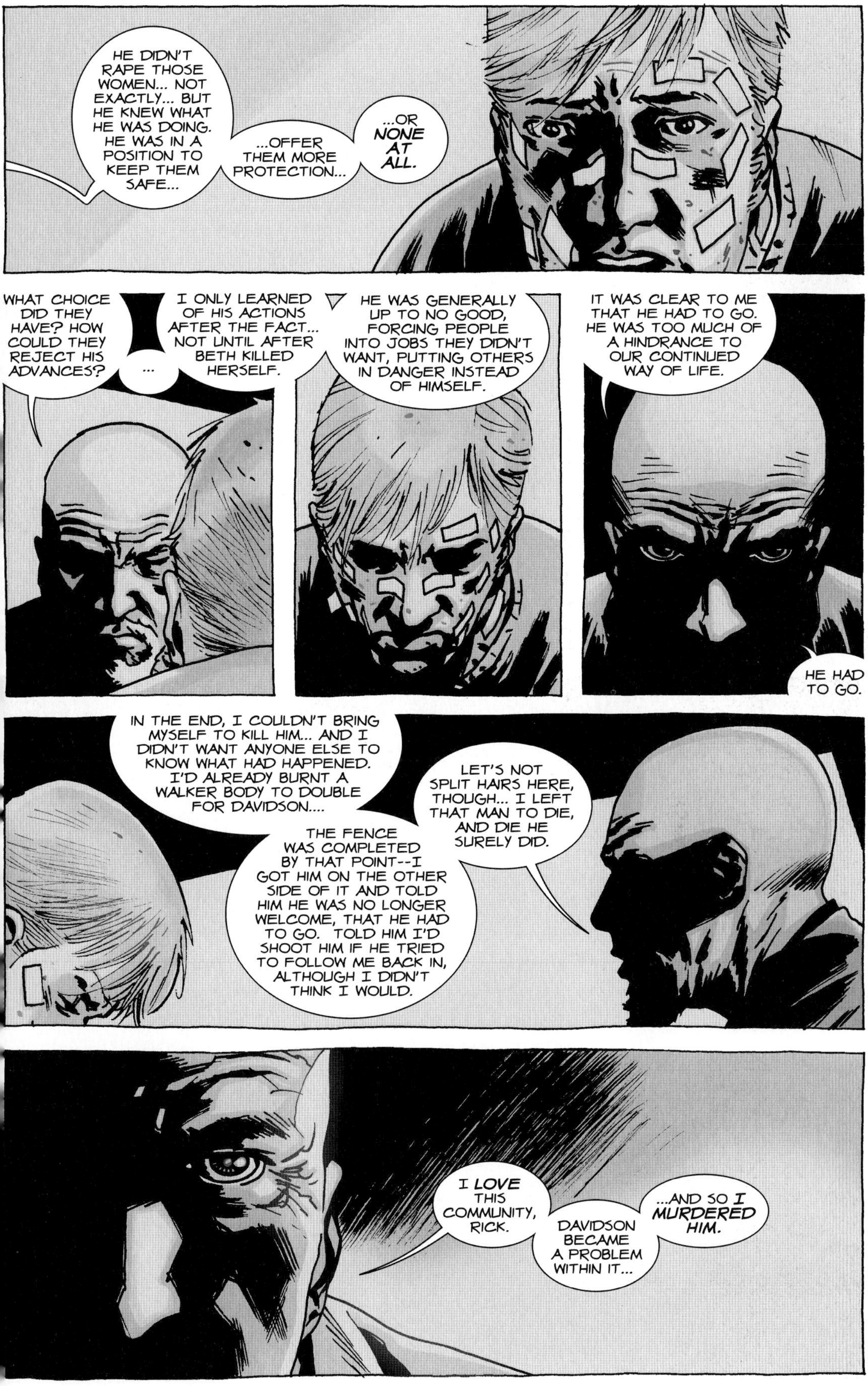
HE DIDN'T RAPE THOSE WOMEN... NOT EXACTLY... BUT HE KNEW WHAT HE WAS DOING. HE WAS IN A POSITION TO KEEP THEM SAFE...
...OFFER THEM MORE PROTECTION...
...OR NONE AT ALL.
WHAT CHOICE DID THEY HAVE? HOW COULD THEY REJECT HIS ADVANCES?
...
I ONLY LEARNED OF HIS ACTIONS AFTER THE FACT... NOT UNTIL AFTER BETH KILLED HERSELF.
HE WAS GENERALLY UP TO NO GOOD, FORCING PEOPLE INTO JOBS THEY DIDN'T WANT, PUTTING OTHERS IN DANGER INSTEAD OF HIMSELF.
IT WAS CLEAR TO ME THAT HE HAD TO GO. HE WAS TOO MUCH OF A HINDRANCE TO OUR CONTINUED WAY OF LIFE.
HE HAD TO GO.
IN THE END, I COULDN'T BRING MYSELF TO KILL HIM... AND I DIDN'T WANT ANYONE ELSE TO KNOW WHAT HAD HAPPENED. I'D ALREADY BURNT A WALKER BODY TO DOUBLE FOR DAVIDSON....
THE FENCE WAS COMPLETED BY THAT POINT--I GOT HIM ON THE OTHER SIDE OF IT AND TOLD HIM HE WAS NO LONGER WELCOME, THAT HE HAD TO GO. TOLD HIM I'D SHOOT HIM IF HE TRIED TO FOLLOW ME BACK IN, ALTHOUGH I DIDN'T THINK I WOULD.
LET'S NOT SPLIT HAIRS HERE, THOUGH... I LEFT THAT MAN TO DIE, AND DIE HE SURELY DID.
I LOVE THIS COMMUNITY, RICK.
DAVIDSON BECAME A PROBLEM WITHIN IT...
...AND SO I MURDERED HIM.

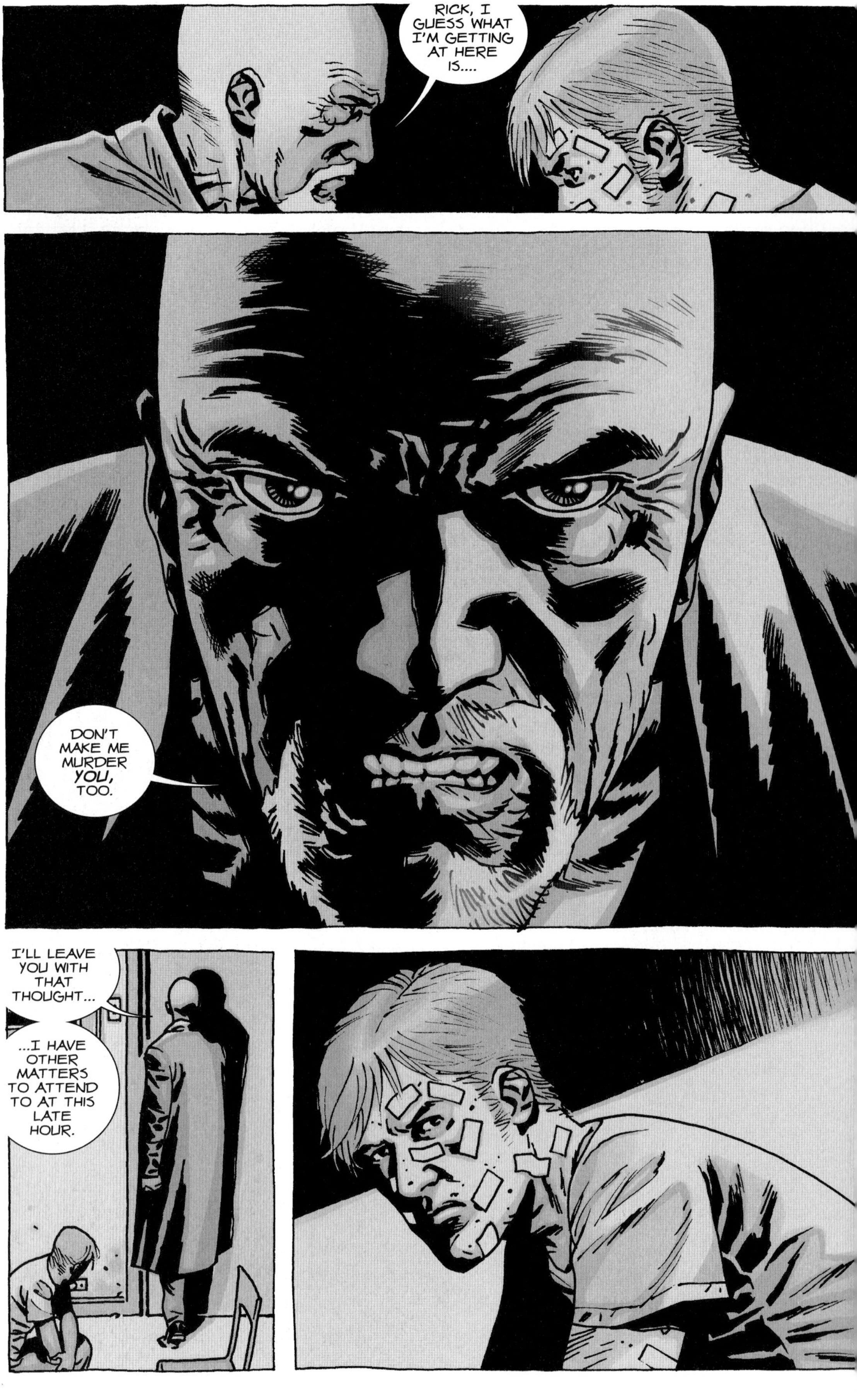
RICK, I GUESS WHAT I'M GETTING AT HERE IS....
DON'T MAKE ME MURDER *YOU,* TOO.
I'LL LEAVE YOU WITH THAT THOUGHT...
...I HAVE OTHER MATTERS TO ATTEND TO AT THIS LATE HOUR.

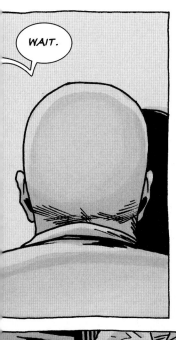

WAIT.

YES?

I NEVER WANTED TO BE A LEADER.

I DIDN'T NEED THE PRESSURE, DIDN'T **WANT** THE RESPONSIBILITY. WITH ALL THAT WAS GOING ON... I HAD OTHER THINGS ON MY MIND. MY WIFE AND SON TO PROTECT.

MY PARTNER SHANE... HE WAS THE LEADER OF OUR GROUP AT FIRST. NOT THAT WE TOOK THE TIME TO MAKE THOSE DISTINCTIONS, BUT HE WAS THE ONE EVERYONE LOOKED TO FOR ANSWERS.

IT DIDN'T REALLY MATTER TO ME UNTIL HE STARTED MAKING DECISIONS THAT WEREN'T GOOD FOR THE GROUP...

HE WANTED TO STAY ON THE OUTSKIRTS OF ATLANTA... BUT IT WAS TOO DANGEROUS. HE THOUGHT HELP WAS COMING. HE HAD HIS REASONS, BUT IT DIDN'T MAKE THINGS ANY LESS DANGEROUS.

WE BUTTED HEADS... THERE WERE A LOT OF ARGUMENTS.

THINGS EVEN GOT HEATED. HE DIDN'T LIKE THAT PEOPLE WERE STARTING TO AGREE WITH ME.

HE HELPED MY WIFE AND SON GET TO ATLANTA... I WAS IN A HOSPITAL HEALING FROM A GUNSHOT WOUND, I CAUGHT UP TO THEM LATER.

I'D DRIFTED INTO A COMA... THEY BOTH THOUGHT I WAS DEAD... THINKING ABOUT IT, WHY WOULDN'T THEY?

THEY WERE ALWAYS CLOSE... HE WAS MY BEST FRIEND, SHE WAS MY WIFE... THEY SPENT A LOT OF TIME TOGETHER BEFORE ALL THIS HAPPENED.

I KNOW SHE SLEPT WITH HIM.

NOT BEFORE... WHEN THEY WERE AT THE CAMP OUTSIDE ATLANTA, BEFORE I ARRIVED. THEY THOUGHT I WAS DEAD...

...WHO COULD BLAME THEM?

I CERTAINLY DIDN'T.

I'M ALMOST CERTAIN THAT MY DAUGHTER WAS ACTUALLY SHANE'S.

WITH ME BACK, LORI NATURALLY SHUNNED SHANE, RETURNING TO ME, PRETENDING NOTHING HAD EVER HAPPENED.

BETWEEN THAT AND SEEING THE GROUP SLOWLY TURN TO ME FOR LEADERSHIP--TAKING MY SIDE IN THE ARGUMENTS... HE STARTED TO CRACK.

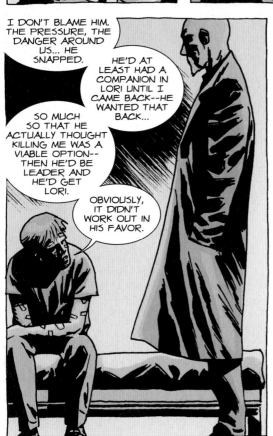

I DON'T BLAME HIM. THE PRESSURE, THE DANGER AROUND US... HE SNAPPED.

HE'D AT LEAST HAD A COMPANION IN LORI UNTIL I CAME BACK--HE WANTED THAT BACK...

SO MUCH SO THAT HE ACTUALLY THOUGHT KILLING ME WAS A VIABLE OPTION-- THEN HE'D BE LEADER AND HE'D GET LORI.

OBVIOUSLY, IT DIDN'T WORK OUT IN HIS FAVOR.

YOU KILLED YOUR BEST FRIEND, TOO?

NO.

MY SON DID IT FOR ME.

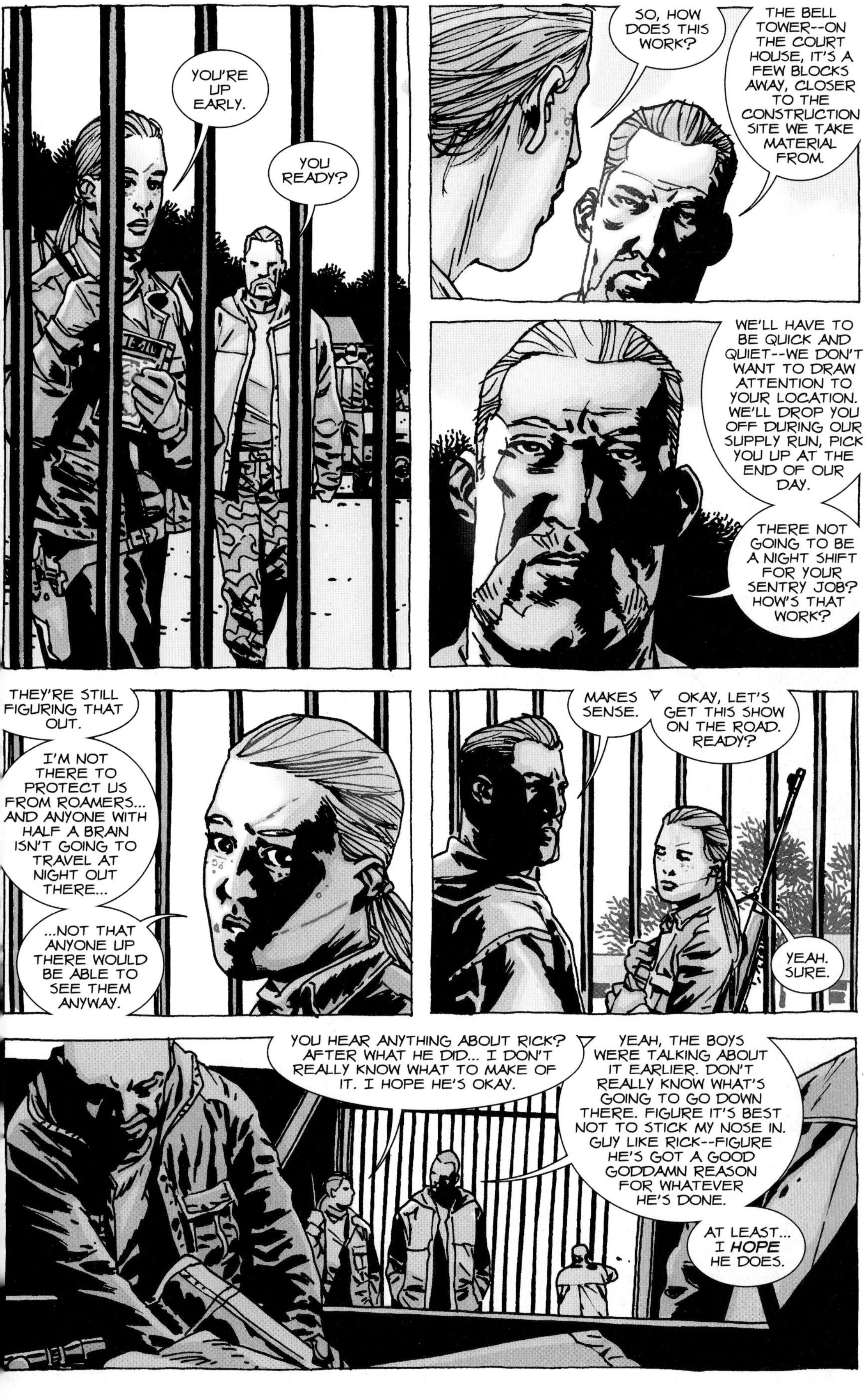
YOU'RE UP EARLY.
YOU READY?
SO, HOW DOES THIS WORK?
THE BELL TOWER--ON THE COURT HOUSE, IT'S A FEW BLOCKS AWAY, CLOSER TO THE CONSTRUCTION SITE WE TAKE MATERIAL FROM.
WE'LL HAVE TO BE QUICK AND QUIET--WE DON'T WANT TO DRAW ATTENTION TO YOUR LOCATION. WE'LL DROP YOU OFF DURING OUR SUPPLY RUN, PICK YOU UP AT THE END OF OUR DAY.
THERE NOT GOING TO BE A NIGHT SHIFT FOR YOUR SENTRY JOB? HOW'S THAT WORK?
THEY'RE STILL FIGURING THAT OUT.
I'M NOT THERE TO PROTECT US FROM ROAMERS... AND ANYONE WITH HALF A BRAIN ISN'T GOING TO TRAVEL AT NIGHT OUT THERE...
...NOT THAT ANYONE UP THERE WOULD BE ABLE TO SEE THEM ANYWAY.
MAKES SENSE.
OKAY, LET'S GET THIS SHOW ON THE ROAD. READY?
YEAH. SURE.
YOU HEAR ANYTHING ABOUT RICK? AFTER WHAT HE DID... I DON'T REALLY KNOW WHAT TO MAKE OF IT. I HOPE HE'S OKAY.
YEAH, THE BOYS WERE TALKING ABOUT IT EARLIER. DON'T REALLY KNOW WHAT'S GOING TO GO DOWN THERE. FIGURE IT'S BEST NOT TO STICK MY NOSE IN. GUY LIKE RICK--FIGURE HE'S GOT A GOOD GODDAMN REASON FOR WHATEVER HE'S DONE.
AT LEAST... I *HOPE* HE DOES.

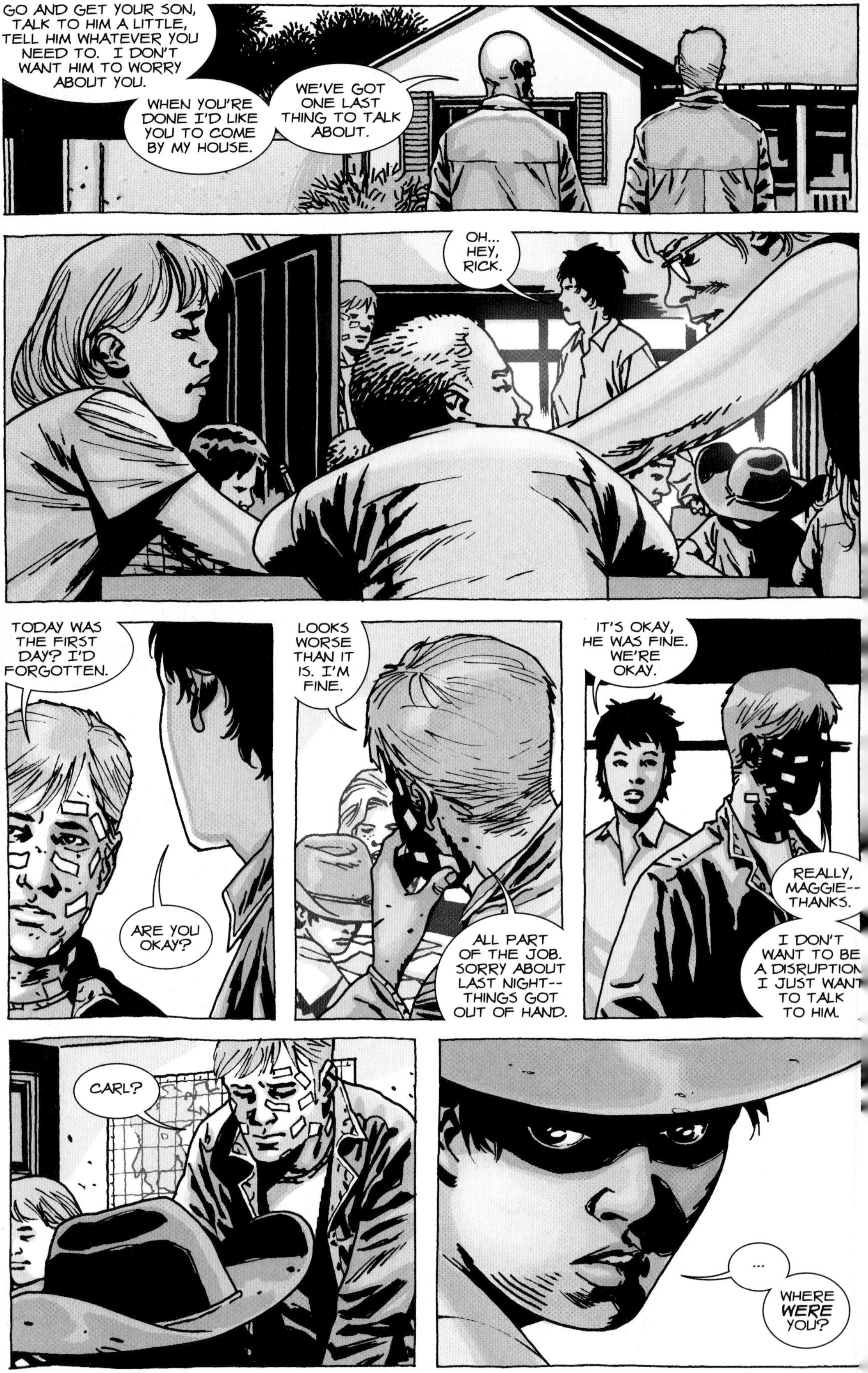
GO AND GET YOUR SON, TALK TO HIM A LITTLE, TELL HIM WHATEVER YOU NEED TO. I DON'T WANT HIM TO WORRY ABOUT YOU.
WHEN YOU'RE DONE I'D LIKE YOU TO COME BY MY HOUSE.
WE'VE GOT ONE LAST THING TO TALK ABOUT.
OH... HEY, RICK.
TODAY WAS THE FIRST DAY? I'D FORGOTTEN.
ARE YOU OKAY?
LOOKS WORSE THAN IT IS. I'M FINE.
ALL PART OF THE JOB. SORRY ABOUT LAST NIGHT-- THINGS GOT OUT OF HAND.
IT'S OKAY, HE WAS FINE. WE'RE OKAY.
REALLY, MAGGIE-- THANKS.
I DON'T WANT TO BE A DISRUPTION I JUST WANT TO TALK TO HIM.
CARL?
...
WHERE *WERE* YOU?

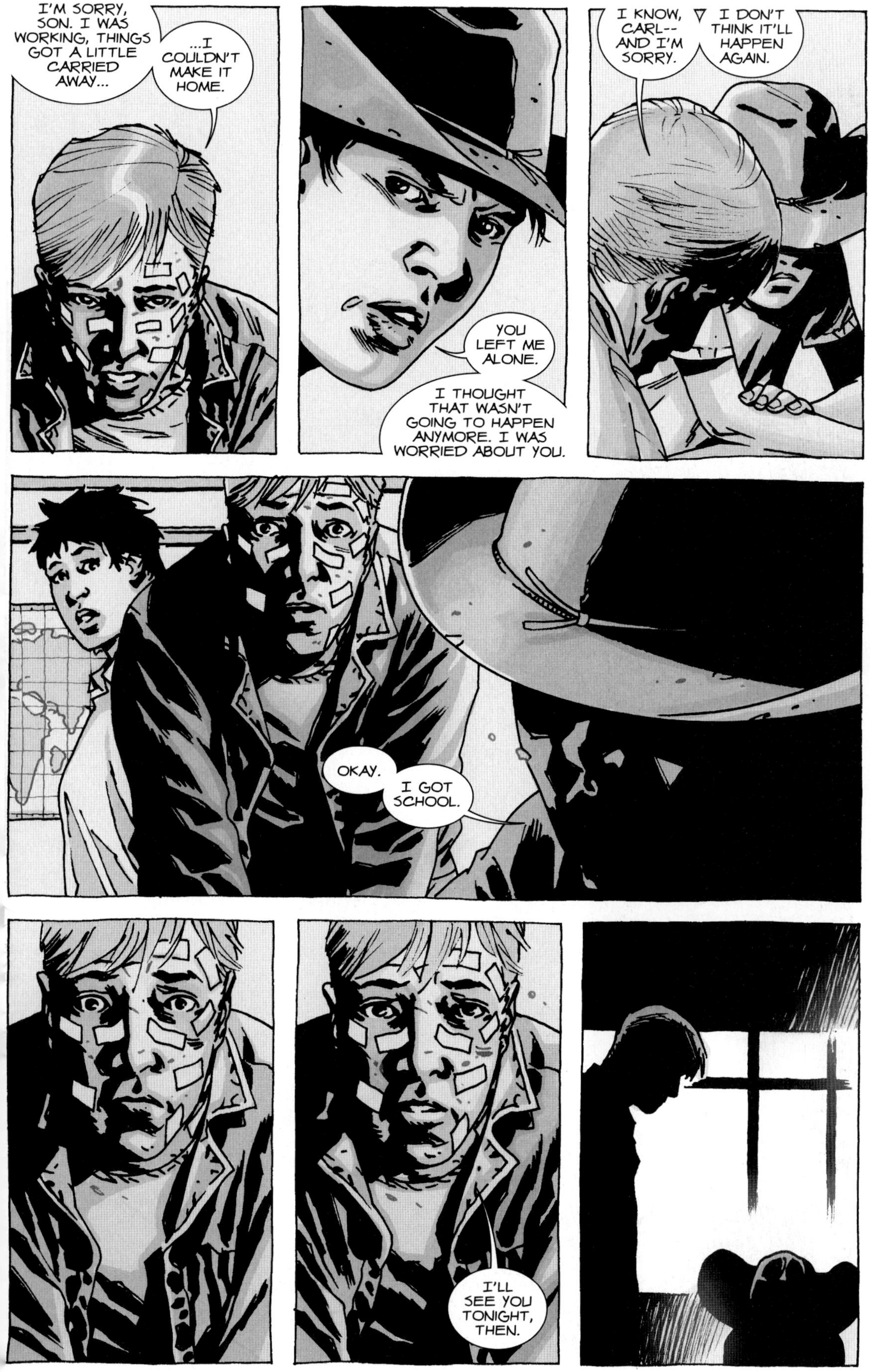
I'M SORRY, SON. I WAS WORKING, THINGS GOT A LITTLE CARRIED AWAY...
...I COULDN'T MAKE IT HOME.
YOU LEFT ME ALONE.
I THOUGHT THAT WASN'T GOING TO HAPPEN ANYMORE. I WAS WORRIED ABOUT YOU.
I KNOW, CARL-- AND I'M SORRY.
I DON'T THINK IT'LL HAPPEN AGAIN.
OKAY.
I GOT SCHOOL.
I'LL SEE YOU TONIGHT, THEN.

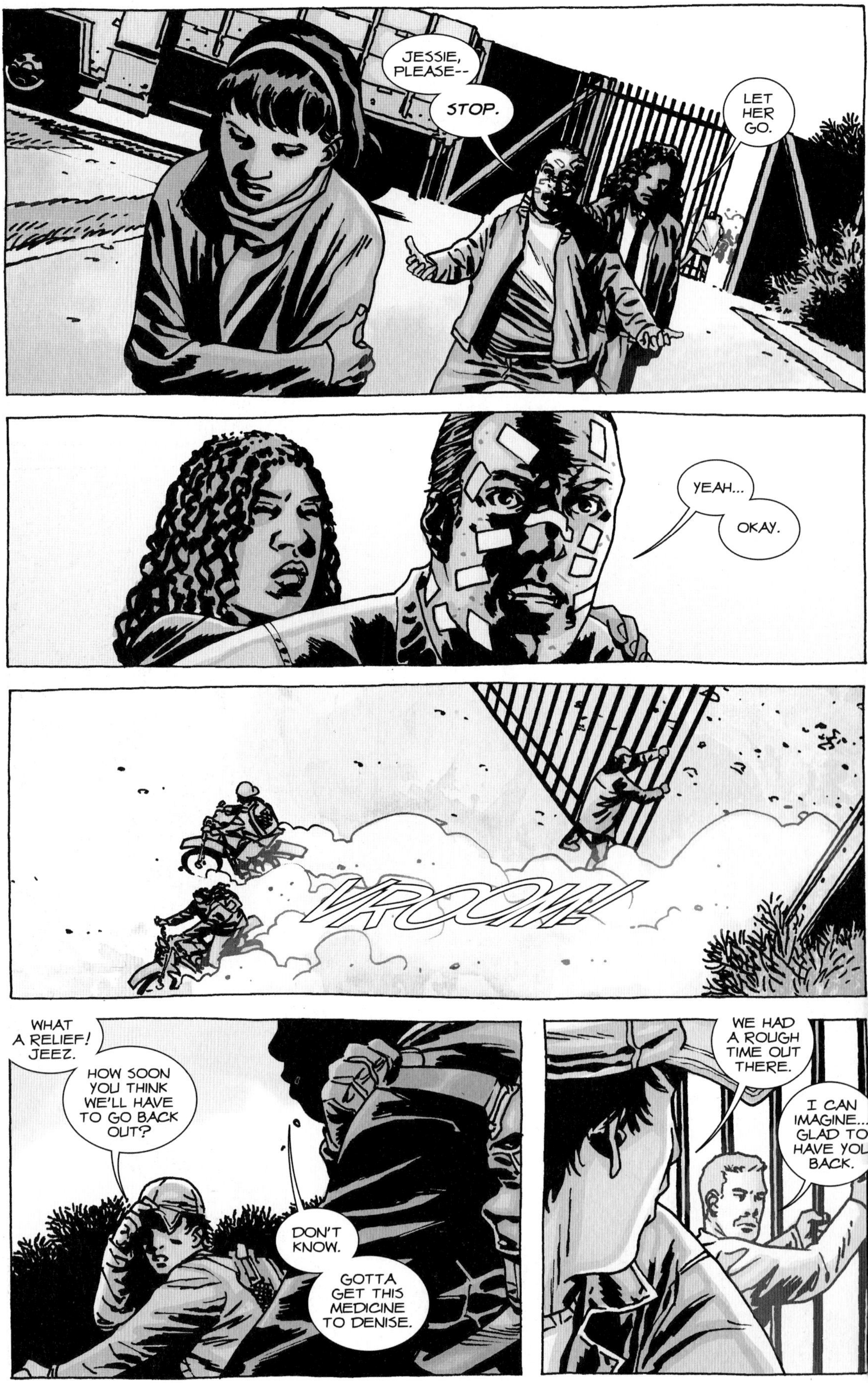
JESSIE, PLEASE--
STOP.
LET HER GO.
YEAH...
OKAY.
VROOOM!
WHAT A RELIEF! JEEZ.
HOW SOON YOU THINK WE'LL HAVE TO GO BACK OUT?
DON'T KNOW.
GOTTA GET THIS MEDICINE TO DENISE.
WE HAD A ROUGH TIME OUT THERE.
I CAN IMAGINE... GLAD TO HAVE YOU BACK.

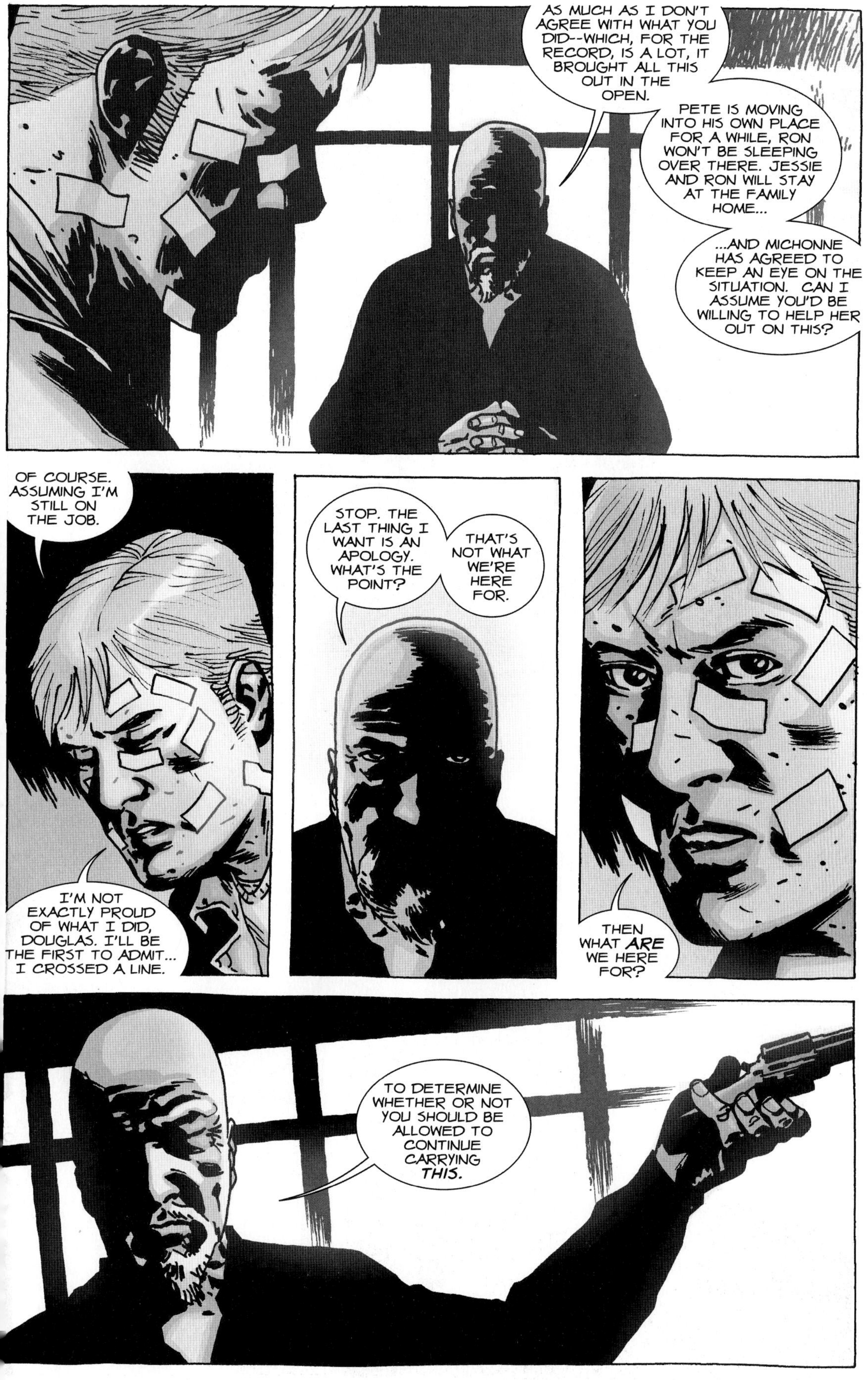
AS MUCH AS I DON'T AGREE WITH WHAT YOU DID--WHICH, FOR THE RECORD, IS A LOT, IT BROUGHT ALL THIS OUT IN THE OPEN.
PETE IS MOVING INTO HIS OWN PLACE FOR A WHILE, RON WON'T BE SLEEPING OVER THERE. JESSIE AND RON WILL STAY AT THE FAMILY HOME...
...AND MICHONNE HAS AGREED TO KEEP AN EYE ON THE SITUATION. CAN I ASSUME YOU'D BE WILLING TO HELP HER OUT ON THIS?
OF COURSE. ASSUMING I'M STILL ON THE JOB.
I'M NOT EXACTLY PROUD OF WHAT I DID, DOUGLAS. I'LL BE THE FIRST TO ADMIT... I CROSSED A LINE.
STOP. THE LAST THING I WANT IS AN APOLOGY. WHAT'S THE POINT?
THAT'S NOT WHAT WE'RE HERE FOR.
THEN WHAT *ARE* WE HERE FOR?
TO DETERMINE WHETHER OR NOT YOU SHOULD BE ALLOWED TO CONTINUE CARRYING *THIS.*

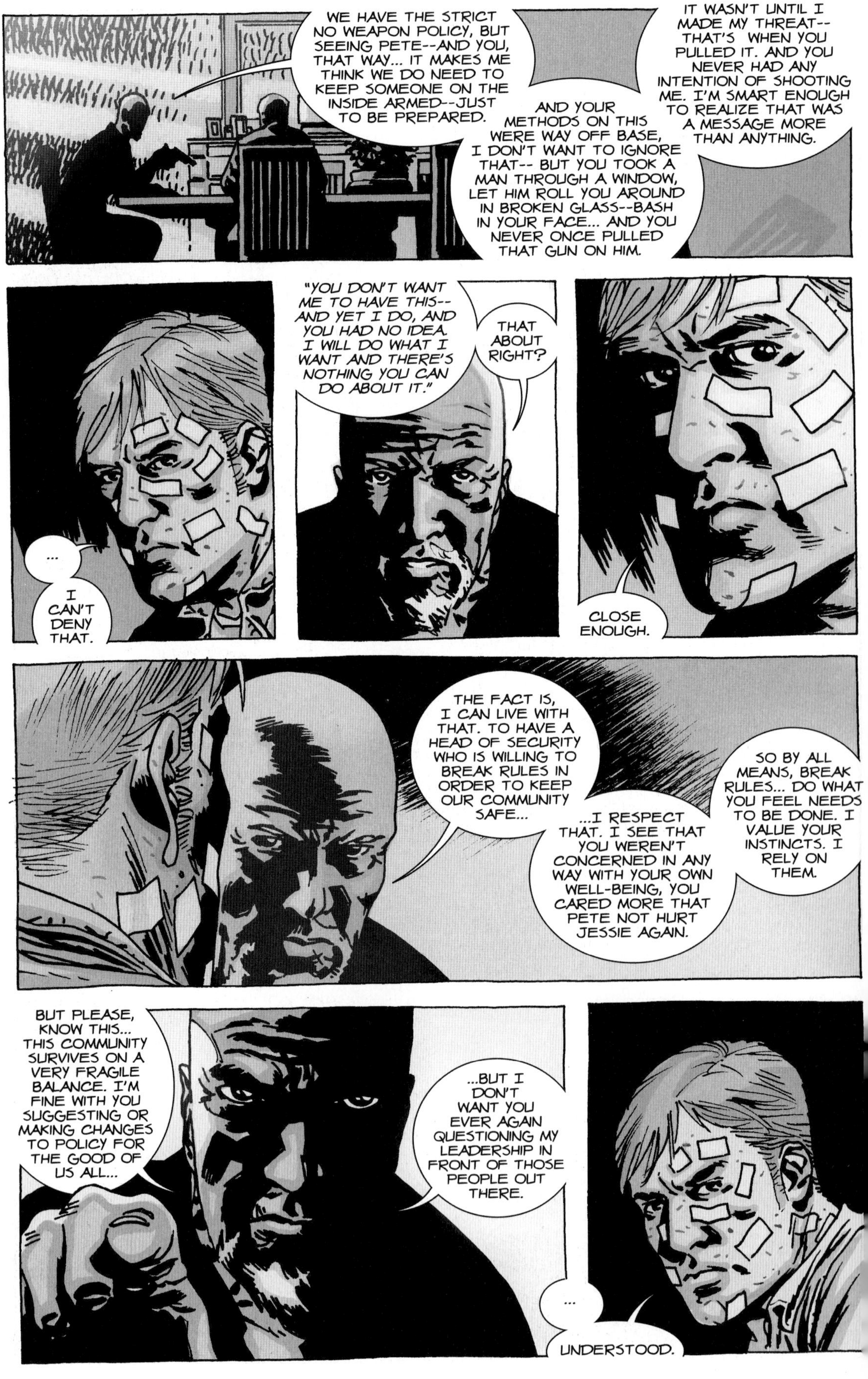
WE HAVE THE STRICT NO WEAPON POLICY, BUT SEEING PETE--AND YOU, THAT WAY... IT MAKES ME THINK WE DO NEED TO KEEP SOMEONE ON THE INSIDE ARMED--JUST TO BE PREPARED.
AND YOUR METHODS ON THIS WERE WAY OFF BASE, I DON'T WANT TO IGNORE THAT-- BUT YOU TOOK A MAN THROUGH A WINDOW, LET HIM ROLL YOU AROUND IN BROKEN GLASS--BASH IN YOUR FACE... AND YOU NEVER ONCE PULLED THAT GUN ON HIM.
IT WASN'T UNTIL I MADE MY THREAT-- THAT'S WHEN YOU PULLED IT. AND YOU NEVER HAD ANY INTENTION OF SHOOTING ME. I'M SMART ENOUGH TO REALIZE THAT WAS A MESSAGE MORE THAN ANYTHING.
...
I CAN'T DENY THAT.
"YOU DON'T WANT ME TO HAVE THIS-- AND YET I DO, AND YOU HAD NO IDEA. I WILL DO WHAT I WANT AND THERE'S NOTHING YOU CAN DO ABOUT IT."
THAT ABOUT RIGHT?
CLOSE ENOUGH.
THE FACT IS, I CAN LIVE WITH THAT. TO HAVE A HEAD OF SECURITY WHO IS WILLING TO BREAK RULES IN ORDER TO KEEP OUR COMMUNITY SAFE...
...I RESPECT THAT. I SEE THAT YOU WEREN'T CONCERNED IN ANY WAY WITH YOUR OWN WELL-BEING, YOU CARED MORE THAT PETE NOT HURT JESSIE AGAIN.
SO BY ALL MEANS, BREAK RULES... DO WHAT YOU FEEL NEEDS TO BE DONE. I VALUE YOUR INSTINCTS. I RELY ON THEM.
BUT PLEASE, KNOW THIS... THIS COMMUNITY SURVIVES ON A VERY FRAGILE BALANCE. I'M FINE WITH YOU SUGGESTING OR MAKING CHANGES TO POLICY FOR THE GOOD OF US ALL...
...BUT I DON'T WANT YOU EVER AGAIN QUESTIONING MY LEADERSHIP IN FRONT OF THOSE PEOPLE OUT THERE.
...
UNDERSTOOD.

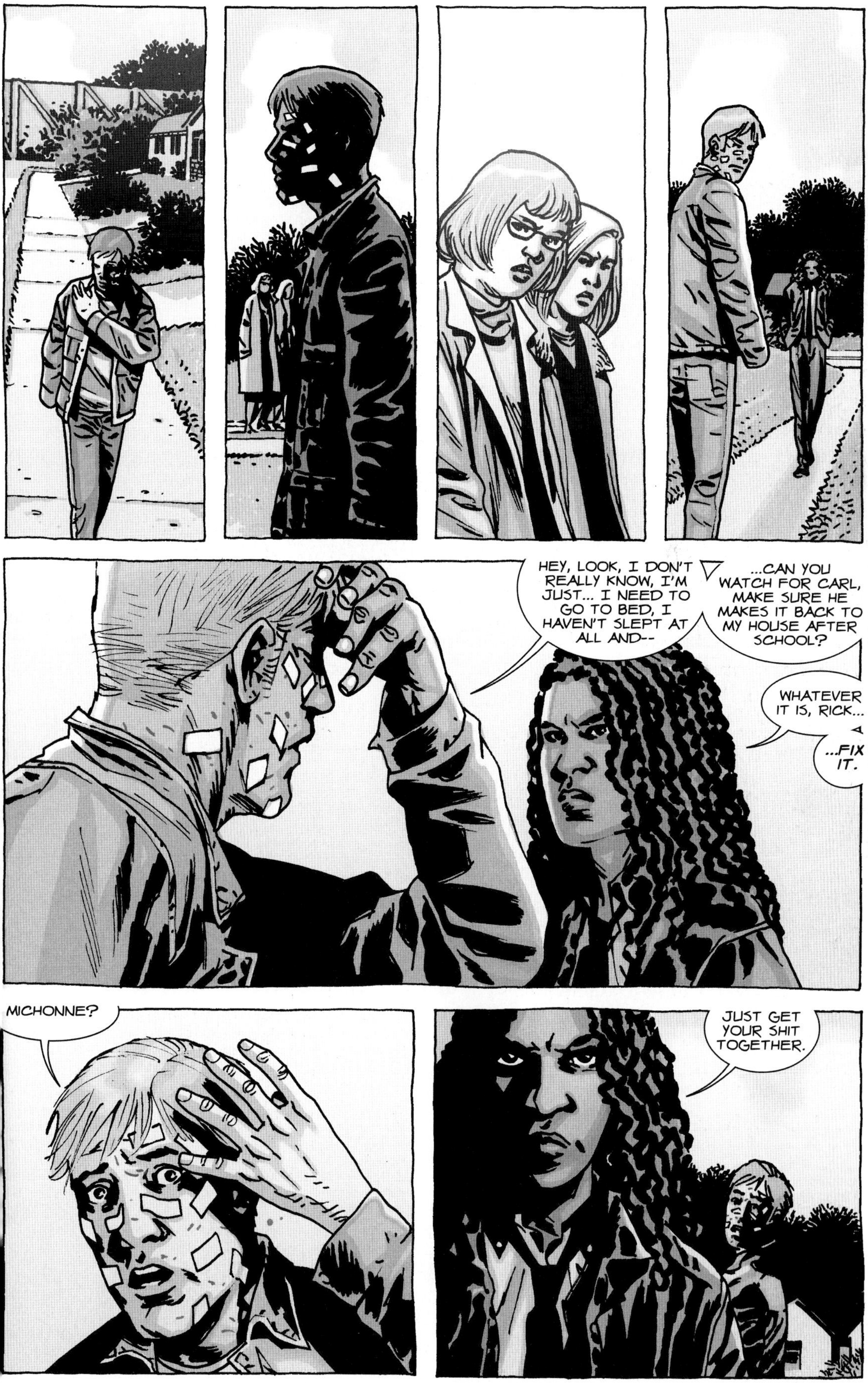
HEY, LOOK, I DON'T REALLY KNOW, I'M JUST... I NEED TO GO TO BED, I HAVEN'T SLEPT AT ALL AND--
...CAN YOU WATCH FOR CARL, MAKE SURE HE MAKES IT BACK TO MY HOUSE AFTER SCHOOL?
WHATEVER IT IS, RICK...
...FIX IT.
MICHONNE?
JUST GET YOUR SHIT TOGETHER.

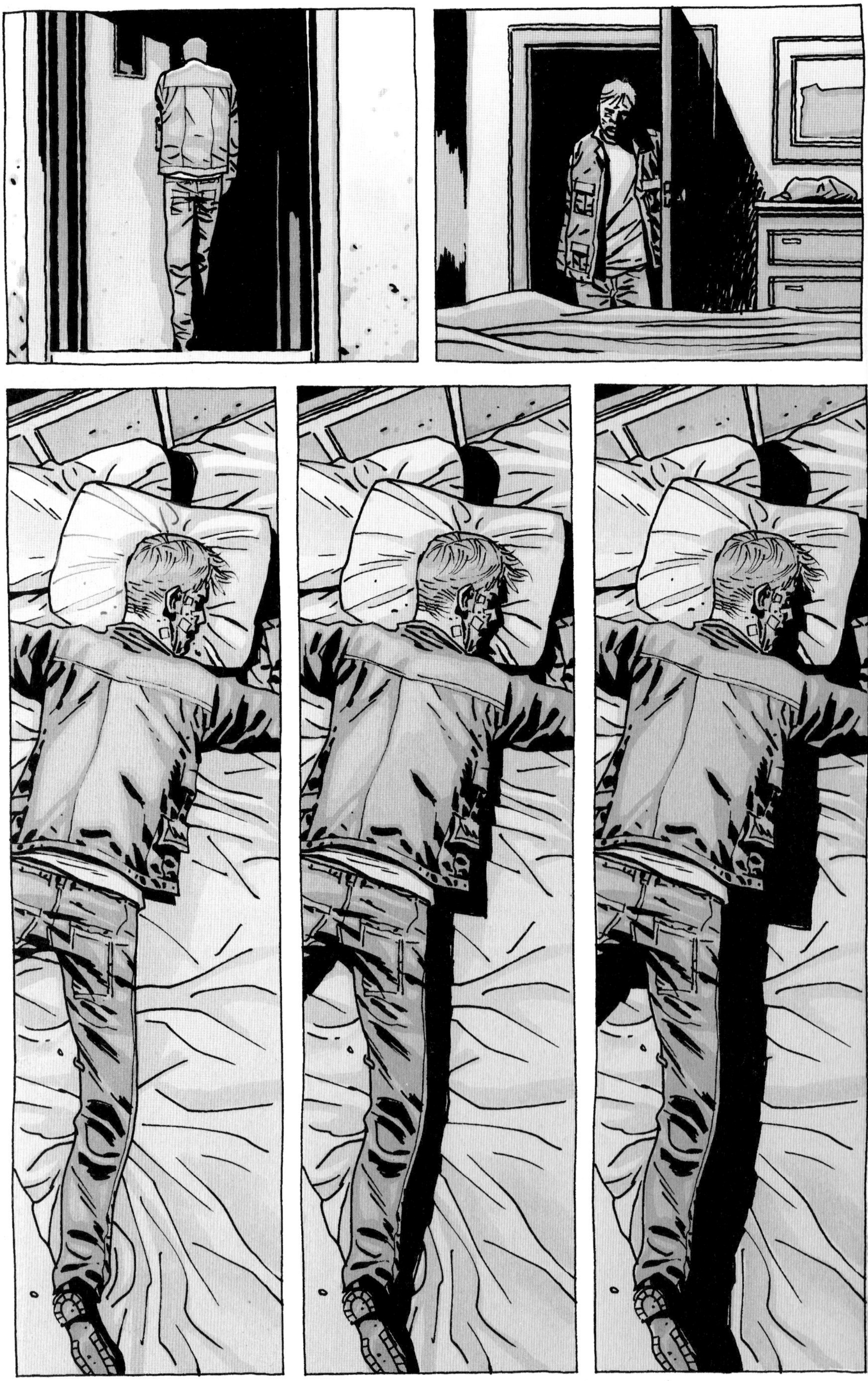

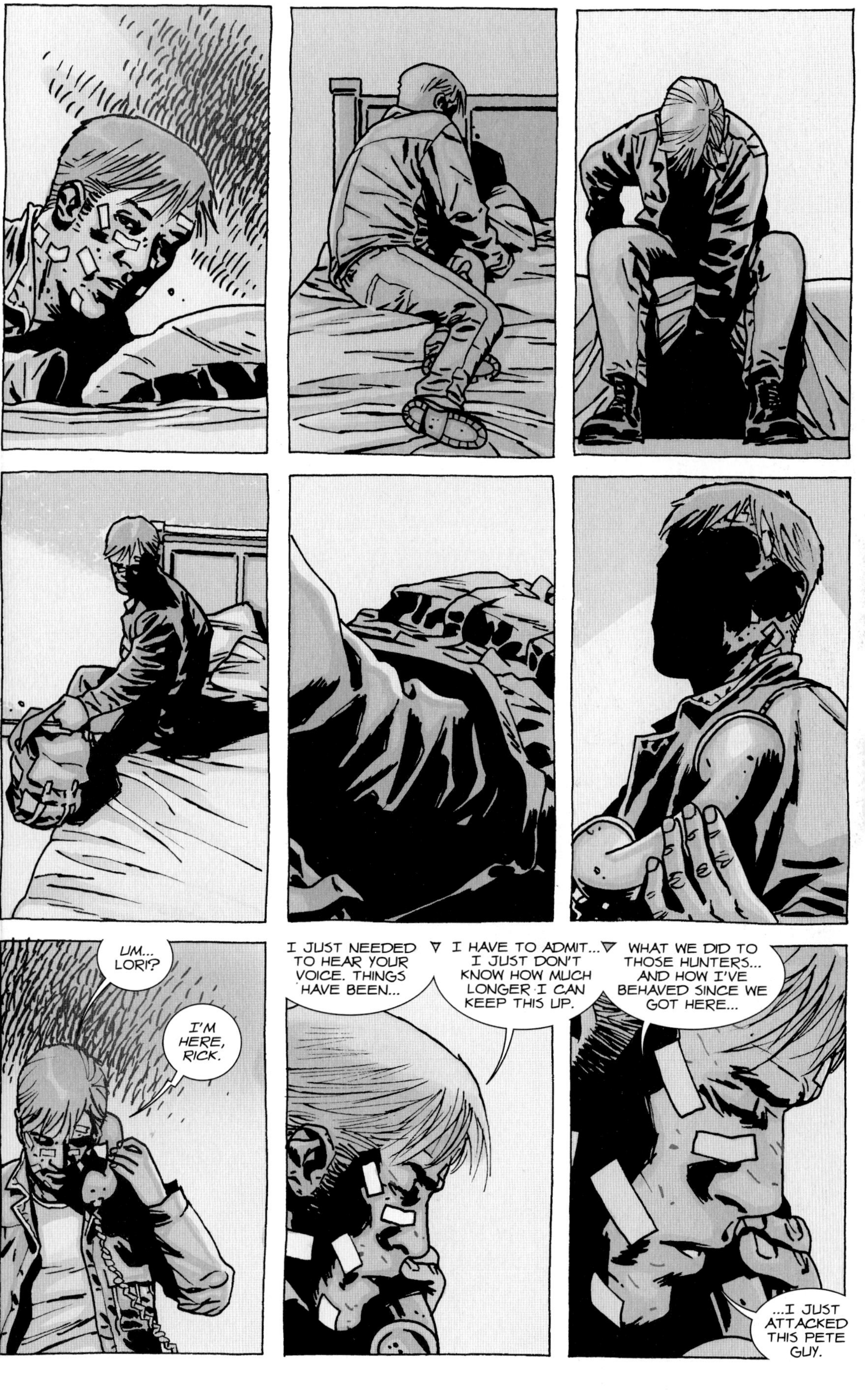
UM... LORI?
I'M HERE, RICK.
I JUST NEEDED TO HEAR YOUR VOICE. THINGS HAVE BEEN...
I HAVE TO ADMIT... I JUST DON'T KNOW HOW MUCH LONGER I CAN KEEP THIS UP.
WHAT WE DID TO THOSE HUNTERS... AND HOW I'VE BEHAVED SINCE WE GOT HERE...
...I JUST ATTACKED THIS PETE GUY.

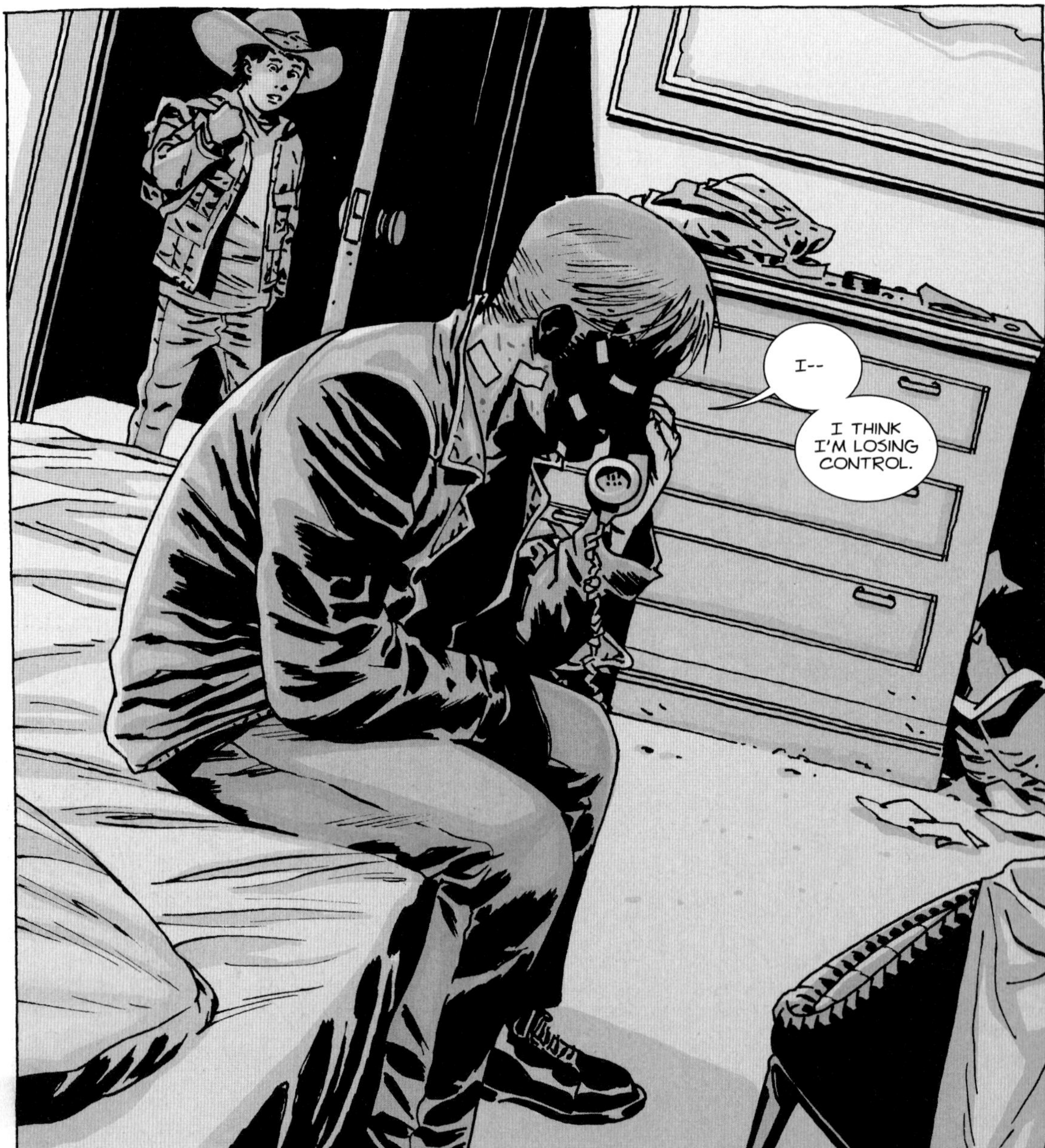
I--
I THINK I'M LOSING CONTROL.

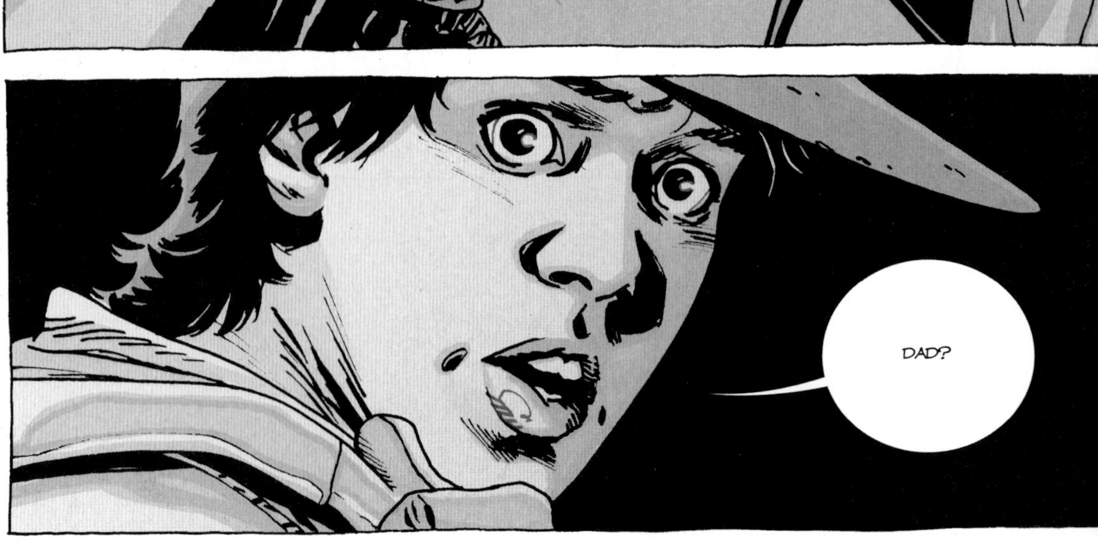
DAD?

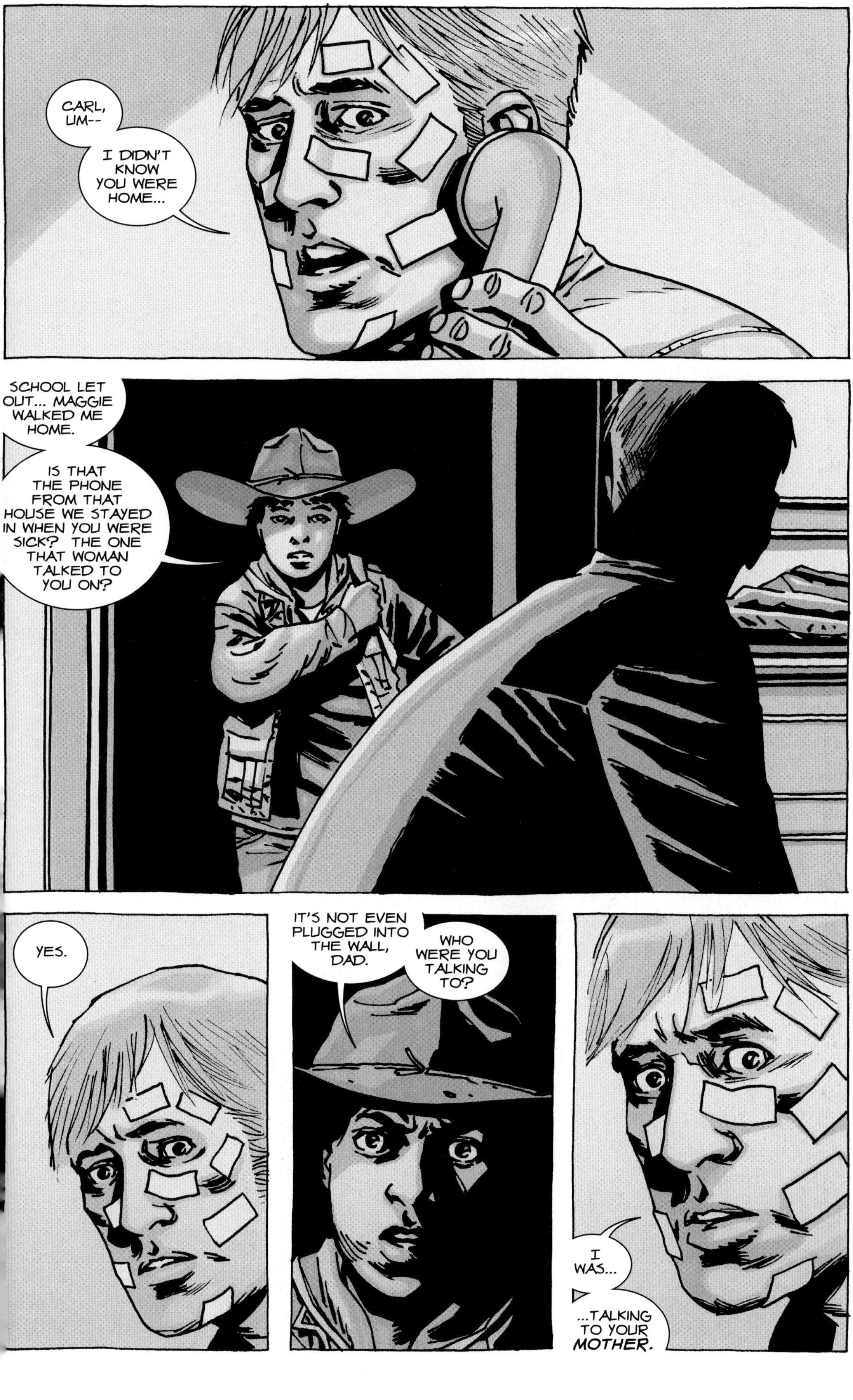
CARL, UM--
I DIDN'T KNOW YOU WERE HOME...
SCHOOL LET OUT... MAGGIE WALKED ME HOME.
IS THAT THE PHONE FROM THAT HOUSE WE STAYED IN WHEN YOU WERE SICK? THE ONE THAT WOMAN TALKED TO YOU ON?
YES.
IT'S NOT EVEN PLUGGED INTO THE WALL, DAD.
WHO WERE YOU TALKING TO?
I WAS...
...TALKING TO YOUR *MOTHER*.

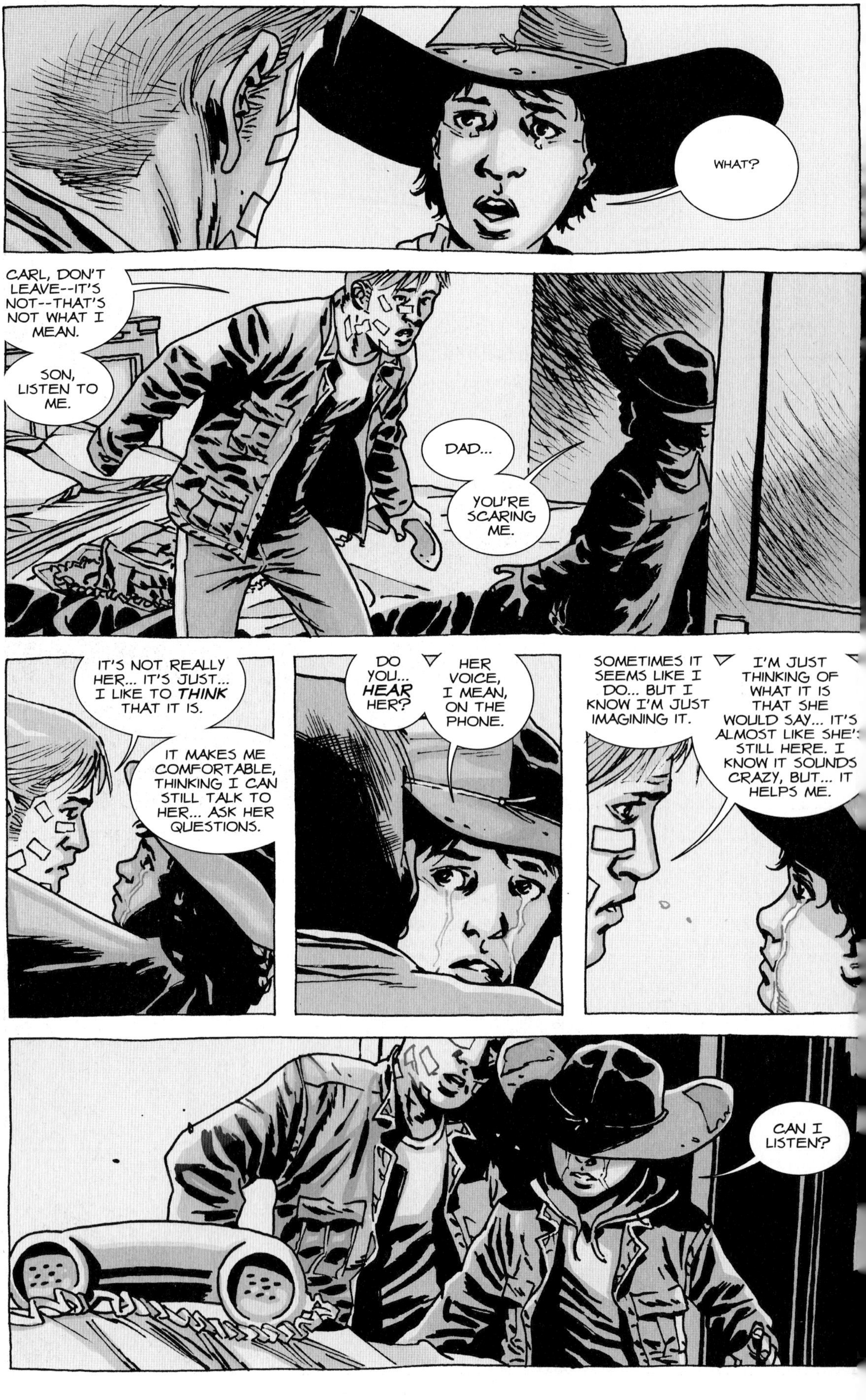
WHAT?
CARL, DON'T LEAVE--IT'S NOT--THAT'S NOT WHAT I MEAN.
SON, LISTEN TO ME.
DAD...
YOU'RE SCARING ME.
IT'S NOT REALLY HER... IT'S JUST... I LIKE TO THINK THAT IT IS.
IT MAKES ME COMFORTABLE, THINKING I CAN STILL TALK TO HER... ASK HER QUESTIONS.
DO YOU... HEAR HER?
HER VOICE, I MEAN, ON THE PHONE.
SOMETIMES IT SEEMS LIKE I DO... BUT I KNOW I'M JUST IMAGINING IT.
I'M JUST THINKING OF WHAT IT IS THAT SHE WOULD SAY... IT'S ALMOST LIKE SHE'S STILL HERE. I KNOW IT SOUNDS CRAZY, BUT... IT HELPS ME.
CAN I LISTEN?

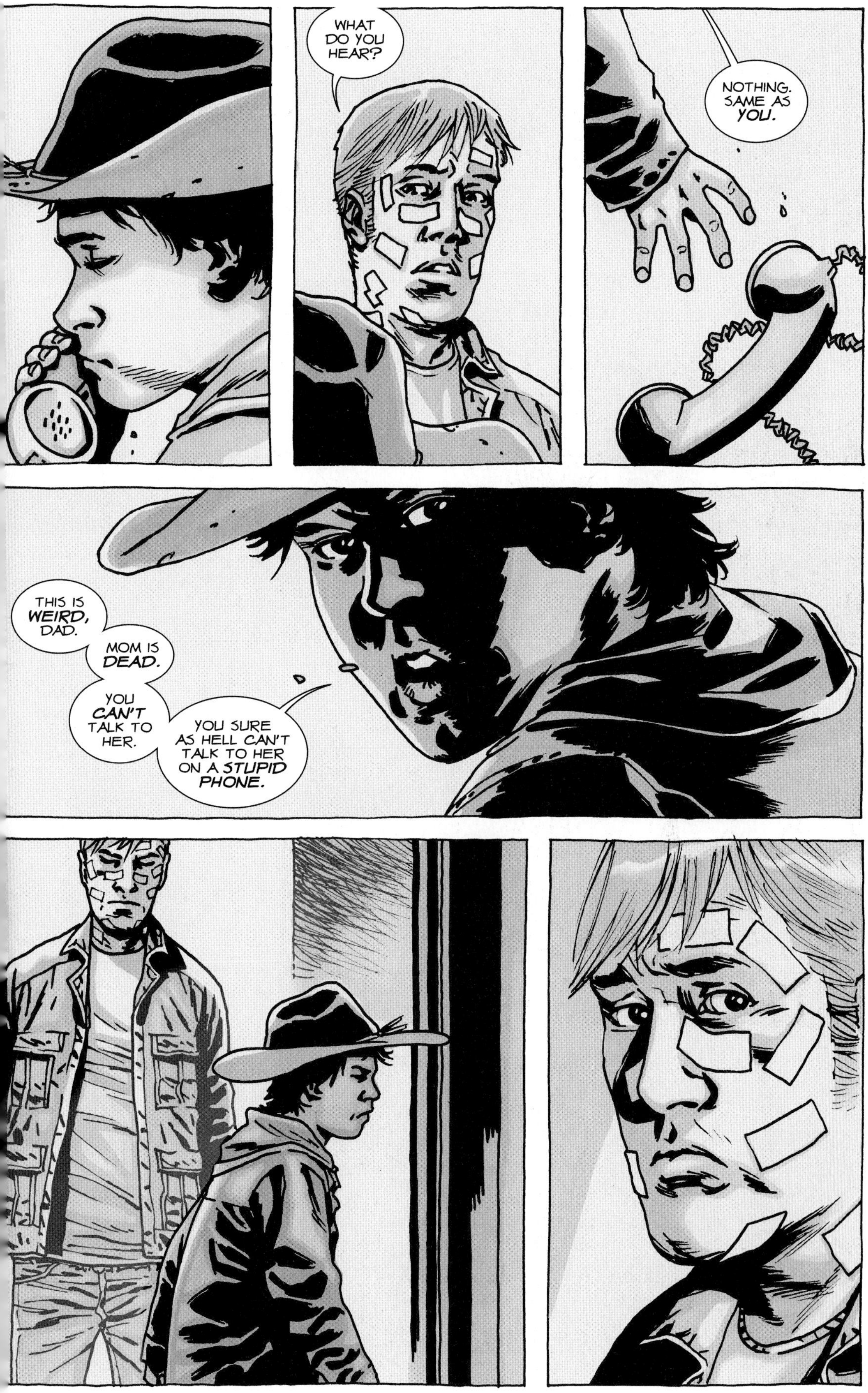
WHAT DO YOU HEAR?
NOTHING. SAME AS YOU.
THIS IS WEIRD, DAD.
MOM IS DEAD.
YOU CAN'T TALK TO HER.
YOU SURE AS HELL CAN'T TALK TO HER ON A STUPID PHONE.

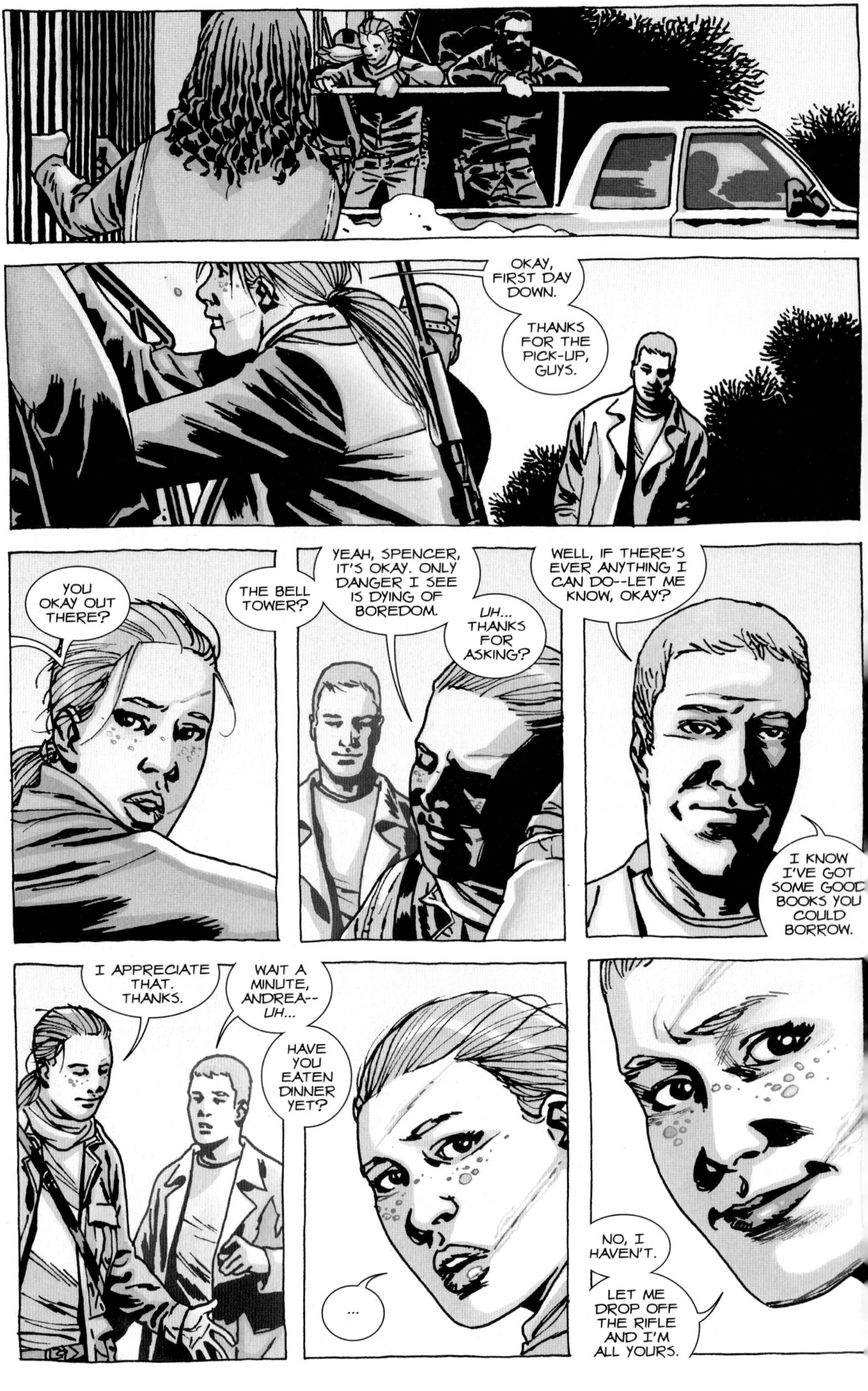
OKAY, FIRST DAY DOWN.
THANKS FOR THE PICK-UP, GUYS.
YOU OKAY OUT THERE?
THE BELL TOWER?
YEAH, SPENCER, IT'S OKAY. ONLY DANGER I SEE IS DYING OF BOREDOM.
UH... THANKS FOR ASKING?
WELL, IF THERE'S EVER ANYTHING I CAN DO--LET ME KNOW, OKAY?
I KNOW I'VE GOT SOME GOOD BOOKS YOU COULD BORROW.
I APPRECIATE THAT. THANKS.
WAIT A MINUTE, ANDREA--UH...
HAVE YOU EATEN DINNER YET?
...
NO, I HAVEN'T.
LET ME DROP OFF THE RIFLE AND I'M ALL YOURS.

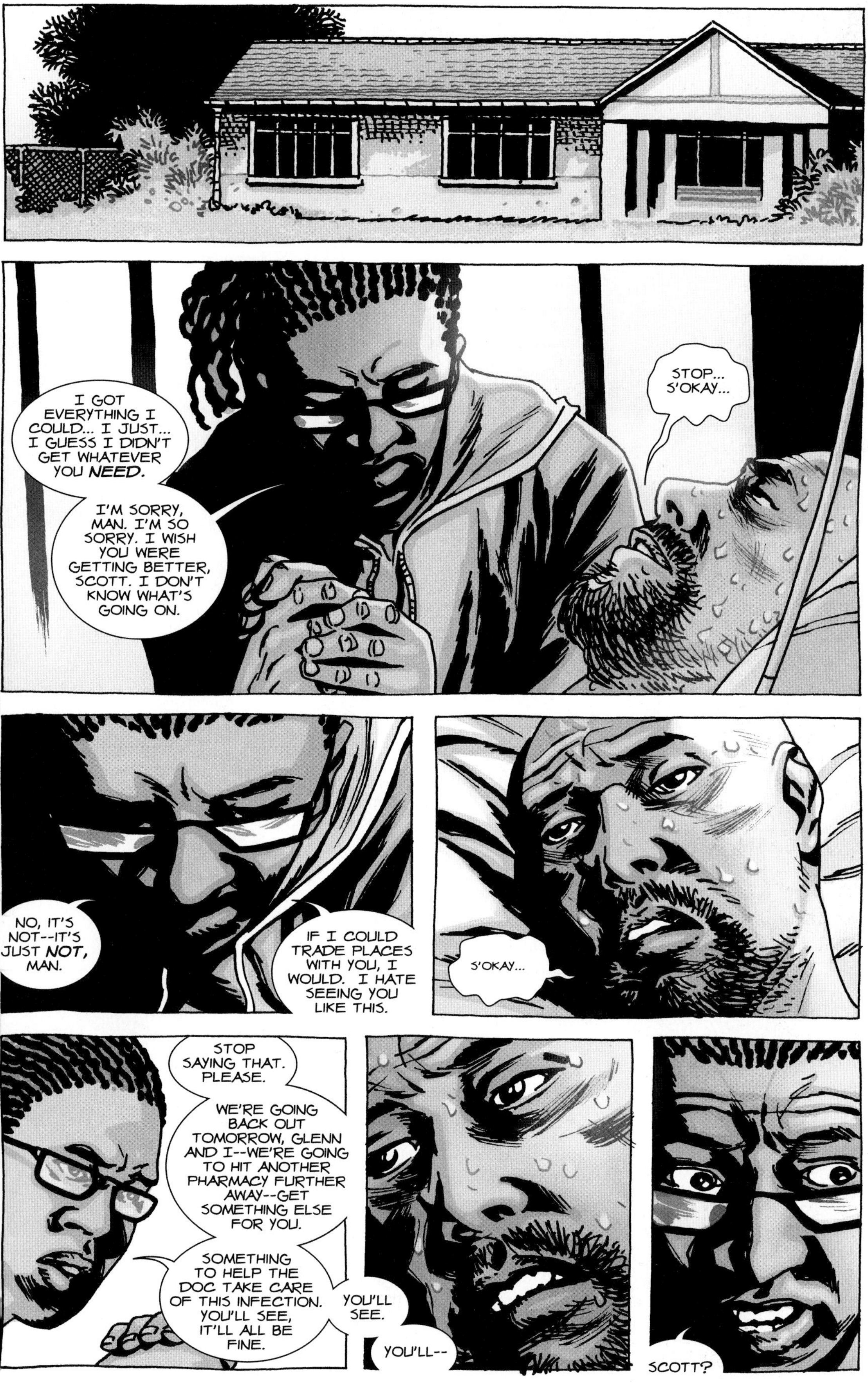
I GOT EVERYTHING I COULD... I JUST... I GUESS I DIDN'T GET WHATEVER YOU NEED.
I'M SORRY, MAN. I'M SO SORRY. I WISH YOU WERE GETTING BETTER, SCOTT. I DON'T KNOW WHAT'S GOING ON.
STOP... S'OKAY...
NO, IT'S NOT--IT'S JUST NOT, MAN.
IF I COULD TRADE PLACES WITH YOU, I WOULD. I HATE SEEING YOU LIKE THIS.
S'OKAY...
STOP SAYING THAT. PLEASE.
WE'RE GOING BACK OUT TOMORROW, GLENN AND I--WE'RE GOING TO HIT ANOTHER PHARMACY FURTHER AWAY--GET SOMETHING ELSE FOR YOU.
SOMETHING TO HELP THE DOC TAKE CARE OF THIS INFECTION. YOU'LL SEE, IT'LL ALL BE FINE.
YOU'LL SEE.
YOU'LL--
SCOTT?

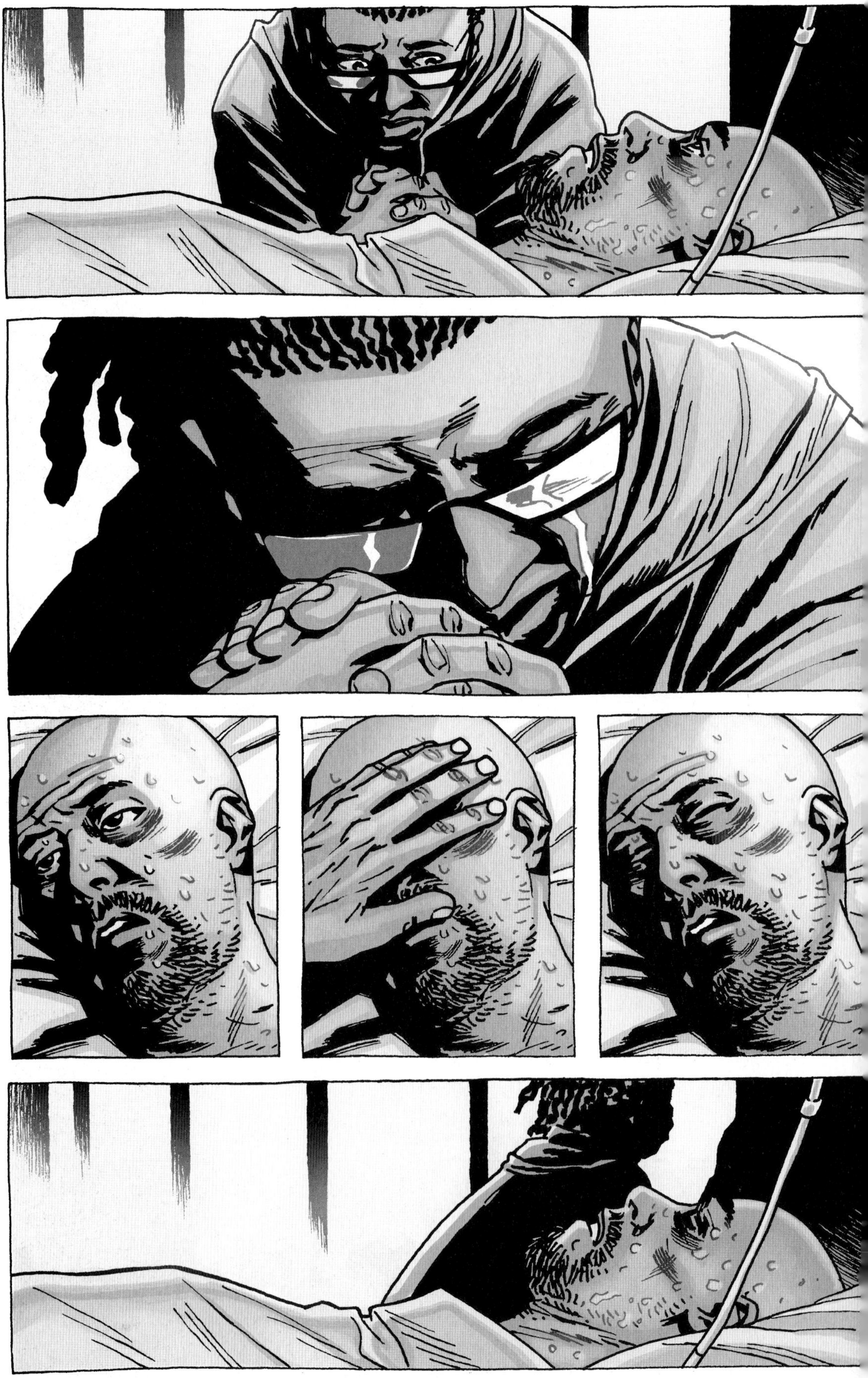

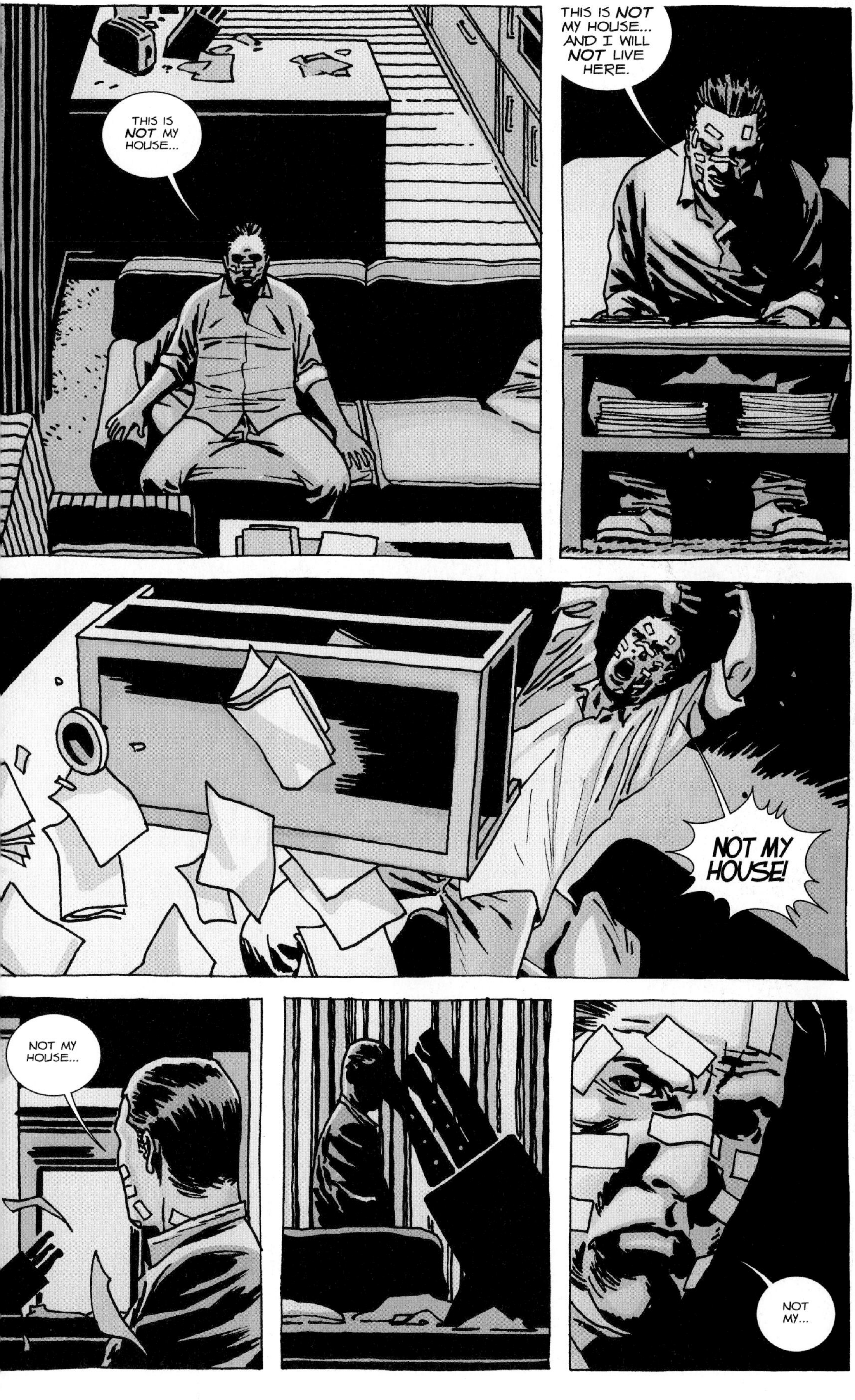
THIS IS NOT MY HOUSE...
THIS IS NOT MY HOUSE... AND I WILL NOT LIVE HERE.
NOT MY HOUSE!
NOT MY HOUSE...
NOT MY...

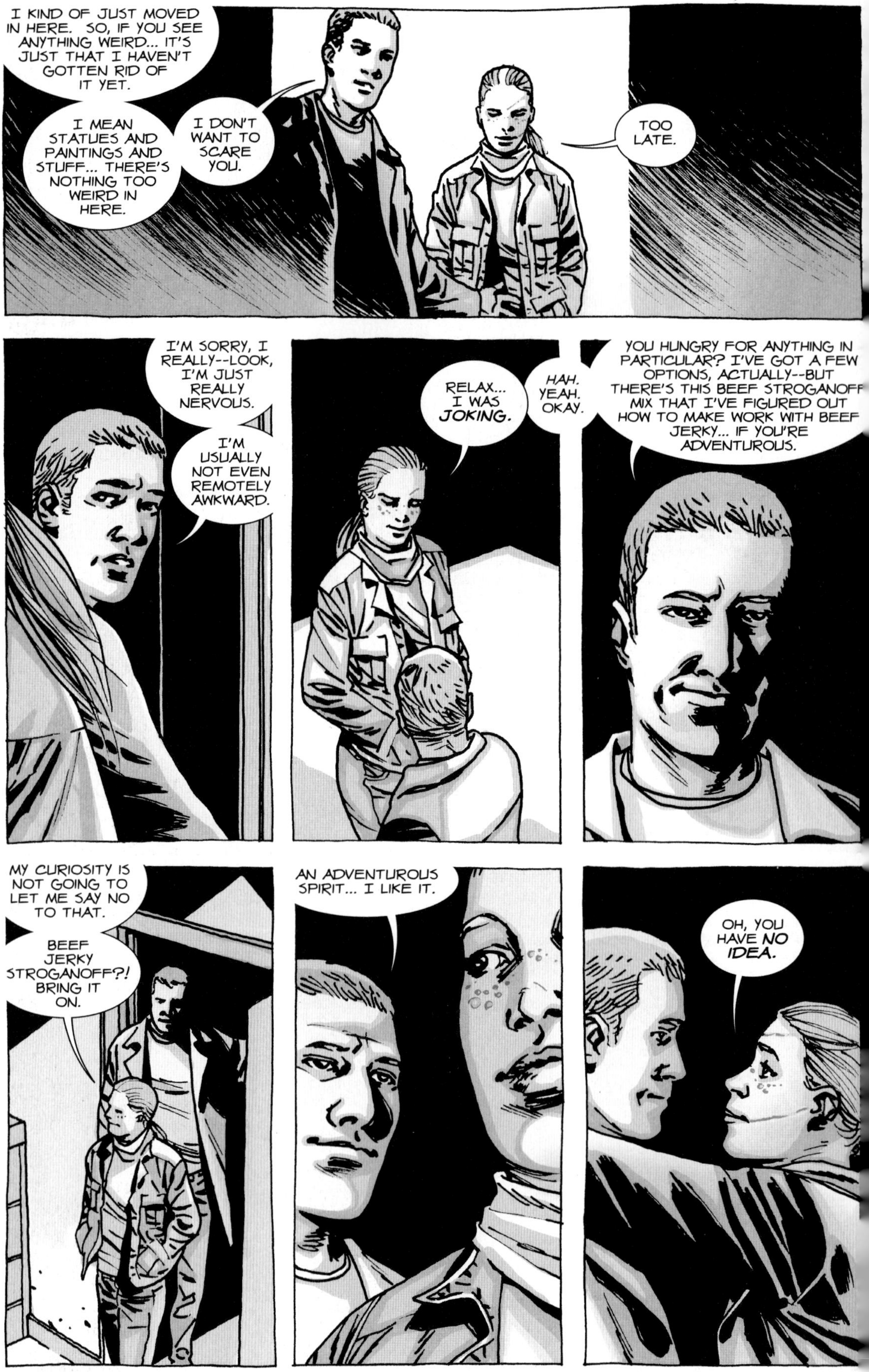
I KIND OF JUST MOVED IN HERE. SO, IF YOU SEE ANYTHING WEIRD... IT'S JUST THAT I HAVEN'T GOTTEN RID OF IT YET.
I MEAN STATUES AND PAINTINGS AND STUFF... THERE'S NOTHING TOO WEIRD IN HERE.
I DON'T WANT TO SCARE YOU.
TOO LATE.
I'M SORRY, I REALLY--LOOK, I'M JUST REALLY NERVOUS.
I'M USUALLY NOT EVEN REMOTELY AWKWARD.
RELAX... I WAS JOKING.
HAH. YEAH. OKAY.
YOU HUNGRY FOR ANYTHING IN PARTICULAR? I'VE GOT A FEW OPTIONS, ACTUALLY--BUT THERE'S THIS BEEF STROGANOFF MIX THAT I'VE FIGURED OUT HOW TO MAKE WORK WITH BEEF JERKY... IF YOU'RE ADVENTUROUS.
MY CURIOSITY IS NOT GOING TO LET ME SAY NO TO THAT.
BEEF JERKY STROGANOFF?! BRING IT ON.
AN ADVENTUROUS SPIRIT... I LIKE IT.
OH, YOU HAVE NO IDEA.

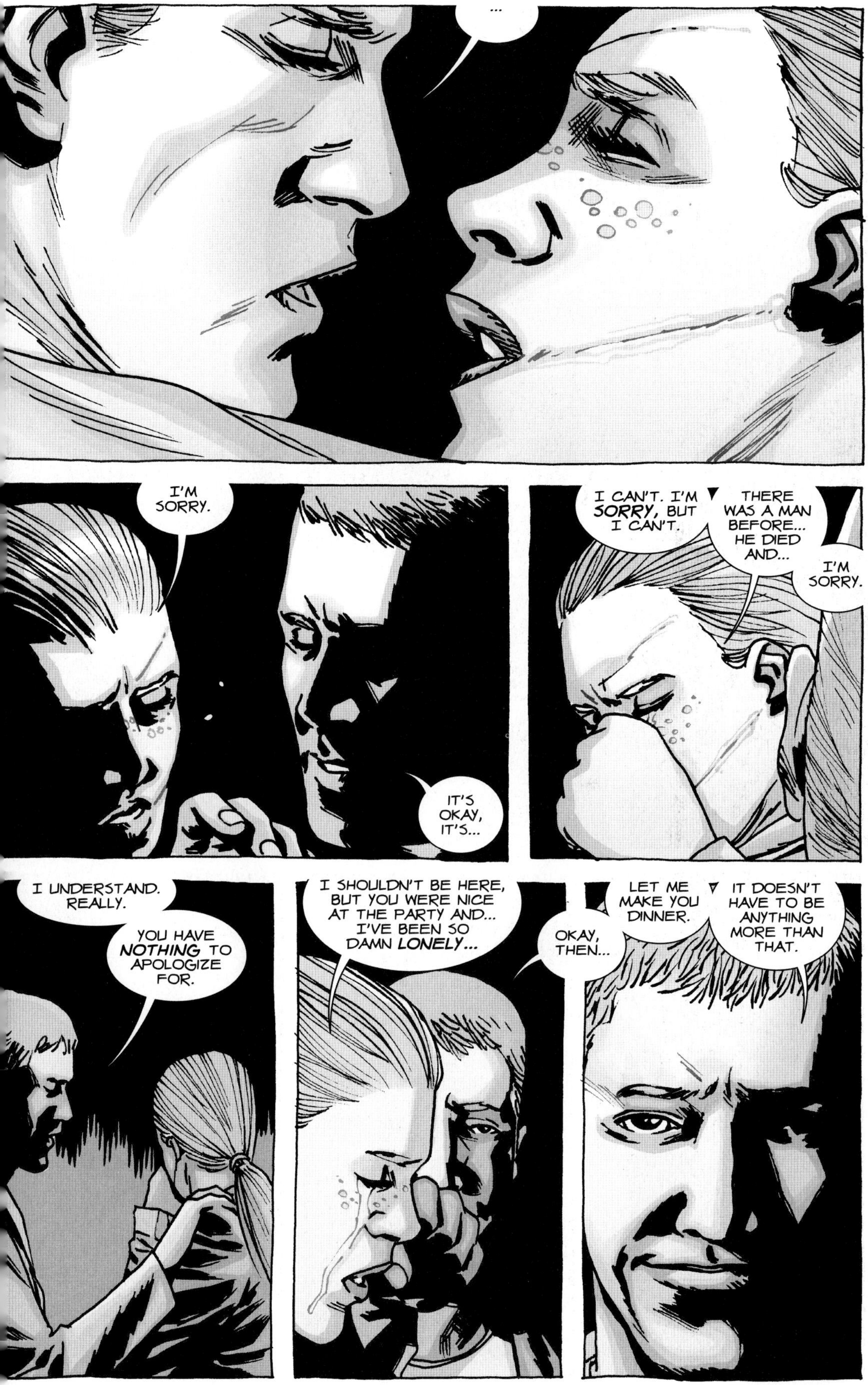
...
I'M SORRY.
IT'S OKAY, IT'S...
I CAN'T. I'M SORRY, BUT I CAN'T.
THERE WAS A MAN BEFORE... HE DIED AND...
I'M SORRY.
I UNDERSTAND. REALLY.
YOU HAVE NOTHING TO APOLOGIZE FOR.
I SHOULDN'T BE HERE, BUT YOU WERE NICE AT THE PARTY AND... I'VE BEEN SO DAMN LONELY...
OKAY, THEN...
LET ME MAKE YOU DINNER.
IT DOESN'T HAVE TO BE ANYTHING MORE THAN THAT.

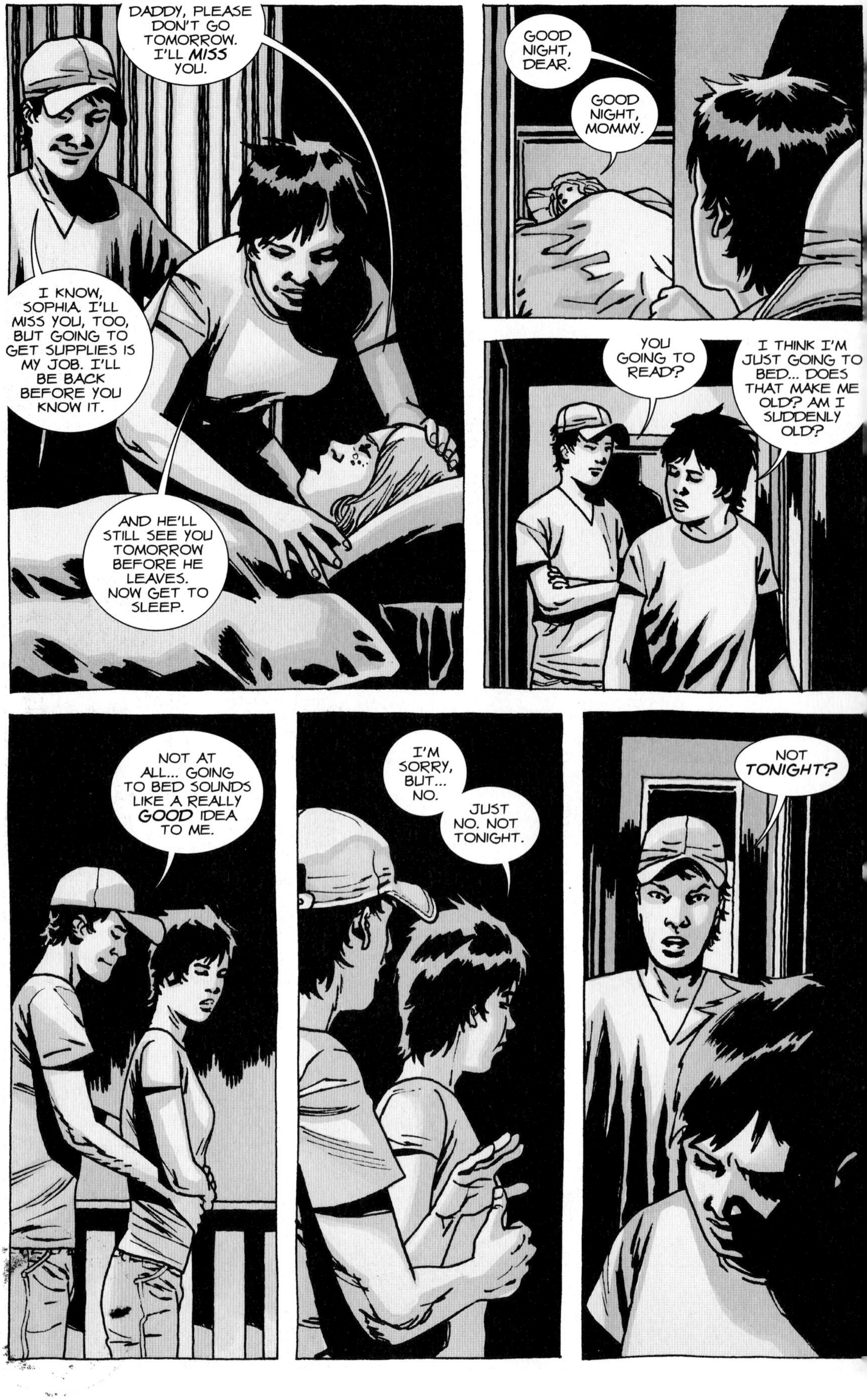
DADDY, PLEASE DON'T GO TOMORROW. I'LL MISS YOU.
I KNOW, SOPHIA. I'LL MISS YOU, TOO, BUT GOING TO GET SUPPLIES IS MY JOB. I'LL BE BACK BEFORE YOU KNOW IT.
AND HE'LL STILL SEE YOU TOMORROW BEFORE HE LEAVES. NOW GET TO SLEEP.
GOOD NIGHT, DEAR.
GOOD NIGHT, MOMMY.
YOU GOING TO READ?
I THINK I'M JUST GOING TO BED... DOES THAT MAKE ME OLD? AM I SUDDENLY OLD?
NOT AT ALL... GOING TO BED SOUNDS LIKE A REALLY GOOD IDEA TO ME.
I'M SORRY, BUT... NO.
JUST NO. NOT TONIGHT.
NOT TONIGHT?

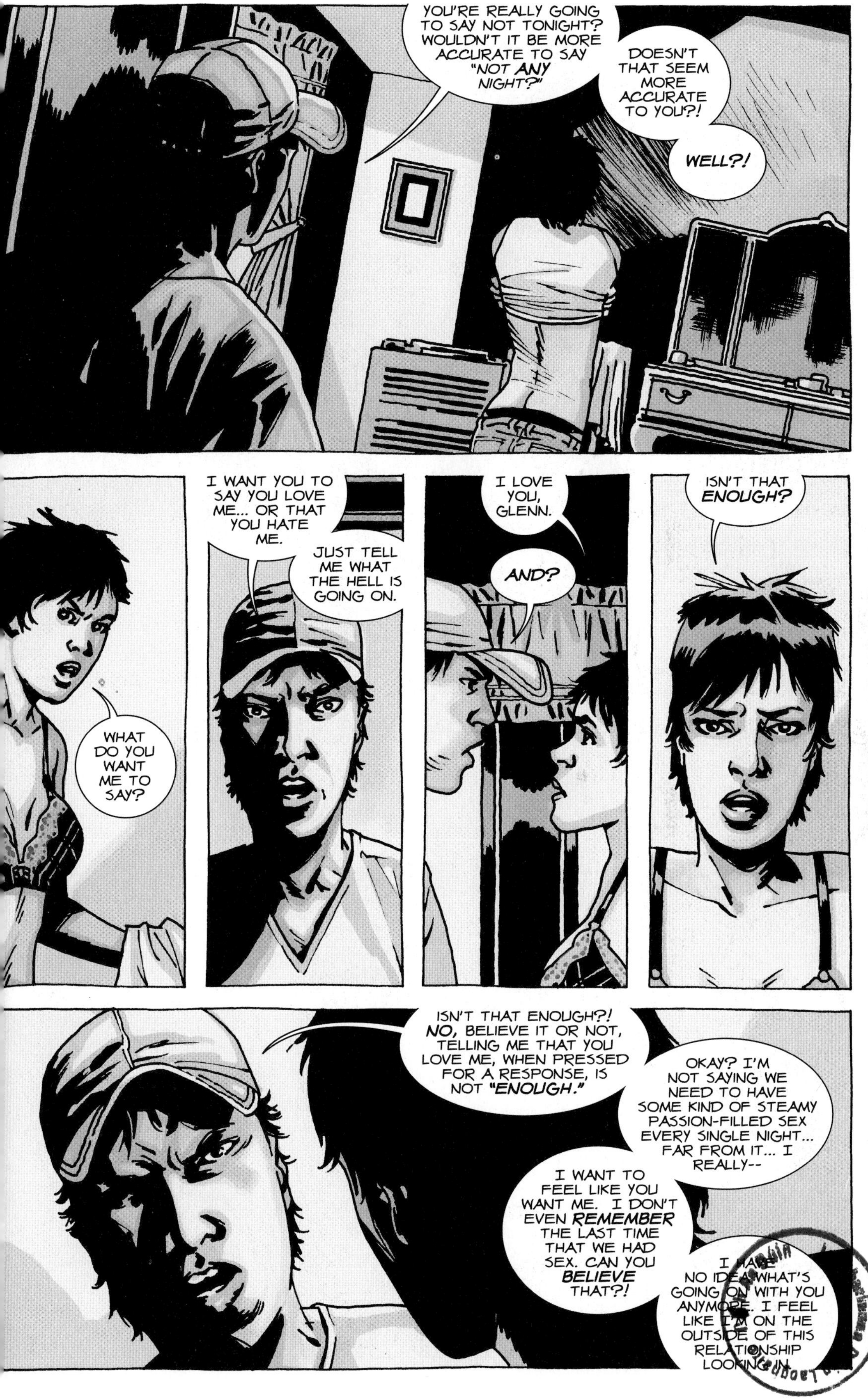

YOU'RE REALLY GOING TO SAY NOT TONIGHT? WOULDN'T IT BE MORE ACCURATE TO SAY "NOT ANY NIGHT?"
DOESN'T THAT SEEM MORE ACCURATE TO YOU?!
WELL?!
WHAT DO YOU WANT ME TO SAY?
I WANT YOU TO SAY YOU LOVE ME... OR THAT YOU HATE ME.
JUST TELL ME WHAT THE HELL IS GOING ON.
I LOVE YOU, GLENN.
AND?
ISN'T THAT ENOUGH?
ISN'T THAT ENOUGH?! NO, BELIEVE IT OR NOT, TELLING ME THAT YOU LOVE ME, WHEN PRESSED FOR A RESPONSE, IS NOT "ENOUGH."
OKAY? I'M NOT SAYING WE NEED TO HAVE SOME KIND OF STEAMY PASSION-FILLED SEX EVERY SINGLE NIGHT... FAR FROM IT... I REALLY--
I WANT TO FEEL LIKE YOU WANT ME. I DON'T EVEN REMEMBER THE LAST TIME THAT WE HAD SEX. CAN YOU BELIEVE THAT?!
I HAVE NO IDEA WHAT'S GOING ON WITH YOU ANYMORE. I FEEL LIKE I'M ON THE OUTSIDE OF THIS RELATIONSHIP LOOKING IN.

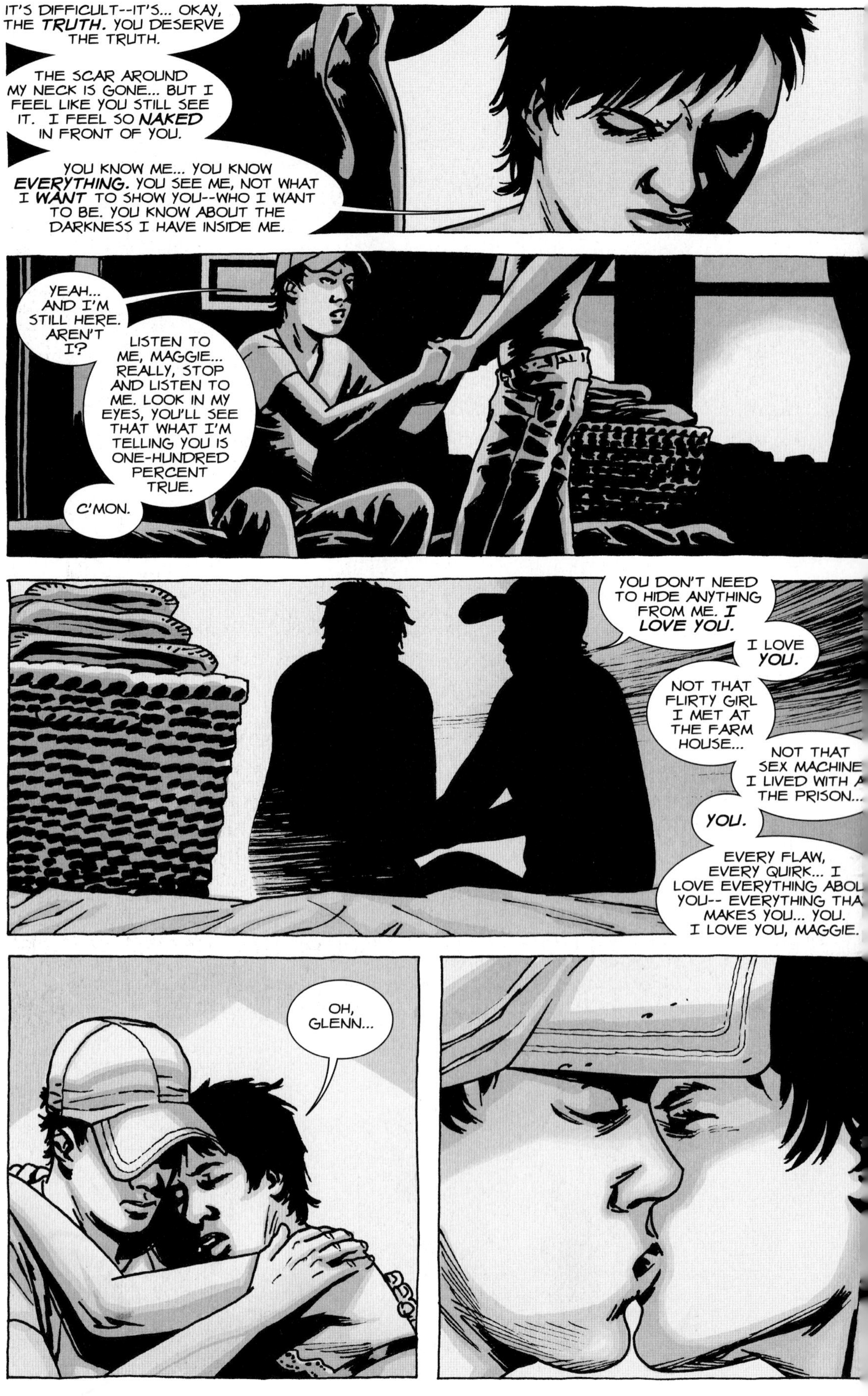
IT'S DIFFICULT--IT'S... OKAY, THE TRUTH. YOU DESERVE THE TRUTH.
THE SCAR AROUND MY NECK IS GONE... BUT I FEEL LIKE YOU STILL SEE IT. I FEEL SO NAKED IN FRONT OF YOU.
YOU KNOW ME... YOU KNOW EVERYTHING. YOU SEE ME, NOT WHAT I WANT TO SHOW YOU--WHO I WANT TO BE. YOU KNOW ABOUT THE DARKNESS I HAVE INSIDE ME.
YEAH... AND I'M STILL HERE. AREN'T I?
LISTEN TO ME, MAGGIE... REALLY, STOP AND LISTEN TO ME. LOOK IN MY EYES, YOU'LL SEE THAT WHAT I'M TELLING YOU IS ONE-HUNDRED PERCENT TRUE.
C'MON.
YOU DON'T NEED TO HIDE ANYTHING FROM ME. I LOVE YOU.
I LOVE YOU.
NOT THAT FLIRTY GIRL I MET AT THE FARM HOUSE...
NOT THAT SEX MACHINE I LIVED WITH A THE PRISON...
YOU.
EVERY FLAW, EVERY QUIRK... I LOVE EVERYTHING ABO YOU-- EVERYTHING THA MAKES YOU... YOU. I LOVE YOU, MAGGIE.
OH, GLENN...

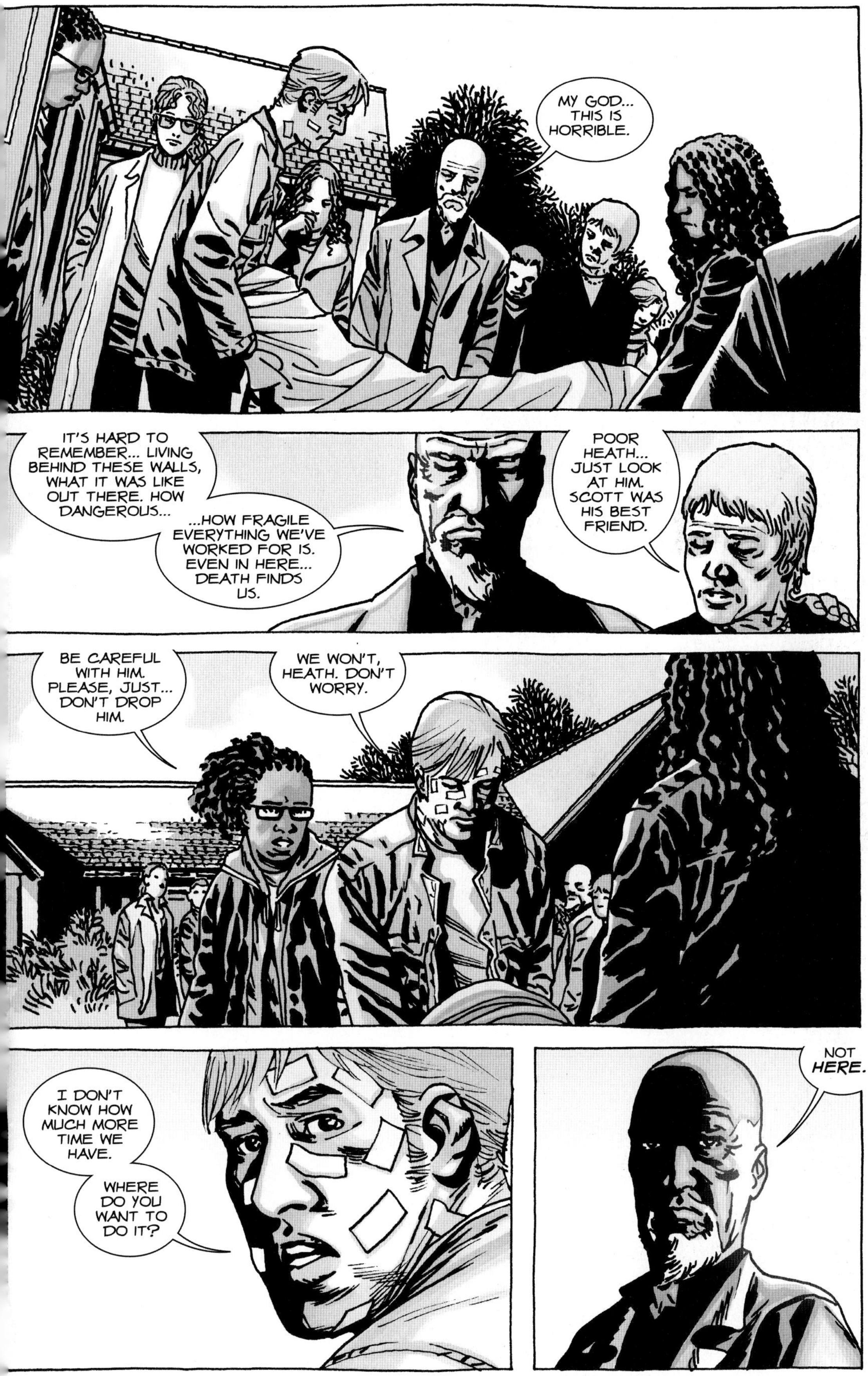
MY GOD... THIS IS HORRIBLE.
IT'S HARD TO REMEMBER... LIVING BEHIND THESE WALLS, WHAT IT WAS LIKE OUT THERE. HOW DANGEROUS...
...HOW FRAGILE EVERYTHING WE'VE WORKED FOR IS. EVEN IN HERE... DEATH FINDS US.
POOR HEATH... JUST LOOK AT HIM. SCOTT WAS HIS BEST FRIEND.
BE CAREFUL WITH HIM. PLEASE, JUST... DON'T DROP HIM.
WE WON'T, HEATH. DON'T WORRY.
I DON'T KNOW HOW MUCH MORE TIME WE HAVE.
WHERE DO YOU WANT TO DO IT?
NOT *HERE.*

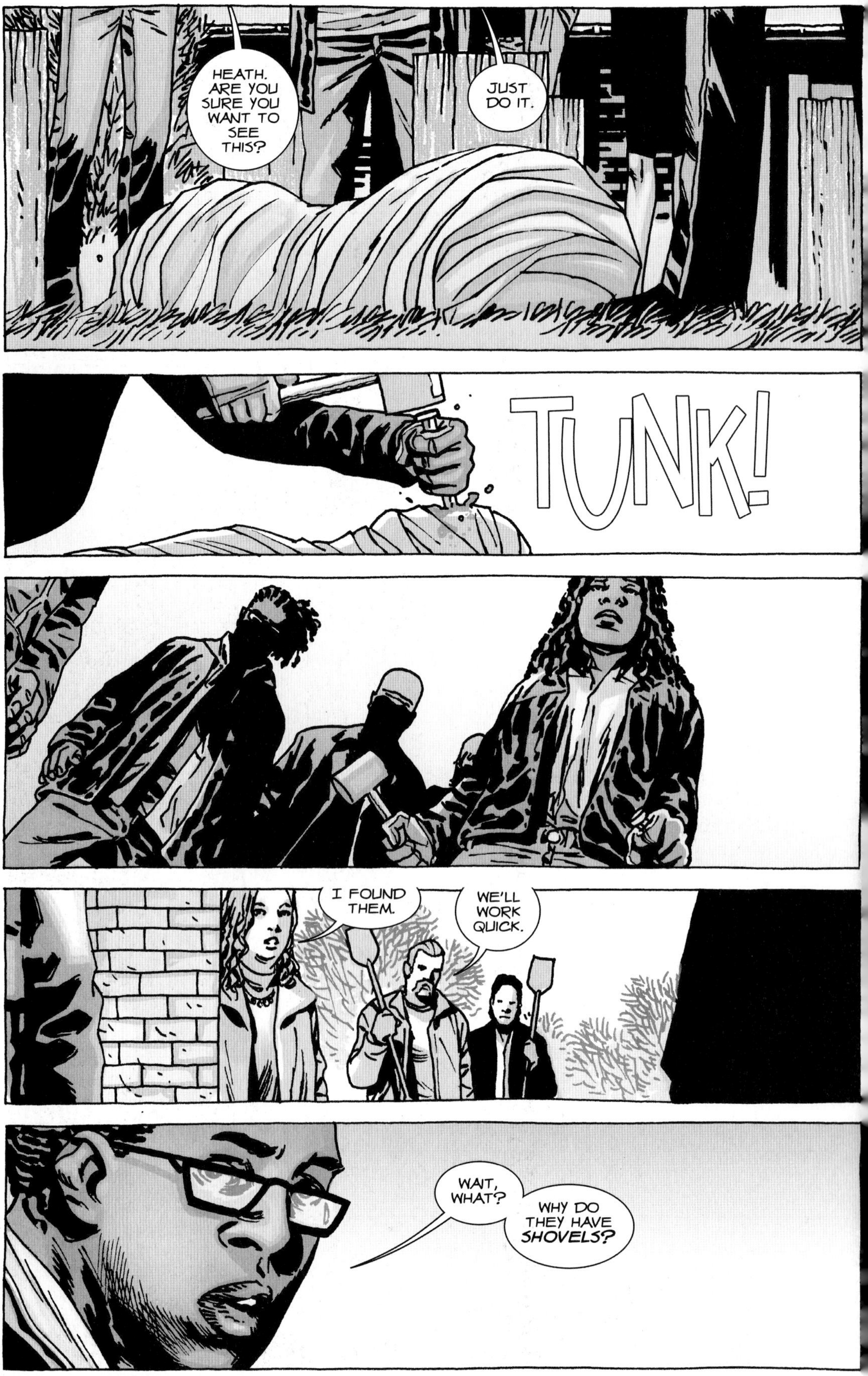
HEATH, ARE YOU SURE YOU WANT TO SEE THIS?
JUST DO IT.
TUNK!
I FOUND THEM.
WE'LL WORK QUICK.
WAIT, WHAT?
WHY DO THEY HAVE *SHOVELS?*

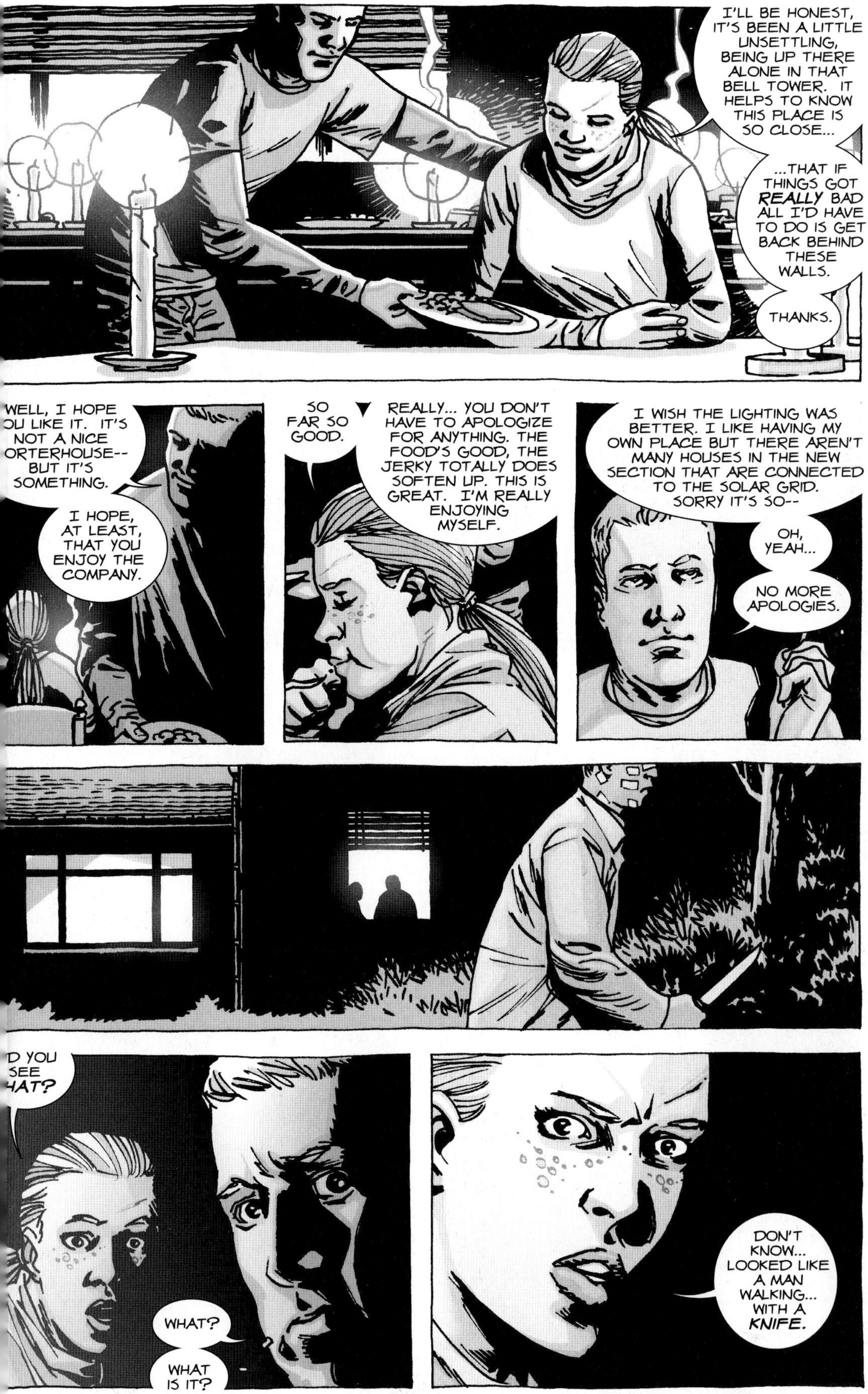
I'LL BE HONEST, IT'S BEEN A LITTLE UNSETTLING, BEING UP THERE ALONE IN THAT BELL TOWER. IT HELPS TO KNOW THIS PLACE IS SO CLOSE...
...THAT IF THINGS GOT *REALLY* BAD ALL I'D HAVE TO DO IS GET BACK BEHIND THESE WALLS.
THANKS.
WELL, I HOPE OU LIKE IT. IT'S NOT A NICE ORTERHOUSE-- BUT IT'S SOMETHING.
I HOPE, AT LEAST, THAT YOU ENJOY THE COMPANY.
SO FAR SO GOOD.
REALLY... YOU DON'T HAVE TO APOLOGIZE FOR ANYTHING. THE FOOD'S GOOD, THE JERKY TOTALLY DOES SOFTEN UP. THIS IS GREAT. I'M REALLY ENJOYING MYSELF.
I WISH THE LIGHTING WAS BETTER. I LIKE HAVING MY OWN PLACE BUT THERE AREN'T MANY HOUSES IN THE NEW SECTION THAT ARE CONNECTED TO THE SOLAR GRID. SORRY IT'S SO--
OH, YEAH...
NO MORE APOLOGIES.
D YOU SEE HAT?
WHAT?
WHAT IS IT?
DON'T KNOW... LOOKED LIKE A MAN WALKING... WITH A *KNIFE.*

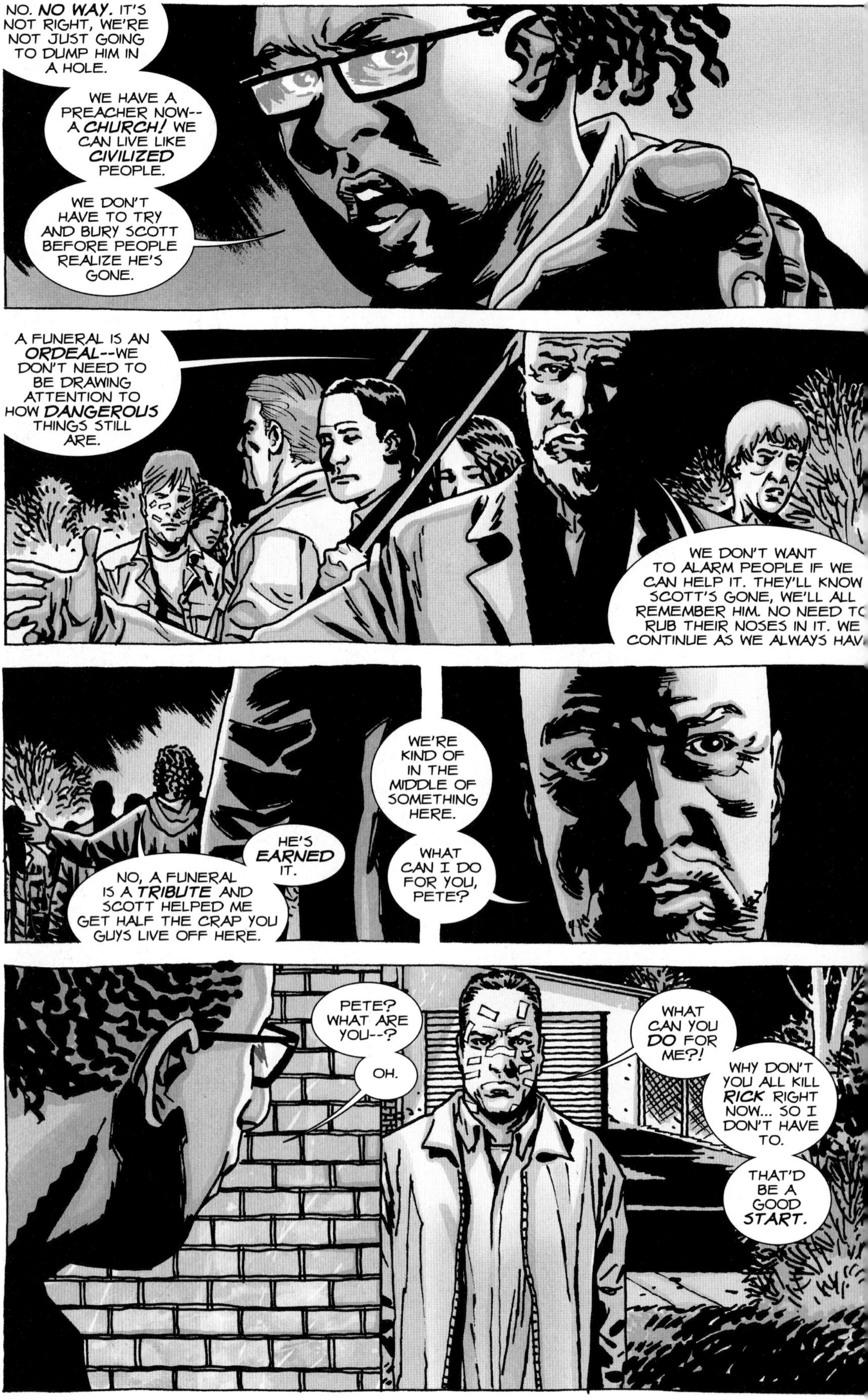
NO. NO WAY. IT'S NOT RIGHT, WE'RE NOT JUST GOING TO DUMP HIM IN A HOLE.
WE HAVE A PREACHER NOW-- A CHURCH! WE CAN LIVE LIKE CIVILIZED PEOPLE.
WE DON'T HAVE TO TRY AND BURY SCOTT BEFORE PEOPLE REALIZE HE'S GONE.
A FUNERAL IS AN ORDEAL--WE DON'T NEED TO BE DRAWING ATTENTION TO HOW DANGEROUS THINGS STILL ARE.
WE DON'T WANT TO ALARM PEOPLE IF WE CAN HELP IT. THEY'LL KNOW SCOTT'S GONE, WE'LL ALL REMEMBER HIM. NO NEED TO RUB THEIR NOSES IN IT. WE CONTINUE AS WE ALWAYS HAV
NO, A FUNERAL IS A TRIBUTE AND SCOTT HELPED ME GET HALF THE CRAP YOU GUYS LIVE OFF HERE.
HE'S EARNED IT.
WE'RE KIND OF IN THE MIDDLE OF SOMETHING HERE.
WHAT CAN I DO FOR YOU, PETE?
PETE? WHAT ARE YOU--?
OH.
WHAT CAN YOU DO FOR ME?!
WHY DON'T YOU ALL KILL RICK RIGHT NOW... SO I DON'T HAVE TO.
THAT'D BE A GOOD START.

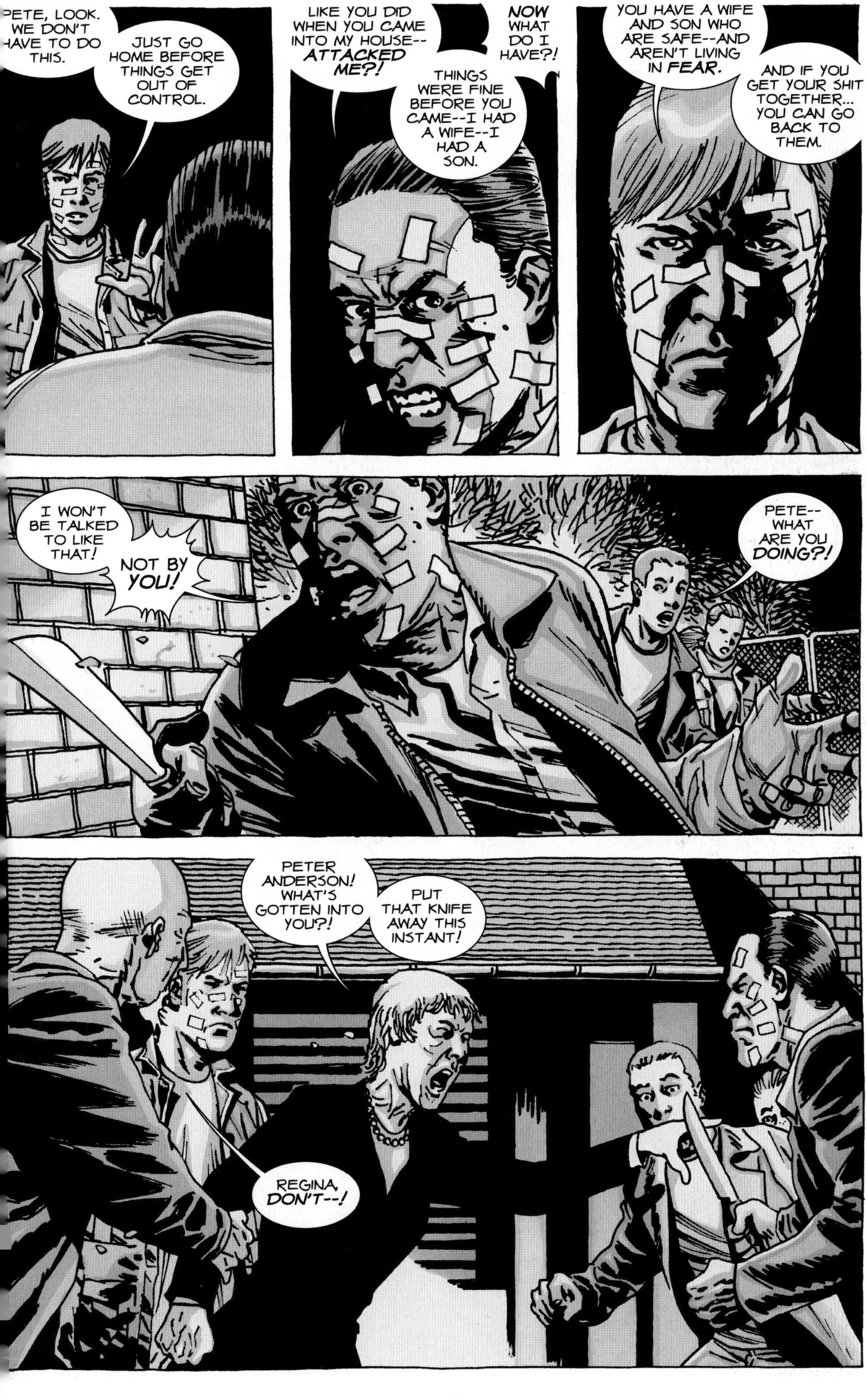
PETE, LOOK. WE DON'T HAVE TO DO THIS.
JUST GO HOME BEFORE THINGS GET OUT OF CONTROL.
LIKE YOU DID WHEN YOU CAME INTO MY HOUSE-- ATTACKED ME?!
THINGS WERE FINE BEFORE YOU CAME--I HAD A WIFE--I HAD A SON.
NOW WHAT DO I HAVE?!
YOU HAVE A WIFE AND SON WHO ARE SAFE--AND AREN'T LIVING IN FEAR.
AND IF YOU GET YOUR SHIT TOGETHER... YOU CAN GO BACK TO THEM.
I WON'T BE TALKED TO LIKE THAT!
NOT BY YOU!
PETE-- WHAT ARE YOU DOING?!
PETER ANDERSON! WHAT'S GOTTEN INTO YOU?!
PUT THAT KNIFE AWAY THIS INSTANT!
REGINA, DON'T--!

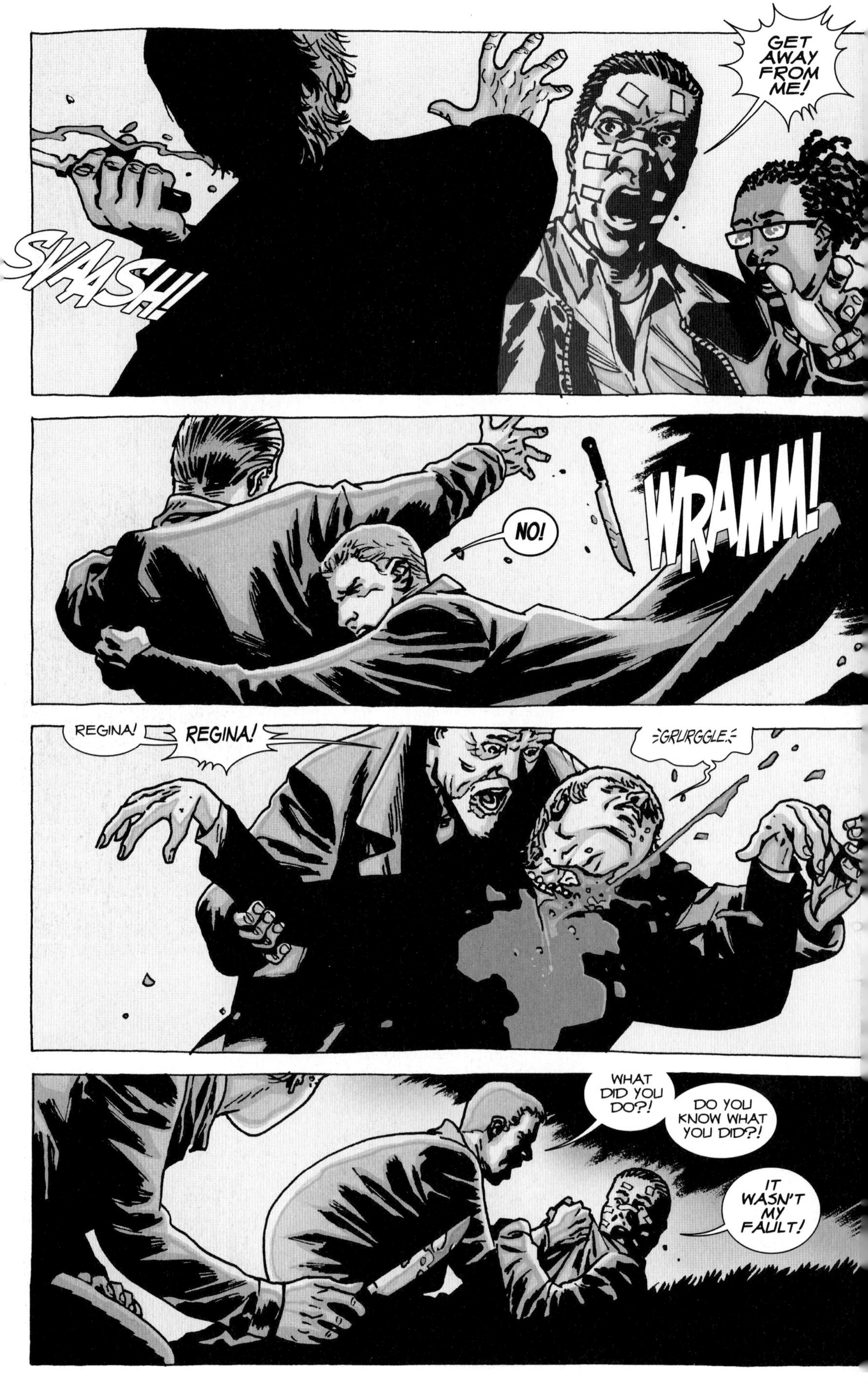
GET AWAY FROM ME!
SWASH!
NO!
WRAMM!
REGINA!
REGINA!
GRURGGLE
WHAT DID YOU DO?!
DO YOU KNOW WHAT YOU DID?!
IT WASN'T MY FAULT!

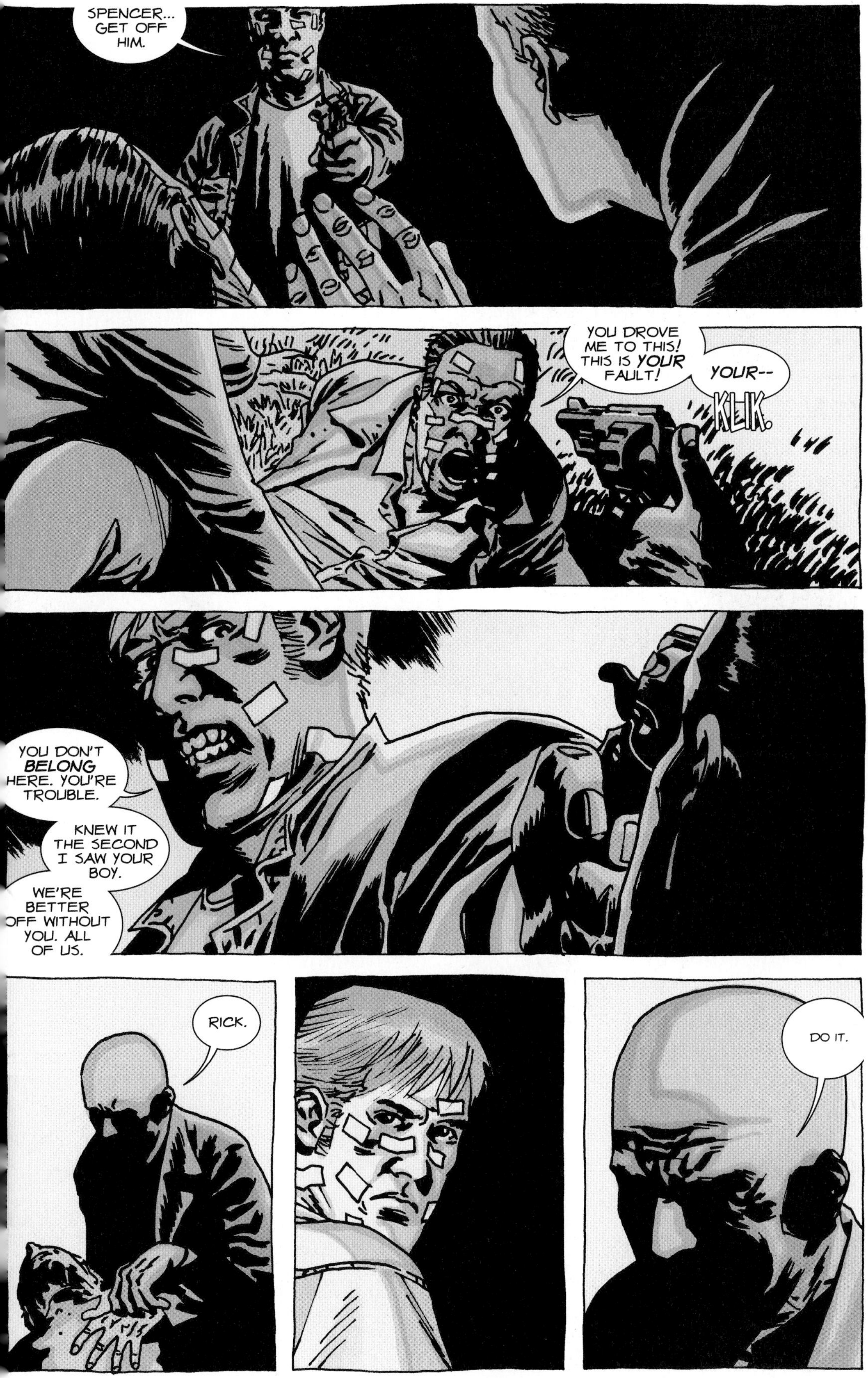
SPENCER... GET OFF HIM.
YOU DROVE ME TO THIS! THIS IS YOUR FAULT!
YOUR--
KLIK.
YOU DON'T BELONG HERE. YOU'RE TROUBLE.
KNEW IT THE SECOND I SAW YOUR BOY.
WE'RE BETTER OFF WITHOUT YOU. ALL OF US.
RICK.
DO IT.

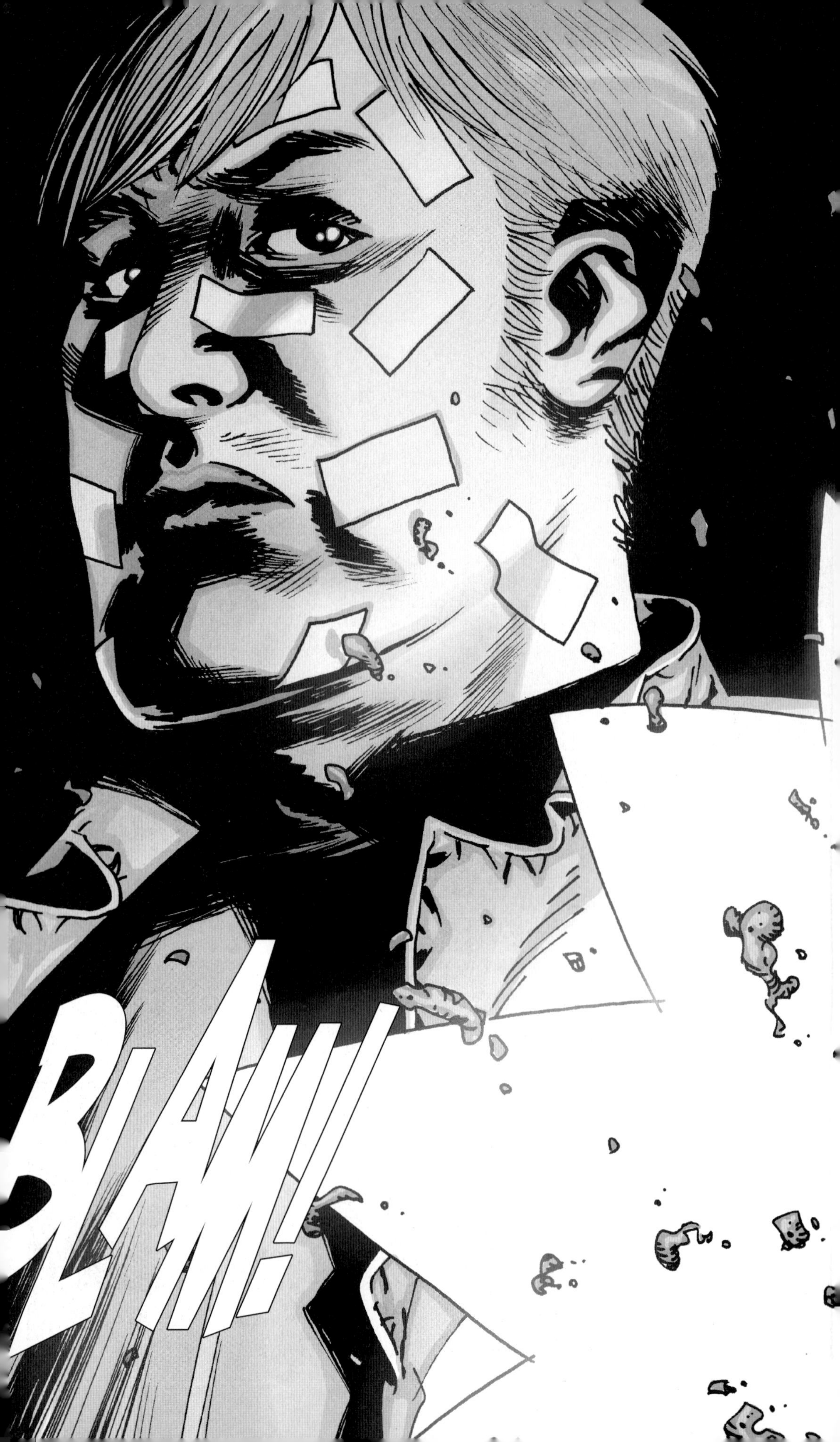
BLAM!

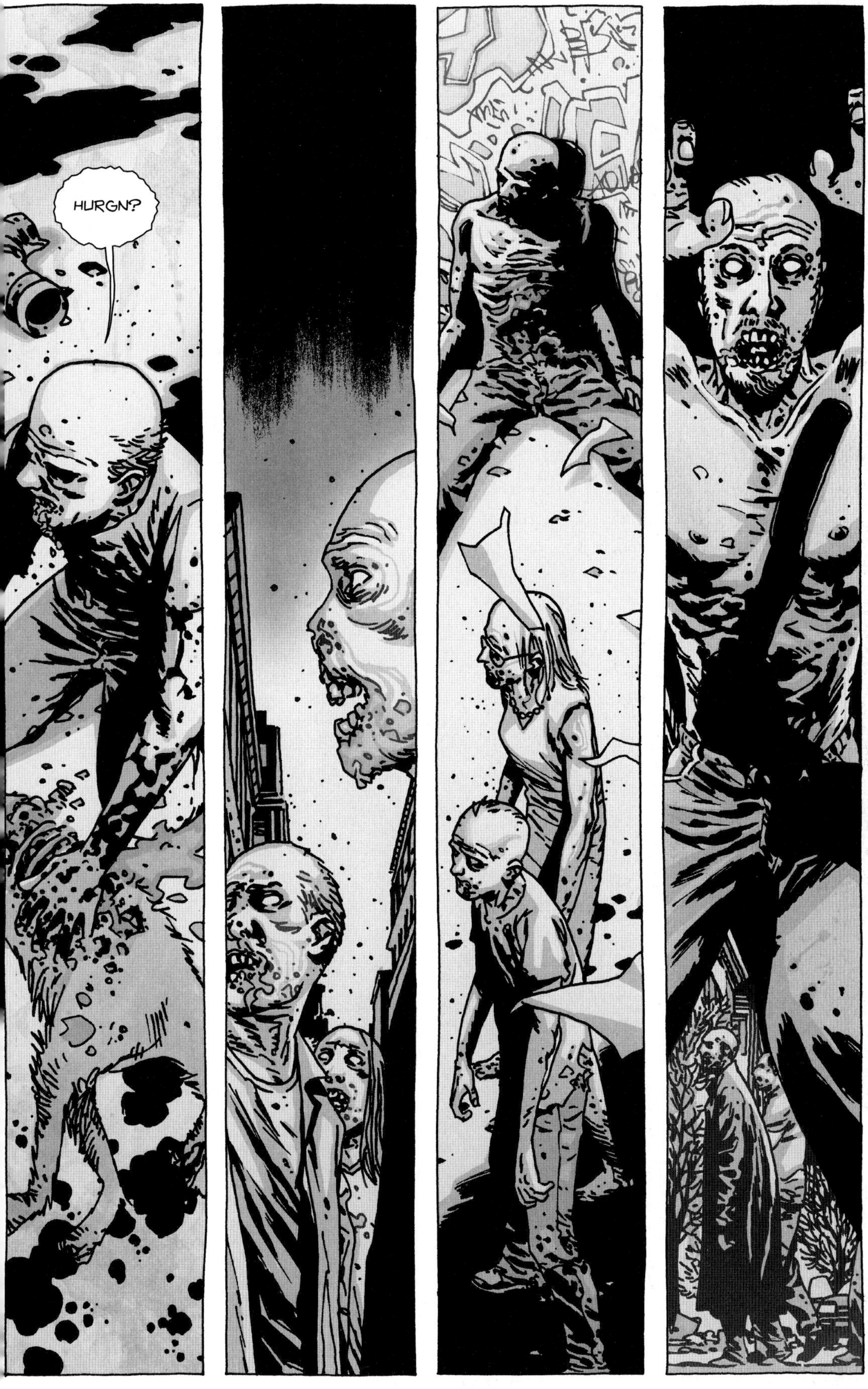
HURGN?

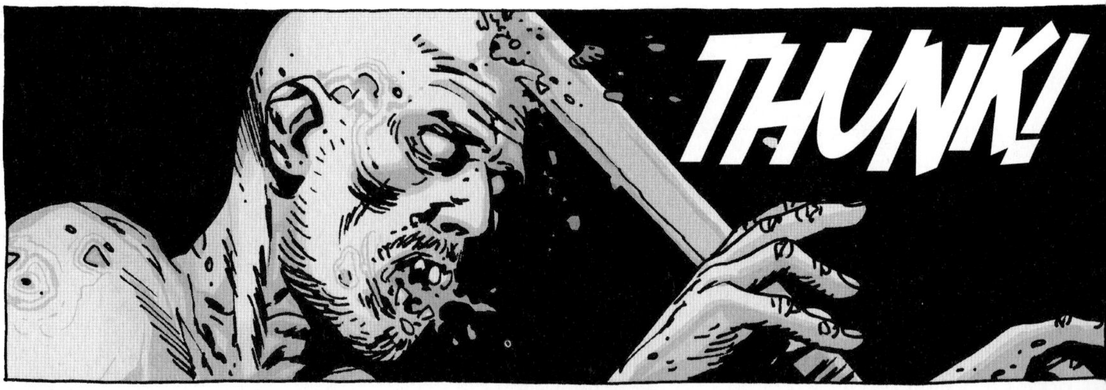
THUNK!

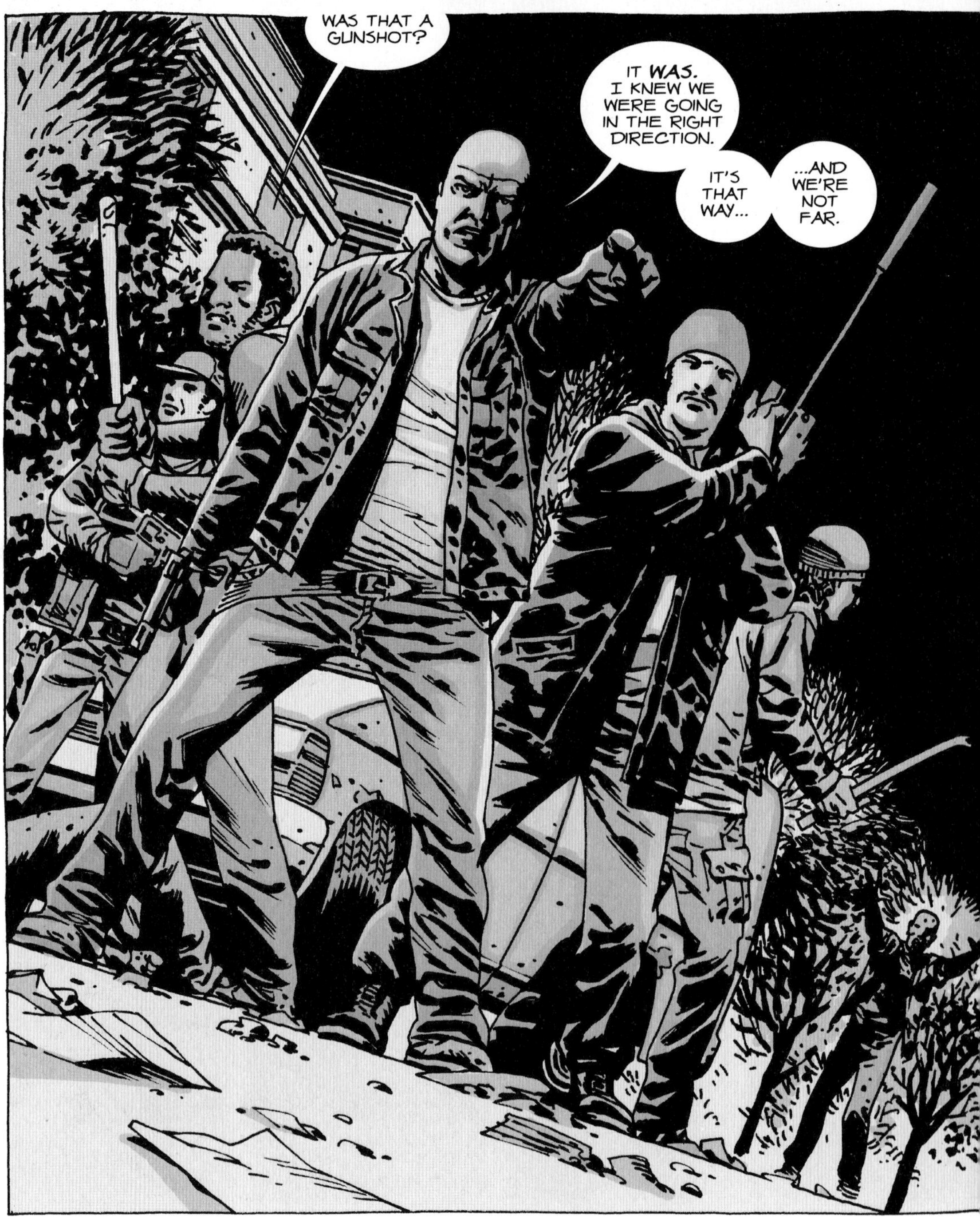
WAS THAT A GUNSHOT?
IT WAS. I KNEW WE WERE GOING IN THE RIGHT DIRECTION.
IT'S THAT WAY...
...AND WE'RE NOT FAR.

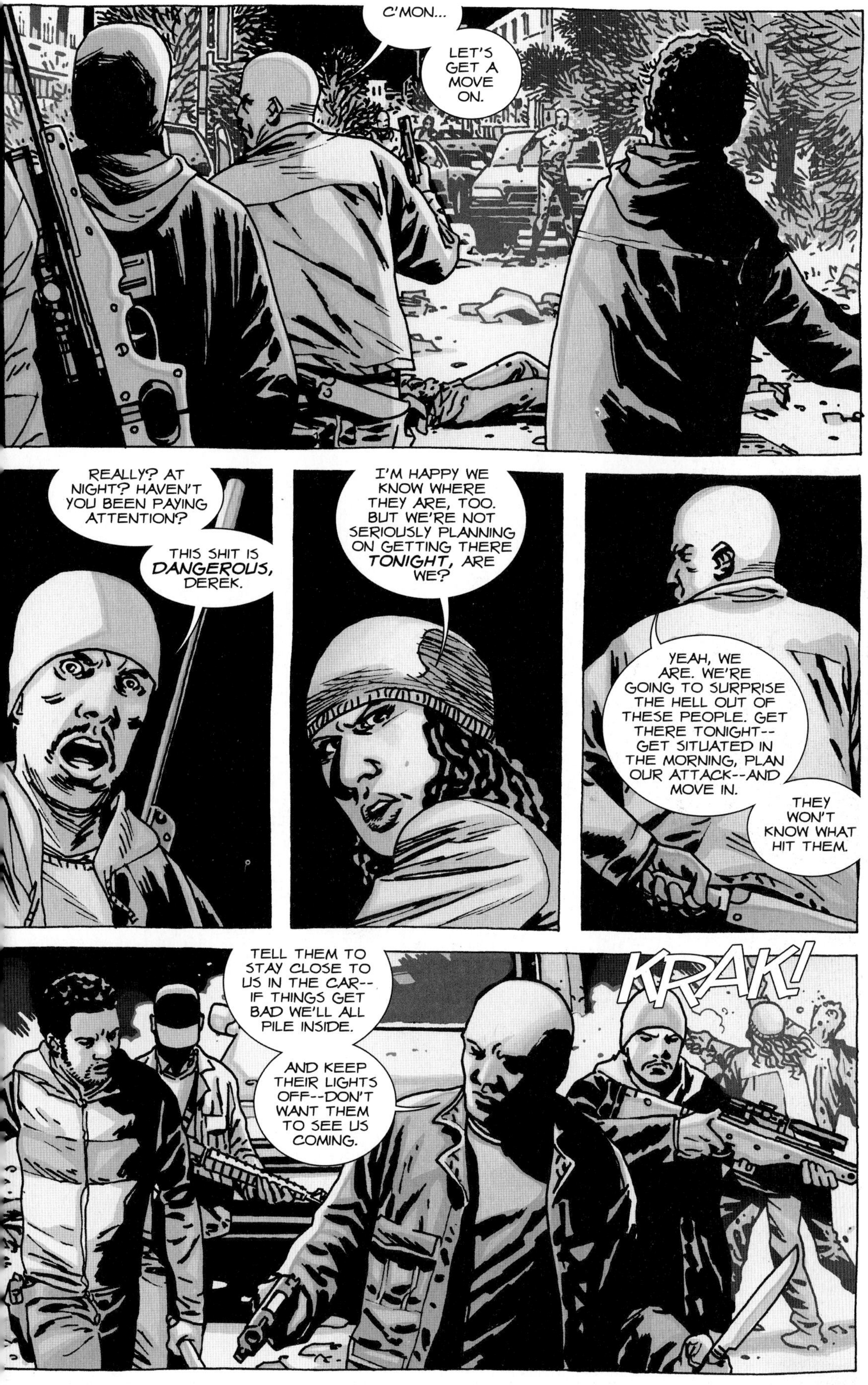
C'MON...
LET'S GET A MOVE ON.
REALLY? AT NIGHT? HAVEN'T YOU BEEN PAYING ATTENTION?
THIS SHIT IS *DANGEROUS,* DEREK.
I'M HAPPY WE KNOW WHERE THEY ARE, TOO. BUT WE'RE NOT SERIOUSLY PLANNING ON GETTING THERE *TONIGHT,* ARE WE?
YEAH, WE ARE. WE'RE GOING TO SURPRISE THE HELL OUT OF THESE PEOPLE. GET THERE TONIGHT-- GET SITUATED IN THE MORNING, PLAN OUR ATTACK--AND MOVE IN.
THEY WON'T KNOW WHAT HIT THEM.
TELL THEM TO STAY CLOSE TO US IN THE CAR-- IF THINGS GET BAD WE'LL ALL PILE INSIDE.
AND KEEP THEIR LIGHTS OFF--DON'T WANT THEM TO SEE US COMING.
KRAK!

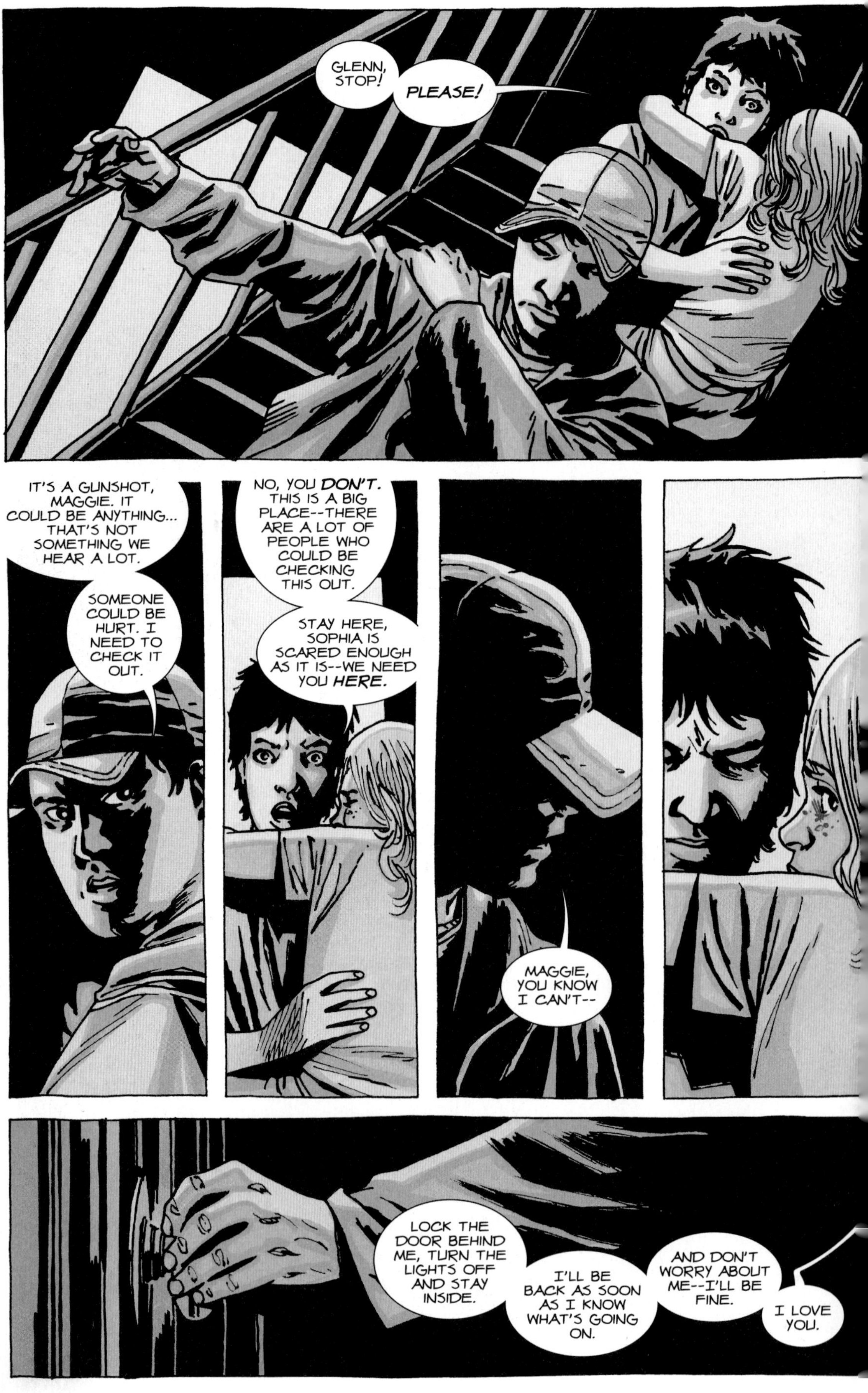
GLENN, STOP!
PLEASE!
IT'S A GUNSHOT, MAGGIE. IT COULD BE ANYTHING... THAT'S NOT SOMETHING WE HEAR A LOT.
SOMEONE COULD BE HURT. I NEED TO CHECK IT OUT.
NO, YOU DON'T. THIS IS A BIG PLACE--THERE ARE A LOT OF PEOPLE WHO COULD BE CHECKING THIS OUT.
STAY HERE, SOPHIA IS SCARED ENOUGH AS IT IS--WE NEED YOU HERE.
MAGGIE, YOU KNOW I CAN'T--
LOCK THE DOOR BEHIND ME, TURN THE LIGHTS OFF AND STAY INSIDE.
I'LL BE BACK AS SOON AS I KNOW WHAT'S GOING ON.
AND DON'T WORRY ABOUT ME--I'LL BE FINE.
I LOVE YOU.

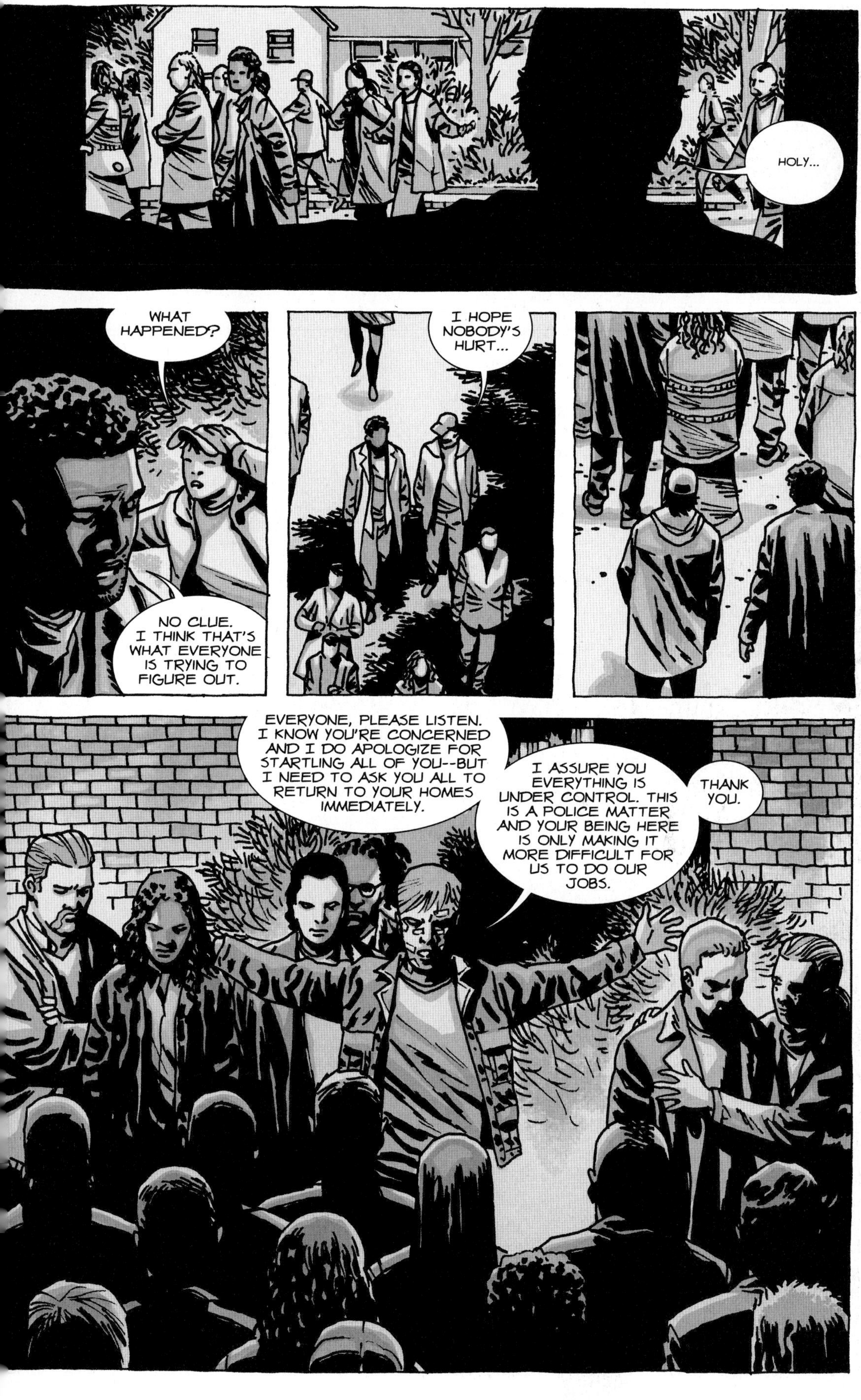
HOLY...
WHAT HAPPENED?
NO CLUE. I THINK THAT'S WHAT EVERYONE IS TRYING TO FIGURE OUT.
I HOPE NOBODY'S HURT...
EVERYONE, PLEASE LISTEN. I KNOW YOU'RE CONCERNED AND I DO APOLOGIZE FOR STARTLING ALL OF YOU--BUT I NEED TO ASK YOU ALL TO RETURN TO YOUR HOMES IMMEDIATELY.
I ASSURE YOU EVERYTHING IS UNDER CONTROL. THIS IS A POLICE MATTER AND YOUR BEING HERE IS ONLY MAKING IT MORE DIFFICULT FOR US TO DO OUR JOBS.
THANK YOU.

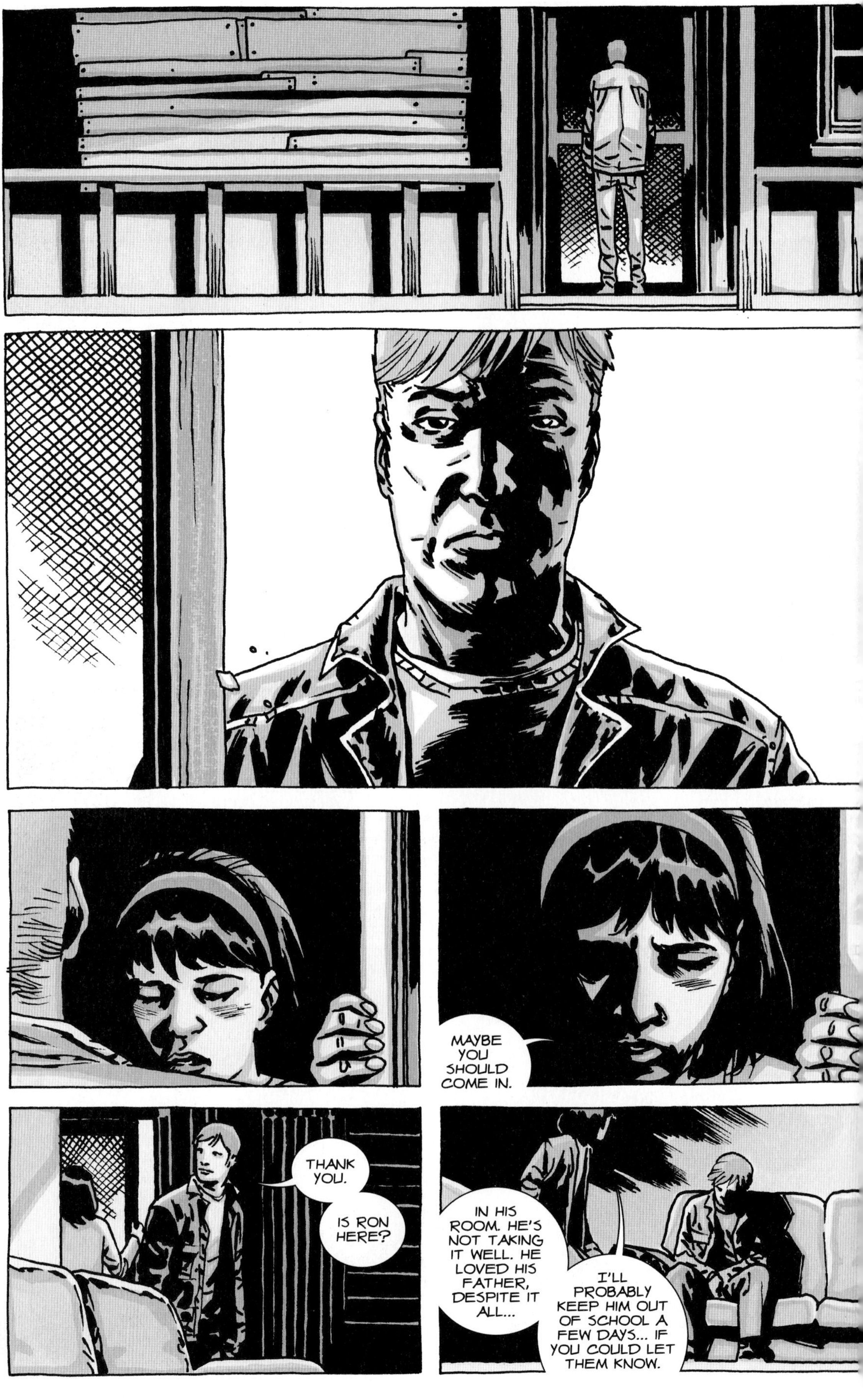
MAYBE YOU SHOULD COME IN.
THANK YOU.
IS RON HERE?
IN HIS ROOM. HE'S NOT TAKING IT WELL. HE LOVED HIS FATHER, DESPITE IT ALL...
I'LL PROBABLY KEEP HIM OUT OF SCHOOL A FEW DAYS... IF YOU COULD LET THEM KNOW.

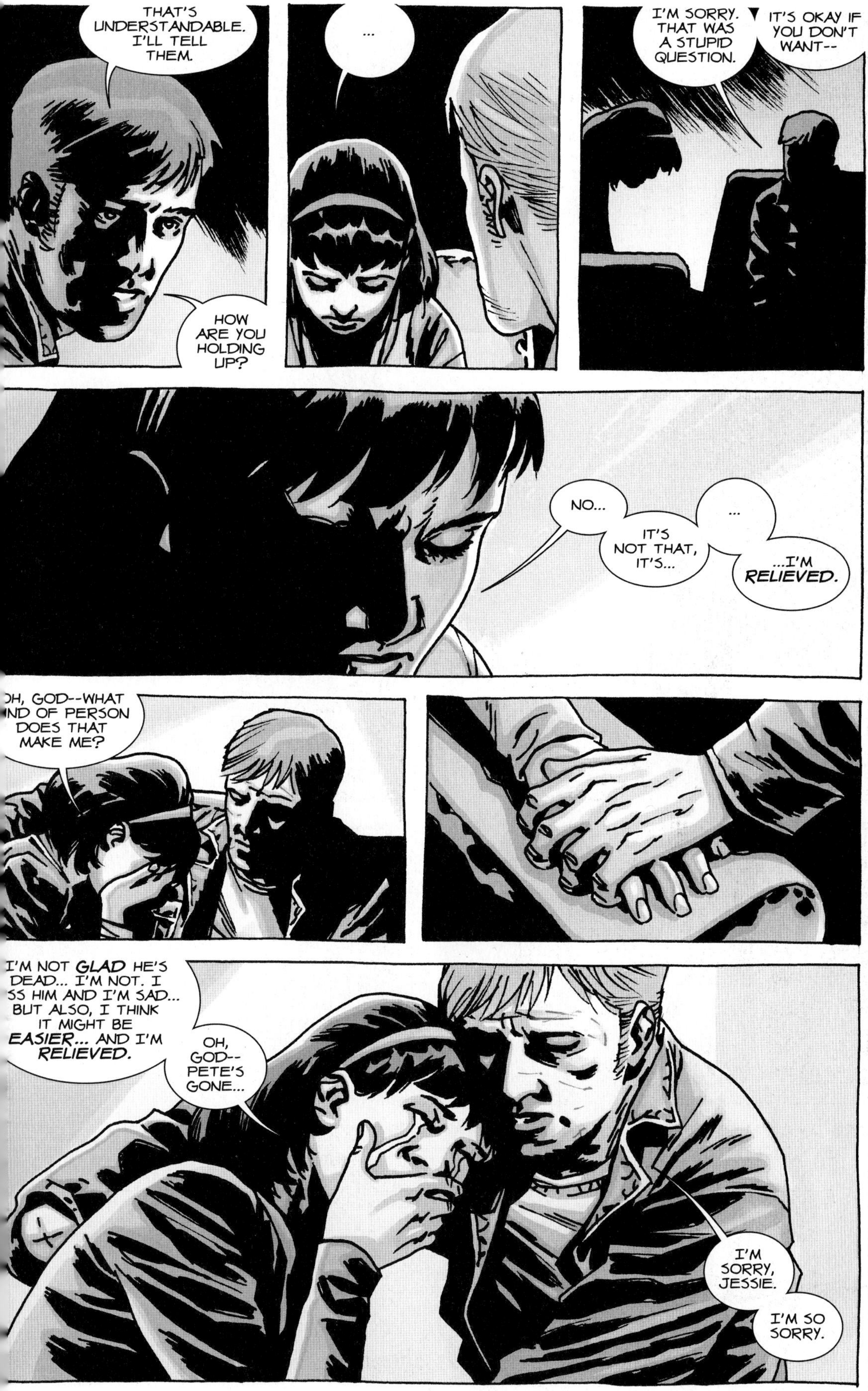

THAT'S UNDERSTANDABLE. I'LL TELL THEM.
HOW ARE YOU HOLDING UP?
...
I'M SORRY. THAT WAS A STUPID QUESTION.
IT'S OKAY IF YOU DON'T WANT--
NO...
IT'S NOT THAT, IT'S...
...
...I'M *RELIEVED.*
OH, GOD--WHAT KIND OF PERSON DOES THAT MAKE ME?
I'M NOT *GLAD* HE'S DEAD... I'M NOT. I MISS HIM AND I'M SAD... BUT ALSO, I THINK IT MIGHT BE *EASIER*... AND I'M *RELIEVED.*
OH, GOD-- PETE'S GONE...
I'M SORRY, JESSIE.
I'M SO SORRY.

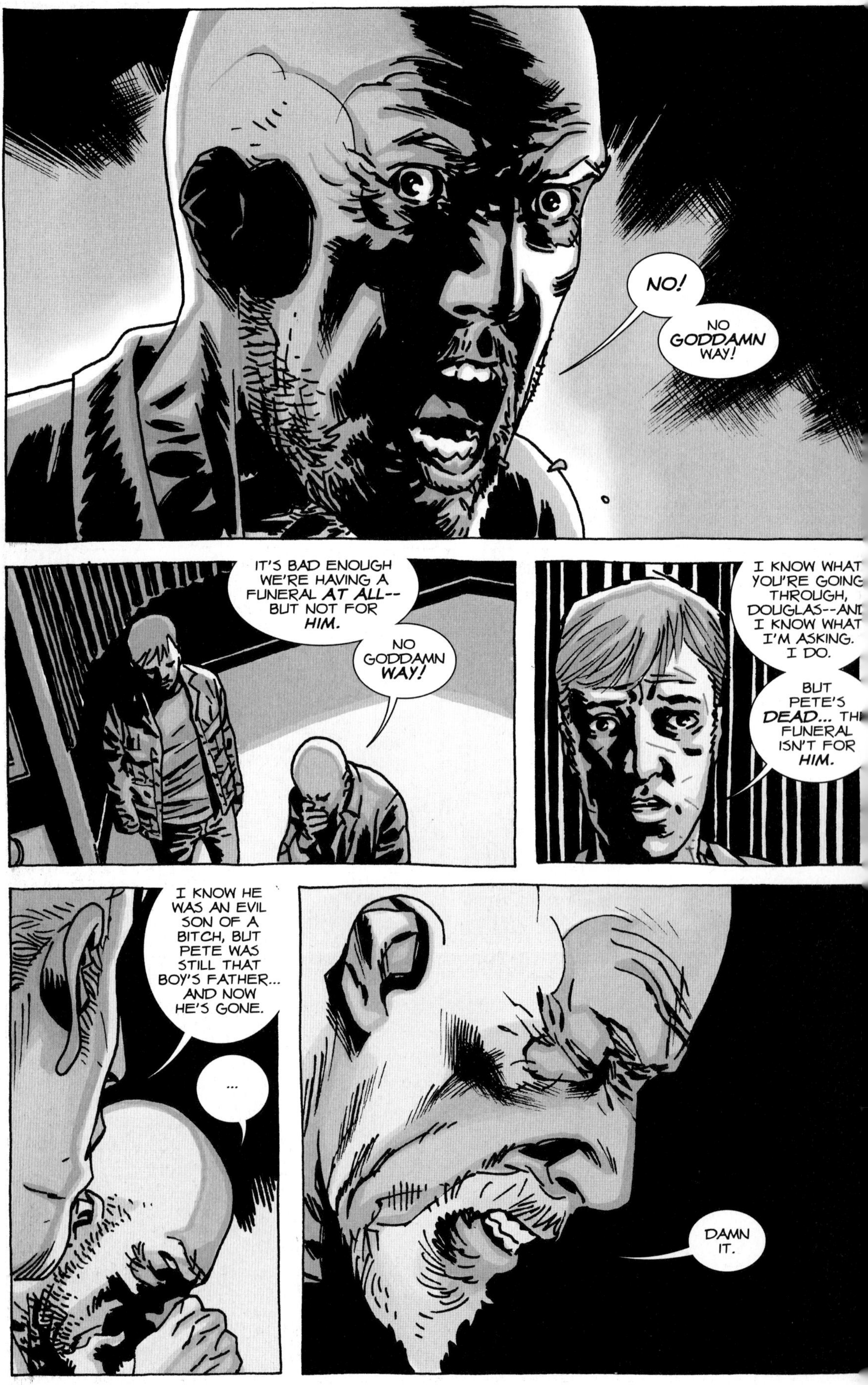
NO!
NO GODDAMN WAY!
IT'S BAD ENOUGH WE'RE HAVING A FUNERAL AT ALL-- BUT NOT FOR HIM.
NO GODDAMN WAY!
I KNOW WHAT YOU'RE GOING THROUGH, DOUGLAS--AND I KNOW WHAT I'M ASKING. I DO.
BUT PETE'S DEAD... THE FUNERAL ISN'T FOR HIM.
I KNOW HE WAS AN EVIL SON OF A BITCH, BUT PETE WAS STILL THAT BOY'S FATHER... AND NOW HE'S GONE.
...
DAMN IT.

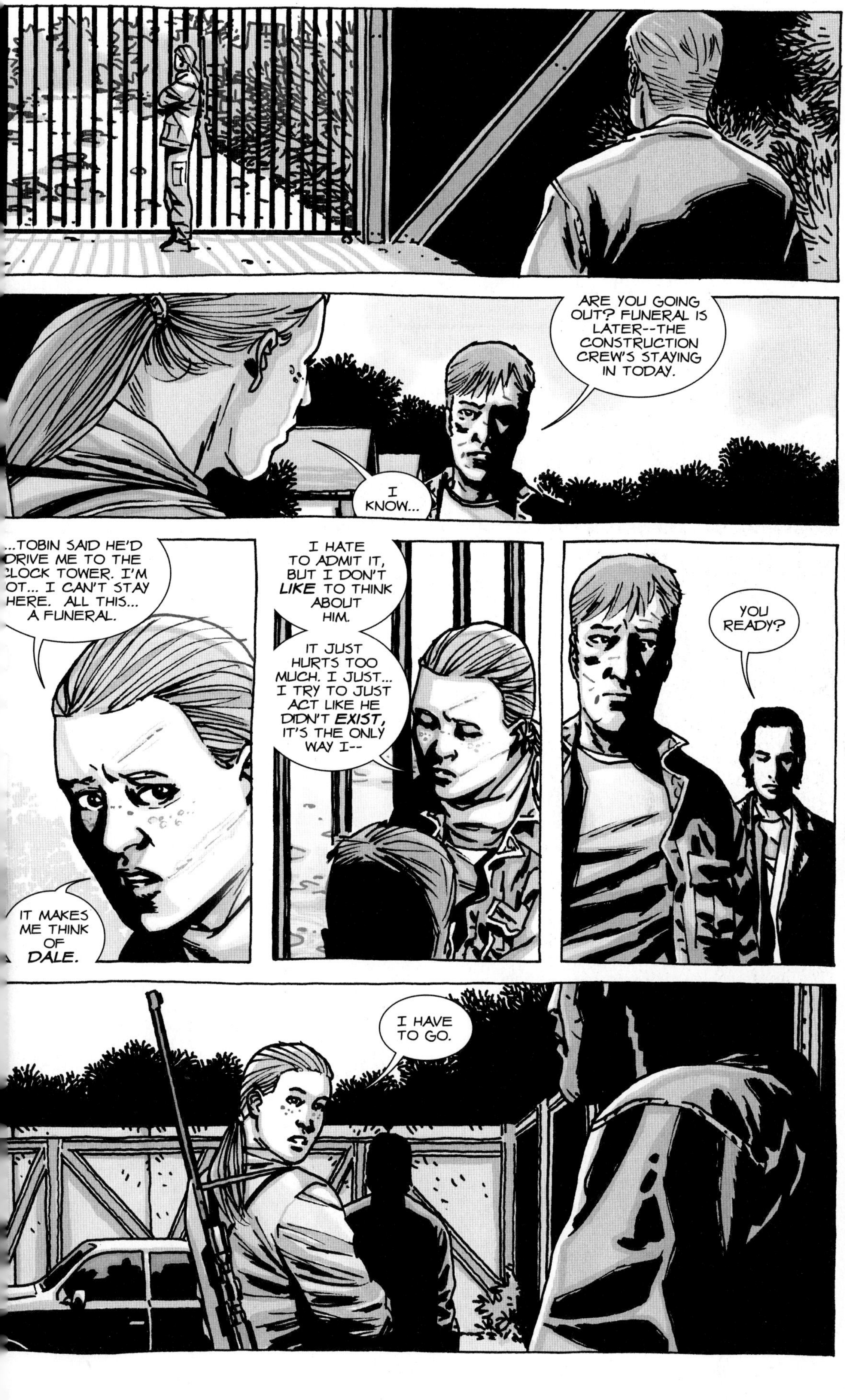

ARE YOU GOING OUT? FUNERAL IS LATER--THE CONSTRUCTION CREW'S STAYING IN TODAY.
I KNOW...
...TOBIN SAID HE'D DRIVE ME TO THE CLOCK TOWER. I'M NOT... I CAN'T STAY HERE. ALL THIS... A FUNERAL.
IT MAKES ME THINK OF DALE.
I HATE TO ADMIT IT, BUT I DON'T LIKE TO THINK ABOUT HIM.
IT JUST HURTS TOO MUCH. I JUST... I TRY TO JUST ACT LIKE HE DIDN'T EXIST, IT'S THE ONLY WAY I--
YOU READY?
I HAVE TO GO.

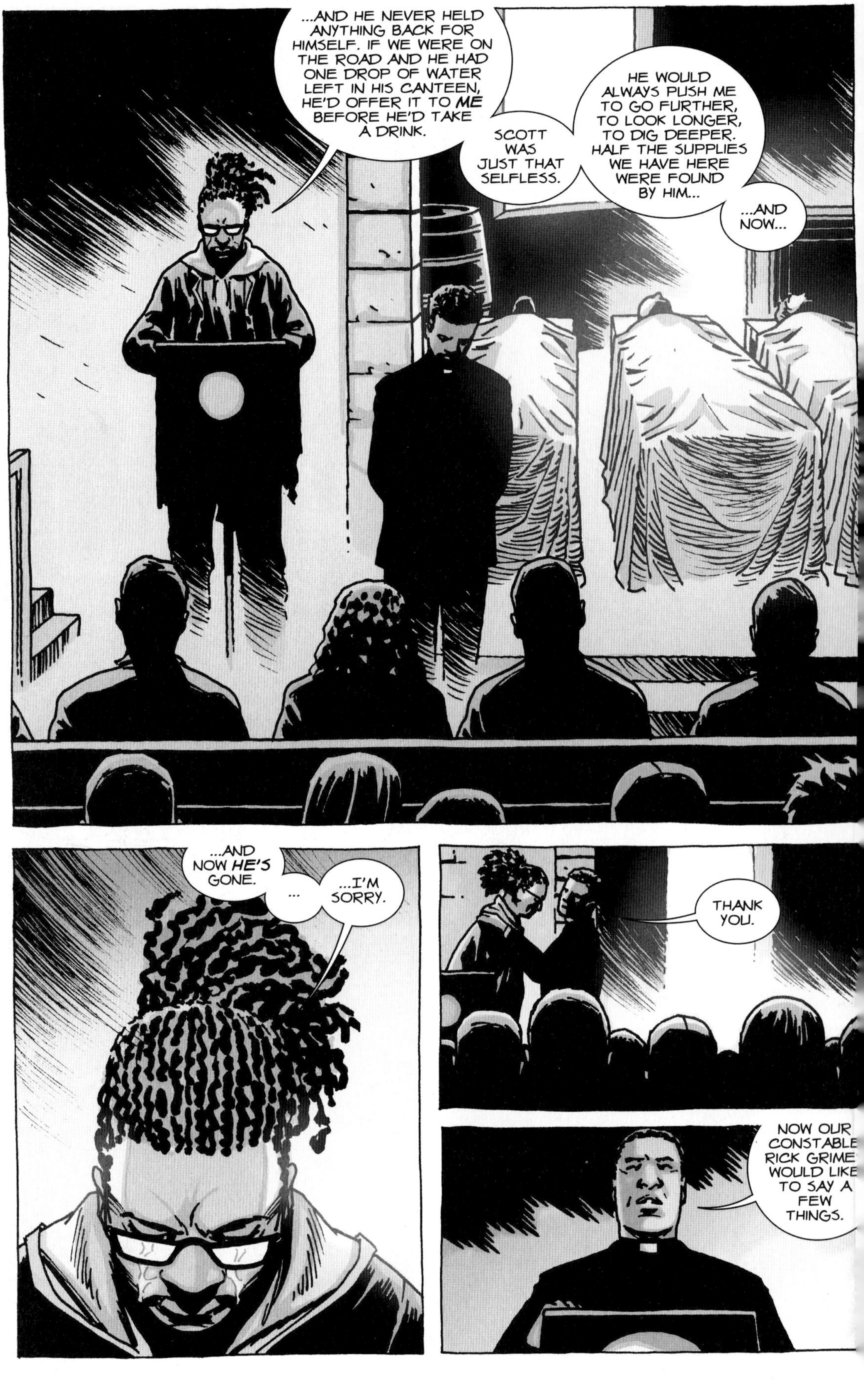
...AND HE NEVER HELD ANYTHING BACK FOR HIMSELF. IF WE WERE ON THE ROAD AND HE HAD ONE DROP OF WATER LEFT IN HIS CANTEEN, HE'D OFFER IT TO ME BEFORE HE'D TAKE A DRINK.
SCOTT WAS JUST THAT SELFLESS.
HE WOULD ALWAYS PUSH ME TO GO FURTHER, TO LOOK LONGER, TO DIG DEEPER. HALF THE SUPPLIES WE HAVE HERE WERE FOUND BY HIM...
...AND NOW...
...AND NOW HE'S GONE.
...
...I'M SORRY.
THANK YOU.
NOW OUR CONSTABLE RICK GRIME WOULD LIKE TO SAY A FEW THINGS.

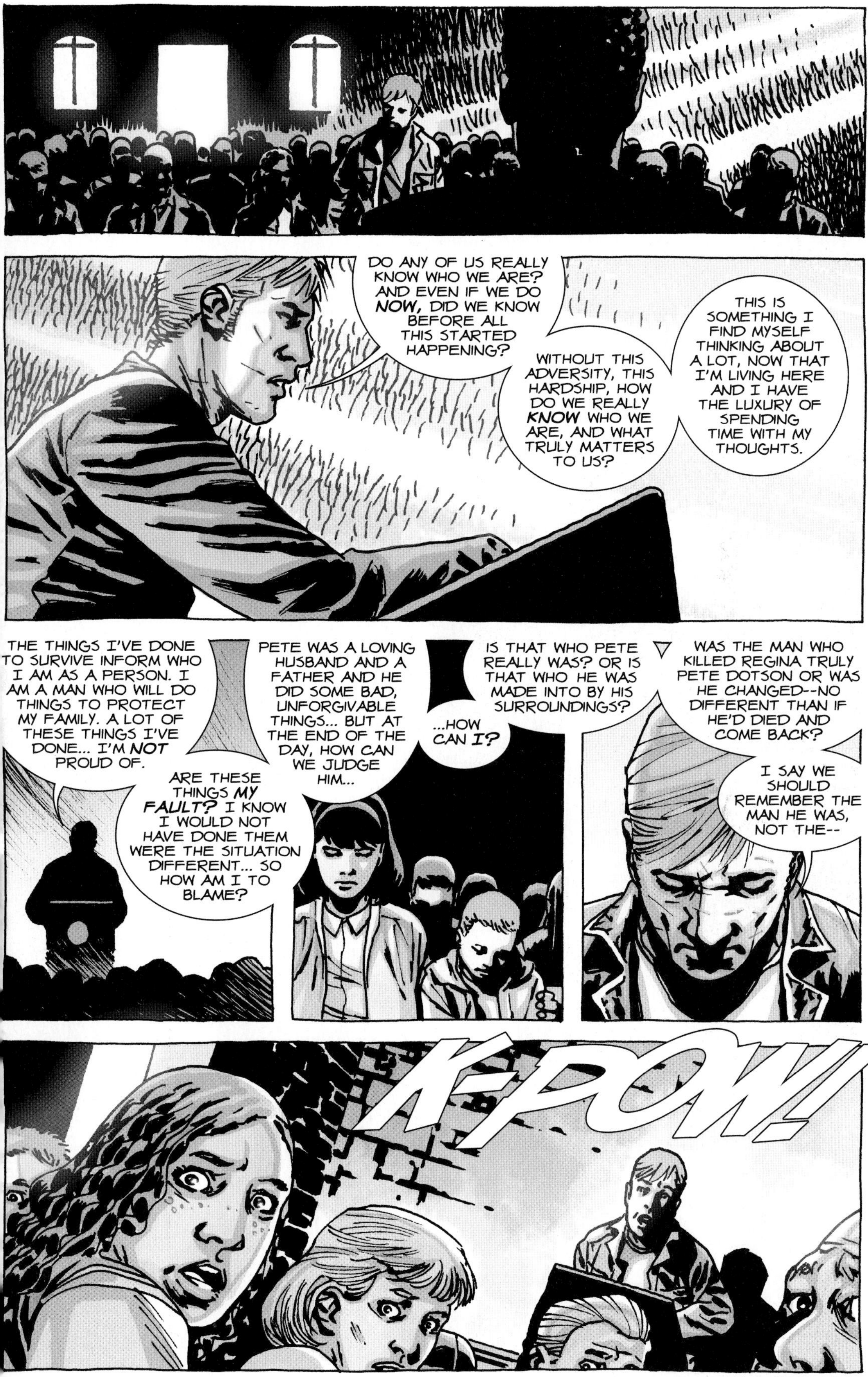
DO ANY OF US REALLY KNOW WHO WE ARE? AND EVEN IF WE DO NOW, DID WE KNOW BEFORE ALL THIS STARTED HAPPENING?
WITHOUT THIS ADVERSITY, THIS HARDSHIP, HOW DO WE REALLY KNOW WHO WE ARE, AND WHAT TRULY MATTERS TO US?
THIS IS SOMETHING I FIND MYSELF THINKING ABOUT A LOT, NOW THAT I'M LIVING HERE AND I HAVE THE LUXURY OF SPENDING TIME WITH MY THOUGHTS.
THE THINGS I'VE DONE TO SURVIVE INFORM WHO I AM AS A PERSON. I AM A MAN WHO WILL DO THINGS TO PROTECT MY FAMILY. A LOT OF THESE THINGS I'VE DONE... I'M NOT PROUD OF.
ARE THESE THINGS MY FAULT? I KNOW I WOULD NOT HAVE DONE THEM WERE THE SITUATION DIFFERENT... SO HOW AM I TO BLAME?
PETE WAS A LOVING HUSBAND AND A FATHER AND HE DID SOME BAD, UNFORGIVABLE THINGS... BUT AT THE END OF THE DAY, HOW CAN WE JUDGE HIM...
...HOW CAN I?
IS THAT WHO PETE REALLY WAS? OR IS THAT WHO HE WAS MADE INTO BY HIS SURROUNDINGS?
WAS THE MAN WHO KILLED REGINA TRULY PETE DOTSON OR WAS HE CHANGED--NO DIFFERENT THAN IF HE'D DIED AND COME BACK?
I SAY WE SHOULD REMEMBER THE MAN HE WAS, NOT THE--
K-POW!

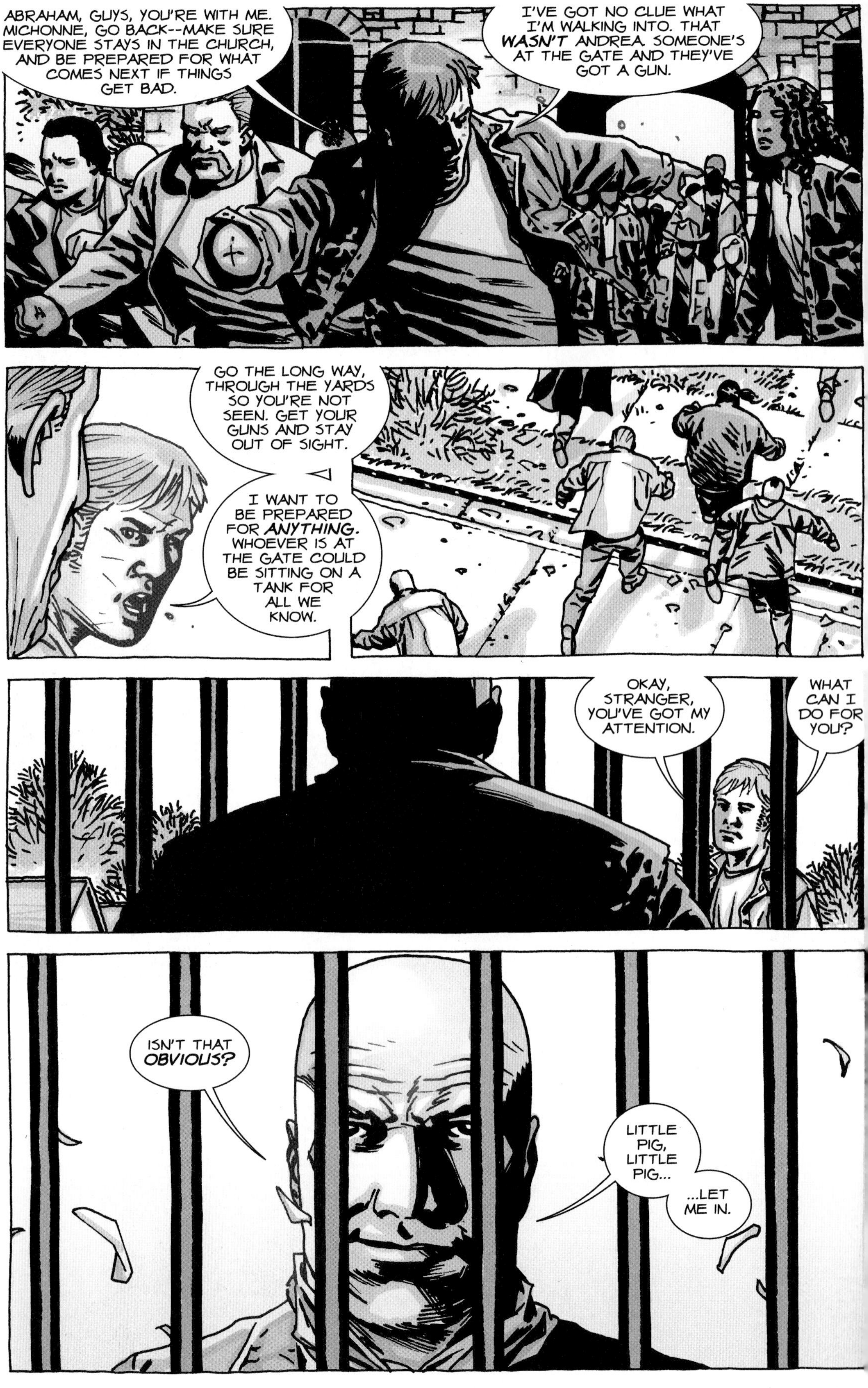
ABRAHAM, GUYS, YOU'RE WITH ME. MICHONNE, GO BACK--MAKE SURE EVERYONE STAYS IN THE CHURCH, AND BE PREPARED FOR WHAT COMES NEXT IF THINGS GET BAD.
I'VE GOT NO CLUE WHAT I'M WALKING INTO. THAT WASN'T ANDREA. SOMEONE'S AT THE GATE AND THEY'VE GOT A GUN.
GO THE LONG WAY, THROUGH THE YARDS SO YOU'RE NOT SEEN. GET YOUR GUNS AND STAY OUT OF SIGHT.
I WANT TO BE PREPARED FOR ANYTHING. WHOEVER IS AT THE GATE COULD BE SITTING ON A TANK FOR ALL WE KNOW.
OKAY, STRANGER, YOU'VE GOT MY ATTENTION.
WHAT CAN I DO FOR YOU?
ISN'T THAT OBVIOUS?
LITTLE PIG, LITTLE PIG...
...LET ME IN.

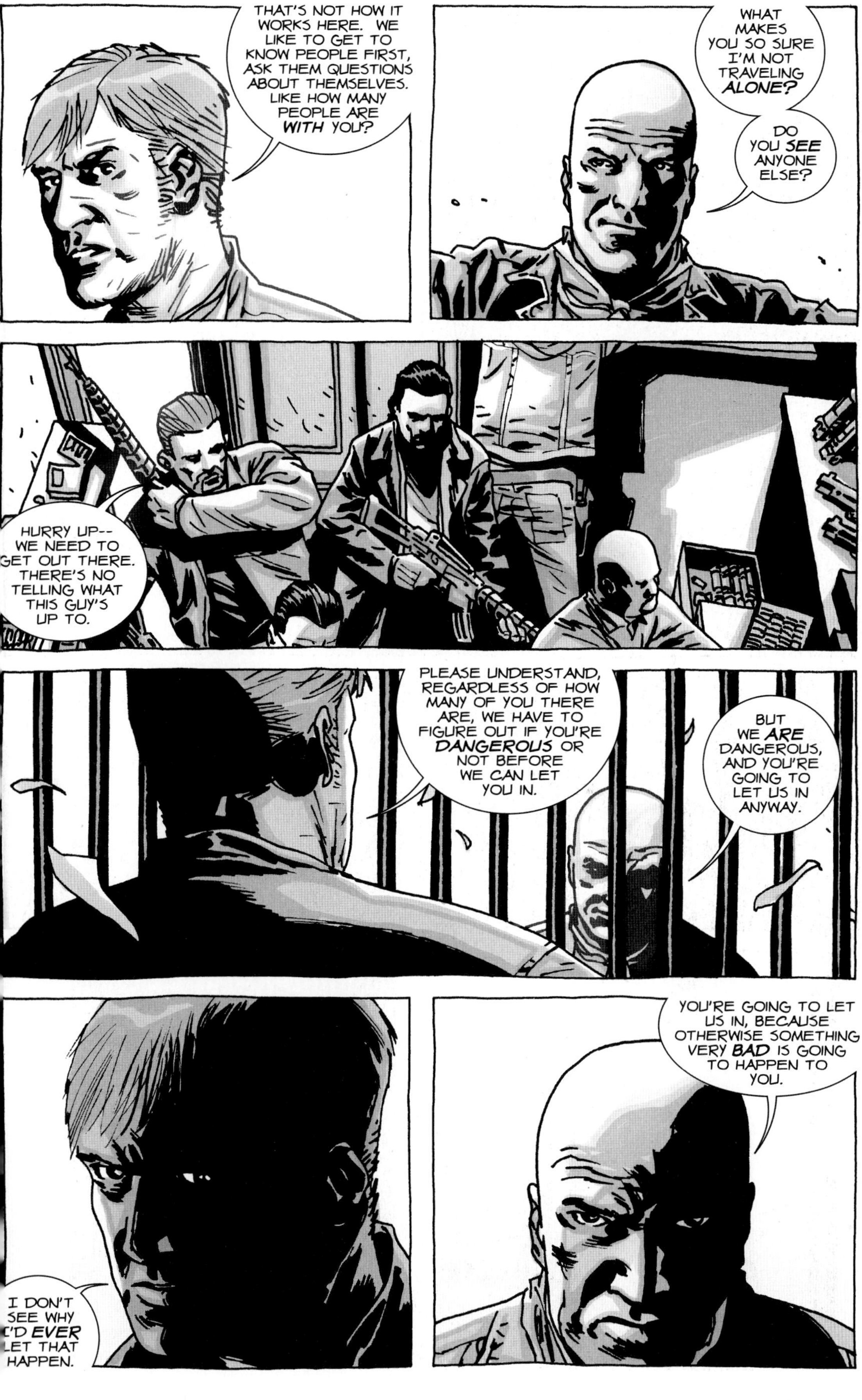
THAT'S NOT HOW IT WORKS HERE. WE LIKE TO GET TO KNOW PEOPLE FIRST, ASK THEM QUESTIONS ABOUT THEMSELVES. LIKE HOW MANY PEOPLE ARE WITH YOU?
WHAT MAKES YOU SO SURE I'M NOT TRAVELING ALONE?
DO YOU SEE ANYONE ELSE?
HURRY UP-- WE NEED TO GET OUT THERE. THERE'S NO TELLING WHAT THIS GUY'S UP TO.
PLEASE UNDERSTAND, REGARDLESS OF HOW MANY OF YOU THERE ARE, WE HAVE TO FIGURE OUT IF YOU'RE DANGEROUS OR NOT BEFORE WE CAN LET YOU IN.
BUT WE ARE DANGEROUS, AND YOU'RE GOING TO LET US IN ANYWAY.
I DON'T SEE WHY I'D EVER LET THAT HAPPEN.
YOU'RE GOING TO LET US IN, BECAUSE OTHERWISE SOMETHING VERY BAD IS GOING TO HAPPEN TO YOU.

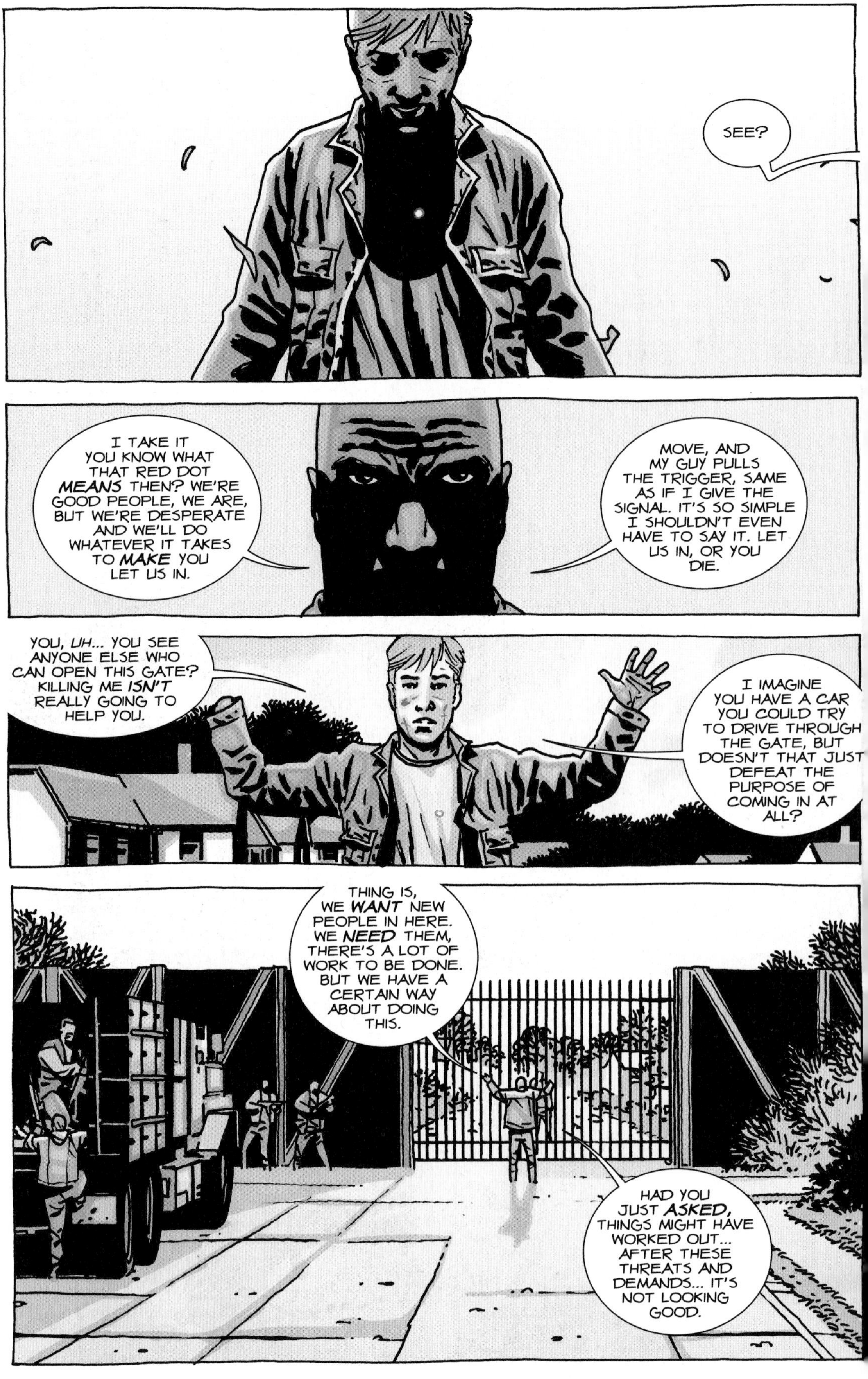
SEE?
I TAKE IT YOU KNOW WHAT THAT RED DOT MEANS THEN? WE'RE GOOD PEOPLE, WE ARE, BUT WE'RE DESPERATE AND WE'LL DO WHATEVER IT TAKES TO MAKE YOU LET US IN.
MOVE, AND MY GUY PULLS THE TRIGGER, SAME AS IF I GIVE THE SIGNAL. IT'S SO SIMPLE I SHOULDN'T EVEN HAVE TO SAY IT. LET US IN, OR YOU DIE.
YOU, UH... YOU SEE ANYONE ELSE WHO CAN OPEN THIS GATE? KILLING ME ISN'T REALLY GOING TO HELP YOU.
I IMAGINE YOU HAVE A CAR YOU COULD TRY TO DRIVE THROUGH THE GATE, BUT DOESN'T THAT JUST DEFEAT THE PURPOSE OF COMING IN AT ALL?
THING IS, WE WANT NEW PEOPLE IN HERE. WE NEED THEM, THERE'S A LOT OF WORK TO BE DONE. BUT WE HAVE A CERTAIN WAY ABOUT DOING THIS.
HAD YOU JUST ASKED, THINGS MIGHT HAVE WORKED OUT... AFTER THESE THREATS AND DEMANDS... IT'S NOT LOOKING GOOD.

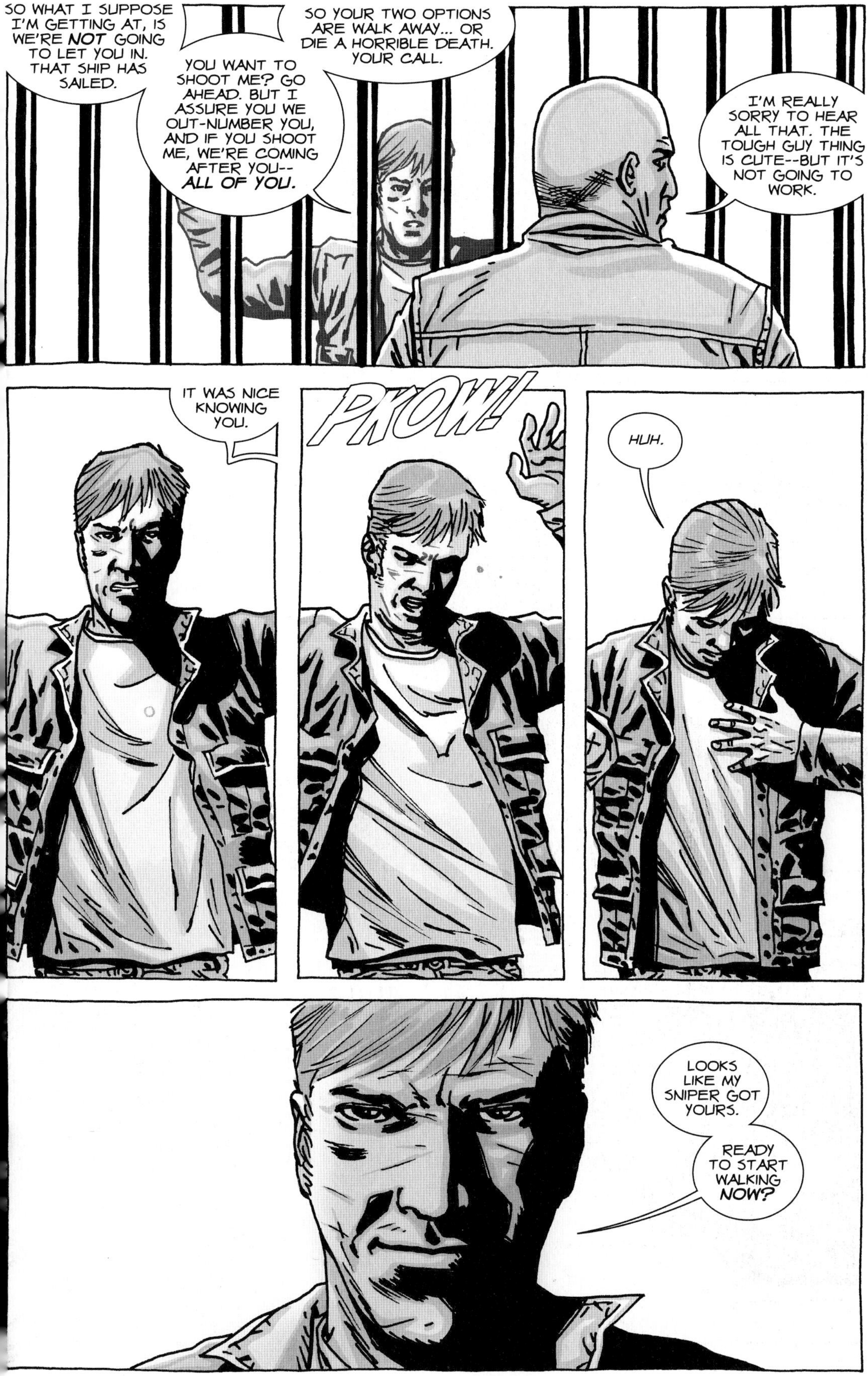
SO WHAT I SUPPOSE I'M GETTING AT, IS WE'RE NOT GOING TO LET YOU IN. THAT SHIP HAS SAILED.
YOU WANT TO SHOOT ME? GO AHEAD. BUT I ASSURE YOU WE OUT-NUMBER YOU, AND IF YOU SHOOT ME, WE'RE COMING AFTER YOU-- ALL OF YOU.
SO YOUR TWO OPTIONS ARE WALK AWAY... OR DIE A HORRIBLE DEATH. YOUR CALL.
I'M REALLY SORRY TO HEAR ALL THAT. THE TOUGH GUY THING IS CUTE--BUT IT'S NOT GOING TO WORK.
IT WAS NICE KNOWING YOU.
PKOW!
HUH.
LOOKS LIKE MY SNIPER GOT YOURS.
READY TO START WALKING NOW?

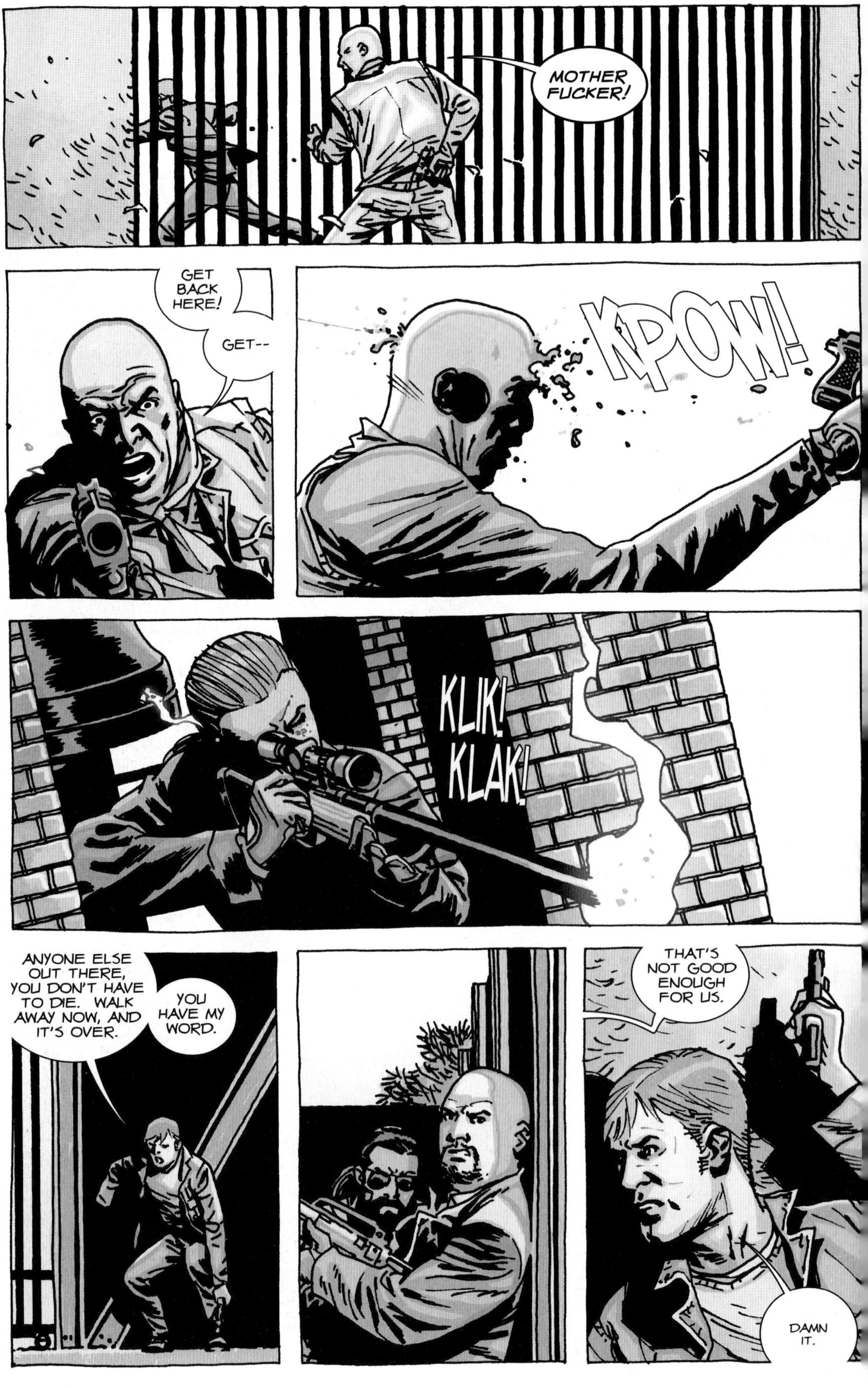
MOTHER FUCKER!
GET BACK HERE!
GET--
KPOW!
KLIK! KLAK!
ANYONE ELSE OUT THERE, YOU DON'T HAVE TO DIE. WALK AWAY NOW, AND IT'S OVER.
YOU HAVE MY WORD.
THAT'S NOT GOOD ENOUGH FOR US.
DAMN IT.

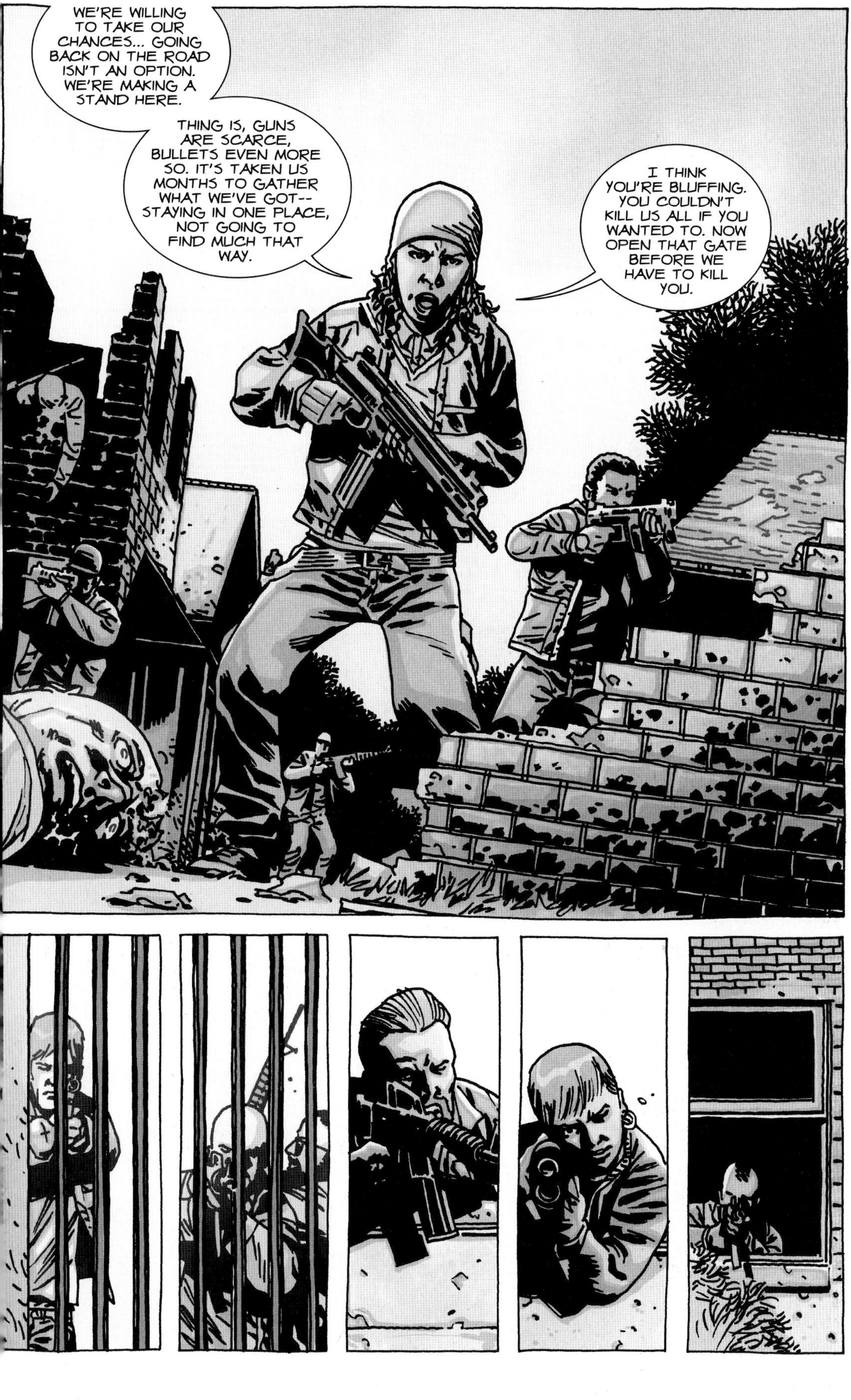
WE'RE WILLING TO TAKE OUR CHANCES... GOING BACK ON THE ROAD ISN'T AN OPTION. WE'RE MAKING A STAND HERE.
THING IS, GUNS ARE SCARCE, BULLETS EVEN MORE SO. IT'S TAKEN US MONTHS TO GATHER WHAT WE'VE GOT-- STAYING IN ONE PLACE, NOT GOING TO FIND MUCH THAT WAY.
I THINK YOU'RE BLUFFING. YOU COULDN'T KILL US ALL IF YOU WANTED TO. NOW OPEN THAT GATE BEFORE WE HAVE TO KILL YOU.

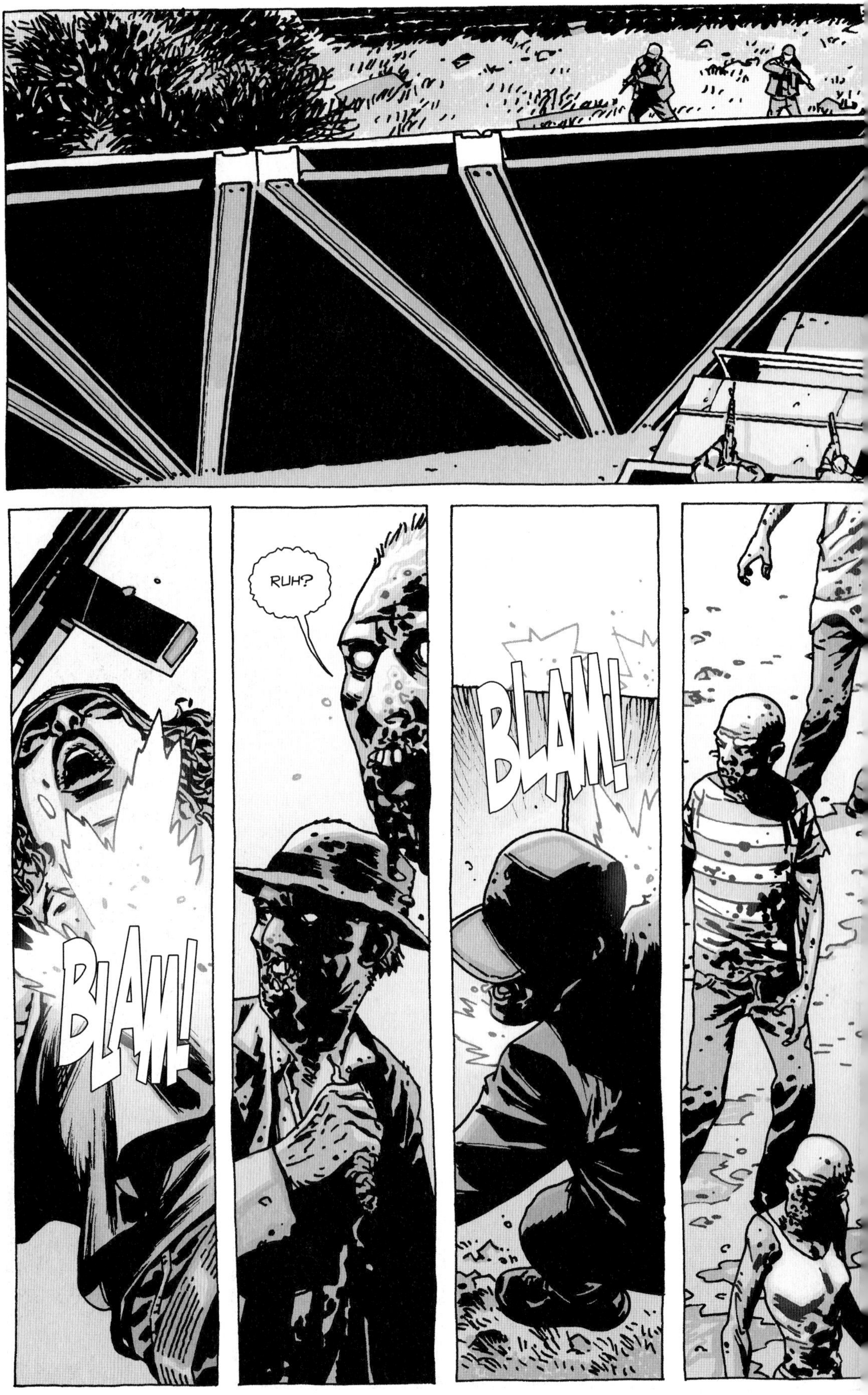
BLAM!
RUH?
BLAM!

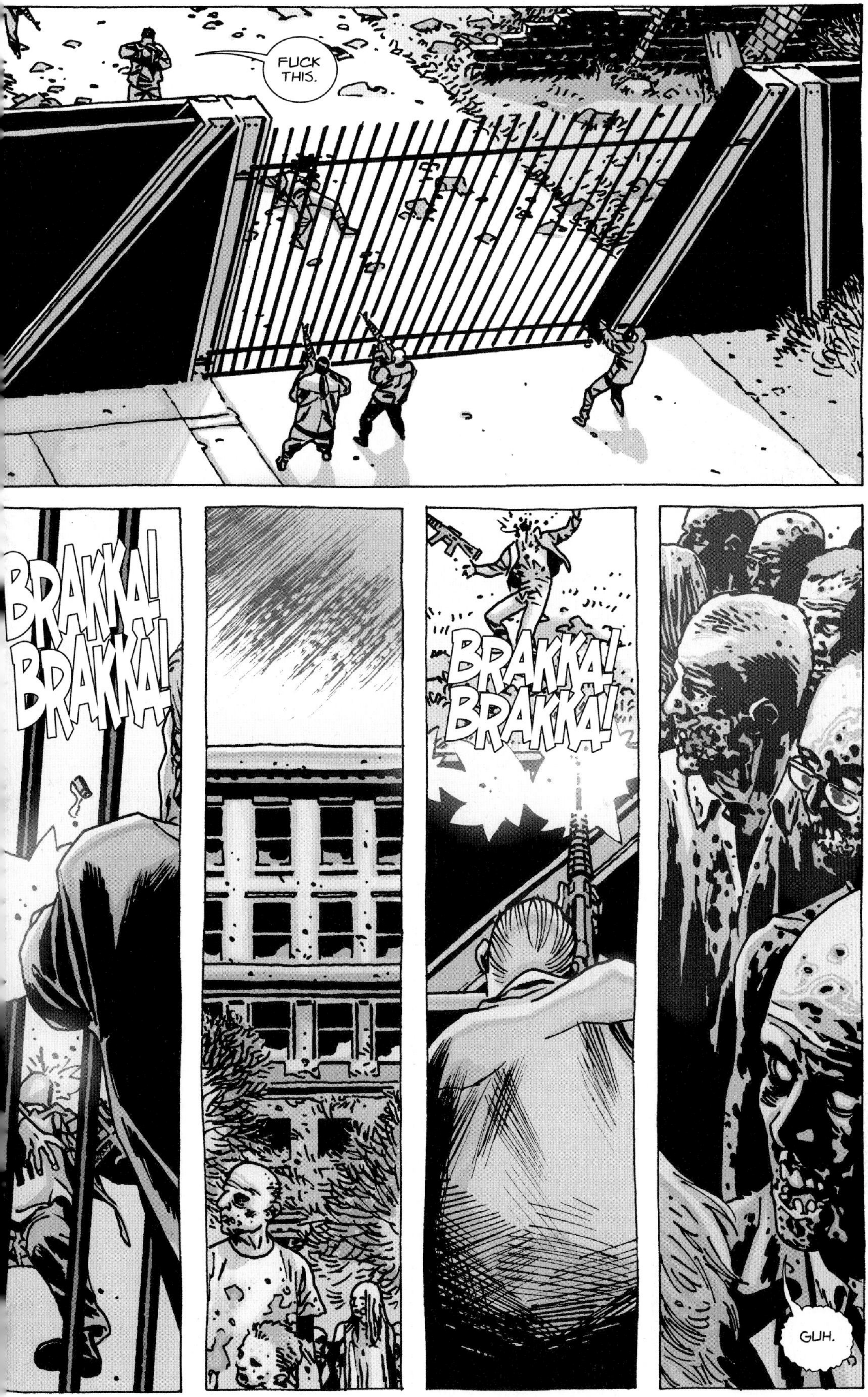
FUCK THIS.
BRAKKA! BRAKKA!
BRAKKA! BRAKKA!
GUH.

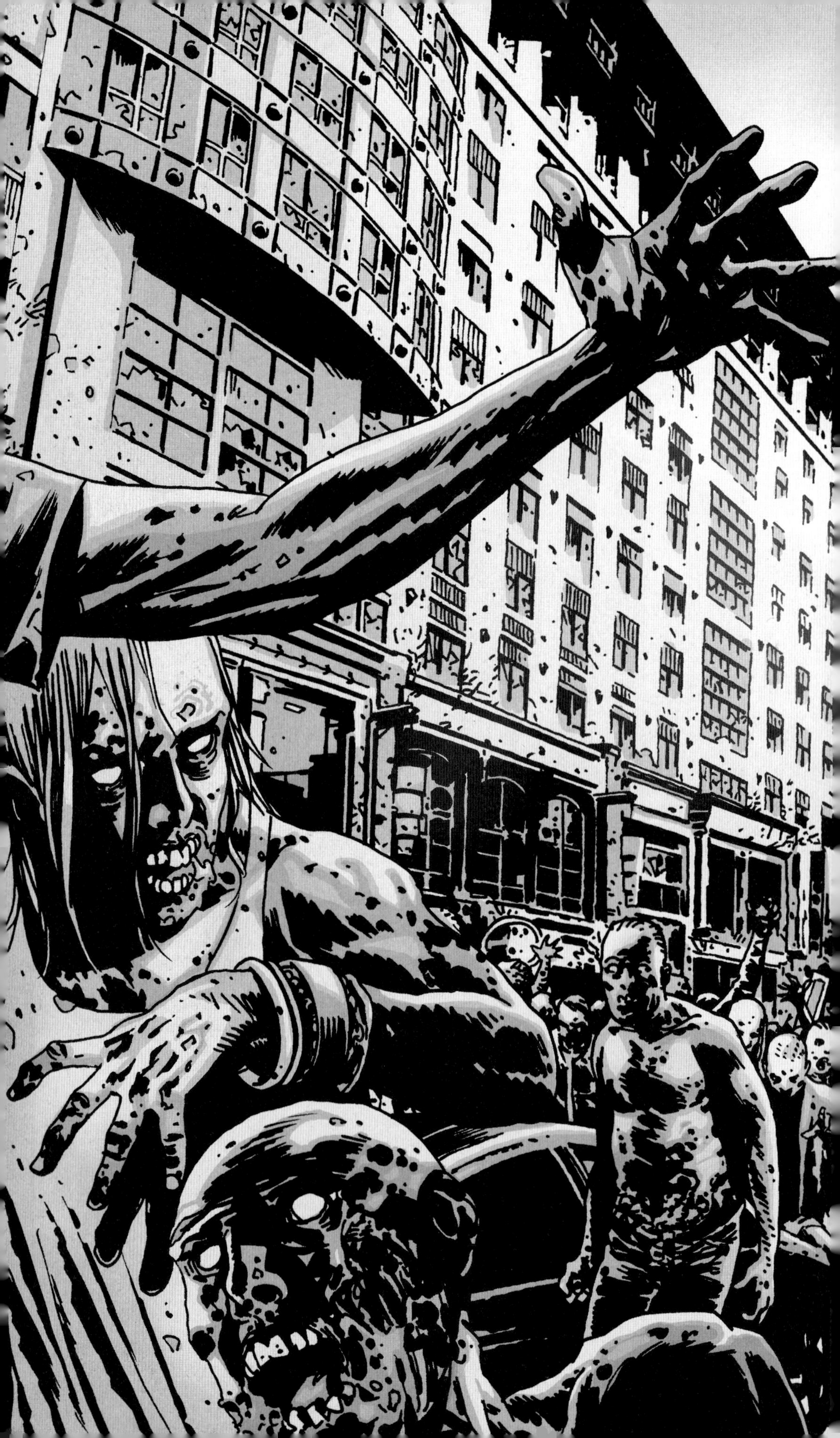

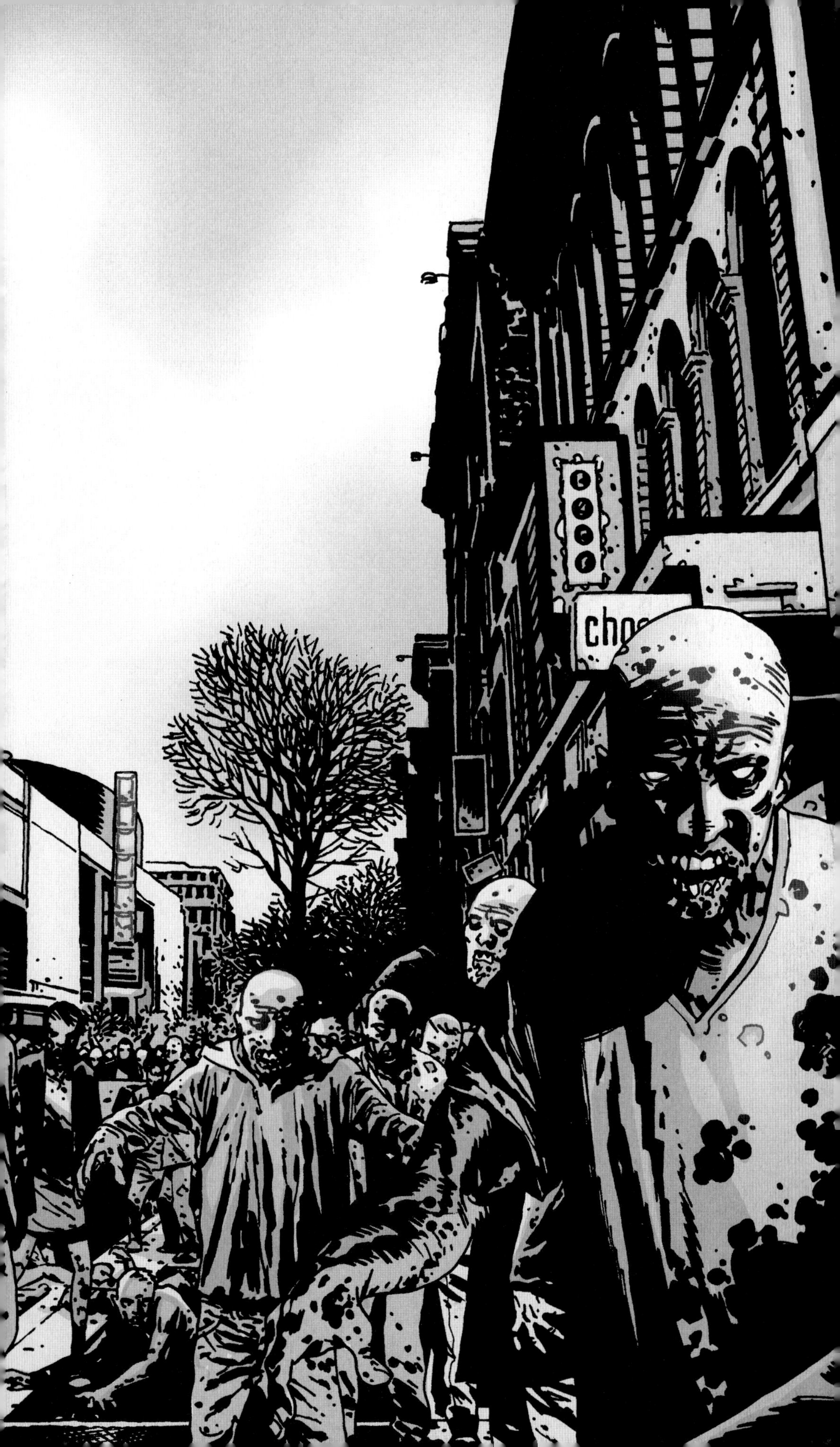
cho

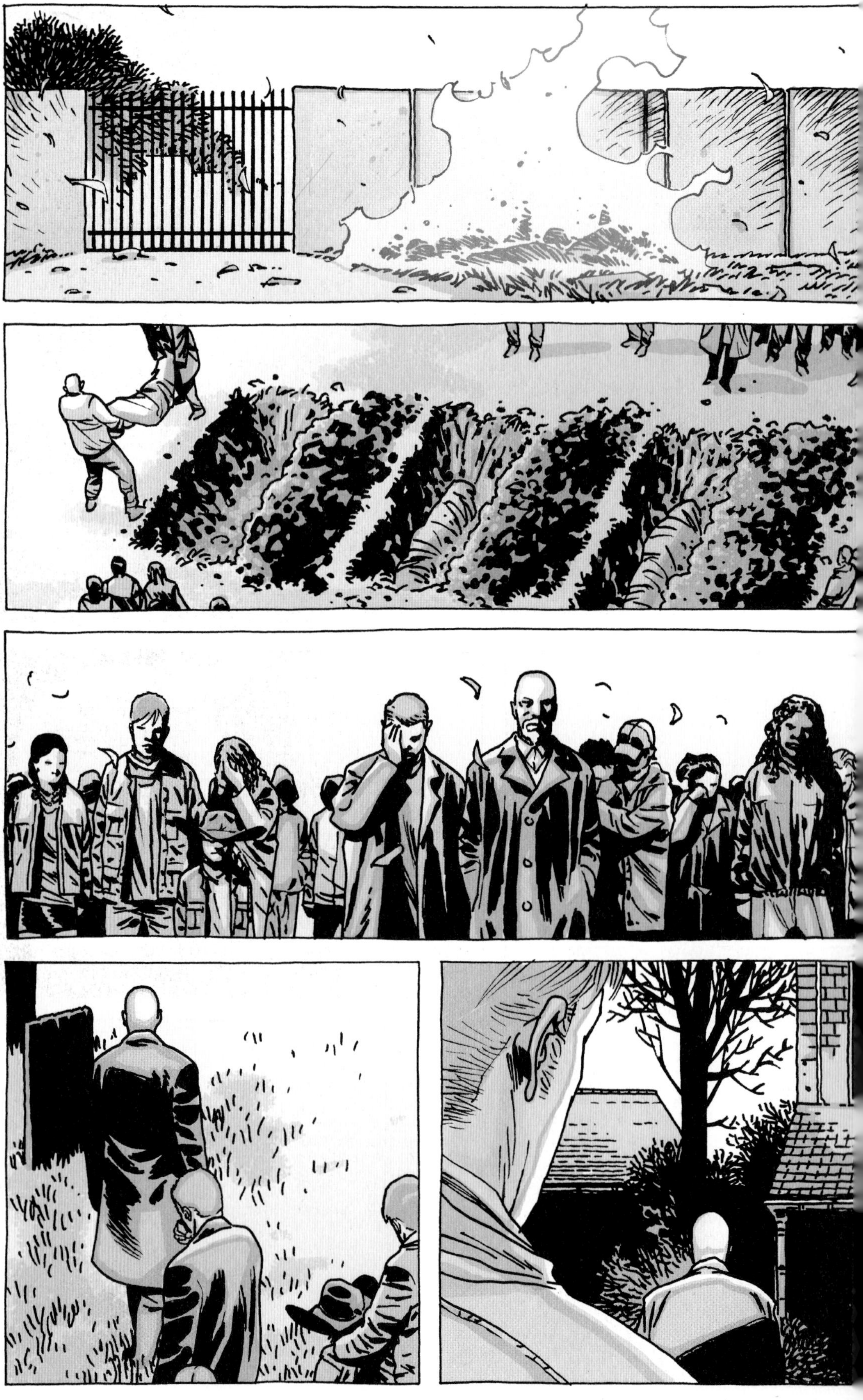

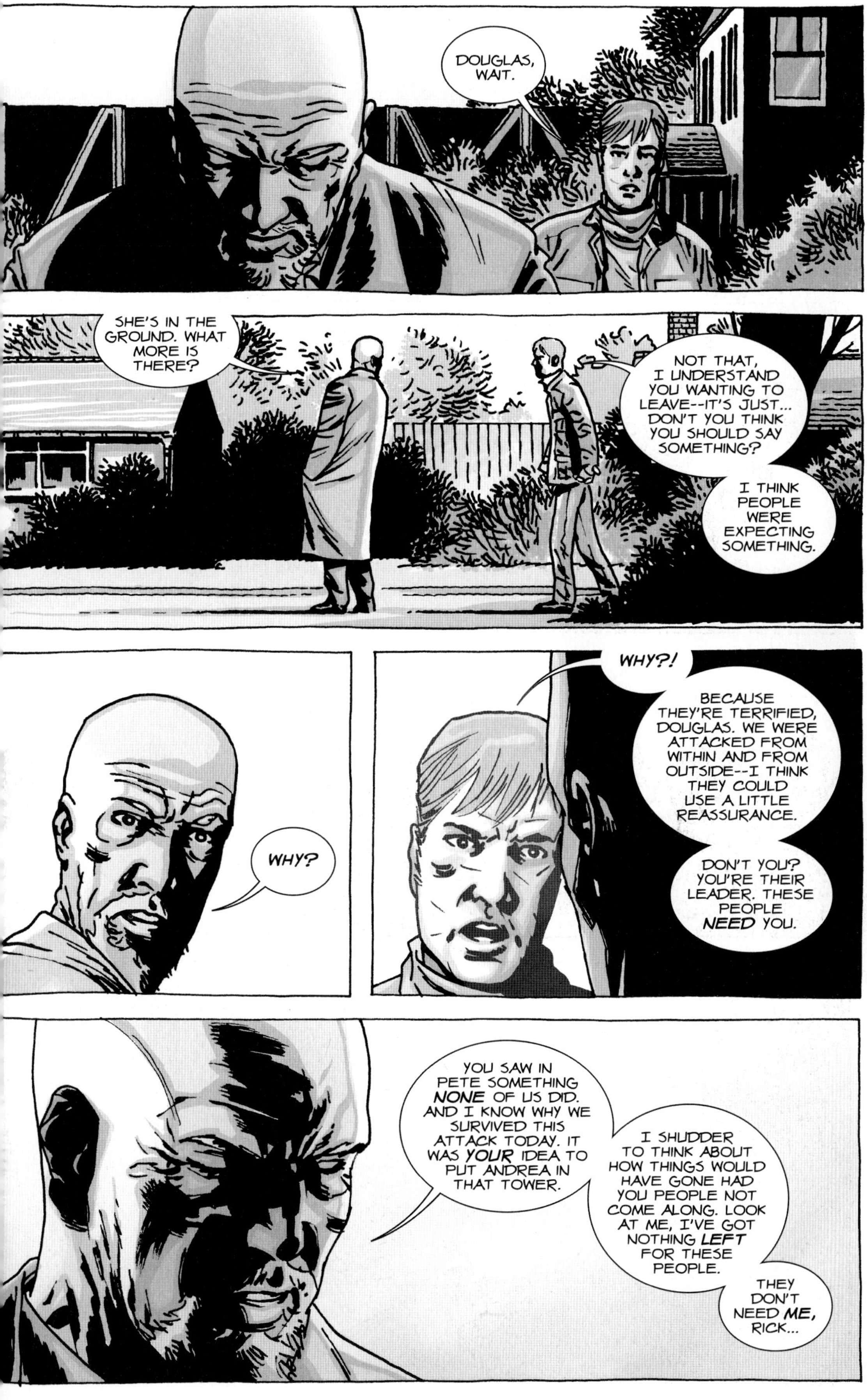
DOUGLAS, WAIT.
SHE'S IN THE GROUND. WHAT MORE IS THERE?
NOT THAT, I UNDERSTAND YOU WANTING TO LEAVE--IT'S JUST... DON'T YOU THINK YOU SHOULD SAY SOMETHING?
I THINK PEOPLE WERE EXPECTING SOMETHING.
WHY?
WHY?!
BECAUSE THEY'RE TERRIFIED, DOUGLAS. WE WERE ATTACKED FROM WITHIN AND FROM OUTSIDE--I THINK THEY COULD USE A LITTLE REASSURANCE.
DON'T YOU? YOU'RE THEIR LEADER. THESE PEOPLE NEED YOU.
YOU SAW IN PETE SOMETHING NONE OF US DID. AND I KNOW WHY WE SURVIVED THIS ATTACK TODAY. IT WAS YOUR IDEA TO PUT ANDREA IN THAT TOWER.
I SHUDDER TO THINK ABOUT HOW THINGS WOULD HAVE GONE HAD YOU PEOPLE NOT COME ALONG. LOOK AT ME, I'VE GOT NOTHING LEFT FOR THESE PEOPLE.
THEY DON'T NEED ME, RICK...

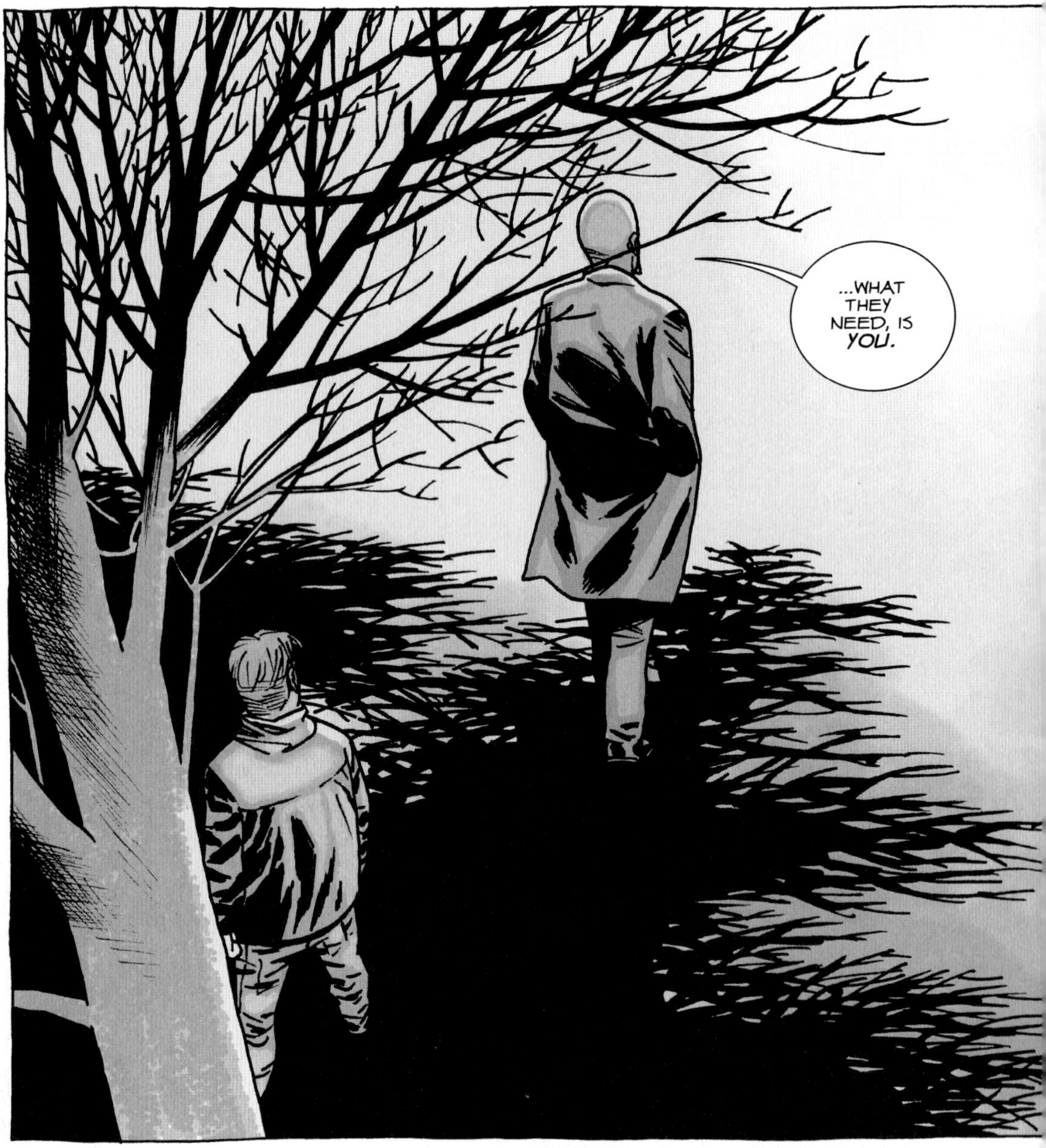
...WHAT THEY NEED, IS YOU.

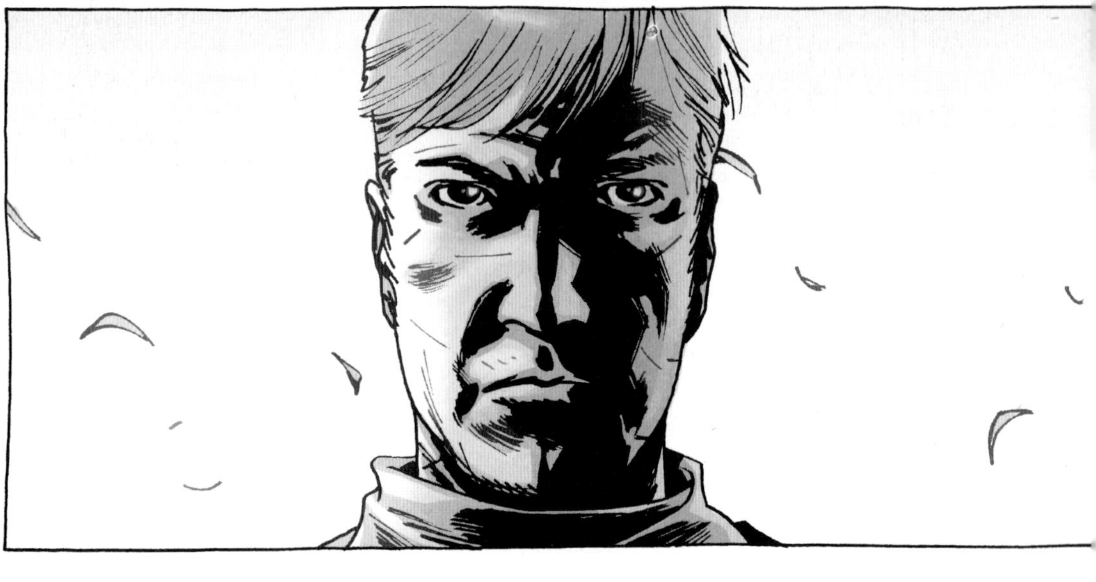

TO BE CONTINUED...

MORE GREAT BOOKS FROM
ROBERT KIRKMAN & IMAGE COMICS!

CAPES
PUNCHING THE CLOCK
BRIT
VOLUME THREE: FUBAR
HAUNT
TECH JACKET
THE BOY FROM EARTH
Battle POPE
Wrath of God

THE ASTOUNDING WOLF-MAN

VOL. 1 TP
ISBN: 978-1-58240-862-0
$14.99

VOL. 2 TP
ISBN: 978-1-60706-007-9
$14.99

VOL. 3 TP
ISBN: 978-1-60706-111-3
$16.99

BATTLE POPE

VOL. 1: GENESIS TP
ISBN: 978-1-58240-572-8
$14.99

VOL. 2: MAYHEM TP
ISBN: 978-1-58240-529-2
$12.99

VOL. 3: PILLOW TALK TP
ISBN: 978-1-58240-677-0
$12.99

VOL. 4: WRATH OF GOD TP
ISBN: 978-1-58240-751-7
$9.99

BRIT

VOL. 1: OLD SOLDIER TP
ISBN: 978-1-58240-678-7
$14.99

VOL. 2: AWOL
ISBN: 978-1-58240-864-4
$14.99

VOL. 3: FUBAR
ISBN: 978-1-60706-061-1
$16.99

CAPES

VOL. 1: PUNCHING THE CLOCK TP
ISBN: 978-1-58240-756-2
$17.99

HAUNT

VOL. 1 TP
ISBN: 978-1-60706-154-0
$9.99

INVINCIBLE

VOL. 1: FAMILY MATTERS TP
ISBN: 978-1-58240-711-1
$12.99

VOL. 2: EIGHT IS ENOUGH TP
ISBN: 978-1-58240-347-2
$12.99

VOL. 3: PERFECT STRANGERS TP
ISBN: 978-1-58240-793-7
$12.99

VOL. 4: HEAD OF THE CLASS TP
ISBN: 978-1-58240-440-2
$14.95

VOL. 5: THE FACTS OF LIFE TP
ISBN: 978-1-58240-554-4
$14.99

VOL. 6: A DIFFERENT WORLD TP
ISBN: 978-1-58240-579-7
$14.99

VOL. 7: THREE'S COMPANY TP
ISBN: 978-1-58240-656-5
$14.99

VOL. 8: MY FAVORITE MARTIAN TP
ISBN: 978-1-58240-683-1
$14.99

VOL. 9: OUT OF THIS WORLD TP
ISBN: 978-1-58240-827-9
$14.99

VOL. 10: WHO'S THE BOSS TP
ISBN: 978-1-60706-013-0
$16.99

VOL. 11: HAPPY DAYS TP
ISBN: 978-1-60706-062-8
$16.99

VOL. 12: STILL STANDING TP
ISBN: 978-1-60706-166-3
$16.99

VOL. 13: GROWING PAINS TP
ISBN: 978-1-60706-251-6
$16.99

ULTIMATE COLLECTION, VOL. 1 HC
ISBN 978-1-58240-500-1
$34.95

ULTIMATE COLLECTION, VOL. 2 HC
ISBN: 978-1-58240-594-0
$34.99

ULTIMATE COLLECTION, VOL. 3 HC
ISBN: 978-1-58240-763-0
$34.99

ULTIMATE COLLECTION, VOL. 4 HC
ISBN: 978-1-58240-989-4
$34.99

ULTIMATE COLLECTION, VOL. 5 HC
ISBN: 978-1-60706-116-8
$34.99

THE OFFICIAL HANDBOOK OF THE INVINCIBLE UNIVERSE TP
ISBN: 978-1-58240-831-6
$12.99

INVINCIBLE PRESENTS, VOL. 1: ATOM EVE & REX SPLODE TP
ISBN: 978-1-60706-255-4
$14.99

THE COMPLETE INVINCIBLE LIBRARY, VOL. 1 HC
ISBN: 978-1-58240-718-0
$125.00

THE COMPLETE INVINCIBLE LIBRARY, VOL. 2 HC
ISBN: 978-1-60706-112-0
$125.00

THE WALKING DEAD

VOL. 1: DAYS GONE BYE TP
ISBN: 978-1-58240-672-5
$9.99

VOL. 2: MILES BEHIND US TP
ISBN: 978-1-58240-775-3
$14.99

VOL. 3: SAFETY BEHIND BARS TP
ISBN: 978-1-58240-805-7
$14.99

VOL. 4: THE HEART'S DESIRE TP
ISBN: 978-1-58240-530-8
$14.99

VOL. 5: THE BEST DEFENSE TP
ISBN: 978-1-58240-612-1
$14.99

VOL. 6: THIS SORROWFUL LIFE TP
ISBN: 978-1-58240-684-8
$14.99

VOL. 7: THE CALM BEFORE TP
ISBN: 978-1-58240-828-6
$14.99

VOL. 8: MADE TO SUFFER TP
ISBN: 978-1-58240-883-5
$14.99

VOL. 9: HERE WE REMAIN TP
ISBN: 978-1-60706-022-2
$14.99

VOL. 10: WHAT WE BECOME TP
ISBN: 978-1-60706-075-8
$14.99

VOL. 11: FEAR THE HUNTERS TP
ISBN: 978-1-60706-181-6
$14.99

VOL. 12: LIFE AMONG THEM TP
ISBN: 978-1-60706-254-7
$14.99

VOL. 13: TOO FAR GONE TP
ISBN: 978-1-60706-329-2
$14.99

BOOK ONE HC
ISBN: 978-1-58240-619-0
$34.99

BOOK TWO HC
ISBN: 978-1-58240-698-5
$34.99

BOOK THREE HC
ISBN: 978-1-58240-825-5
$34.99

BOOK FOUR HC
ISBN: 978-1-60706-000-0
$34.99

BOOK FIVE HC
ISBN: 978-1-60706-171-7
$34.99

BOOK SIX HC
ISBN: 978-1-60706-327-8
$34.99

DELUXE HARDCOVER, VOL. 2
ISBN: 978-1-60706-029-7
$100.00

THE WALKING DEAD: THE COVERS, VOL. 1 HC
ISBN: 978-1-60706-002-4
$24.99

REAPER

GRAPHIC NOVEL
ISBN: 978-1-58240-354-2
$6.95

TECH JACKET

VOL. 1: THE BOY FROM EARTH TP
ISBN: 978-1-58240-771-5
$14.99

TALES OF THE REALM

HARDCOVER
ISBN: 978-1-58240-426-0
$34.95

TRADE PAPERBACK
ISBN: 978-1-58240-394-6
$14.95

INVINCIBLE presents
ATOM EVE & REX SPLODE
THE WALKING DEAD
TOO FAR GONE
THE WALKING DEAD
THE COVERS
REAPER
THE WALKING DEAD
BOOK SIX

TO FIND YOUR NEAREST COMIC BOOK STORE, CALL:
1-888-COMIC-BOOK

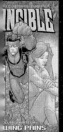

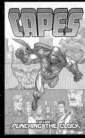

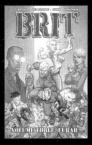

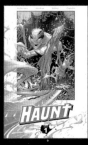

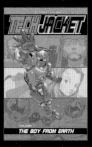

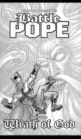

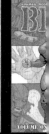

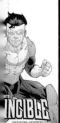

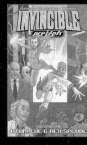

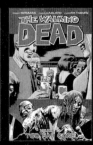

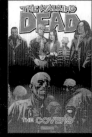

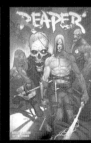

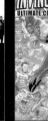

ROBERT KIRKMAN
CREATOR, WRITER

CHARLIE ADLARD
PENCILER, INKER

CLIFF RATHBURN
GRAY TONES

RUS WOOTON
LETTERER

CHARLIE ADLARD & CLIFF RATHBURN
COVER

SINA GRACE
EDITOR

IMAGE COMICS, INC.

Robert Kirkman - chief operating officer
Erik Larsen - chief financial officer
Todd McFarlane - president
Marc Silvestri - chief executive officer
Jim Valentino - vice-president

Eric Stephenson - publisher
Todd Martinez - sales & licensing coordinator
Betsy Gomez - pr & marketing coordinator
Branwyn Bigglestone - accounts manager
Sarah deLaine - administrative assistant
Tyler Shainline - production manager
Drew Gill - art director
Jonathan Chan - production artist
Monica Howard - production artist
Vincent Kukua - production artist
Kevin Yuen - production artist
www.imagecomics.com

For SKYBOUND ENTERTAINMENT

Robert Kirkman - CEO
J.J. Didde - President
Sina Grace - Editorial Director
Chad Manion - Assistant to Mr. Grace
Tim Daniel - Digital Content Manager

WWW.SKYBOUNDENT.COM

THE WALKING DEAD, VOL. 13: TOO FAR GONE. Second Printing. Published by Image Comics, Inc. Office of publication: 2134 Allston Way, 2nd Floor, Berkeley, California 94704.

PRINTED IN USA. For information regarding the CPSIA on this printed material call: 203-595-3636 and provide reference # EAST – 70233

ISBN: 978-1-60706-329-2

image comics presents

THE WALKING DEAD™

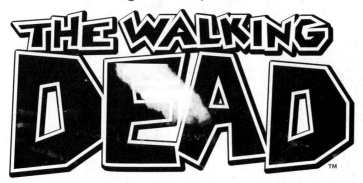